WIRED KINGDOM

RICK CHESLER

DEVIATION

ISBN: 1-935142-07-0
ISBN-13: 978-1-935142-07-2

Published by Deviation Books (USA) an imprint of Variance LLC.
www.variancepublishing.com

Library of Congress Catalog Number: 2010925051

Visit Rick Chesler on the World Wide Web at: http://www.rickchesler.com
You may also email him at rick@rickchesler.com

Cover and interior design by Stanley Tremblay
Printed in the USA

10 9 8 7 6 5 4 3 2 1

Printed on acid-free paper.

Dedication

For my parents, Ron & Lois, and my wife, Tabbatha, for all of their support over the years. For my unborn child, whom we expect in October—I look forward to the day when we can see a whale together!

In memory of Jon Bok, fellow scuba diver and marine biology student. One more dive!

This book is also dedicated to the real-life men and women around the world who work every day in decidedly unglamorous jobs to understand and preserve our planet's living marine resources.

ACKNOWLEDGEMENTS

My heartfelt thanks goes out to the entire team at Variance Publishing: Tim Schulte, for taking a chance on an unknown writer; Shane Thomson, for patient, insightful editing that makes me look better than I am; and Stan Tremblay, for handling the day-to-day details that helped bring this book to life.

I would like to acknowledge the invaluable input of *Meg* author Steve Alten, whose advice on the early drafts of this novel helped make it what it is today.

I would also like to thank the many friends I have met online who became supporters of *Wired Kingdom* long before they could hold the book in their hands (or their Kindles!). Know that I appreciate all of you.

WIRED KINGDOM

To hold as 'twere the mirror up to nature

- Shakespeare

Pleasant it is, when winds disturb the surface of the vast sea, to watch from land another's mighty struggle

-Lucretius

CHAPTER 1

PACIFIC OCEAN

OFF THE SOUTHERN CALIFORNIA COAST

The great whale hung beneath the waves, surveying her domain. At ninety-seven feet and one hundred tons, she was the largest animal in creation, even larger than the dinosaurs that once roamed the land and seas; yet she was still vulnerable to her enemies.

The behemoth generated a sound that disturbed the Pacific. It was a low groan, comparable to a jet engine in terms of sheer decibels. Though she could not reach the seafloor miles below, the blue whale's biological sonar allowed her to scan its depths.

This time, it had identified something unusual.

With an almost imperceptible movement of her powerful fluke, the whale began a patient ascent.

WIRED KINGDOM TECH SUPPORT FACILITY

Hundreds of miles away in California's San Fernando Valley, Trevor Lane's computer speakers rattled to life on his desk, snapping him awake. He had heard the sound they produced only once before, and it had not been as loud or sustained as this. He removed his glasses, rubbed his eyes and glanced at the clock on his PC: 8:02 A.M. He'd been staring at the monitor for almost three straight hours before he dozed off. He reached for a half-empty can of Red Bull without taking his eyes off the screen.

His monitor displayed a panoramic view of blue ocean, and in the foreground, the back of a blue whale. The live images, transmitted via satellite, originated from a remote camera attached to the whale's dorsal fin. The angle reminded Trevor of the over-the-shoulder point–of-view camera angles used in the video games he had designed to pay his way through a computer science degree.

He had been watching the video for days, and although many times there was nothing to look at but varying shades of blue and green, it fascinated him nonetheless. It was as if one were swimming along with the whale, holding onto its dorsal fin as it traversed thousands of miles of open ocean. What made it engaging to the millions of paying Internet users was that it wasn't simply video being viewed over the web—it was a live streaming audio/video feed. What made it especially enthralling to Trevor was that he had invented it. It was his technology that had been used to put a tiny, waterproof web-cam on a blue whale. Of all Trevor's technical accomplishments, this was by far the most impressive.

Over the past several days Trevor had electronically followed the whale as it trolled its camera across the planet's largest body of water. He knew exactly where it was on the globe, because its GPS coordinates were embedded in the upper left corner of the streaming video. Since it was currently well off the coast, there was not much to see other than the whale's body itself amidst a sea of blue. Although, every twenty minutes or so the blue whale's spout interrupted the monotony with an explosive burst as it came to the surface to breathe, offering Trevor brief glimpses of sky and swells before the animal dove again. He marveled at how loud it was. Sometimes his onscreen view became whitewashed by a glaring sun. Once he'd even seen a bird soaring high overhead. Other than that, he'd mostly seen open blue water.

Trevor rubbed sleep from his eyes, waiting for the whale to surface again. He was anxious for another GPS reading; the last one had contained incomplete data. His eyes wandered to information posted on the web site, his most recent obsession:

"This is the official web site of the *Wired Kingdom* television show. All content herein is the sole property of *Wired Kingdom*."

He clicked the "Contest Information" link:

"*Wired Kingdom* strives to present a thoroughly

absorbing and unique educational experience for all of its viewers. A large component of our programming involves this web site. Viewers are encouraged to participate by entering weekly contests sponsored by *Wired Kingdom* in conjunction with its television nature series. Most of our contests revolve around online inter-action with our free-ranging wild animals featuring live web-cams. These audio/visual feeds are streamed through our web site completely unaltered in real time through our privately owned satellite network."

With an amused sort of detachment at what had been done with his technical creation, Trevor clicked the listing for the current week's contest:

"A cash prize of one million U.S. dollars will be awarded to the contestant who submits a screen-captured image from our web site's *Wired Animal* streaming broadcast, demonstrating a '*spectacular and clearly visible example of human presence in the ocean*.'

"All entries must be submitted no later than midnight, July 23. Winners will be announced live on the following Friday night's 8:00 P.M. television broadcast. In the event that two identical images are submitted, the winner will be that with the earliest submission date/time stamp.

"Only one entry per contestant per week. Once a contestant has submitted their entry, the entry is final.

Contest only open to *Wired Kingdom* web subscribers.

"Good luck!"

As an employee of *Wired Kingdom*, Trevor was ineligible for the show's cash prize. But human presence in the ocean? At first he thought there would be a lot to choose from; however, the whale had remained hundreds of miles from land, avoiding the major shipping lanes. At an entry fee of fifty dollars, potential contestants were passing on the occasional plastic six-pack tie, shopping bag or miscellaneous piece of fishing gear in hopes of snapping a one-in-a-million shot of some icon of the sea: a message in a bottle or perhaps a sunken Spanish galleon loaded with gold doubloons that every sea aficionado dreams of discovering.

He wondered if he'd missed anything while asleep, but the web site's message boards confirmed that other users had so far not seen anything noteworthy. Trevor clicked back to the whale's live feed. More blue, but the water was lightening in color. Trevor guessed the whale was drifting up to the surface for air. He hunched forward in his chair, watching, waiting in vain anticipation, as though something interesting might happen this time. A plume of mist shot thirty feet skyward, accompanied by a thunderous grating sound that reminded him of gravel being dumped from a truck bed. Nothing unusual here.

And then he heard something else.

A voice.

Trevor turned up his speakers.

A female voice.

The video showed only the whale's back slicing through calm, blue water.

Now he could make out words . . . distant, as if carried by a breeze, yet distinct.

"Please no. Please—"

Gunfire.

Two shots, about a second apart.

A splash.

"What the . . ." Trevor muttered.

Water washed over the camera's lens as the animal submerged.

Did someone shoot the whale?

The curtain of swirling bubbles dissipated, revealing a quick shot of bare legs and feet kicking in a cloud of greenish blood. Before Trevor could freeze the image, the whale rolled to one side, returning the monitor to its familiar blue.

"Damn it!" *Was that real*?

The whale moved and again the view changed.

A flash of bare breasts.

Bits of flesh and blood.

Then the screen went to static.

"No!" Trevor grabbed the monitor and shook it. "Come on!" He checked the connections, knowing full well the interference came from the satellite transmission. Although the broadcast was susceptible to occasional interruptions of service resulting from bad weather—similar to consumer satellite television feeds—he had never seen this type of sustained interference before. And the weather was perfect.

He was considering possible sources of interference without success when the garbled transmission on screen suddenly cleared.

Sharks!

Trevor froze as blue sharks swarmed through the greenish sea, inflicting savage bites on the woman, removing a ten-pound chunk from the gushing torso. Clouds of blood obscured her upper body and head. And then, once more, the scene plunged into indecipherable snow.

Trevor slammed a fist into his desk in frustration.

"Bastards!" he yelled at the empty room. *They said they wouldn't stage anything. Millions of dollars worth of cutting-edge R&D being used for entertainment?* The contract he had signed with the show guaranteed that his device would be used solely for scientific purposes and to promote awareness of the marine environment. He recalled painfully that it also tied his salary to the performance of the whale-cam and web site.

He continued to watch. The static intensified, rendering the transmission worthless. This concerned Trevor even more than what he had seen—his testing had been exhaustive. On a second computer monitor, he consulted a stream of technical data that acted as the vital signs for the constellation of private satellites transmitting the signals from the telemetry device to the Internet. Nothing appeared out of the ordinary.

To confirm that the show's web site had broadcast the actual data stream from the satellites, he bypassed the commercial web site and used his secure account to view the satellite transmission directly, only to find that they were exactly the same. Unfortunately, it wasn't a simple hack whereby someone had substituted a pre-made video for the satellite feed as a hoax. *The satellites are transmitting this! Maybe the show staged some kind of surprise publicity event. But why the interference?*

His other monitor flickered back to life, displaying an empty blue frame, with the exception of the whale itself. He glanced at the GPS coordinates. Jotted them down. The whale was far out to sea off the Southern California coast. The whale rose again, breaking the surface. Sun-dappled open water. Calm, but no longer mirror flat. A light breeze whistled through the mic. Although he had integrated a windscreen into the device to prevent the annoying *whooshing* noise familiar to camcorder users, if the angle was right it couldn't be completely stopped.

Again, the image returned to a scrambled mess. When the picture returned a few seconds later, he heard a sound he couldn't place. Something vaguely familiar.

Then nothing.

The connection now appeared to be lost entirely as the screen went black, leaving Trevor to stare at his own reflection. His brown eyes betrayed a lack of sleep. His wavy dark hair needed cutting. He thought he appeared much older than a recent graduate. Finally, he banished his mirror image by clicking out of the video feed.

A quick check of the site's chat room and message boards revealed only the impassioned confusion of people wondering what was going on, whether what they had just witnessed was real. Trevor placed a call to Anthony Silveras, one of *Wired Kingdom*'s many producers, but the only one who seemed able to get things done. Anthony picked up on the first ring, his voice strained.

"Trevor—"

"Did you see—"

"I was about to call you. My phone's ring—"

"Tony, listen."

"What's going on, Trevor?"

The open line went quiet. "Looks like we just broadcast a murder live on our web site."

CHAPTER 2

BAJA CALIFORNIA, MEXICO

Héctor González drove his old but reliable pickup truck at a leisurely pace up the wide dirt road of his rural coastal village. Tejano music poured from the blown speakers as he lit a cigarette, shook out the match and rested his arm in the open window. The neighborhood children playing soccer in the street parted to let him pass and waved. But as he waved back, despite the easy smile he wore, he failed to hear the music, taste the tobacco or take comfort in the familiarity of his surroundings.

He crested the hill and began the descent to his street. Even the splendid view of the blue Pacific in the distance, which had never before failed to lift his spirits after a long day of work, left him numb. He rolled past a row of shacks set back from the road until the ground leveled out at an intersection just off the town square. He was about to turn left when a man came running out of an old fishing shop, waving with one hand, a small Styrofoam cooler in the other.

"*Hola*, Héctor!" the man shouted, smiling broadly.

Héctor stopped the truck. "*Hola*, Arturo, need a ride?" The local fisherman was a friend of Héctor's who had steady work as a deckhand on a sport fishing boat. He owned no car, and each day his boss would drop him off at the shop, where he would walk or catch a lift the rest of the way home with someone. More than a few times that someone was Héctor, who was usually glad for the company, if not today.

"Yeah." Arturo nodded and climbed into the vehicle, placing his cooler on the floorboard at his feet. "Thanks," he said.

"Good fishing?" Héctor asked, pulling back onto the road.

"Not bad. Ready for *siesta*."

Héctor forced a smile. Normally he would be too by late morning, but he could not allow himself to rest now.

They rolled on in silence for a time, the balding tires stirring up a cloud of dust in their wake. Arturo glanced at Héctor. "How is Rosa?"

He shook his head. "Not now, my friend, please."

Arturo nodded, looked out the window. He grinned as a basset hound wobbled after a clutch of roosters on the side of the road, the dog's testicles hanging so low that they hit the ground as it walked. "Faster, Diego!" he called to the hound. "You know that dog is a miracle?" he said to Héctor. "All day, he drags his balls on the ground and yet he's fathered every mutt from here to Las Palmas."

Héctor forced another smile. "Yes, I know. He must have brass *cojones*." Héctor pulled the truck to a stop in the middle of the road. There was of course no other traffic to block.

Arturo opened the door and got out. He lifted the lid from his cooler and took out a Ziploc bag bulging with fish filets. "Have yourself a good lunch," he said, handing Héctor the bag. Héctor nodded his thanks.

Driving again, he continued on in a daze, reaching his house by instinct. Rolling past a stand of towering fan palms that marked the northern edge of his property, he pictured the trees as they had been decades ago, shortly after his father had planted them. Back then they had been close enough to the ground to be run over by careless drivers, and some had succumbed to that fate. But the rest had survived, outliving even Hector's father, who had lived to a ripe old age before leaving the house to his son.

Héctor pulled into the narrow driveway of his one-story home, the nicest on the block. He took the three steps to his front porch and flung open the screen door. "How is she?" he said without preamble. Their living room was well worn, lived in. A battered old upright piano occupied part of one wall, its top decorated with figurines of Jesus and Mary and framed photographs of their extended family. His wife of twenty-three years did not look up from her position on the floor as she knelt in the corner in front of a homemade altar, a semi-circle of lit candles arrayed before her. She was praying feverishly, hands clasped in front, lips moving rapidly with quiet intonations. Héctor looked down at the tired figure she had become. She had aged in the past months, lines of gray streaking her rich black hair, creases marring her smooth complexion and once-bright eyes. She was still beautiful, but so sad, even in her faith. He himself had been unable to do anything, after all, so she would appeal to God. He waited for her to finish; who was he to disrupt her pleas?

After another few moments his wife rose and turned to face him with wet eyes. She spoke rapidly. “Héctor, the news from the hospital today is very bad. Rosa has been transferred back to the critical care unit. Her doctors report that the complications from surgery have gotten worse. Her body has rejected the donor tissue. They say she is starting to die, Héctor, and that all they can do where she is now is to make her passing more comfortable.” At this she broke into a sob, dropping to the floor one knee at a time. “Eleven years old, Héctor. She is only a child! Why?”

Héctor went to her, knelt with her, held her.

“But what about the advanced treatment? They told us that if the surgery failed, something could be done in Mexico City.”

His wife wiped her nose, shaking her head. “They do want to move her.”

“But if they can save her—”

“We cannot afford the treatment. Even if we sold our house, Héctor, and your business, borrowed from everyone we know . . . it wouldn't be enough.” She broke down again, weeping.

"Listen to me, Carla. Listen." She stopped sniffling and looked him in the eye. "When you go back to the hospital to visit Rosa—"

"Me? Aren't you coming? Rosa will want to see you."

"Listen. I want you to tell the doctors to notify the surgeons in Mexico City." Héctor stood, his wife rising with him.

"I am flying to the United States this afternoon, near Los Angeles. I will be gone for at least a day, maybe a few days."

"Héctor . . . she may not have much time."

"It will be okay," Héctor reassured her.

"But *Los Angeles*? Why?" She grabbed the bag of fish from his hand and went to the kitchen. He followed her but said nothing as she laid the filets in a pan and began to season them. He deliberated carefully while she worked on the fish. After she had lit the burner under the pan, he spoke.

"I have accepted a job."

"A job? What is wrong with your usual trips?"

An air charter operator, Héctor had built a successful business around his piloting skills and Cessna seaplane to run eco-tours for a wealthy American clientele. He thought about how many trips he would have to make, ferrying adventurous San Diego surfers to Todos Santos Island or weekend kayakers to the Coronados to earn what he had already been wired in advance for this mission.

"This job will pay for Rosa's procedure."

"Héctor, most of the money must be paid before they will treat her. You know this."

"It pays well, *cariño* . . . enough to pay for the entire treatment."

Carla whirled around, shaking a spatula at him. "Héctor Jesús González! What is this crazy talk? You tell me that you are not planning anything illegal. You tell me this instant!"

"It is nothing illegal." *Liar!* his inner voice screamed. In fact, his new job was illegal, but not in the way his wife meant. There were drug traffickers, human smugglers who would contract his aerial services for uncommonly high pay. But he would not allow his wife to suffer the indignity of returning home one day to find his head on their doorstep. Abhorrently violent crime was on the rise in Mexico as drug gangs battled over turf. And, he thought, it was too far beneath him. Using his airplane—the centerpiece of his professional accomplishments, his most prized possession—to enable a pathway of devastation and misery for drugs and sexual slavery was not something that was inside him, not something he could redeem in the eyes of his God, even to save the life of his little girl.

But this new job . . . against the law, yes, but it only involved violating U.S. airspace in order to retrieve a piece of technical equipment from a whale. That was all he knew. He would receive further instructions later, but what could be so wrong? No one would be hurt, not even the animal.

"Do not take too much risk, Héctor. God will take care of Rosa; He does not need to watch over you, too."

"I will be performing a simple aerial survey of the Channel Islands. It is no more risky than normal, but since their usual seaplane service is unavailable they are paying me extra for rapid response."

His wife clucked her disapproval before returning to the preparation of their meal. While she busied herself in the kitchen, Héctor frowned as his mind wrestled the tangled calculus of the logistics required to complete his new assignment. While not as dangerous as working with violent criminals, the job was rife with its own special hazards.

There were the extra fuel tanks he had outfitted his plane with that would convert it into a volatile flying gas tank. There was the low-altitude flying over water for hours on end, over rough seas, in unpredictable weather. He could have mechanical problems far out to sea, unable to radio for help for fear of drawing the attention of the authorities, unable to do anything but drift helplessly hundreds of miles from land. Landing on open ocean posed enough of a challenge, not to mention putting down near a large wild animal. Then there was the real possibility of being sighted by the U.S. Coast Guard ships or aircraft, chased down and detained—maybe jailed—before being deported without his plane, his livelihood, and never again allowed to enter the U.S. That would leave his family considerably worse off than they were now.

Furthermore, he was proud of the relationship he had built and maintained over the years the with American aviation authorities. These ties had enabled him to build a lucrative business, making trips to the Coronados, an island group straddling Mexican and U.S. waters near San Diego. The thought of deliberately defying their trust left a bitter taste.

As Héctor smelled something starting to burn in the kitchen, yet another possible outcome rattled his brain: he might simply fail to locate the piece of gear or be unable to retrieve it. Fly all that way and undergo all that risk for nothing. His instructions had been clear and simple: deliver the whale's tag and collect a tremendous cash reward.

Then Carla was telling him to sit at the table, sliding a plate of *dorado* in front of him. Badly burnt. She was typically an excellent cook, but her mind had not been on the task. He broke off a piece with his fork and forced himself to eat. It would be his last home-cooked meal for some time.

She asked him how the fish was with a glance.

"Good fish," he said, crunching a mouthful into submission. Another lie. Was it getting easier? But he could no longer savor food; the finest, freshest bluefin tuna would be tasteless mush to him now.

"Good fish," he said again.

CHAPTER 3

FBI FIELD OFFICE, LOS ANGELES

Special Agent Tara Shores did not like what her boss was telling her.

"You're saying you don't want me working the First National case, sir?" she asked. "I wrapped up the identity-theft thing yesterday. You got my report, right?" A string of recent bank robberies had left Los Angeles authorities on high alert. As a five-year FBI veteran based with the Los Angeles Field Office, Shores had expected to be added to the case when another bank was robbed the previous day.

Will Branson, special agent in charge of the L.A. field office, leaned back in his chair and regarded his subordinate. She was still a few months shy of her thirtieth birthday, single and attractive, her black hair kept short in something of a pageboy cut. As far as he knew she wasn't dating anyone. Incidents had occurred from time to time, causing Branson serious headaches, but he had been glad to see Shores manage each situation on her own. She'd made it clear over the years that she was off limits to the male agents who sought her attention. He had seen more than a few female agents quit over less.

In an agency of professionals skilled at uncovering things about people, Shores herself had proven tough to figure out. At times she was a stubborn, by-the-book agent, while on other occasions she was fiercely . . . innovative. Recently, though, in those instances where she had chosen to act independently, her actions had verged on those of an unstable rogue, which concerned Branson's superiors. Nevertheless, Tara had built a reputation for closing cases—including highly dangerous cases—and closing them fast. Branson needed that ability now. The bank jobs were becoming an embarrassment. What Shores didn't know was that although he wanted her on the bank case the order had come from on high to put her on the whale incident.

"I got the report, Shores. Good work. But the First National case is fully staffed at the moment. I need you to investigate this whale thing."

Tara's mouth dropped open in disbelief. "Sir, with all due respect, don't we have trainees who can take care of this?"

Branson fidgeted. He'd wondered the same thing himself, but orders were orders; and he had to admit that he was curious to see how she would handle it. He suspected his superiors were interested in this as well.

"This isn't exactly a low-profile case," he said, tossing her a thin folder. "It's on all the news shows and the Internet. That little snuff film, or whatever the hell it is, has already gotten millions of YouTube views."

"It's a publicity gimmick for the TV show," she said, flipping through the file.

"I'm not interested in your opinion, Agent Shores. Grill the show's producers, find out what they know. We may not have a body, but we've got two million witnesses who claim something happened out there."

"Okay, sir, let's assume a crime has been committed. We don't even know if this is within our jurisdiction. Did the murder take place in international waters? Was it aboard an American-registered vessel? There's nothing to work with here. Maybe someone could look into that while I join the First—"

Branson cut her off with a wave of his hand. "That someone is *you*, Shores. Check out the ports and marinas. Find out who's missing. Do the legwork." He pushed his hand through his hair and sighed. "C'mon, you didn't used to be such an adrenaline junky. Have you forgotten how to be a detective?"

That hurt. Five years ago she had been regarded as one of the agency's brightest stars. *Unusually high IQ. Bachelor's degree in criminology from UCLA. Top of her FBI Academy class, academically. Streetwise situational awareness. Adept with ambiguous circumstances. Expert pistol shooter and hand-to-hand fighter. Physical abilities excellent . . .*

She locked eyes with her supervisor, suppressing a

nightmare. *Was Branson challenging her?*

"Tell you what," he said, sensing her determination, "wrap this up quickly and I'll see what I can do about getting you on the First National case."

Tara snatched the case file and stood up. "Yes sir," she said, smiling. She would knock this case out of the way and move onto more important things. And, she thought, she would do it without being bitter.

She opened the folder. A phrase on the first page of the file caught her attention. "Reality TV, eh?" she said looking up from the case file. Branson nodded. "Finally, my chance to be discovered!"

Branson chuckled. Then he grew serious. "Look, even with the bank hits, I'm under some pressure here to identify what the hell this whale incident was, one way or the other. The entire Internet is asking what happened, and no one seems to have an answer. I'm hoping that by assigning an agent with some experience I'll be able to settle this thing sooner rather than later. So try to take it seriously."

"Oh, I will." She started for the door, ticking things off on her fingers as she went. "I'll have to get my hair styled, my nails done. . . . You think my ID headshot is okay for an eight-by-ten glossy?" She held the plastic-encased badge she wore on a lanyard up for Branson, then flipped it around to look at it herself, shrugging.

Branson waved at the door, but was unable to suppress a smile. "Godspeed, Shores. I hope you remember us little people when you're a big star."

"I'll have my people call your people," she quipped

on the way out. "We'll do lunch."

"Shores, one more thing," he said as she reached the door.

"Sir?"

"Keep me informed."

The smile vanished. *Short leash.*

"Of course, sir."

Tara read the case file as she walked down the hall. She felt a stab of surprise upon learning the full premise of the show. This was not the type of reality TV she was familiar with, she had to admit. No one on this show was competing for a mate by participating in silly games. She stopped walking for a minute after reading about the whale's onboard computer. Was this nothing more than some kind of unorthodox Bureau psych evaluation?

She doubted Branson would test her mettle that way, but she wouldn't put it past some of his superiors. Male superiors. Tara was not oblivious to the fact that there were still men in Herbert Hoover's distinguished organization who wouldn't mind seeing her fail. While the rest of the government and the private sector seemed to have caught up when it came to women in the workforce, the Bureau still clung to old stereotypes. Tara had heard other female agents describe it as having to wear a mask to work, a façade that hid their true self to assimilate into the culture. But for Tara it had been the opposite. From the day she set foot in the academy at Quantico, she felt like she'd taken the mask *off*, that her true identity had been revealed by the culture rather than hidden.

She shook her head and continued on past a wall-mounted plaque which read: Fidelity, Bravery, Integrity. She felt the weight of this decoration every time she saw it. For Tara, its meaning went beyond that of a familiar motto. Single, with no parents, no siblings, the Bureau was her family. And now her family seemed to be testing her.

Flipping the case file shut, she had to laugh. *This* was her big test? The reason they'd kept her from the city's top priority case? Some viral web video? *Fine.* She hadn't flinched. She'd requested the bank case, but what agent in her right mind wouldn't? That's where the visibility was; that's where the chance to save people from serious harm was.

BEL AIR

Less than an hour later Tara flashed her badge to a gate guard in an elite Los Angeles suburb. Known for its density of movie and sports stars, it boasted some of the priciest real estate in the world. The guard waved her in.

She slid her spruce-green Crown Victoria up to the curb in front of the home of Mr. and Mrs. George Reed and double-checked the address. They were listed in the case file as the owners of *Wired Kingdom*. She observed the property. An expansive lawn sloped up to a sprawling mansion. A marble fountain bubbled in the center of a circular drive in front of the home.

She took the winding, brick-paved driveway to the house and strode to the front door. She rang the chime and waited. No response. She rang again, wondering how long it would take for "the help" to get to the front door from the far reaches of the home. She heard approaching footsteps, then the door swung open.

"May I help you?" asked a young, eye-catching Latina maid wearing a black-and-white uniform that fell somewhere between something a maid would actually wear and those worn in adult fantasies. A little racy, but somehow still functional. The two working women gave each other a once-over, each sensing that the real divide between them was not race or sex appeal, but economic class.

"Mr. Reed, please," Tara said.

"One moment," the maid said before disappearing back into the house, leaving Tara to wait on the doorstep.

A man Tara judged to be fifty-five years of age appeared in the entrance hall. He wore a casual business outfit, with designer sunglasses perched atop his nearly bald head. "Morning, sir." She flashed her credentials. "I'm Special Agent Tara Shores with the Federal Bureau of Investigation. Are you Mr. George Reed?"

"Yes. Is there a problem?" he asked, still blocking the doorway. A woman appeared behind him, a concerned look in sharp contrast to her tropical sun dress. She appeared to be the same age. Tara guessed she was his wife.

“I need to ask you and your wife a few questions about the content broadcast over the *Wired Kingdom* web site this morning,” she began.

“We don’t really know anything about it,” he said, starting to close the door.

“That's unfortunate, sir, because I was hoping you could explain what has been reported as a possible murder. But since you can't, or won’t, I've no choice now but to conduct a more thorough interview at the field office.” She paused to let this sink in while looking around the property. “I’m sure it’s a lot more comfortable here.” That was an understatement. No doubt the Reeds' pantry would be bigger than the interview rooms at the field office.

Reluctantly, Mr. Reed invited the agent inside, but only long enough to walk through an immense foyer that eventually opened up on the other side of the house. As she kept up with the Reeds at a near trot, Tara caught glimpses of framed photographs on the wall—Mr. Reed posing with Ronald Reagan; Mr. and Mrs. Reed on the cover of *People*; a shot of the much younger couple on the deck of a sailing yacht, Mr. Reed at the wheel, guiding the hands of a young girl. *Their daughter?*

Mrs. Reed held open double French doors leading out on to a flagstone patio littered with wicker chairs and wrought-iron tables topped with umbrellas matching the decor. Her outstretched arm, wrist jangling with pricey baubles, all but shooed Tara from the mansion as though she were a day laborer done with a one-time job. A circular black-bottomed pool dominated the lower patio level. The Reeds guided Tara to an ivy-laced gazebo to the side. Some distance away, a gardener with clippers tamed a menagerie of topiary animals.

"Look," Mr. Reed said, "the truth is, we don't really know what happened."

Tara glanced at Mrs. Reed, who appeared bored, examining her French-manicured nails. *Need to wake her up.* "Sir, lying to a federal officer is a serious crime. You and your wife run *Wired Kingdom.* Do you honestly expect me to believe you have no clue what took place?"

Mrs. Reed shot Tara a look to kill. "Look, Agent . . ."

"Shores."

"Agent Shores. Just as the web site states, we don't alter images in any way, nor do we stage events. This is reality TV. The whale's camera records whatever it happens to record."

A cell phone rang. Mr. Reed pulled it from a pocket and switched it off. "Sorry. Damn reporters."

Tara nodded. "What about the possibility that someone hacked into your web site and altered or substituted the images?"

"I don't think so," Mr. Reed said. "Of course, my wife and I are far from technicians. You really need to talk with our technical director, the man who invented the whale-cam—Trevor Lane."

"I'm going to ask you both one more time, just so

we're clear. I remind you that if you are lying or omitting any part of the truth, you will be held accountable under federal law. Neither of you have any idea what those images were?"

"Correct," Mr. Reed said.

Mrs. Reed shrugged and said, "No idea."

Tara gave Mrs. Reed a hard look. Her eye makeup was smudged, her eyes red, slightly swollen.

"If that's all, I'll be going inside," Mrs. Reed said, clearly uncomfortable with the scrutiny. Mr. Reed made a subtle motion for his wife to remain seated but she responded with a scowl. Tara sighed, allowing her impatience to surface. "I'll tell you when we're finished, Mrs. Reed. Sit down, or we take a ride. Your choice." Mr. Reed couldn't hold back a smile as his wife sat.

"What the hell are you smirking at?" she said to her husband. The tone was venomous.

Mr. Reed avoided further confrontation, scratching his temple while pretending to monitor the gardener's progress across the yard.

"Your daughter, Anastasia, is the host of the show. She's spent a lot of time around the whale. Have you seen or spoken with her since the incident?" *Make sure it wasn't her in the video?*

Mr. Reed nodded. "Talked to her on the phone right after it happened," he said. "She has no idea what it was, either."

She watched the gardener for a moment as he maintained a dolphin-shaped hedge. The ocean was a big place, and the chances of this whale randomly encountering an act of violence were slim to non-existent. For the first time since she'd been given the case, Tara allowed herself to consider the possibility that the video represented a real murder.

"Tell me more about these million-dollar contests. How many people have entered to win this week?"

"I'd have to talk to my people—" Mr. Reed began.

"I'll speak with your people myself if I need to. Just give me a ballpark estimate. Let's start with how many entered last week."

"Quarter of a million," Mrs. Reed said in an icy tone. Tara made a notation in her pad. The Reeds assumed she was simply recording the figure, but she actually multiplied 250,000 by $50, the contest entrance fee, and subtracted $1,000,000, the prize money.

$11,500,000 per week revenue, not counting the web site subscription fees. Lotta cash floating around this whale.

"Have you had more or less contest entries this week?"

"Quite a few more," Mr. Reed said, sounding pleased.

Tara tossed an eight-by-ten print of a frame from the video onto the table. It was the clearest shot of the victim. A savage gash ran from her belly to her breasts. The right leg was fully extended in some kind of death kick. Mrs. Reed recoiled at the sight of it.

"How many entries are of this woman?"

CHAPTER 4

WIRED KINGDOM TECH SUPPORT FACILITY

"Four thousand six hundred and ninety-seven," Trevor Lane said, looking up from his computer monitor at the special agent standing next to him.

Tara stood in the office of *Wired Kingdom*'s technical operations, in an industrial section of the San Fernando Valley. A trash can overflowed with crumpled printouts of computer code. Stacks of technical manuals engulfed the desk, competing for space with empty caffeinated-beverage cans. Only twenty minutes from the Reeds' idyllic neighborhood, but a world away.

The number Trevor recited was much larger than Tara had hoped to hear. She wondered if one of those 4,697 contestants could have orchestrated an oceanic scene in an attempt to win the million dollars.

"That's almost a thousand entries per minute for the duration of the video," Trevor continued, clearly excited. Tara had learned from the Reeds that his average salary was augmented with handsome bonuses based on the performance of the whale-cam and web site. She noted the dark circles under his eyes.

"Let's back up a bit. Start with the telemetry device itself. Tell me how it works."

"In terms of satellite communications protocols, or video capture, data acquisition, power supply, or what?"

"Just give me a general, non-technical rundown on how it functions and what it's supposed to do," she said, scanning the room. Her eyes lingered on a binder with the logo for a well-known national defense contractor entitled "Fundamentals of Satellite Communications Protocols." *His phrasing was identical.*

"The unit is implanted on the whale's body," Trevor began. "It—"

"Excuse me, just one thing," Tara said, taking the binder from the desk. "Did you work for Martin-Northstar?"

Trevor's eyes widened a bit as she opened the manual. "Uh, no."

She shifted her gaze from the binder to Trevor, then back again. The introduction page caught her attention. *When all other resources for solving political problems have been exhausted, countries sometimes resort to the utilization of military force. The tools of this force are weapons, which, in the past, sometimes destroyed more than the intended target.* . . . She doubted the manual, stamped CONFIDENTIAL, was ever meant to be taken off the defense contractor giant's property.

"That's my father's; he's retired from Martin-Northstar."

Tara flipped through, pausing at the dog-eared pages, noting that several lines of complex equations had been highlighted. "Why do you have it?" she asked without looking up. *If the whale-cam is based on stolen defense technology . . .*

"It's just an interesting reference. I considered majoring in engineering instead of computer science, and so I asked my Dad if I could see some examples of his work."

"And you graduated how many years ago?"

An awkward hesitation.

"Seven." Trevor drummed his fingers on the desk and stared uncomfortably at the monitor, which showed a whale's back plowing through blue water.

Tara decided that at this point the origins of the whale-cam's technology were tangential to her specific case but that the potential threat of an investigation might increase Lane's level of cooperation. She handed the manual back to him, offering him a half-smile. He stuck it in a drawer.

"So the whale-cam is implanted in the whale's body?" Tara prompted.

"Right," Trevor said, glad to change subjects. "It contains a data logger that collects oceanographic data like temperature, salinity, dissolved oxygen, and what biologists call a 'depth profile' of the whale's dives. A tiny camera also captures color video; a hydrophone records audio. GPS coordinates are also recorded. These *in situ* data are then encrypted before being transmitted to the closest of our satellites in geosynchronous orbit. From there they're relayed to our secure servers, where the information is decrypted and broadcast on the show's commercial web site."

"Sounds simple enough," Tara joked. Trevor smiled condescendingly as she continued. "But I thought GPS didn't work underwater?" Tara couldn't help but watch on the monitor as a school of baitfish balled up in front of the whale. Their collective shape shifted and darted while Trevor talked.

"It doesn't work *under* water, but when the whale comes to the surface to breathe, the GPS coordinates are transmitted then. You want some coffee?" he asked, gesturing toward a pot brewing on a filing cabinet.

"No, thank you." Tara made a note in her pad.

Trevor poured himself a cup.

"Do you archive the transmitted data?"

Trevor nodded. "A copy of everything streamed to the web site is also stored on separate machines."

"I need to see the stored copy of the incident from this morning."

"Sure, but it's exactly the same as what was transmitted. The interference happened as a result of the satellite transmission."

"I still need to see it."

He led her around a corner into a glassed-in room

filled with servers and tape drives. Stepping inside, she was glad she hadn't taken off her jacket.

"It's air conditioned in here for the benefit of the machines," Trevor said, out of habit. "Several terabytes of data are recorded each week from the whale. It's all stored here."

"So all these computers are to handle the whale's telemetry feed? Or is one of them for the whale and the rest are for your online role-playing games? What's the hot game these days—I haven't evolved much past Tetris and solitaire."

"The hot game these days is *Wired Kingdom*. A million bucks a week . . . play from anywhere . . . everyone's in. All this equipment is for the whale and the *Wired Kingdom* web site."

"What do you do with all the whale's data after it streams onto the web site?"

"Nothing yet. Eventually, it will be made available via on-line subscription for anyone who wants to pay."

"Who would want to pay?"

"Researchers. Similar to how biotech companies with proprietary gene sequences make their data available to pharmaceuticals to develop new drugs with—an ocean science version of that. The database has a name already: MS. ANASTASIA REED. Or ANASTASIA for short."

"She named it after herself?" Tara asked, unimpressed. Scientists were known for personalizing important accomplishments, such as discovering new species, but this seemed unusually vain.

"Yeah, but it's also an acronym that describes the service."

"Acronym for what?"

He indicated some text on a screen.

"Marine Science Animal Network And Satellite Telemetry-ASsisted Information Archives of Real-time Environmental and Ecological Data."

"Cute," Tara said, adding to her notebook.

"I guess she wanted it so that whenever anyone needs to look at the data they have to go through MS. ANASTASIA REED."

Takes all kinds, Tara thought. She reminded him that she needed to see the video.

He pressed a key, and a copy of the transmitted footage played. Tara noted that it was indeed the same as what was broadcast. She watched the unknown woman struggling yet again. *Who are you?*

"Make me a copy of the tape, eight hours prior to the incident to right now." She observed him closely for signs of discomfort. If he had anything to hide, he'd stall, claiming that he had to obtain permission from his boss or that it would be too difficult and time-consuming to download so much data.

"Sure, it'll take a minute," he said, turning back to the machines. Tara watched him start the transfer process.

"So you have no idea what caused the interference on the video?" she continued.

"Not yet. That's what I'm trying to figure out today."

"And so there is no copy of the video unaffected by the interference?" she asked, wishing she could see through the static on the screen.

"I didn't say that," Trevor said, eyebrows raised. She waited for him to explain. He hit some keys and turned to face her. "On the whale."

"On the whale?"

"Right. The telemetry tag on the whale has its own special hard disc. That disc contains the original data—unaffected by any interference from transmission."

Okay, now I'm getting somewhere. Trevor handed her a set of computer discs containing a copy of the incident. She would submit the digital footage to an FBI lab for image analysis; they'd be able to verify its authenticity.

"Where's the whale now?" Tara asked, pocketing the discs.

"C'mon, I'll show you." Trevor exited the data storage room. Tara was glad to return to the warmth of the main office.

"These are the GPS coordinates," he said, pointing to the video feed from the whale. He saw her writing in her notepad and added, "These are always displayed here, so you can check on its position any time." The animal rested on the surface, alone in mild swells. Foamy water sluiced off its broad back. "So far it's stayed way off . . . the . . . coast," he said, his voice trailing off as he noticed a scrap of paper with his handwriting.

"What's wrong?"

"These are the GPS coordinates I wrote down at the time of the interference," he said, extricating the paper from beneath a pile of empty energy drinks. "They haven't changed on the video feed."

"Maybe the whale's still in the same location," she offered.

Trevor shook his head. "No way it can be in the *exact* same location. This isn't your standard consumer GPS. These coordinates are accurate to the nearest inch. Normally, when the whale is on the surface, you can see the coordinates changing in real time, even if she looks like she's just floating in one place."

Tara eyed the GPS data on the screen. They remained fixed, the same digits as those Trevor had copied earlier. "Has this happened before?"

"Never." A current of stress transformed his voice. "Whatever caused the interference apparently disabled the GPS function of the telemetry unit."

"And there are no other tracking devices on this whale besides yours?" she asked, hopeful.

He shook his head. "None. Animal rights groups gave the show enough of a problem over this one tag, even though it's feather-light and minimally invasive. A lot of people are against endangered mammals being turned into floating Radio Shacks."

"So there's no way to tell where the whale is now?"

It was Trevor's turn to sense her concern. He glared at the screen, frustrated. They both knew he wouldn't be getting any bonuses until the GPS was restored.

"Without the GPS, all we have is its last known location."

CHAPTER 5

WIRED KINGDOM HEADQUARTERS,
LOS ANGELES

The Los Angeles set of *Wired Kingdom* buzzed with activity. A live studio audience waited for the taping of the show. Behind the set, dozens of television studio employees scurried about making last-minute preparations. Among them was producer Anthony Silveras, who checked his watch as he spoke with a nervous assistant producer. Silveras was a stocky Mexican American in his late forties with salt-and-pepper hair. He wore his usual outfit of jeans and a Polo shirt, with cowboy boots.

"Five minutes, everybody." He held a hand up, fingers outstretched. "I just talked to Trevor and he's still got no idea what's up with the GPS."

"As long as Anastasia knows how to handle it—I hope somebody pried her out of her lab," one of Silveras' assistants said. Anastasia was known for being late, ostensibly because she was always working overtime to meet submission and publishing deadlines. "Publish or perish!" she would say, breezing onto the set minutes before airtime. Her tardiness was tolerated, due to the fact that it was her very scientific reputation that lent the show its credibility. "I still can't get over the fact that the star of the show works a real job," he added, shaking his head.

"It took a lot of convincing to get her to do the show at all; it's not like she's in it for the money."

"Yeah, well, if I had her parents . . ."

Silveras shrugged. "I still don't think–" He cut himself short as he saw a brunette of medium height, long hair tied in a ponytail, wind her way through an army of production assistants.

Anastasia waved to Anthony. She wore the same featureless, black outfit she wore for each episode. She had defended it, saying that she wanted viewers to focus on what she said as opposed to what she looked like. She couldn't find work as a fashion model, but she had been dubbed easy on the eyes by the show's producers after a test screening.

Anthony walked to greet her. "Anastasia, c'mon, you need to get to makeup right away–four minutes!" He knew that she refused all but the most basic makeup required by anyone appearing under television studio lights, but even so, she was cutting it close.

"On my way," she said, breezing past him.

"You got the script revisions?" he called after her. She gave him a wave without looking back.

Minutes later, a studio camera's red light blinked to life. Celebrated scientist Dr. Anastasia Reed began her broadcast. She sat at a low-profile computer workstation on a reflective black floor. A glass-etched wall map of the world spread out behind her, from which most of the light on the set emanated. The oceans fluoresced a deep electric blue while the continents were a dimmer green or brown. White lights indicated major metropolitan areas; a whale icon glowed red against the blue, off the Southern California coast. Ethereal electronic mood music pulsated in the background.

Several screens were visible over the map, some playing whale videos, others showing different pages of the *Wired Kingdom* web site. One screen showed nothing but an enlarged counter depicting in real time the number of Internet users currently hitting the site. The number was in the millions, the digits on the right side of the counter a blur as they turned over. A large overhead monitor descended from above, displaying the whale's live feed. To the viewers, Anastasia looked like a mysterious, pale face floating in blackness in front of a computer screen.

"Good evening ladies and gentlemen," she began, "I'm your host, Dr. Anastasia Reed, marine biologist. Welcome to *Wired Kingdom*. I know there are many questions about what our wired whale broadcast on the Internet earlier this morning. We can only say at this time that what you saw on the web is what the whale-cam transmitted. Nothing was modified or enhanced by us in any way.

"Our wired whale is an early example of using

computer engineering to answer questions about marine biology. As humans' ability to monitor the seas is extended via telepresence, we will continue to see things that would otherwise remain unknown. It's a big ocean out there, with a lot going on. Some of these things will involve people, and some may even be unpleasant. But this increased awareness of our planet's most ubiquitous environment will ultimately benefit us all."

A screen behind her changed to show a map of the whale's last known position.

"Thank you for the many e-mails and phone calls letting us know that the whale-cam's GPS unit is not working properly. Our team of technical experts is working hard to fix this problem. Until it is resolved, the whale's exact location remains unknown, although we can continue to view the animal and its surroundings."

Anastasia then launched into the main part of the show, in which she presented in detail the highlights of the whale's movements and behavior of the last week. She discussed its feeding activities, solitary lifestyle and diving abilities while referring to video clips throughout. When it was time to announce the winner of the week's contest, an overhead screen changed from a view of the whale's feed to the logo of a national telecommunications company.

"This week we asked you to look for examples of human presence in the ocean. There were many interesting entries, but after much thought, we managed to single one out. The person whose name I announce after the break will talk with us via videophone about their winning screen capture and will become the latest *Wired Kingdom* millionaire. Be right back."

The lights dimmed and videos played to entertain the studio audience as Anastasia left the stage. Although her script called for her to act as though she knew the contest winner in advance, the winning entry was chosen by a panel of producers and not known to her until it was time to give it away.

"Great job, Anastasia," Anthony said just off stage. "Going well." He handed her a folder. She nodded absentmindedly as she examined the folder's contents—the winning contest image and identity of the winner.

Her features contorted into a mask of disbelief as she saw the photo: the leg of a woman firmly in the grasp of two blue sharks; an alabaster hand pressed against the snout of one of the attackers, hopelessly outclassed by the predator's instinctive power; a river of green issuing from her ruined leg.

"You're kidding, right Anthony?" She tore her gaze from the image long enough to look him in the eye. He held his hands up in a gesture of surrender.

"No possible way!"

"Look, Anastasia, this is the winning entry. It was voted on by the panel."

"Why wasn't I—I can't believe you'd pull a stunt like this. When I agreed to do this show, it was under the condition that it be oriented towards education and awareness, not shock-value crap."

"Anastasia, maybe if you were around a little more often, instead of always showing up at the last—"

"Oh, please." She turned away in disgust, then whirled back around. "What's wrong with the oil tanker? Why couldn't that be the winner?"

"You can't be serious. A shot of an old, rusty oil tanker doesn't stand a chance against this. If we announced it as the winner, we'd lose what little credibility we have. 'Reality TV,' remember?"

"This is a family show, Anthony. How can we get away with showing something like this on prime time?" She gawked at the explicit image with open disgust.

"You'll deliver a 'graphic content' warning—just follow the teleprompter."

She shook her head. "Unbelievable."

"Try to relax, please. We're not going to play any of the actual video. Just show the still shot for five seconds and refer to the web site where they can download it along with the rest of the winners."

A cameraman started his countdown.

Anastasia shook her head and stalked away. For one terrifying moment, Silveras thought she was going to walk off the set, but she stepped around a tangle of cables on the floor and made her way back to the stage. Fumbling in his pocket for a bottle he knew was there, he swallowed a fistful of extra-strength Tylenol, dry.

Back under the harsh stage lights, Anastasia made a conscious effort to avoid revealing her distaste as she read the lines from the teleprompter.

"And now it's time to announce our contest winner for this week—the newest *Wired Kingdom* millionaire. But first I must warn you: the winning image you are about to see is extremely graphic and may not be suitable for all viewers. Parents, if you're watching tonight with young children, you may want to supervise them closely." It was an obvious ploy by the network to stimulate interest. "Here is the image submitted by our contest winner." Anastasia displayed the photo for the studio audience, who responded with a collective gasp.

After allowing them a moment to absorb the impact of the picture, she announced, "Our winner is Jerod Wilderson, of Lincoln, Nebraska." The audience applauded as a voluptuous blonde model, walking to the beat of the music playing over the loudspeakers, brought out a giant cardboard check in the amount of one million dollars and placed it on a stand. Although the show was educational in nature, even Anastasia hadn't been able to convince her father to completely strip it of the fluff which had made his earlier shows so successful. "Jerod is a nineteen-year-old college student, and he's been previously notified of his winning entry. He's waiting to chat with us now via videophone."

The screen with the corporate logo came to life and a pimply-faced teen with bad teeth greeted the audience. Anastasia went through a routine interview with the winner, thanked him for his entry, and then told the audience it was time to announce the theme of the new week's contest.

"Next week at this time, we're going to award *another* one million dollars to the most striking screen-captured image that depicts another cetacean—that is, another whale, dolphin or porpoise."

She waited for the clapping to subside before continuing.

"This—"

Shouting erupted from the studio audience. Two young men in scruffy dress near the back row unfurled a banner reading FREE THE WORLDWIDE WHALE, holding it high. Others who had been occupying the back rows, posing as mild-mannered fans, suddenly became demonstrators, parading other signs like, WHALES ARE MEANT TO BE WIRELESS, WHALE 1.0: NATURE'S VERSION RULES, and DR. ANASTASIA *GREED*.

Stage lights prevented Anastasia from seeing anything beyond the first row of seats. She continued with her concluding remarks, although the audience's attention was now focused in the opposite direction.

A squadron of headset-wearing security officers flanked the protestors, who stood their ground, becoming more vociferous. One man wielded a placard's wooden stake like a weapon from his perch on the backs of two seats in parallel rows. As two of the staff approached him from either side, the protestor leapt away, apparently intending to land astride two other seats several rows down; but he lost his footing and went down straddling a seatback, his face slamming into a chair arm. The sound of teeth rattling across the concrete floor was drowned out by screams from the audience. Moments later security guards from adjacent studios poured into the back rows and the protest was quelled.

Four bouncers carried one demonstrator from the building in a prone position, followed by a cameraman with a shoulder-cam. The protestor screamed "Ocean Liberation Front!" and spit on the camera's lens as he was taken outside, where chanting had already begun: "OLF! OLF! OLF!"

Someone killed the stage lights, and Anastasia was surprised to see the seats nearly empty and people scrambling for the exits. She was also surprised to see a woman in a dark suit standing calmly in front of her, a smallish gym bag slung over one shoulder, presenting a badge.

"You here about the protestors?" Anastasia asked, stepping down from the stage.

"Protestors? You mean they're not your fan club?" Tara started with a smile. "Special Agent Tara Shores, FBI. I'm only interested in them if they had something to do with the web video your show broadcast this morning. I'm here because I understand you're the foremost expert on this wired whale."

"You could do worse. What is it you want?"

"The FBI needs to recover the hard drive from the

whale's telemetry unit as soon as possible."

Anastasia laughed softly. "Join the club."

"I intend to get that hard drive, Dr. Reed."

"I believe you do." Anastasia paused, frowning as the audience members were ushered from the building under heavy security. Angry shouts still punctuated the roar of the evacuating crowd. "Have you thought about *how* you're going to get it?"

"I have." Anastasia appeared surprised to hear an answer in the affirmative.

"Do tell. In case you haven't noticed, we're having a little GPS problem with the tag, and we'd kind of like to get it back, too."

"We're going use a helicopter to run search patterns from the whale's last known GPS coordinates."

"You'll be wasting your time."

"By *we* I meant you and I. And we'll use a grid in whichever direction your expert opinion deems to be the most likely."

Anastasia considered this. "I suppose there's not much else you can do besides that," she said. "And I would like to go. I can have a copter reserved for the morning out of Long Beach."

"No need. I've already got one waiting, closer than that. We can be at the whale's last known coordinates with daylight to spare."

Anastasia threw up her hands. "Free helicopter ride to look for my whale on a Friday night? It's a date."

CHAPTER 6

Tara sensed Anastasia's surprise deepening as she led the marine biologist into the studio's main office building.

"There's one thing you may not have thought about," Anastasia said as they approached the elevators in the central lobby.

Tara pressed a button and turned to face her. "What's that?"

"If we do find the whale, what then? You gonna jump out of the helicopter, swim over to a ninety-seven-foot sea mammal and hope it cooperates while you rip the cam from its body?"

Tara shuddered at the thought. "As enjoyable as that sounds, bear with me while I assess my options. How is the tag attached to the whale?"

"It's embedded in the blubber layer at the base of the dorsal fin. The attachment protocol involved a crossbow for propulsion to implant a deployment dart fitted with the tag. The dart breaks away once the tag is embedded in the blubber layer, leaving the antenna, sensors and camera lens outside. The tag has a medical grade titanium housing with four holes drilled in it, covering a broad-spectrum antibiotic gel so that it's bio-inert and won't cause infections. The whole thing is smaller than a soda can, cylindrical, but tapered at both ends to reduce drag."

"How is it designed to be retrieved?"

"Unless I calculated incorrectly, and the blubber layer thickens too much during the summer feeding season, we should be able to trigger the release mechanism by passing a magnet over the saltwater switch. The unit can then be extracted by hand—in theory, anyway. I've had problems with the pop-up tags that were designed to automatically drop off the animal after a certain amount of time. Hopefully I didn't overcompensate. But this one is a real breakthrough, both in terms of long-term retention and the increased sampling schedule. I didn't want it coming off, especially knowing what the thing cost."

"So you need to physically touch it with a magnet?"

"Yes. If a strong magnet passes over the tag, it triggers a rapid mechanical process that retracts a flared collar at the base of the unit. Then it can be pulled out by hand from the blubber layer."

"Okay. If we see the whale, I'll radio its GPS coordinates and current heading to our Underwater Evidence Search Team, and then pick up the search with them at first light."

They entered the elevator. The truth was that although the FBI did have a specialized underwater unit, it was headquartered in New York. It handled elite underwater tasks such as helping NASA to recover space shuttle debris after an accident, and there was no way Tara could appropriate its resources on such short notice. She'd had to pay back enough favors as it was to requisition the helicopter. However, Tara saw no reason to downplay the resources available to her while in the field on a case.

"I didn't know the FBI had an underwater search team," Anastasia said as they began their ascent.

"It's pretty low profile, but they've got technical divers and Remotely Operated Vehicles."

"Still, you'd have to find the whale *again* after waiting for first light, and the boat trip back out."

They exited the elevator on the top floor and Tara held out her gym bag. "Besides relaying information to the underwater team, I'm hoping that if the opportunity presents itself I might be able to make their work a bit easier." She unzipped the duffel.

"What special agent worth her salt doesn't carry a bag of tricks?" Anastasia said, watching as Tara removed something from the bag. "But whatever's in there, I doubt it can help."

Tara was irritated with Anastasia's constant reminders of the slim odds of recovering the whale's device anytime soon. She removed a two-foot-long contraption that looked like a weapon, but instead of something lethal on the business end of it there was a large-diameter suction cup. A small boxy object with an antenna was attached to the cup. Tara held the device up for Anastasia's inspection.

"I see you brought your own tracking dart. What is that thing, ten years old?"

Tara shrugged. "Wouldn't surprise me. FBI keeps all kinds of stuff around for decades. But it doesn't have to shoot video or do Twitter updates, it just needs to mark the whale's position. The techies assure me it'll do that."

Anastasia chuckled. "It works for a few hours before it pops off the host and floats around until you pick it up again—and even that's only if you know how to use it." She shook her head in a silent laugh of incomprehension before continuing. "I definitely give you an 'A' for effort. But seriously, you need to decide what exactly it is you want to do."

"Got any better ideas? I don't know how to use it, but you do, right?"

Anastasia grew serious. "I'm only trying to help. Let me explain. Those guns are meant to be used from boats to deploy tags at close range."

"So?"

"So, you said we have a helicopter waiting, not a boat." Tara nodded and started walking down the hall toward a door marked ROOF while she put the tagger back in the bag.

She opened the door to gusts of warm air. A dark blue Schweizer 300C piston engine helicopter sat at the ready on a marked helipad, door open. The two women stood in the doorway where they could still hear over the engine.

"With the resources *Wired Kingdom* has, I'm surprised you haven't already used a helicopter *and* boats together to slap a basic GPS locator on your whale," Tara called back.

"Not that simple." Anastasia raised her voice as they approached the helo. "For one thing, I haven't filed for a permit on a new tracker yet. Federal regs are strict. I'm not allowed to go shooting the thing with whatever I want, whenever I want. When we go out on a tagging cruise, our permit contract specifies the exact number of times we're allowed to approach the whale, how many shots we're allowed to take, with precisely what equipment, the number of personnel on board—everything down to the smallest detail. Any amount of variance with the filed plan triggers a mandatory incident report."

"Ah, government bureaucracy. So what's the other thing?"

"The other thing is that *Wired Kingdom*'s tag has only been malfunctioning for a few hours. It could be due to some temporary atmospheric disturbance—solar winds or something—that could resolve itself any minute. Trevor's looking into it. Anyway, I'm not going to launch a full-scale recovery operation only to have the tag start working on its own the minute we set off. In this business you learn to deal with unpredictability. Of course, had I known there would be a murder investigation involving the tag, I would have acted sooner."

Tara warned Anastasia to duck under the rotors as

they jogged forward. Entering the cockpit, they sat three across with the pilot, who sported a dark crew cut behind a headset and mirrored sunglasses. “Name’s Rob Tanner, FBI pilot,” he said, nodding to Anastasia.

Tara occupied the middle seat, as she wanted her whale expert to have an unobstructed view. “This is his first solo flight, so bear with him!” Rob laughed while Anastasia's eyes widened in alarm.

“She says that every time,” Rob said, flipping some switches on the control panel. “I've been flying for over twenty years.” Anastasia eyed Tara with doubtful curiosity.

They lifted off into the L.A. skyline and headed towards the ocean, already visible as a shimmering band of silver to the west. As they passed over the Century Plaza Towers, Tara turned to Anastasia. “Have you had trouble with protestors before?”

“Not like today. There have been threats in the past, but never any violence.”

“What kind of threats?”

“That wacko group, Ocean Liberation Front, they want us to take the tag off the whale. We knew there’d be some protestors going into this, but I had no idea they were so extreme. These guys have members in prison for blowing up SUV dealerships and killing Japanese whalers.”

“Is it possible the woman in the video is an OLF activist who was killed in an attempt to remove the tag? Maybe they damaged it and that’s why the GPS stopped working?"

Anastasia shrugged. "It's possible, but they haven't claimed responsibility yet. They're like terrorists that way, they crave publicity."

Tara considered this as the pilot engaged in some technical chatter with a control tower. If the video was a botched tag-removal attempt by a radical environmental group, the tactics represented a significant departure from their known methods.

"I don't understand why people get so upset over it, anyway," Anastasia continued. "The technology empowers the animals; it doesn't hurt them. It enables them to protect themselves by using information as a weapon. Who's going to poach a whale or a tiger or an elephant, knowing they could be caught on video for the whole world to see?"

"The same type of people who rob banks, knowing they're full of security cameras, I guess. Desperate people. But the thing about these animal cams is that they do also give away the animal's location to potential poachers. Is that why Ocean Liberation Front is so angry—because you plan to tag more animals with this technology?"

"We haven't said as much, publicly, but we are in the permitting process for more whales and for some African predators, mostly big cats."

As they flew over a beach dotted with city dwellers escaping the heat, water stretched before them to the horizon, interrupted briefly by the mountainous Channel Islands. Taking in the vast expanse with their objective in mind, Tara realized how daunting her task was. *Maybe Dr. Reed is right after all. This whale might as well be the proverbial needle in a haystack.* But she had to try. Bigger and better cases were waiting for her as soon as she exposed this silly goose chase for what it was.

"Rob," Tara began, "are the whale's last known GPS coordinates set?"

"That's affirmative," he replied as he banked the craft northwest.

"Couldn't hope for better weather," Anastasia said. Tara agreed with a nod. That was one small factor in her favor. The late summer afternoon sun blazed in a cloudless, blue sky and, far below them, the sea was calm as they hurtled out over the Pacific.

The wired whale was not alone.

Driven to the cooler, temperate waters off the California coast after enduring a long fall and winter in the nutrient-poor tropics, she gorged herself on fields of shrimp-like crustaceans known as krill. The paradox of the planet's largest animals sustaining themselves by feeding on some of the smallest has long fascinated naturalists. The closer to the bottom of the food chain the organism is, the more efficient it is at meeting its energetic needs. Plants are at the bottom of this food chain and, in the ocean, microscopic plants called phytoplankton harvest energy directly from its ultimate source: the sun. These so-called "primary producers" are then consumed by microscopic animals termed zooplankton, which in turn are eaten by krill, which are themselves eaten by larger animals. Each step up this chain, or "trophic level," represents a significant loss of energy efficiency. Because baleen whales (those that filter feed for krill and copepods as opposed to toothed whales, which eat meat) feed so low on the food chain, they are able to take advantage of high levels of available energy in order to fuel their enormous bodies. Blue whales must eat about three million calories per day, or about three to four tons of krill.

The wired "Blue" now found herself in an area where this requirement could be effortlessly exceeded. Nothing could distract the animal from this kind of bounty—not even the white seaplane that had landed nearby.

Héctor González brought his amphibious craft to an easy halt, bobbing atop large but orderly swells, as his two scuba divers tested their underwater communications gear. The divers exclaimed to one another in rapid, excited bursts how much larger the Blue was than the gray whales they had dived with at home, until Héctor told them to shut up. They protested that even if someone had managed to intercept their secure frequencies, the language barrier would likely keep them from being understood.

Behind his baseball cap and sunglasses, Héctor's face reddened as he looked back at his men. "Listen to me! Our language itself is an identifier. When using the communications units, you will speak only when absolutely necessary to coordinate your activities. Every second that passes puts us at greater risk."

His men were excellent divers and all-around watermen, but were not accustomed to the precise, almost paramilitary tactics they were now forced to employ. The limited time he'd had for briefings back home would have to suffice, Héctor thought. He eyed the whale. In it, he saw his daughter's future and prayed inwardly that it would not dive.

Even when the two divers jumped from the aircraft and began swimming toward the Blue, she refused to interrupt her feeding.

But suddenly, the goliath registered a new presence.

Multiple contacts. Large. Fast.

Orca.

The pod racing towards her was unusual in that it consisted of so many members—about forty in all—representing every strata of killer whale society. Male and female hunters led the pursuit. Older adults guarded the calves near the rear of the pod. An Orca mother who had carried her stillborn calf in her mouth for the last twenty-four hours finally relinquished her lifeless offspring to the sea. Her own life had a new purpose now: the ultimate sustenance . . . an adult blue whale. A Blue was far too massive an animal for any one Orca to challenge, but for a coordinated team, even the largest creature ever to inhabit the planet was fair game.

The hunters split into several groups, two to six in each. They shadowed the Blue, their intent to surround her. The Blue dove. She needed to survey the area without remaining vulnerable on the surface. Three hundred feet down in near darkness she hung vertically. The sea filled with staccato bursts of echolocation as predators and prey each sought information about the other.

While the Blue could hold her breath three times longer than her adversaries—almost an hour—the killers were well aware she'd have to surface before long. Patience was second nature to Orca; they would not waste their energy diving. The Blue wanted to control when and where she surfaced. Otherwise she might find herself forced to come up to breathe in the middle of the marauders, gasping and weak while they ambushed her.

She sliced upward at an oblique angle, aiming for an open patch of water. Reaching the surface, she ignored the two scuba divers now swimming much closer. In a display of raw power that said *leave me alone* to humans and Orca alike, the whale raised her fluke, twenty-three feet across, and slammed it against the surface. The sound carried underwater for miles, chased the humans back, and gave the Orca pause.

But the Orca had numbers. The lead group, consisting of two twenty-six-foot-plus males, accelerated.

The fight for life was on.

WIRED KINGDOM TECH SUPPORT FACILITY

At his computer, Trevor Lane jumped in his chair at the explosive sound made by the whale's fluke slap, knocking over his latest mug of coffee. Ignoring the spill as it dripped onto his jeans, he studied the whale's feed on the monitor. A pair of six-foot, black dorsal fins porpoised across the screen. Seabirds dashed, making shallow test-dives, waiting for a probable meal.

Trevor hurried over to the server room to monitor the machines carefully, optimizing them for the onslaught of activity he expected to hit the web site. *Killer whales attacking the Blue live on the web. Here comes my bonus.*

It was a different sound which drew his attention back to his desk.

A rhythmic thumping grew steadily louder.

33° 24' 23.1" N AND 118° 04' 86.3" W

Orca groups took flank positions around the Blue while six individuals cut off her forward flight. Panicking at the sharp bites along her pleated belly, the Blue charged. The lead Orca leapt from the sea, unable to stop its prey's forward momentum, while other Orca inflicted nasty bites on her pectoral fins as she passed. With blood flowing freely, more Orca moved into position, cutting off the Blue again.

Over the next ten minutes the dance was repeated, the Blue showing visible signs of fatigue and stress.

Circling warily on the surface, ragged breaths sputtering from her double blowhole, she again slapped her fluke, this time scattering far fewer of her adversaries.

Two adult males rushed at her head.

Neither predators nor prey noticed the two humans closing in from behind.

The Blue executed a series of shallow dives meant to break the attacker's concentration, but the Orca regrouped each time she surfaced. The Blue kept her mouth shut, knowing the Orca would rip her tongue out if they could. Then the largest Orca, a weathered, twenty-seven-foot male, saw an opportunity. The Blue's left side was exposed when she lunged at attackers to the right and front.

The killer barreled in, jaws bared to remove a lamb-sized portion of flesh from the whale's left flank. Instead, it detected an unusual signal, electrical in nature, stronger than the familiar biological impulses. Cocking its head to one side, it *ping*ed its prey's dorsal fin, allowing the Blue the seconds she needed to defend herself.

In an agile feat of maneuverability, the 100-ton animal rolled to one side, thrust her head down and, in one motion, raised her great fluke nearly vertical out of the water. Then she smashed it down onto the attacking Orca's melon. The concussive impact rendered the Orca unconscious. As its limp body began sinking into the depths, the trailing elders broke from the attack to prod their fallen comrade back to the surface. Frustrated, one of the lead hunters paused to assess the miniscule, clumsy mammals which still flitted about the Blue like oversized cleaner fish.

As they flew over the Blue's last known coordinates, Tara realized this was her first look at the crime scene . . . if in fact it was a crime scene, she reminded herself. The featureless plane of open sea did not offer many clues. She was used to being able to at least walk around a crime scene and examine things; to collect fibers, shell casings, weapons, fingerprints; or extract DNA from hair samples or skin tissue. Peering down from the helicopter, all she saw was a barren, unforgiving environment.

"What's the water temperature right now?" she asked Anastasia.

"Sixty-four, a little cooler than last summer."

"How long could a person survive out here in sixty-four-degree water?"

"For most people you're looking at about four hours max, maybe up to eight with a wetsuit. Any kind of flotation device increases the odds of survival, too."

"And how deep is it?"

"About sixteen hundred feet."

"Anything unusual about this area of ocean?"

"Not in a Bermuda Triangle sense if that's what you mean. But the whales come here for a reason. Animal and plant life in the sea are not distributed randomly; they follow complex patterns. This area represents a boundary between cold northern currents and warmer southern currents."

She was in the process of explaining the cycles of seasonal upwelling and krill blooms when they saw movement and splashing ahead. Anastasia grabbed a set of binoculars and focused on the activity. "Whale!" she called, still looking through the lenses. "It's a *Balaenoptera*—a blue. Could be our girl, but she's not alone."

"What do you mean?" Tara asked, shifting to get a better view over Anastasia's shoulder.

"Orca. Big pod, and they're hunting her—wait," she broke off, scanning the scene through binoculars as the pilot reduced altitude, "there's a plane."

"Let me see." Tara grabbed the binoculars from Anastasia and trained them on a white speck near the commotion. "White seaplane," she said to Rob, glancing at the radio.

Taking the radio transmitter, the pilot called for the aircraft to identify itself.

No response.

"Did you send out spotter planes?" Anastasia asked. Tara shook her head while continuing to peer through the lenses. She ignored the plane for the moment and zoomed in on the whale's dorsal fin. She waited for the water lapping over the animal to subside, and then she saw it: a glint of metal.

"That's it! That's the whale. I can see the tag," she said. She handed the binoculars back to Anastasia for confirmation.

"Yeah, there she is."

If the Orca succeeded in killing the whale, its corpse would sink to the bottom and the device would be lost forever.

"They're going to eat that whale?" Tara asked, incredulous. It didn't seem possible for such a large animal to be eaten.

"They're going to try, anyway. They're not always successful, but this pod is unusually large. We don't have much data on this—we're extremely lucky to see it."

"So are millions of web viewers," the pilot pointed out.

Scanning the water close to the Blue, Tara spotted something alarming. "Is that a—*a diver on the surface, surrounded by Orca*," she finished in her head. *Why is he there?*

He was a scary distance from his plane. The aircraft began a cautious taxi closer to the Blue. Tara had to do something to stop the diver from getting the whale's tag . . . or being killed by Orca before she could question him.

She outlined a simple plan to Rob.

CHAPTER 7

WIRED KINGDOM TECH SUPPORT FACILITY

Glued to his monitor, Trevor could hear an engine nearing the whale. That alone was odd enough, but it was the image on screen that now commanded his attention. A human figure approached the tagged cetacean. The diver occupied more of the screen as he neared the camera. He was encased in black gear, including a full face mask with a tinted faceplate, making it impossible to see anything behind it. The diver's gloved hand seemed to be reaching out to grab Trevor as it enveloped the camera, plunging the screen into darkness. *What the hell? I didn't hear anything about an expedition to get the tag back.*

The gloved hand lifted and Trevor could see again. The blue undercarriage of a helicopter came into view and then disappeared as the whale rolled in a swirl of bubbles. When the water cleared, he saw the fingers of one gloved hand obscuring the left part of the screen.

The computer speakers shook with the rapid throb of the chopper.

Why are they so close?

The diver's other hand appeared on screen, holding an object. Trevor leaned forward, squinting. A square piece of metal.

A magnet.

The computer whiz thought about what he'd gone through at Martin-Northstar in order to gain what he thought of as his inspiration for the tag's design. *Could these guys be from M-N?*

The hand with the magnet grew larger on Trevor's screen. The percussive beat of the helicopter's blades chopping at the air came in uneven bursts as waves lapped over the hydrophone. Then the unmistakable black and white of an Orca, slicing across the field of view, hammered into the diver, cracking his faceplate and knocking the piece of metal free from the black glove.

The Blue moved off. The diver was nowhere to be seen.

Did he trigger the release?

Trevor kicked his chair out of the way and shifted to a second computer. He scanned its technical information, looking for the line of code that would tell him whether the tag's release mechanism had been triggered. *Please don't say* True.

He found the line:

STATUS.RELEASE("ACTIVATION") = FALSE

Trevor breathed a sigh of relief. The tag was still attached to the Blue.

Unnerved, he picked up a phone and got Anthony

Silveras after a single ring. "Who's trying to get the tag?" Trevor demanded without preamble.

"Don't know. Anastasia took a chopper ride with the FBI agent to see if they could get a spot on the whale, but they didn't mention anything to me about divers."

"That tag is my technology, Anthony. If the show is trying to take it from me by pretending to have it stolen—"

"Hey, take it easy, Trevor. It's not us. Try some decaf."

Trevor made an effort to relax. "The release wasn't triggered," he managed.

"Doesn't surprise me. Probably some weekend thrill-seekers with money to burn. They don't know what they're doing."

Trevor wasn't a diver, but he didn't think the tinted facemasks he'd seen looked like typical sport-diving gear. "How much of the feed did you see?"

"None, I was in the editing room. I just heard about it."

Trevor suspected as much, given Silveras' casual tone. "I wouldn't say they didn't know what they were doing."

"Why's that?"

"Tell me this: have any of the shows ever talked about the release mechanism?"

"No, we agreed not cover the specifics on that."

"It's never been on the web site anywhere, either."

"So?"

"So . . . how'd they know to bring a *magnet*?" He raised his voice at the end of the sentence, too loud to hear the cacophony of shouting and ringing phones on the other end of the receiver.

"They read up on wildlife tracking technology, big deal. Look, Trevor, I gotta take some of these calls. Make sure the web site's ready for heavy traffic."

Trevor returned his attention to the Blue's feed. Something on screen wasn't right. At the moment there was only the Blue's back and water, but it didn't look like normal water. Trevor checked the tint and contrast settings for his monitor. DEFAULT. Still, the water was too dark, too . . . red. *Blood? Killers got the Blue.* He imagined the tag sinking to the black depths of the sea on the remnants of the giant carcass, or even being swallowed whole by a ravenous Orca, broadcasting on its way down the beast's gullet. . . .

Then the perspective on screen changed, and Trevor could see all too clearly that the blood was not from the Blue.

33° 25' 25.4" N AND 118° 03' 87.7" W

"Hover. No, Lower. Bring it down."

The helicopter bore down on the Blue's dorsal fin. The seaplane was less than a football field away, bounding toward them on the surface like a skipped stone.

"Any lower than this, we'll land on the whale's back," Rob shouted back to Tara. Rotor wash churned the sea to froth. They had hoped to scare the Blue into diving before the diver could get near the tag, but she'd stubbornly held her position on the surface, fending off Orca.

Tara watched in disbelief as the fully geared scuba diver was launched into the air, arms flailing. Unable to take down the Blue, the Orca batted this new victim around like a seal, dragging him under by an arm before resurfacing.

Tara yelled for Anastasia to switch seats with her. She removed her Glock .40 caliber from a shoulder harness worn under her suit jacket. Anastasia looked in shock at the gun and tore off her seatbelt. They scrambled around each other and Tara leaned out the window, taking aim.

The diver floated motionless, face down. An Orca nosed under him, ready to fling its new toy to the others. Breath held, Tara was about to fire warning shots near the Orca when the Blue exhaled beneath them, coating the aircraft in blinding respiratory mist. No longer able to see what she was aiming at and gagging on the rank smell filling her mouth and lungs, she lowered her weapon. As she did so, her eyes lit on the gym bag at her feet. At the same time, flying blind, Rob eyed the altimeter and yanked on the collective, putting more sky between them and the water. He flicked on the windscreen wipers and activated the defogging system once they had reached a safe altitude.

Eighty vertical feet and a few seconds later the

windscreen cleared. They could see the Blue moving, her torpedo shape beginning to slide out of sight beneath the surface, and the seaplane drifting much closer, a diver struggling to pull himself aboard. The other diver floated listlessly among the pod of killers beneath the helicopter.

Tara yanked the tracking dart out of the bag. She handed it to Anastasia with the instruction, “Set it up and give it back to me.” Anastasia took the tagger while Tara looked down at the scene unfolding below. “Rob, look, there’s a second diver. Take us back down.”

Rob nodded and eased them to a mere ten feet over the swells.

“Ready to go,” Anastasia declared. She handed the tagging gun back to Tara. “Want me to take the shot?” Anastasia asked. “I presume you haven’t tagged a whale before?”

Tara thought fast as she considered this. The diver still floated there, the plane was still nearby, but the whale was leaving. Now. “No time to switch seats again.” Tara said as she opened the cockpit door. “How much recoil does it have compared to a regular gun?”

“I’ve never fired a regular gun,” Anastasia said. “But it does kick back a little.”

“What are you doing?” Rob shouted after Tara. Ignoring his protests, Tara stepped out onto the skid and, bracing herself on the doorframe with one hand, she pointed the big suction cup dart at the whale’s back. The old phrase about hitting the side of a barn ran through her head. She'd never fired anything like this before, but she was an expert markswoman with a variety of traditional weapons. From this distance, even in motion the Blue presented a can't-miss target to Tara. The familiar sense of focus that aided her when target shooting came over the special agent as she held her breath. The whale's back was arching into a diving maneuver almost directly under the helicopter. With Rob screaming at her to get back inside, Tara squeezed the trigger. She felt rather than heard the dart leave the firing mechanism.

Tara watched as the dart impacted with the Blue's hide. The suction cup hit where she'd intended, on a patch of skin that appeared free of barnacles, and stuck there.

"It's on. It's on!" She handed the now dartless gun back to Anastasia.

They watched as the Blue submerged, positioning itself for a deep dive.

Seconds later, something appeared on the surface, bobbing in the swells.

The suction cup dart with its attached GPS transponder. It had come free of the whale.

Tara couldn't hide her disappointment. Her eyes bored into the water but there was now no sign whatsoever of the Blue.

Anastasia put a hand on Tara's shoulder. "The cup slid off when it submerged. Don't feel bad, your shot was pretty good. Happens all the time."

A black form below commanded Tara's attention. The diver. Tara shifted her thoughts to how she would get the body aboard. The identification of the dead man could break open the case. Looking under the seat she found only a coil of thin, yellow polypropylene line.

"We got a harness or a grappling hook, something to haul the body in with?"

"Hell no!" Rob said. "This isn't a search-and-rescue bird. Strictly survey. Don't do anything stupid," he said, casting a quick but concerned glance her way.

"Lifejackets?"

"Negative."

She hesitated. He pressed his case. "Look, Agent Shores, this wasn't part of the plan. I said we'd chase the whale off; that's what we did. It's gone. I didn't agree to any tagging or body recovery. We are not equipped for that."

A red indicator light started blinking in the dash, as if to agree. He pointed to it. "We go in now or we won't have enough fuel to make it back," he said, relieved to be saved by the bell. Nobody argued with the fuel light.

"Can't you do something?" Tara argued.

"Yeah, I can bring us back in."

"What about the reserve?" Tara asked, turning her attention to the poly line. She could tie it off to the aircraft and then fasten the other end to the diver's body to keep it from drifting away while they pulled it aboard. But where to tie the line? This was not a utility helicopter with an abundance of straps and D-rings. Her eyes darted about the cabin. She saw only smooth upholstery.

"We need all the reserve as it is now," Rob said.

Tara shook her head. "There must be something you can do." She wrapped the free end of the poly line through a seatbelt clip and was fumbling with a crude knot when Anastasia put down the binoculars and grabbed the line.

"Let me do that," she said. Tara let go and watched closely. Anastasia's hands worked the line while Rob continued to argue with Tara.

"You can record the coordinates from my plotter, Shores; that's what you can do. We'll send back a search-and-rescue team." Tara glared at him, testing his resolve. A veteran military pilot who had flown missions in the Gulf War, Rob was not used to passengers—even law enforcement professionals—questioning his judgment. "You have sixty seconds."

"I'll take it," she said, giving Anastasia's now completed knot a violent tug. It was remarkably solid for the few seconds she'd had to work on it, and she'd further reinforced it with a complex noose arrangement that spiraled up the strap. "Thanks," Tara said.

Anastasia shrugged. "You won't need it anyway. Those Orca are having too much fun with their new toy. They won't be going anywhere." Below, several killer whales had surfaced near the unresponsive diver. One of the younger ones nosed the lost suction cup tag along like a plaything.

"Trust me, they'll be leaving," Tara said, climbing back out onto the skid.

Taking aim in a one-handed grip with her Glock, she fired four rounds above the Orca, and the pod started to move away.

At a short distance, two Orca stopped to spyhop, assuming a vertical posture with their heads out of water, to assess the new threat. Tara placed two more warning shots well over their melons. She knew she'd be roasted alive by animal rights groups and the public in general if the Blue's web-cam caught her shooting at the popular creatures. The Orca dove to escape the sharp *pop*s and fled, leaving the motionless diver behind to mark the center of a spreading blood cloud.

The floatplane taxied around, one diver safely back on board. Tara shouted to Rob through the open window, "Tell the plane to stop."

Rob addressed the plane through the helicopter's loudhailer: "White Cessna seaplane, this is the FBI. Turn off your engine now. Repeat, this is the FBI—turn off your engine."

The plane turned tail and throttled up for takeoff. It would soon be gone. Tara looked down at the body floating beneath her. She'd been unable to place a working locator tag on the whale, and they'd never catch the plane, but the body would be almost as good. She squatted, still standing on the skid and, finding a lower handhold, leaned out to grab the man.

Rob was red-faced. "Agent Shores! I cannot allow—"

"Just bring me a little closer. I'll pull in the body

and we're outta here."

"There's no time!"

Just focus on the body, she told herself. *Focus . . .* The water was so blue. So clear. She felt as though she could see all the way through the water column to the bottom thousands of feet below. The sunlight flashed off the topping swells and a brilliant rainbow rose in the mist surrounding the helicopter. An overwhelming sense of vertigo seized her, made her weak. She clutched the rim of the door tighter and forced herself to breathe. "Closer!"

Shaking his head and muttering something about a crazy bitch, something about putting this in his report, Rob nosed the helicopter closer to the diver.

Tara saw a glint from the diver's cracked faceplate as he crested a swell. She inched the hand with the line out a little farther.

One more swell . . .

She eyed the diver's weight belt, readying herself to snare it. *Focus . . .* The diver's body began to lift with a rising swell. Rob's expert piloting kept the craft positioned just over the surface. The wave reached Tara's runner, washing over her feet. She stretched out and grabbed for the diver.

Then an Orca slammed into the chopper from the pilot's side, the impact pitching Special Agent Tara Shores into the cool Pacific.

CHAPTER 8

Every one of Tara's nerve endings protested the cold. After the cozy confines of the helicopter, the frigid water was shocking. Angry. Salt water stung her eyes, but she kept them open for fear of swimming down instead of up. She hadn't felt this like this since . . .

Don't think. Just swim.

The urge to breathe wrenched her back to reality. Her head broke the surface. She shrieked for breath, her ears assaulted with a cacophony of wind, waves and chopper wash. Then she remembered: *Orca!*

The realization that she was in close proximity to animals that had just killed a man only made things worse. Panic began to wash over her with the surrounding swells. Still dressed in business attire, Tara struggled to keep her head up. She kicked hard, feeling a shoe come loose. As she sputtered for breath between cresting waves, she saw the diver float innately over a swell. Using a crawl stroke that had been dubbed "ungainly and inefficient" by an FBI swim instructor during her academy days, she made her way toward the body. She recalled her instructor's words: *You've really got no business being in the water at all, you know, Shores.* She agreed, but never thought it would matter.

A strident hissing came from the direction of the diver. Then she caught a glimpse of a severed regulator hose whipping about, spewing compressed air, before another swell slapped her in the face. Currents and wind narrowed the gap between her and the diver, and she saw what had really happened for the first time. A riot of shredded neoprene told its own horror story. Feeling her ability to reason abandoning her, she tried to flip the lifeless body over to see if she could establish a better hold, only to find that the right arm was missing.

A mouthful of water stifled her startled gasp. She choked and sputtered and coughed, and held on tight. The dead man lay face down. Tara felt the sickening warmth of his blood spilling out around her. Now feeling not only nausea but terror, she tried to scramble atop the fresh corpse, the buoyancy control vest still inflated with enough air to keep them both afloat. For now.

The helicopter hovered over Tara as she wrestled with the diver before falling back in the water.

"What is she doing?"

Rob shook his head. "I don't know, but we need to pick her up and get out of here."

Below, Tara continued to flail about ineffectively.

"I could swim out—" Anastasia started.

"No. You just sit right there."

"She needs help!"

"I'll bring us closer. She can swim over. You pull her in." But to Anastasia it didn't look like Tara was capable of swimming anywhere.

Rob maneuvered the aircraft so that the landing gear kissed the water's surface, but the rotor wash pushed Tara and the body farther away. Rob pounded the dash in frustration. "What the hell is she doing?"

Anastasia grabbed the line tied to the seatbelt and hauled on it. Tara struggled to stay above water while she clung to the diver. The vest was losing air, and his heavy weight belt was dragging him—and Tara—underwater. Worse, the way blood issued from the corpse, it wouldn't be long before sharks were drawn to the scene.

"Let go of the diver," Rob called through the loud hailer. "You've got to get back in the chopper. I can't maintain this position."

But Tara's dread was such that she could do nothing but grip the sinking body. She still clutched the poly line in one hand but could not concentrate enough to attach it to the diver.

Anastasia felt the sea spray on her face as she drew in the line hand over hand. The slack ran out and she pulled harder to overcome the resistance. Tara, white-knuckling the line in one hand, was pulled away from the diver. She tried to protest against losing her crucial evidence, but her words were cut short by another mouthful of bloody saltwater.

Anastasia continued to reel her in. As Tara reached the helicopter, a rolling swell caught the side of the craft. Water entered through the open door. Numerous splashes from unseen creatures peppered the surface around them as blood continued to disperse in a thousand microcurrents.

Anastasia sat on the helicopter's skid and lugged the FBI agent onto the hovering skid.

"The body—help me get the body," Tara called out.

Anastasia shook her head. "Are you crazy? Sharks! No more fuel! C'mon!"

Rob was hollering for both of them to get back in the helicopter as Anastasia pulled Tara up by her belt and made sure she was securely on the skid before they lifted off.

Anastasia pulled Tara inside the cockpit. Rob glared at the detective as she took a seat next to him. Tara examined the sea below as they rose above the surface. They looked on as the unidentified body slipped beneath the waves, its black-clad form dissolving into the watery gloom before their eyes.

The Blue was nowhere to be seen. The divers and their plane . . . gone. Empty ocean sprawled for miles in every direction. For all appearances, Tara thought, holding her feet out of the water sloshing around on the cabin floor, nothing had ever happened.

CHAPTER 9

SANTA MONICA MUNICIPAL AIRPORT

Two disheveled women stepped from the helicopter that had just touched down on the tarmac, one soaking wet. A crowd of waiting reporters shouted questions. “Is it true, Agent Shores, that you’re investigating the first ever murder broadcast live over the Internet?”

“No comment.” She pushed through the reporters, Anastasia close behind. The show host put an arm around Tara, falling into step with her. She spoke softly into the detective’s ear. “Why don’t we catch a taxi to my place and dry off. You look like you’re about my size; I’m sure I can come up with an outfit for you.”

Tara stopped walking and turned to Anastasia, conscious of the reporters. Anastasia traced her fingers lightly along Tara’s arm. Before Tara could answer, a black Town Car rolled to a stop a short distance away. Tara slipped away. “This is my ride. I’ve got to get back to work.”

“Chauffeured limo, cool. They stock champagne in there?”

Tara was surprised to see her boss, Special Agent in Charge Will Branson, step from the car. It wasn't often that he visited the field. *Wonder if he saw it on the web.* Branson walked briskly toward her, shaking his head. *Yep. He saw it.*

"Agent Shores, are you hurt?" he asked. He threw a blanket over her while other FBI personnel escorted Anastasia away from the throng of reporters.

"No, sir. My outfit is done for," she said, looking at her soaked and ripped pants, "but I'm in one piece."

"Get in the car." Before he shut the door behind her, he added, "Somebody sure as hell wants that video unit, Shores. Get it before they do. That's an order."

SANTA MONICA BEACH

Private Investigator Roger Carr checked his cell phone for the tenth time in as many minutes. Still on, ready to receive calls, though none came. He shifted his considerable bulk in the sand as his head turned to soak up the scenery. Beautiful day, he thought. The only thing preventing his full enjoyment of it was the no smoking signs. He chortled aloud at the absurdity of it. No smoking on the beach. Only in L.A.

The floral-print shirt, floppy hat and cheap sunglasses pegged him for a tourist, but in fact Mr. Carr was a longtime resident of the City of Angels. He was here in connection with his lone client, although the P.I. would be the first to admit that his current undertaking was a long shot more aimed at giving him time to indulge in some girl-watching than it was serious work. But one never knew, he thought, looking around. That fat cat television producer had told his bimbo to meet her here today. And *that* little stakeout had been rather rewarding, hadn't it, Roger mused to himself. Sure, the pay was good—better than he was used to—but the photo that it had produced was exceptional!

Which reminded him. Were they going to call, or what? Pictures like that didn't come around every day. One more day, Roger told himself. If he didn't hear from them by this time tomorrow, he'd offer the images to another magazine. There'd be plenty of takers.

In the meantime, he was bored, fixating on a pair of women in skimpy two-piece suits, tops undone, lying down by the water. He thought about walking over there for a better look, but decided against it. It was a huge beach, not crowded on this late weekday afternoon, and he knew the girls would become uncomfortable if an overweight, old curmudgeon such as himself were to take one step within a hundred feet of them.

His elbow hit something in his backpack as he shifted positions, and a smile crossed his face. He fished out his Pentax and uncapped the long zoom lens. Here we go, he thought, bringing the viewfinder to his eye. He was trying to decide which sunbather he admired more when a voice mere feet away spiked his heart rate. He lowered the camera and turned around to see a pair of policemen on quadrunner ATVs. How did they manage to sneak up on him like that? Some P.I., he thought bitterly.

"Hey, Mr. Wildlife Photographer," one of the cops said, nodding at the camera. "Maybe that's okay in Europe, or wherever you come from, but not on this beach. This is your one warning. Put that thing away and move on, you got it? You're done here for the day."

Roger mumbled something about a lens check as he gathered his things. The ATVs left him in a cloud of sand and rolled away toward a bike path. The revving engines came close to drowning out the sound of Roger's cell phone.

Clutching it tight against his head, he trundled across the sand back into the city.

Tara wanted nothing more than to go home and take a shower. But on the trip back to the field office, FBI personnel in the car informed her of the diver seen on the web with a hand on the tag. The full video during the helicopter trip would have to be carefully reviewed.

"And this came back," the agent said, holding out a file with the results of the background check she'd ordered on Trevor. "I could run over there and put some serious pressure on this tech nerd, given—"

"Thanks. I got it," she said, cutting him off, and took the file out of his hand. The case was bigtime news now. She was its lead investigator and wanted to keep it that way.

WIRED KINGDOM TECH SUPPORT FACILITY

Tara took the few steps to the door and knocked. It was now Friday evening, but everyone she'd talked to said Trevor was a workaholic. She held her badge up to the peephole as she heard footsteps approaching. Trevor opened the door.

"Evening, Mr. Lane. I need to see what the whale recorded during the last few hours."

"Right this way, detective. Been out jogging?" he asked, noting the sweatsuit and running shoes she now wore in place of the suit she'd been in earlier.

"Yeah, something like that." She had stopped in at the field office just long enough to change into the clothes she kept there for her daily gym workouts before driving to Trevor's office. Out of habit, her eyes swept the room before entering. "You the only one here?" she asked, stepping inside.

"Yeah. They're way too cheap to hire any staff for me." He gestured toward the server room. "This way."

She followed him through the office.

"Looked like quite a ride you had."

Great. "I do what I have to do." The curt response made it clear she wouldn't discuss the case. She had learned on the ride over that only the helicopter itself, and not her in-water experience, was visible to the whale-cam. For that, she was thankful.

They entered the server room. Tara surveyed the

cramped space and its walls of floor-to-ceiling computers and racks of electronics. Trevor slid a keyboard out from one of the machines and hit some keys. The unknown diver's cracked faceplate appeared on the monitor, then spun away at a crazy angle as the whale rolled.

"Run that again."

Trevor replayed the segment.

"Again," Tara said, moving closer to Trevor's shoulder for a better look at the monitor. He did as he was told, but Tara was still unable to recognize any of the diver's features.

"What are we looking for?" Trevor asked.

"Don't worry about it."

"Oooookay." Feeling awkward, and put out, he replayed the scene three more times without being told and wondered how long they'd be at it. And then it occurred to him that the diver's identity might be of interest in the investigation. He opened his mouth as if to speak but stopped himself when he saw Agent Shores' reflection in the screen, lost in thought, her expression hard. "You okay, detective?"

Shores bit back a sarcastic reply. *Fantastic, I just saw a killer whale use a man as a chew toy.* "Back it up three hours and record from there," was what actually came out of her mouth, and she turned away.

Trevor set up the file transfer and initiated the burn.

"What would happen if all this equipment was destroyed somehow—say in a fire? Is the data backed up somewhere off site?"

"Right now, this is it. I recommended to the producers that the data be replicated in a second location, but they didn't want to get involved with setting that up yet."

"So if this building were destroyed, they'd lose all the data?"

"Not all of it. Dr. Reed backs up her own stuff." Tara's mind flashed to the scientist asking her to accompany her to her place. She shivered. ". . . ANASTASIA REED database at her university office," Trevor was saying. "But it doesn't have the actual video, just the oceanographic data from the telemetry stream, and a pointer to the video time code so it can be located from the archives. So if something were to happen to this equipment, they would lose the thousands of hours of blue water, but footage with something happening, they could probably get back."

"What do you mean?"

"Once something gets on the Internet, it can never be completely destroyed. It ends up on a million PCs, laptops, servers, PDAs, smart phones, and various storage appliances. I guarantee every piece of footage from that whale exists somewhere in the world outside this room; it's just locating it when you need to that might be tricky. But with the resources of the FBI, you could do it. Especially the video segments with something happening–like the murder, or the Orca diver. Those little clips are sure to be around forever, whether you want them to be or not. I heard somebody's already posted the murder video clip on YouTube," he said, before hastily adding, "but it wasn't me."

Tara studied Trevor as he tended to a machine. He was comfortable in his environment, in control. Meanwhile, she was getting nowhere. *Time to shake things up and see what falls* out.

"Mr. Lane, there's one thing I don't understand."

"What's that?"

"How were you able to develop the whale-cam?"

"I'm sorry?" He turned to face her.

"Our records indicate that you have a background in computer science—worked as a programmer and software developer—but the whale-cam uses state-of-the-art telecommunications engineering that doesn't fit with your training and work history. So how did you develop it?"

"Well, as I told you before, my father was a telecom engineer, before he retired—"

"Retired from Martin-Northstar."

"That's right."

"But according to our records, your father hadn't actually worked in that capacity for years. He'd been transferred to a management position where he was in charge of the hiring program for new telecom engineers. He hadn't worked on any designs himself for about ten years, so he wasn't giving you cutting-edge ideas."

Trevor said nothing, but she noticed a tremor in his lower lip. She went on. "The FBI's engineering consultants tell me that they've got no idea how certain aspects of that whale-cam work, Mr. Lane," she continued matter-of-factly. "And for these consultants—some of whom have access to top secret military technology—to have *no idea* about how something works can mean only one thing: it's brand new technology, still in the pipeline."

The whir of a disc ejecting cut through the awkward silence that followed.

"Video's ready." He retrieved the disc and held it out to her, an offering.

She ignored it.

"We understand that you personally visited your father's office at Martin-Northstar on several occasions, the first of which was a career day where you accompanied him to work."

"Yes, yes I did. He brought me there on a routine visitor's pass, which I signed for."

"You could have used your time there to set up remote access for yourself that would look authorized to the system administrators. Is that something I should look into, Mr. Lane?" Tara knew she was pushing hard, reaching even. But she'd been pushed pretty hard herself by the men in the bureau. She wanted to bust this whale B.S. wide open so she could prove her real worth.

Trevor laughed in response. "If you think you can enlighten a bunch of frickin' rocket scientists as to the vulnerabilities in their networks, then be my guest."

"Show me the Martin-Northstar manual I saw the

last time I was here. I'd like to see its publication date."

His pale face expressed annoyance more than concern. "I gave it back to my father. He said he would return it to the company."

"Maybe you should get a lawyer, Mr. Lane."

He shrugged. "I will if I have to, but I've done nothing wrong."

She stared again at the bloody Orca scene on the monitor, but she wasn't seeing it. She whirled around and left the server room. "I'll be back with a search warrant, Mr. Lane," she said, heading for the front door.

"That's fine, detective. I've got nothing to hide," he called after her.

"I hope not, because until that whale's GPS is working again, I've got nothing better to do than crawl through your life with a microscope."

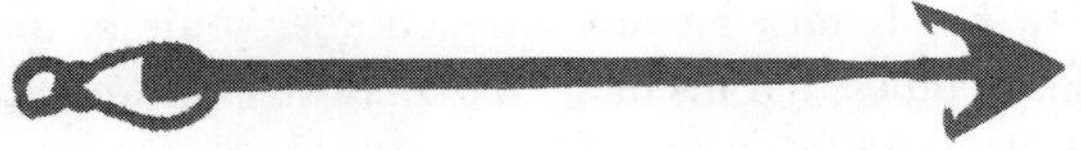

CHAPTER 10

WEST LOS ANGELES

Rivulets of steaming water raced down the curves of Tara Shore's body, washing away the salty residue left by the ocean's brine, and in spite its warmth, she shivered as she recalled being in the cold ocean with the dead diver. It frustrated her to no end that she'd gone through such an ordeal for nothing.

She left the shower, wrapping herself in a towel, and walked to her living room. Its Spartan simplicity reflected the fact that she didn't spend much time there. On a small table next to an easy chair sat a framed photograph of a ten-year-old Tara with her father. He had been an L.A. cop. After confiding in her father that she, too, wanted to become a police officer, his face had become stern.

"You can do better than that. You're FBI material, girl. Never forget that."

"Do they shoot guns in the FBI?" She loved guns. She often sat with her father as he cleaned and maintained his extensive firearms collection. He had taught her to target shoot on a Remington .22-caliber Scoremaster at the age of nine. When she was ten, he won a few hundred bucks when he bet some of his police buddies that his daughter could strip down and reassemble their standard-issue Beretta 9mms faster than they could—blindfolded.

"Yes, they use guns," he had explained, "but there's more to the FBI than just shooting. You have to be smart too, and you're a smart cookie, girl. Remember that."

Tara's eyes lingered on the picture. A handsome dark-haired man in his thirties cradled his daughter in his arms on the deck of a small sailboat. The picture had been taken by Tara's mother on their last day together during their fateful vacation to south Florida.

A succession of grief counselors had enabled Tara to cope with her parents' sudden death as well as could be expected. But they couldn't fix everything.

Tara traced her fingers lightly over her father's stern face in the picture. *It's not about guns, Dad. I know that now. You taught me that. You—*

The phone rang, snapping her thoughts back to the present. She picked it up.

"Agent Shores, this is Trevor Lane. Check the whale-cam now. You've got to see this."

Tara rooted her laptop out from under a pile of *Guns N Ammo* magazines. Activating the computer, she told Trevor to hold while she accessed the whale's live feed.

She stared in disbelief at the scene on her monitor.

The whale-cam's night vision enabled a clear, but grayish green-tinged view. The blue whale's back was split open. Copious amounts of blood—appearing black in the light from a rising moon—drained in sheets from the cavernous wound, coating the leviathan's sides. More startling was the whale's environment. The view around the marine mammal was not of water, but rocks. Tara cringed as a low moan sounded through the speaker. The cetacean exhaled bloody froth from its blowhole.

Tara scrambled for the phone.

"What happened?"

"She beached herself, to die. Because of the Orca injuries. You didn't know?"

For the first time, Tara saw the whale not simply as the bearer of a key piece of evidence, but as an animal, a sentient being capable of suffering. She averted her gaze from the tortured beast long enough to look at the GPS coordinates in the corner of the screen: still frozen.

"No. But the GPS is still out. So where is this?"

"It's on a rocky point not too far from here."

"Maybe I should give Anastasia a call, see if she's seen this," Tara said.

"I wouldn't do that if you want to be the first one to get that tag."

"Why not?" She heard Trevor exhale sharply.

"Interrupt her precious data stream that's making her famous? No way. She knows you'll want not just the video from it, but the whole device, to hold as evidence. So if she can, she'll get it and put it on a different whale. Or a great white shark, or who knows what she and her show think will make even more money. But what they won't be doing is looking forward to having it sit in an FBI evidence locker."

Tara shook her head, now pacing her living room, looking down at the evening traffic on Wilshire. "She'd be interfering with a federal investigation. We can get a court order to make her hand it over to us."

"But how long would that take? The network can afford an army of attorneys that can generate a hurricane of red tape. Sure, the FBI would probably win in the end, but that could take years. Every week that goes by is *millions* of dollars they're making off that whale-cam."

Tara was silent for a moment while she considered this. Maybe Trevor had a point. She needed her involvement in the case to end with a murderer in jail, not a tangled legal fiasco. "If the tag's GPS is still out, how do you know where the whale is?"

"I have some special GIS (Geographic Information Systems) software that I used to analyze local shorelines for a terrain match with what's on the video feed. Right now I have a ninety-percent match. If you want to meet me at Marina del Rey, by the time we reach open waters I'll know exactly where it is."

"Tell me where you think it is, and I'll go there to check it out."

"Look, Agent Shores, I'm not officially admitting anything here, okay. I'm not *on the record.* But let's just say that some people might not believe I didn't borrow part of the design for that device. So if I'm publicly seen helping the FBI to recover it, that should help my situation, right?"

"Yes, but just telling me the information that leads to the tag's recovery is enough—"

"It's not good enough! I want to be seen on camera. I want to be there when you come back with the tag to a bunch of reporters, so that everyone can *see* that I'm helping."

"You ready to go now?"

"Meet me at the marina in thirty minutes." He gave her a slip number.

"Oh, and Lane?"

"Yes?"

"This had better work. I'm really tired right now and I can name about a hundred things I'd rather be doing than going out in a boat at night with you. If this dead ends, I'll see you tomorrow with search warrants for your office and your apartment while I wait for this whale to wash up somewhere. You got that?"

He clicked off.

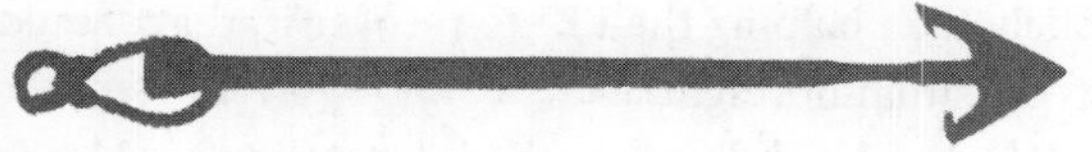

CHAPTER II

MARINA DEL REY

An hour later Trevor Lane leaned on the throttle of a twenty-four-foot, open-cockpit Sea Ray Sundeck as he and Tara left behind the marina breakwater for the open ocean. For Tara, the boat was small to the point of being claustrophobic. And Trevor's inexperience as a boat operator only added to her anxiety.

With the darkness making it difficult to judge the sea state, Trevor took the boat over a swell too fast and they went airborne before slamming back down.

"Who was crazy enough to give you a license for this thing?" Tara chided, rubbing an elbow that had bashed into the boat's rail.

"Sorry."

Tara was glad for the seasickness patch behind her left ear. She watched the lights of the beach towns grow dimmer as they motored out. After thirty bone-jarring minutes Trevor cut speed as they approached a rocky point. A lighthouse beamed atop a cliff, a warning. The area was littered with the wrecks of vessels that had come too close.

Tara aimed a searchlight ashore, illuminating a formidable landscape. Steep cliffs shot up from the water. Access to the narrow band of jumbled boulders looked equally difficult from water or land. If she did see the whale there, how would she get to it?

Trevor read her thoughts as he watched her play the beam along the treacherous shoreline. He paused a moment to witness a thunderous explosion of whitewater as sea met rock. "The area she beached at looks easier to get to than this," he said.

"Where?" Tara saw no signs of a whale.

"According to the GIS"—he briefly consulted a handheld device—"it's right around this point."

They approached the end of a rocky promontory jutting out to sea. Random pinnacles of rock thrust out around them. Trevor had to slow the boat to a controlled drift. He asked Tara to use her light to watch for rocks while they picked their way around the point. Before long Trevor asked her to take the wheel.

"I need to check the GIS before we get too far," he said, indicating his laptop in the cuddy cabin, and retreated into the bow of the vessel.

Tara scanned the rocks with her searchlight, looking for signs of the Blue. She saw none. The first symptoms of irritation were gnawing at her when Trevor emerged from the cabin—

—pointing a pistol at her.

"What are you doing? Put that thing down!"

"Shut the hell up and turn off the light!" Lane kept

the weapon leveled at her head.

Despite the intimidating posture, Tara recognized his choice of target as a sign of an inexperienced shooter, a headshot requiring more precise aim and reaction time than a shot to the torso. A professional killer would never take the risk of missing his shot in the dark on a moving boat.

Still, she was now one-on-one with an armed suspect, a situation she had been trained to avoid at all costs.

Her finger reached for the light switch. Sudden darkness would require Trevor's eyes to readjust, if only for a second. But a second was all she needed.

She killed the light and slammed the throttle full ahead while ducking behind the steering console. The instant acceleration launched Trevor toward the stern. He flew by Tara, firing the gun twice on his way past, the bullets embedding in the console.

Tara's Glock was out before Trevor smashed into the transom and his gun clattered across the deck. Too dark to see where it went. She trained her weapon on Trevor's chest. He held a hand out and whimpered—he thought he was about to die—but she kept her pistol silent. She wouldn't kill him if she didn't have to, but considering the mood she was in if he moved the wrong way, she'd finish what he started.

Trevor pointed past the bow.

"Rocks!" he yelled.

Tara was not going to turn around to have Trevor rush at her or pick up his gun. But she was acutely aware that the boat was plowing along unpiloted at full speed. Keeping her weapon on Trevor, she glued her eyes to him while her left hand crossed over and found the throttle.

She was easing the throttle back when they felt a sickening *thud* as the boat struck a submerged rock. The impact threw the two of them against the door to the cabin as the craft came to a sudden stop. Tara lost her gun when her head slammed into the doorframe.

Trevor piled into her and groped about looking for her weapon. In a move calculated to bring horrific pain, Tara wrenched Trevor's pinky finger out to the side, severing the tendon so that the digit only dangled uselessly. He gave a pitiful shriek and then tried to knee her in the groin. Tara turned her hip to deflect the blow and countered with a heel to Trevor's gut, dropping him to the deck gasping for air.

Tara used the seconds she had bought sweeping the deck on all fours looking for a gun, and she realized somewhere in the back of her mind that she was getting wet. The boat was turning a slow, wobbly circle. It listed badly. Water lapped at the port rail. Worse, a steady stream of ocean poured in from the cabin.

Tara's foot came into contact with something heavy and she caught hold of it. Trevor threw himself on top of her and broke her grip. She watched the object skid out of reach.

There was more scuffling, but Tara would not remember the details of it. The next thing she would recall, however, was producing her handcuffs and slapping a bracelet on Trevor's wrist as it came at her face. She yanked on the free end of the cuffs, pulling Trevor back to the deck, and lunged for the rail. He let her pull his arm by the cuff, concentrating instead on the gun he'd found. Then he heard a ratcheting *click click click* of the other cuff locking to a metal cleat, handcuffing him to the boat.

Tara's eyes swept the deck. Saw Trevor's foot on her Glock. He followed her gaze to his foot and began sliding the gun toward his free hand. She stepped on his mangled finger just as his hand reached the pistol.

He blacked out before he could scream.

When he came to, she was standing at the console, shining the searchlight around the deck. She held her gun in her other hand, pointed at him. She spotted Trevor's gun near the stern. Went to it and picked it up. It was an old .38. Nothing special, but deadly all the same. She tucked it into her waistband.

Turning her attention to the condition of their craft, Tara noted with horror that the water on deck was now ankle deep. The boat slanted undeniably towards the bow, where the rock had ripped a gaping hole.

They were sinking.

Tara searched the console for the marine radio. Found it on top, with a bullet hole smack in the middle of the digital display. Her cell phone dripped water when she pulled it from her pocket. Tried it anyway. Nothing. She pointed the pistol at Trevor and asked him if he had a cell phone. Slowly, he removed it and he tossed it to her, but it too was wet; and its faceplate had been smashed during the fight.

Tara spun around in a slow and deliberate circle, searching the distance for running lights.

They were alone.

Trevor, who had been sitting quietly with his knees drawn up to his chest, started crying and repeatedly knocking his head into the rail. He reminded Tara of a crazy guy getting busted on *COPS*. She'd arrested more people than she could remember—white-collar felons, violent criminals, bad cops—and if she'd learned anything, it was that you could never predict someone's reaction when they felt those cuffs for the first time. Here was a highly educated computer expert behaving like an indigent drug addict. A sense of imminent loss of freedom could do that to a person. But she felt no pity for him. He had tried to kill her. She would use him to survive, and to advance her knowledge of the case.

"Trevor, do we have a life raft?" She hoped they wouldn't need one, but if all else failed she would cling to it like life itself.

He continued butting his head into the rail, adding an accompaniment of "No, no, no . . ."

Deciding she couldn't trust him, she tore the boat apart looking for an emergency flotation device—inflatable diving vest, ski vest, rescue buoy, anything. Lifted all the seat cushions in the rear, probed every corner of the craft with the searchlight. With only the cabin left to search, she glanced at Trevor to make sure he was still chained down and then opened the cabin door.

She entered the small compartment. It was free of clutter, which meant she could see right away that there was no raft. The forward-most area of the cabin was underwater. If there were life jackets on board, they were stowed here, but she couldn't bring herself stay in the flooding compartment long enough to check. Hanging on the wall over the flooded section was a white life ring.

Better than nothing.

She inched forward, reaching a hand out for it. As she stepped, the bow tilted and took on more water. Screaming as cold ocean assaulted her for the second time that day, she snatched the ring and made her way back. She saw Trevor's laptop sitting near the door on a bench. Grabbed it seconds before it would have been claimed by a surge of incoming water.

She stepped out to the deck. Trevor's eyes widened when he saw her emerge with the life ring. "The boat's sinking. You've got to unlock me."

Tara ignored him, shining her light at the rocks on shore while trying to gauge their distance. An eighth of a mile? A quarter? And in a choppy, confused sea.

"Start the pump," Trevor said. He pointed to a small bilge pump attached to an old car battery. She went to it and fired it up. She doubted it could have much effect. So did Trevor. "Please," he continued. "When it sinks it'll happen fast, and you might not have time to unlock me." Tara's gaze turned his blood to ice.

"Regained what little sense you had, have you?"

A wave washed over the rail, taking Trevor's feet out from under him. "I wasn't go—going to kill you," he said, choking on sea water.

Tara stepped back to the console and turned their foundering craft toward shore. They limped toward the rocky beach.

"You fired at me twice."

"I . . . Look, there's no time to talk right now, okay? Please unlock me from the boat—keep me handcuffed if you want, just get me off the boat so I have a chance."

The investigator in Tara made her forget her predicament for the time being. She took the life ring and climbed on top of the console. "Oh, I think we've got plenty of time," she said, dropping the ring around her neck, oozing false confidence. *We'll never make it to shore.*

Only the rails of the deck were clear of the sea now. Trevor's eyes radiated the fear of a trapped animal. A thin trail of bloody spittle hung from his mouth. "What do you want me to do?"

Tara held up the laptop. "Can I send an e-mail from this thing?"

"Yes. Satellite linkup. Just open Internet Explorer."

She logged onto her Internet mail and sent a message to FBI staff who would be monitoring her case activities. She wrote, in typo-ridden shorthand, that she was with a combative suspect in a sinking boat. She described her position both visually and with the GPS coordinates she took from the open GIS program. Clicked SEND and looked up at Trevor. "Okay, now. If you want me to unlock you, you'll need to answer my questions. What are you into that you would kill an FBI agent for? Did you kill that girl in the video?"

"No! I didn't kill h—her." He spat out invading seawater.

"Who did?"

Another wave swamped Trevor's head. Panicking, he tried to free himself. He jerked his chained arm from the rail in a motion that was far more damaging to his wrist than to the boat. He tried it two more times. The cleat held.

"Who did, Lane? There's not much time." Tara knew that soon her desire for answers would be outweighed by her instinct for self-preservation. She was losing focus.

"I don't know. I swear. I don't know that." He lost his footing and slipped beneath the water on deck. Atop the console, Tara felt a twinge of fear. What would she do if he didn't come back up? Part of her wondered if she wasn't a little too fascinated with watching this guy suffer. Then he pulled himself back up by the handcuff, retching water.

Just a little more. "In another couple of minutes you're gonna be part of L.A.'s newest artificial reef if you don't answer me. There's no whale beached on these rocks, is there? You tricked me with some kind of computer-generated scene. That demonstrates serious premeditation, Lane."

"Arrest me. I want to talk to my lawyer. Just get me outta here."

"You tried to kill me—the ballistics report will bear that out—and so I had to handcuff you to the rail to control you. Also true. But then the boat sank so fast I barely had time to save myself." She hung her head in a mock show of sadness.

"You sick bitch! You can't do that. That would make you a murderer."

"Who was in that floatplane earlier today?" *That's it. Last question.*

He screamed his entire reply at the top of his lungs, head thrown back to the sky, yanking spastically on the handcuff as bloody spittle erupted from his mouth. "I don't know! I don't know! All right? I don't know! I was being blackmailed by some guys at Martin-Northstar—system administrators with access. I told them I was interested in certain types of telemetry for web sites, and I paid them five grand to hook me up with technology I was able to modify for the whale-cam. But when they found out I made a deal with *Wired Kingdom,* they started threatening me. E-mailing me pictures they'd taken from security cameras showing me in restricted areas, saying they had fingerprints of mine they'd lifted from keyboards, computer routing records with my home IP address logging on to secure systems. Said they would send it all to the FBI if I didn't wire them fifty thousand dollars."

"What did you do then?"

He took a deep breath and slumped against the rail. "I wired them the money. Took everything I had—my signing bonus from the show, my savings, borrowed from my parents, sold some computer equipment. Everything I could get. Then they contacted me two weeks later and said if I didn't wire them another twenty-five grand they'd turn me in anyway."

"And you thought by killing me those problems would just go away?"

"When they asked for the twenty-five I decided to fight back. I said I'd turn them in for their part in getting me the original designs if they didn't lay off. They said they'd be sending someone for me if they didn't get the cash. I refused to wire it—couldn't get it anyway—so when you started coming around I figured you were the one they sent to kill me. Posing as FBI."

"It didn't occur to you after the girl was murdered live on the web that authorities might be looking into it?"

He shook his head. "At first I really thought it was part of the show somehow, like everyone else. A media-hype thing. I called a producer right after it happened and asked him that. Anthony Silveras. You can ask him yourself. He'll remember my calling."

Tara shook her head in amazement. "Newsflash, Lane: I'm a real FBI agent. And right now you're a real attempted-murder suspect. It's time to go."

She forced herself to get down from the console into the swirling water on deck. Let the laptop fall into the water. She waded toward Trevor, familiar sensations of panic welling up within as the water roiled around her. Too risky to come within arm's reach of him.

"Trevor, I don't trust you. So if you want to live, keep quiet and do exactly as I say."

He glared up at her before ducking another wave.

She held up a small key. "I'm going to toss this to you. You need to catch it."

If possible, his eyes got even wider. "Why can't you just hand it to me? I'll stick my hand out and you drop it into my palm."

"No deal. One chance is all anyone gets to kill this agent. I'll toss you the key from here. Take it or leave it."

"Okay. Okay. Just give it to me!"

Under ordinary circumstances it was a trivial toss, but at night, handcuffed to a sinking boat, knowing you're dead if you don't catch the damn thing, Trevor knew it was a different story. He pleaded with Tara once more to just hand him the key.

"One . . ."

Bait wrappers, Styrofoam coffee cups and other flotsam drifted away from the small cruiser as it began to slide under for good. Tara had already started to shiver.

"I'll keep the light steady on your hand."

"D—don't, please. Just hand it to me, I w—"

"Two . . ."

As the water drained from his face, leaving him stammering and sputtering, Tara shot forward, thrust the key directly into Trevor's palm, and retreated to beyond arm's length. "Don't drop it."

He didn't look up at her or offer any kind of thanks, but simply bent to the task of freeing himself. She held the light so he could see what he was doing. The beam jumped in her shaky grip.

No sooner had Trevor removed the bracelet from his wrist than the entire boat was swallowed by the sea. Life ring around her waist, Tara jumped clear of the sinking cruiser. She was shocked at how fast it happened. Ten more seconds and Trevor would have had to unlock himself on the way to the seafloor. They heard the discordant shriek of fiberglass grating against rock as the craft scuffed along the bottom only a few feet beneath them.

Tara said a silent prayer of thanks that their foundering vessel had made progress toward shore.

CHAPTER 12

Trevor moved to put a hand on the life ring. Tara waved her Glock at him. "Off."

He backpaddled.

Neither knew just how close to shore they were until the next wave came. A gurgling river of surge whisked them through a barnacle-encrusted cut in the rocks. Trevor, somewhere ahead of Tara in the darkness, cried out in pain as his skin was sliced by the sharp crustaceans. He and Tara were washed through the channel and deposited in a shallow open area. Tara was grateful to scrabble over the uneven rocks.

Trevor scrambled up to a rocky shelf and collapsed there in a tide pool. Emboldened by having two feet on solid ground, Tara approached him, gun at the ready. But he only lay there on his back, motionless in a bed of green sea anemones.

"I like it here," he said, not looking at Tara, but staring up at the dark sky. He closed his eyes. Trevor would be of no help to her.

Tara took in their surroundings, looking for a way

off the surf-swept shelf. She saw none. A near-vertical wall of rock and scrub brush rose into the night sky. A treacherous array of jagged tide pools stretched endlessly in either direction. Buffeted by strong winds, she wondered if it was high or low tide, and if they would be able to last through the night without being swept from their rocky perch. Tara thought back to Trevor's laptop, now on the sea bottom. Did her e-mail get through to the field office?

Sitting on a pile of kelp, she had almost nodded off for the umpteenth time when a faint rhythmic thumping caught her attention. Suddenly a helicopter buzzed in low, searing the tide pools with a high candlepower spotlight.

"FBI. Don't move. We're coming down," a voice boomed from a loudspeaker. A line was dropped from the aircraft and the first man from a SWAT team rappelled to the rocky shelf.

L.A. COUNTY JAIL

After receiving medical treatment for the injuries he had sustained in the fight with Tara, and from being dragged across the rocks, Trevor Lane was taken to L.A. County Jail and booked for the attempted murder of a federal agent. He was then placed in an interrogation room. Tara, in a borrowed suit one size too small, which earned several glances from her male associates, watched Trevor from the dark side of the one-way glass. Two of the SWAT team members who had rescued them watched with her. Trevor sat with his head buried in his elbow on the tabletop.

"You think he knows anything else?" one of the SWAT guys asked.

Tara shook her head. "If he didn't tell me what he knows while he was handcuffed to a sinking boat . . ."

The SWAT men exchanged approving glances. "Give us five minutes alone with him to find out for sure," one of them said.

Tara shrugged. "Go for it."

The pair of SWAT operators entered the holding room. Trevor remained still as they entered.

"Have anything to say for yourself?" one agent repeated, kicking the table leg.

Trevor tilted his head to one side, looking up, but said nothing.

The other agent jerked the table away from Trevor, forcing him to sit up in his chair. "So I hear you're a real genius, stealing national defense technology to sell to some game show. Proud of yourself, dickhead?"

Trevor only hung his head.

"Like shooting at FBI agents, huh?"

As she watched the questioning begin, Tara thought about the computer programmer's role in the case. He said that he was being blackmailed. He perceived the threat to his own safety as real enough to kill for. But was that connected to the murder victim? Was the dead woman somehow involved in the theft of the engineering designs that led to

Trevor's development of the whale-cam?

In the room, Trevor grunted in pain as one of the SWAT team slugged him in the gut. She went to join the interrogation. "Thank you, gentlemen," she said, "I'll take it from here."

"I want to speak to a lawyer," Trevor said as soon as he could breathe again. A tear rolled down his cheek. She pitied him at this point, but reminded herself that he had tried to kill her.

"Trevor, your cooperation here could determine whether any of the charges against you are reduced or dropped. If there's someone else involved in this with you, now's the time to give us their names. You're looking at an attempted murder charge for starters, and that's before we talk to Martin-Northstar and get your involvement in any design theft ironed out."

He sniffled and wiped snot on his sleeve before answering. "Anything I could tell you is only related to these guys who were blackmailing me."

"Could the murdered girl be someone who found out what was going on at Martin-Northstar, maybe a whistle-blower who threatened to expose your blackmailers?"

He stared blankly into space. One of the SWAT agents grabbed his mangled finger, now in a brace. "The lady asked you a question."

"Okay, okay, let me think." But he only shook his head and vomited a little down the front of his shirt.

Then the door to the interrogation room burst open. A man Tara recognized from newspaper photos as a prominent L.A. trial lawyer was escorted inside by a uniformed police officer.

"Trevor Lane, I'm Lance Wozniak, attorney." He started to thrust a hand out before seeing that Trevor's wrists were handcuffed behind the chair. He motioned irritably to the police officer to unlock him. The officer nodded to the FBI agents.

"Mr. Lane," Wozniak said as Trevor's hands were freed, "I've been retained by *Wired Kingdom* to take your case. Your bail has been paid. Let's go."

"Wait a minute," one of the SWAT officers protested. "This guy's up for attempted murder of a federal agent and he makes bail?"

"That's *alleged* attempted murder. His employer paid the four hundred grand. No priors," Wozniak said, motioning for Trevor to get up.

Tara took a step toward Trevor, who was staggering up from the chair. "Was she a whistle-blower?"

The lawyer held out a hand, palm first. "That's enough, Agent Shores. Mr. Lane, as your attorney I advise you to say nothing further."

He turned to the agents. "Look at the condition this man is in. This treatment is nothing short of criminal."

Trevor averted his eyes from Tara's as he was led from the room by his attorney. On the way out, Tara could hear the lawyer asking Trevor how long he'd been talking.

33° 36' 25.2" N AND 119° 69' 78.9"

Mountains of rock rose from the seafloor to within two hundred feet of the surface. Currents ran strong here, and an array of information tickled the wired whale's senses. A complex, high-energy environment, this place was cold and murky, and of interest to myriad marine creatures. The unusual geology of the area stood apart from the featureless desert of the deep seafloor far below. Large pelagic predators, including great white sharks, frequented the perimeter of this zone, while the rocky crags, caves and shelves of the seamount itself were home to invertebrates such as lobster, sea stars and octopi. The upper reaches of the undersea mountain were festooned with billowing strands of kelp and varieties of colorful algae.

Diving for the first time since the Orca attack, the Blue neared the seamount. In the wake of her narrow escape, her movements were tentative, restrained. Still, she had a caloric intake to sustain. Her echo-location depicted a pinched, M-shaped summit that dropped into an abyss. She hovered above the "M." The smell of food was intoxicating. The locale was rich in the zooplankton that comprised her diet, but this was something more. A rich beacon of nutrients called to the animal's most primal instincts.

She moved in. No fewer than sixteen pinpoint sources of high-quality sustenance assailed her senses.

Sixteen perforated 55-gallon drums, each oozing a

protein-rich cocktail of krill, copepods and anchovies, suspended in a massive monofilament net invisible to sight and sonar.

CHAPTER 13

AVALON, CATALINA ISLAND

While the northern Channel Islands made up a remote marine sanctuary, Catalina to the south was L.A.'s aquatic playground. The island lay twenty-two miles off the coast, with regular high-speed ferry service bringing thousands of passengers each day. Private boat traffic brought still more. And then there were chartered helicopter and small plane flights.

The tourist-oriented city of Avalon was home to about three thousand permanent residents. But behind the waterfront tourist area with its harbor and pier, crowded beach, quaint cobblestone walkways and carefully decorated establishments, there was a quieter part of town. A few blocks inland, before the chaparral-covered hills began their march up to form the island's spine, a local business district clung to the island like the barnacles covering the rocks of its shores. Stripped-down stores with unpretentious signs sold fishing and diving gear, offered outboard motor repairs, carried general hardware and—for those with the patience or connections to beat the ten-year waiting list to bring a car or truck onto the island—auto repair. Most people drove golf carts, which were more suited to the island's narrow roads. Presently one of those carts, driven by a man who, in a town with more than its fair share of drunks, was known as "the town drunk," wound its way down from the hills.

Ernie Hollister remembered to turn the cart's headlights on when he passed under a thick stand of eucalyptus trees that filtered the moonlight. Beyond his inebriated condition, his lack of attention to the road was particularly dangerous because of the animals that roamed Catalina's hillsides. Buffalo, left behind from a 1920s movie shoot, were not unknown to venture into the upper reaches of town at night, and wild boar or feral goats could emerge just about anywhere en route to a food source.

A long-time Avalon resident, if anything Ernie was a little too familiar a sight on the island roads for his own good. His near-silent electric vehicle allowed him to enjoy the sound of leaves crunching under the cart's wheels as he made his way into town, catching unsuspecting victims unawares. Reaching for the cup holder, he lifted a can of beer and finished it off with one hand on the wheel. He crumpled the can and tossed it into a stand of ironwood trees before reaching the level, street-lit avenue marking the edge of the business district.

Most of the lights were off inside the weathered

one- and two-story facades lining the street. Drifting up the island on a sea breeze from the beachfront were the faraway sounds of weekend revelers escaping the mainland metropolis. The waterfront was not Ernie's destination, although he was looking for drink and company. As usual, he knew where to find it.

The Pelican's Nest was the hub of Ernie's social life. The Nest, as it was affectionately known around town, was a dive bar favored by old salts. When he saw the flood of smoky light coming from the open doorway Ernie angled his cart toward the miniature parking lot and hit the brake, as was his habit. Only this time the brake pedal gave no resistance.

Ernie approached the building at top speed as he pumped the brake. When it became apparent he would not be able to stop in time, he bailed out of the cart, leaving it to ramp over the curbstone and smash into The Nest as his stout body thudded onto the sidewalk. He lay there for a moment, listening to the clatter of an errant beer can that had shaken loose from somewhere in the cart.

A figure took up the entranceway. "Oh c'mon, Ernie, not again," said a wiry, aged man with silver hair. He stepped through the doorway to inspect the damage, absently drying a beer glass with a white dishtowel as he did so. The bartender was also the sole proprietor, and he knew Ernie well, as he did most of the patrons who frequented his establishment. Small towns and islands were places where folks knew each other's business, and Catalina was both.

Ernie staggered up from the ground. He pried the cart's fender out of the doorjamb and gave it an angry shove. It landed on the ground again with a thud. Ernie dusted off his pants with great care, as if they weren't tattered, oil-stained work clothes, while a smattering of applause came from the regulars inside the bar.

"Sorry 'bout that, Bill," Ernie said, removing a baseball cap from his bald head to give an exaggerated stage bow. The hat had a logo patch sewn on the bill. It was too soiled with grime to be readable, but Bill knew that in years past it had read *The Pelican's Nest*.

Bill traced his fingers along the impact crater left by the cart's fender.

"Damn rinky-dink cart," Ernie said. "This year better be my year to get my truck out to this blasted rock." Ernie's name had been on the waiting list for twelve years already, and he'd been making a louder stink each time the list was read in the town hall meetings and his wasn't on it.

Behind closed doors, though, most of the locals were all too glad that he wasn't driving a real car through their tourist-filled streets and winding mountain roads. There were even rumors that the sheriff had seen to it that Ernie's name would somehow drop a little farther down the list with each passing year.

Ernie staggered into The Nest. On his way to the bar, he passed under a large Japanese glass fishing float, which dangled from the ceiling. The "disco ball," Ernie called it. The watering hole was filled with older blue-collar men, but there were a few women in the back around a pool table. The rest of California had a no-smoking-indoors policy, and the tourist establishments of Catalina followed it, but someone forgot to tell the Pelican's Nest.

Ernie took a rusty stool at the bar and accepted the mug of brew passed to him by another regular. Mounted on a wall over the bar was a television set tuned to that day's *Wired Kingdom* studio broadcast, from which the OLF disturbance had been edited out. On screen, Anastasia was about to announce the contest winner.

Watching a clip, courtesy of the Blue's camera, reminded Ernie that he couldn't remember the last time he'd had his fishing boat out. It had once been his livelihood, but had fallen into disrepair over the years as his drinking increased, as did the cost of fuel. At first the repairs kept him dry-docked for a few days, then a few weeks and months, until he'd been living from one odd job to another on land. Ernie's boat still sat in dry dock. He'd even been offered a token sum for it, but he had refused because the boat, even though it was no longer seaworthy, was still a boat. And he knew he'd never be able to afford another one. He wasn't even able to maintain his golf cart.

Looking up at the TV now, at the clean, blue water the whale swam through, Ernie wondered if he'd ever be his own captain again. Then he was invited to a game of eight-ball by a guy he'd beaten before, and he turned his back on the tube.

CHAPTER 14

THE CALIFORNIA CHANNEL ISLANDS

"There are only four more aspirin, Guillermo," Héctor González said to his diver. "Perhaps you should save them—you may need to thin your blood later."

"I need them now!" Guillermo countered, slamming his fist against the plane's backseat. He lay in the cramped cargo space sweating, crippled with acute pain in his joints.

"Let's give you more oxygen." Héctor retrieved a portable 02 bottle and placed a respirator over Guillermo's face. Tears traced the edges of the mask as the man's body was racked with agony again. Five minutes of oxygen appeared to improve the diver's condition slightly, and the mask was removed.

"Oxygen is almost out too," Héctor said.

"Please. The aspirin. Let me have them now, I beg you."

The pilot considered the near-empty pill bottle. Reluctantly, he opened it and pressed the four remaining tablets into his diver's good hand. He noted with mounting unease that the fingers of the other were curled into a gnarled, useless claw.

"How deep did you go?"

"Not sure." Guillermo grunted in pain as he brought the aspirin to his mouth.

"Where is your dive computer?"

The diver indicated his gear bag under the seat. He chugged down a bottle of water while Héctor consulted the profile of the most recent dive. He crossed himself after reading the numbers.

"Ay, Guillermo. Over two hundred feet? Are you crazy? One fifty was supposed to be the maximum. And what happened to your decompression schedule? The planned stops?"

"The currents made it impossible to stay at twenty feet. The upwelling . . . it was like being in a whirlpool. I was too tired to fight. And after Carlos . . . I could not do the work of two men."

Héctor winced at the reminder of his other diver's death. His hopes of snatching the device from the whale upon first sighting had been ripped from him. The mission would not be only one day. He fought for control of his fears.

"You should have told me when you came back to the plane. You could have gone immediately back down to do your decompression on a fresh tank."

"I didn't think—I couldn't—I would have been okay if you hadn't flown so high." Scuba divers were not supposed to fly within twenty-four hours after diving because the reduced-pressure at altitude could lead to "the bends"—a condition resulting from nitrogen bubbles in the bloodstream, with painful and potentially deadly complications.

"We had to reach the cloud layer to conceal ourselves. Do not blame me for that."

"I need a recompression chamber!"

"Guillermo, you know that is . . . Just wait. Get some sleep. And if your condition does not improve by morning, I'll take you then."

The diver shifted on the seat, seeking a resting posture that his screaming joints would tolerate. "I do not like this whale, *señor*. It has been made . . . unnatural. I fear it will kill us all."

An electronic warbling sounded from the front seat. Héctor grabbed an Iridium satellite phone and stepped from the plane. His head emerged from a stand of trees and brush that obscured their aircraft at the rear of a secluded cove. The inlet was so small as to be almost claustrophobic. Even to a boater cruising the shore of this barren outcropping of rock thirty miles from the mainland, the isolated beach could only be seen from a certain angle of approach. It had not been easy to drag the seaplane up onto the beach, but with the aid of high tide they had managed it.

Héctor's eyes swept the cobblestone beach and out over the water while his ears probed for aberrant sound. Satisfied that he and his surviving partner were the only people within earshot, he answered the phone.

"*Bueno*."

The voice on the other end was demanding. “Are you on the island? Are you safe?”

The pilot glanced out at the empty sea. A small animal rustled somewhere nearby. Winged creatures he thought might be bats dashed overhead. An anguished cry emanated from within the plane.

“For the moment, we are the only ones here. But *jefe*, listen, circumstances have become very complex. The job is more than what I am comfortable with. It is too dangerous to continue.”

“Had you not failed today, you’d already be collecting your fortune instead of hiding on that godforsaken rock. Were you able to set the trap?”

“Yes, but it was not easy—my remaining diver has the bends. He needs a recompression chamber. He will not be able to dive tomorrow.”

“No recompression chambers. If your man can no longer work, you get rid of him. Perhaps you should consider the consequences of not completing the job. That could be costly, too.”

“I do not unders—”

“I know that Rosa is on hold to go to Mexico City. I might be able to help.”

Héctor suppressed a gasp. He hadn't thought his boss would know that much about him. “Alright, but I must emphasize that it is risky to continue now. One man is dead, another crippled and likely to die without medical attention. We haven’t had enough time to prepare.”

“So get another man.”

"The authorities will be looking for my plane, and trying to identify Javier. His death was filmed on the Internet—"

"In dive gear that made him totally unrecognizable. Have your new recruits bring you another plane. It's not like you can't afford it with what you're being paid. Work it out. I'll triple your fee, and will wire you a bonus today that will allow Rosa's treatment to begin."

Héctor didn't know what else to say. He thought of Rosa spending another night in the hospital, and then there was only one thing *to* say. "Okay, *jefe*, thank you. We leave at dawn, before any boats arrive."

"Good. You are aware of the FBI agent after the whale's tag?"

"Yes, from the helicopter. It is good she could not swim so well, no?"

"Let me just add that were she to meet with some kind of accident, your bank account would benefit even more handsomely."

Silence.

"One more thing. I had a package shipped to your office. It will arrive today. I want it available as a last resort."

"What is its purpose?"

"You'll know when you see it."

"Very well, *jefe*."

"Tie up the loose ends. You do that, and I'll take care of Rosa."

Héctor hesitated, but then forced himself to respond. "Yes, *jefe*." He terminated the call and placed another, to his office in Baja.

WEST LOS ANGELES

Tara had been asleep for less than four hours when her phone rang. She snatched it up off the floor. A young case assistant she'd assigned to watch the whale's feed overnight apologized for waking her.

"That's okay. What have you got?"

"The whale appears to be caught in a fishing net. Location unknown—still no GPS. I haven't got an expert opinion yet, but in the chat rooms they're saying the whale may drown if someone doesn't cut it loose."

"Any signs of people in the vicinity?"

"No. It appears she's only just gotten tangled."

Tara thanked the assistant and hung up.

THE CALIFORNIA CHANNEL ISLANDS

The sound of an engine shattered the pre-dawn stillness, awakening Héctor from a vague nightmare starring his daughter. He cast a worried glance at his stricken diver, who stirred in fitful sleep, a line of drool snaking from his mouth to a puddle on the plane's floor. Héctor exited the plane and walked out onto the beach in time to see a blue seaplane—another Cessna, identical to his except for the paint—make a perfect landing a hundred yards away.

Consulting a pair of binoculars, he was pleased to count a total of three persons inside, including the pilot. Just enough personnel to get the job done, he thought. He would have liked more divers, perhaps even an inflatable boat, but that would mean involving more people. The less who knew of his expedition to U.S. coastal waters the better.

Activating a secure channel on his handheld marine radio, Héctor rattled off a string of call-sign letters that would identify him to his contacts in the plane. Once the authentication was completed, he said, "You've made good time. I am glad you are here."

He instructed them to paddle the plane quietly to the beach while he prepared to depart, but the new-comer pilot ignored the command, rapidly eating up the distance to shore.

"I said cut the engines!"

"As you requested, we have a laptop with satellite Internet connection to view the whale's transmission. We are watching it now, and the whale is in the trap. I repeat, it is caught in the trap now. We must hurry."

Cursing, Héctor dropped his cigarette and ran back to the beached plane. He parted the shroud of foliage at its doors and then entered. "Guillermo, we need to—" he began, but stopped in mid-sentence as it dawned on him how much the diver's condition had deter-iorated in the last few hours.

"You called . . . a plane . . . for me. Thank you," Guillermo said, his voice barely above a whisper.

Héctor hung his head, ashamed. "I'm sorry, Guillermo, but that plane is here to take us to the whale. Your excellent work has trapped it. Can you walk?"

"But, *señor*! . . . I—no. I cannot move my legs . . . my hand. I cannot feel the left . . . my face."

This confirmed the pilot's worst fear. The only real treatment for the bends was to be placed in a recompression chamber, which would recreate the pressure of ocean depths, allowing nitrogen bubbles to return to the bloodstream. Anything he could do for him in the field was only a minor stopgap meant to serve as an emergency precaution until a chamber could be reached.

"The chamber, *señor*. You promised. . . ."

Recalling the sat-phone conversation with his boss, the pilot ran his fingers through his thick but graying hair, which was usually covered by a baseball cap. The newly arrived plane cut its engines as it reached the beach.

"Okay, Guillermo, let me get ready."

The diver closed his eyes and sighed in relief as his boss started for the front seat. Héctor picked up the radio, staring at the transmitter. To use it was to save Guillermo and condemn his own daughter. He could hear the door opening on the other plane, the splashy footfalls as his reinforcements jumped out and waded onto the island. Héctor dropped the transmitter. He whirled back around, moving behind the diver's head. He quickly reached over and covered the man's mouth and nose with both hands and pressed, his forearms rippling with the effort.

"*Lo siento, amigo*."

The diver struggled in the wake of the apology but,

unable to fully command his limbs, he couldn't lessen Héctor's vice grip. Guillermo's body twitched and jerked for want of air. Tears welled in Héctor's eyes as he tightened his grasp.

"Relax, Guillermo. Relax. You are going to be with God. Your net captured the whale. Your share of the money will go to your family. It will take care of them for the rest of their lives. I promise you. I promise you that."

Guillermo's eyes flickered with recognition, and gratitude, before his body went limp.

CHAPTER 15

33° 36' 25.8" N AND 119° 69' 78.4" W

Sport fisherman Joe Roberts cursed the misfortune that had befallen him. After motoring nearly forty miles offshore through most of the night, he had cast his first line with the sunrise, hoping for a prize tuna. What he got was a hopeless snag.

Jerking the line yet again, Joe asked his fishing buddy, Dean Farley, to confirm their position. The two were construction contractors in their forties who had been fishing together for years.

"We're right over the seamount," Dean said after consulting a chart. He picked up a pair of binoculars. "You got yourself a net."

"Crap. Another eighty-dollar lure. Maybe we can drift over and cut it loose."

"Not worth it. We get that crap wrapped around the prop . . ."

"Hell, you're right. You know, every year we go farther out and catch less fish. I think I've about had it. You think Mike would buy my half of the boat?"

Reluctantly, Joe produced a knife. He was about to cut the line when Dean told him to wait.

"Hang on. I saw something. In the net, I think. Something big."

"A commercial net, just my damn luck."

"Don't see any marker buoys."

"Maybe they broke off."

"Maybe."

A series of frenzied splashes disrupted the glassy surface. A mammoth, dark shape tore through the water. Dean picked up the glasses.

"Shark?" Joe asked.

"Don't think so. It's . . . it's too big."

Then a colossal fluke scratched at the sky, a web of glistening nylon mesh enveloping the appendage like a shroud.

"Whale!" Dean shouted. "It's a whale!"

Joe stared in awe as the enormous creature slapped its tail against the surface, producing a tremendous spattering of foamy water. Dean stared wide-eyed at the taut fishing line stretching in the direction of the netted giant.

"Cut your line," he said.

Joe pulled the line toward him with a finger.

"Wait, never mind," Dean said.

Joe looked at his friend, knife poised over the rigid line. "What is it?"

"I think if you come across a whale in distress like this, you're supposed to call it in so rescuers can find it. We can give our GPS coordinates, but if we cut the line they might not be able to find it later.

"Look, if I hooked a damn whale I don't *want* anyone to know about it, okay? We report the thing in trouble, we're heroes; we say we hooked it, we're animal killers. I'm cutting my line."

"I can see it now," Dean said, eyes glued to the binoculars. "You didn't hook the whale. Your lure's in the net. I'm looking at it."

"I'm still cuttin' loose. Call the Coast Guard. Tell 'em we found a trapped whale. We'll follow it if we can, until they get here, but I don't wanna be hooked to it."

As soon as he finished his sentence the whale attempted to breach, pulling the net with it and ripping the fishing rod from Joe's hands. He swore as rod and reel flew over the transom into the water and out of sight.

The blue seaplane banked sharply as it approached the ensnared whale.

"These are the coordinates where the trap was set," Héctor González, now riding co-pilot, announced.

The pilot of the new plane pointed toward the trap site. "What is that?"

"A fishing vessel," Héctor said. "Land us as planned."

He picked up the radio while scoping the boat through binoculars. He said into the transmitter, "Fishing vessel . . . *Beeracuda* . . . this is the seaplane overhead. Acknowledge, please." He repeated the message. Thirty seconds passed as their plane descended into a landing pattern, and then a response crackled through the cockpit.

"Seaplane, this is *Beeracuda.* What's up?"

"How's the fishing?"

"Not good so far. There's a gill net or something with what looks like a whale stuck in it. We just called the coordinates in to the Coast Guard. You with the park services?"

Héctor held up a hand to silence the grumbling of his crew as they digested the news. He pressed the transmit button. "Copy that," he said. "We will be landing to rescue the whale. Thank you for your help, but now we need you to please keep your vessel clear of the site."

A tense moment passed in the plane while they waited for a reaction. Would the fishermen be cooperative, or pesky hangers-on? Were they really even fishermen? All speculation ceased as the radio came to life.

"Roger that, seaplane. We're outta here. Good luck."

The first diver hit the water while the airplane still bounced across the surface. Although he was highly experienced and outfitted with state-of-the-art gear, he could not have faced more hazardous diving conditions.

Weak early-morning light struggled to pierce the murky water—a krill-laden maelstrom of converging currents and upwelling that swirled around the undersea mountain like a whiteout atop Mount Everest. The seamount's twin peaks lay two hundred feet below, but they were a deceptive target, rapidly succumbing to thousands of feet of inky blackness. Somewhere in this unforgiving realm, nearly a square mile of invisible nylon mesh was being thrashed about by a petrified, ninety-seven-foot beast fighting for its life.

The diver tested his communications unit. "Visibility poor. Following compass heading toward the trap."

Then he kicked off into the gloom.

MARINA DEL REY

Tara eased her Crown Victoria off the 405 toward the same marina she'd left from only hours earlier with Trevor. Caught up in a heated argument on her cell phone, she earned a nasty glance and creative gesture from a motorist attempting an aggressive merge. He was talking on a cell *and* shaving with an electric razor, Tara wasn't surprised to notice.

After learning of the Blue's predicament, she had phoned Anastasia to see if the marine mammal expert was aware of the situation. She was.

"We can't wait," Anastasia declared as Tara switched lanes to avoid a collision. Tara heard her giving terse orders to a boat crew as they prepared to leave the dock. "If you're here, fine, we'll take you. But we can't afford to wait—the whale can't afford to wait."

"I'll be there." Deciding she'd better concentrate on her driving, Tara dropped her cell and punched the gas. She plowed through the rapidly filling streets of Venice and Marina del Rey until she hit a string of stubborn red lights on Lincoln.

Less than a mile from the boat slip, she called Anastasia again. The scientist picked up, and this time Tara heard the throaty sound of engines revving.

"Dr. Reed, have you left yet?" She pulled up to another red light and sat.

"Not yet, but they're casting off the lines. What's your twenty, girl? I told you, we can't wait."

Girl? She couldn't remember the last time anyone had referred to her as *girl*. She was about to remind Anastasia that she was not some production assistant she could boss around, when she realized she'd better be nice if she didn't want to literally miss the boat.

She could just make out the tops of masts bobbing in the distance. "I can see the boats, but still have to turn into the marina."

"I don't know what to say. If you're here, you're here. If you miss us you can—Hey buddy, what're you thinking leaving that tank standing up there!—catch a ride with one of the hundred other boats gearing up to save the whale."

"That many?" She did her best to ignore the driver still gesturing wildly next to her.

"Looks that way. A couple of fishermen broadcast the whale's GPS coordinates to the Coast Guard on an open frequency. Look, I gotta go. *Ciao*, girl!"

The call went dead. Tara fumed at the next red light, the last one standing between her and the marina entrance. Between her and the whale.

The guy she'd almost hit pulled up next to her and was rolling down his passenger-side window to have a little chat about the finer points of driving etiquette when he saw her point something that looked like a garage-door opener at the traffic signal. The light changed from red to green and Tara shot across the intersection into the marina. The other driver calmly rolled his window back up.

Tara parked her car and ran toward the dock. Anastasia's boat was hard to miss. The Scarab racer was already prowling its way from its berth toward the main marina channel. Anastasia stood at the wheel. TV cameras, dive gear and a crew of half a dozen men busied themselves securing things on the rear deck. Pressed for time as she was, Tara couldn't help but marvel at the glitzy watercraft. Plastered along the hull were the logos of various corporate sponsors, the largest of which was *Wired Kingdom* featuring an airbrushed blue whale, complete with enlarged web-cam tag, wrapping around the stern.

Tara stopped ogling the vessel long enough to raise Anastasia's phone once again.

"Sorry, not enough time to turn this beast around."

"I was told the FBI could expect your full cooperation."

"This is cooperation. I want the whale; you want the whale. But if I wait for you, neither of us will get what we want. The whale needs to be freed now or it will die. I'm doing you a favor."

Tara stopped running as it became clear she wouldn't catch up with the boat. "Some favor . . ."

"It's not like you can't find another ride," Anastasia continued. Tara saw her wave an arm at the small armada of watercraft readying to set sail. "Can't you commandeer one?" she added, laughing. "They just won't be as fast as us, that's all."

"Is this because I wouldn't go home with you yesterday?" Tara asked.

Before Anastasia could answer, a black wooden schooner under power turned itself broadside in the narrow waterway, obstructing the entrance to the main channel. Anastasia stared at Tara for a moment and then picked up a megaphone and directed it at the vessel blocking her path.

"Move that old scow!"

A tanned young man wearing only a pair of surfer board shorts and long dreadlocks appeared on deck. He ambled to the port side of his vessel and sat facing the idling Scarab, his legs dangling over the side of the ship.

"Well, if it isn't the environmental rebel himself. Long time no see—but not long enough. Move out of the way, Eric!" Anastasia's megaphone boomed.

The sailor lifted a hand, middle finger extended, and remained seated, idly swinging his feet. Another young man appeared on deck and hoisted a flag up the mainmast. Everyone aboard the Scarab muttered some kind of epithet when they read the letters *OLF* stenciled on the hull. Two more OLF crewmembers appeared on deck and anchors dropped from the bow and stern, locking the schooner in position.

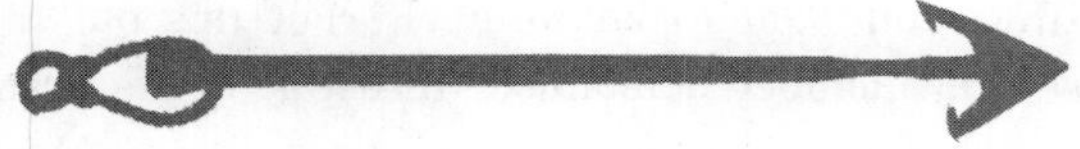

CHAPTER 16

ABOARD PANDORA'S BOX

Eric Stein ordered his crew not to move the schooner while he went below decks. He made his way through the well-worn passageway to the captain's quarters, shut his door and sat on his bunk. He massaged his temples while he grappled with a tempest of memories dredged up upon seeing Anastasia. Their relationship had spanned the course of three years while both studied marine biology at the same university, but it was one recollection in particular which plagued him now: their time together in the environmental awareness group GreenAction.

For Anastasia, the GreenAction experience had been a summer stint between graduating college and beginning a PhD program. For Eric, it marked the end of his collegiate career, without earning a degree, and the true beginning of his own rival environmental organization.

The ship R/V *Green Resistance* was as unforgettable for him as the place: Antarctica. They had been searching for a Japanese whaling vessel. Stein still flashed on the experience like it was yesterday. . . .

"Eric, you want to kill yourself? Put this on!" a fellow crewmember demanded, thrusting a life vest into his chest.

Stein fended him off. "Screw it, man. No time." He started for the Zodiac. He felt a strong hand grip his shoulder.

"I don't think so, Eric. You wear it or you don't take the Zodiac. You know the regulations."

Eric's eyes blazed, but he donned the life vest. He ran over to the rail where several crew balked as they looked out on a rough sea. "Gotta be fifteen-, maybe twenty-foot swells. I don't think we should launch it," one of them said, eyeing the Zodiac as it dangled from the crane.

The very act of launching the small boat was treacherous. The launch procedure, on which they ran drills during calm weather when there were no whaling ships in the vicinity, called for the Zodiac's passengers to sit in the boat while it was lowered into the water by winch.

Simple in concept, but not in practice. A crewmember had died once because the boat had blown into the side of the ship on the way down and flipped over. The person who had fallen out simply disappeared under the ship's hull. End of story. This was why running interference with the small boat in conditions such as these was strictly optional.

But Stein had a gift for rallying the troops, and

sitting in the galley around hot coffee, he had ten men willing to put their lives on the line. By the time they walked outside into the freezing wind, huddled around the Zodiac while it swayed under the crane like a kite in the breeze, six had changed their minds. One more backed out when it came time to actually board the Zodiac dangling over the angry sea.

Anastasia ran down from the bridge, where her talent as a marine mammalogist was being put to work tracking whales. She was so good at it, the captain of the *Resistance* famously remarked, that he became concerned the Japanese were following *them*, since they always seemed to be first on the whales.

"Don't do it, Eric," Anastasia implored. "It's not worth it."

He shook his head. "I'm going."

She pulled him to her. "Please don't go. They'll only be able to take one whale, anyway. The pod will make it into the ice pack, south."

"It's always one more. One more whale. One more tuna. One more whaling season. I'm sick of it. *No* more." He broke free from her embrace. In retrospect, Stein would later understand that this was the exact moment—with one gloved hand gripping the ice-covered rail of a protest ship in howling Antarctic seas, a coterie of men standing around nervously watching for his cue—that he had pulled away from her forever.

While Anastasia marched back up to her station in the bridge, Eric clenched the hand straps in the boat as the winch operator lowered them to the shifting water.

Eric untethered them from the winch cable just as the Zodiac hit the top of a swell, and the Zodiac captain—a former Alaska crab fisherman—gunned the outboard to get them a safe distance from the ship.

The launch successful, they rocketed toward the Japanese whaler, a huge factory of a ship that could go about business as usual for months at a time in conditions like these. Stein white-knuckled the cargo netting to remain in the Zodiac as it skied down mountainous waves.

Then the communications man received a spot from the *Resistance* over the radio. He pointed the way toward the pod of whales. The idea was to maneuver the Zodiac between the whaling ship and their intended targets so that the harpoon gunner would hesitate to fire long enough for the whales to leave the area.

The whalers had grown increasingly tired of the interference with what they saw as their national right, however, and the conflicts had escalated to physical confrontations—which was fine with Eric Stein. Given the chance, he would personally board the whaling ship and choke the life out of the harpooner until somebody did the same to him. To Eric it was a personal affront to kill these whales, which belonged to everyone.

But this time the Japanese were ready. Tired of the Americans endangering all who ventured into the Southern Ocean with their self-righteous antics and racking up huge financial losses, they took action.

They aimed a water cannon at the small boat, blasting it with a torrent of icy seawater, ripping the radio out of the communication man's hands and flinging it into the sea.

No longer able to receive reports from the *Resistance*, the men in the inflatable had to wait until a wave lifted them high enough to see what was happening around them. The whalers, from their perch towering above the decks of their factory-ship, could easily track the protestors. The activists carried no weapons, which were strictly forbidden by GreenAction, but Eric incited the harpoon gunner by buzzing the Zodiac around the whaler, shouting profanities and slogans, then stopping between it and the intended target.

But Stein's use of force—even if largely symbolic—was more than the whalers would tolerate. A salvo of water hit the Zodiac's driver square in the gut, knocking the wind out of him and sending their boat into an uncontrolled spin. The next moments were a blur to Stein. Like some kind of sensory kaleidoscope, at once he recalled the odor of the captain's vomit, the shouts of a crewman, the sneer on the Japanese harpoon gunner's face, and lightning passing through his shoulder.

The images ceased when Stein hit the polar water.

The pain had been caused by a direct hit from the water cannon. His shoulder, dislocated when he slammed into the outboard before tumbling overboard, would bear a dark and deep bruise for over a month. When a wave lifted him, Stein could see the Zodiac, maybe ten yards away, catching air as a swell dropped out from under it, the two men inside flailing to stay aboard. No way he could move himself to it.

The water temperature was like nothing Stein had experienced before. *Cold* didn't begin to describe the paralyzing force that began shutting down his physiology within seconds. Even with the life vest buoying him, he could barely muster the coordination to breathe. Peripherally, Eric saw the whaling ship's metal hull rising above him, then bearing down on him. He knew that he lacked the power to swim away from it, and even if they wanted to, the whalers wouldn't be able to move such a hulk of a ship quickly enough to avoid him. Eric faded in and out of consciousness as the swells took him. He heard the buzzing of the Zodiac as the crewman still on board took the driver's place at the outboard.

Were it not for the orange streak of the life vest, Stein would have been invisible in the frothy sea. The last thing he would remember was being yanked aboard the Zodiac, and then bouncing painfully on the floorboards as the inflatable raced back to the *Resistance*.

Upon reviving him, the crew told him that after five minutes in the Antarctic sea without an exposure suit, he should have been dead when they pulled him aboard. He spent the next hour wrapped in a blanket and sipping hot coffee in front of a window, where he watched as blood poured from the fin whale he'd tried to save.

Once tensions had subsided, Stein was rebuked by his fellow GreenAction activists, who praised the gunner's restraint. The harpoon gunner had been tracking him with the grenade-tipped harpoon gun on its rotating turret, his finger on the trigger. Eric's response to the criticism was that floating idly nearby and filming the Japanese slaughter of whales was a sham; all it accomplished was to get GreenAction's name in the media so they could return next season and document more whaling.

"I'm not interested in filming whales dying," Stein spat at his colleagues. "I want to save them. That's what I tried to do out there today."

He was reminded in no uncertain terms that he had almost died doing it, endangering the crew in the process. Stein's acidic retort sealed his fate within the organization.

"At least I tried. Out of a whole ship of so-called protestors who sailed to the bottom of the Earth, I'm the only one who actually did anything once we got there. I can see this is just a job for you people; you wouldn't want to jeopardize your precious funding by actually doing anything. Better to just cruise around and film the animals you pretend to protect while they go extinct. It beats working, right?"

Stein was terminated from GreenAction, and from that point forward he had conducted his own brand of activism, his own way. He had surprised even himself when, two years later, he had 1,000 members of an organization that was defined to its very core by him and him alone. Without the checks and balances of a more traditional group like GreenAction, Stein's rancor compounded exponentially, made manifest in targeted protests that almost always ended in violent, newsworthy mayhem. By the time he had two full-time criminal defense attorneys on OLF's payroll, Stein had become an international pariah.

Even so, he recalled the shock and surprise he'd felt the first time he saw the label "eco-terrorist" next to his name. *Eco-terrorist Eric Stein . . .* he'd read one day in the *L.A. Times.* Is that what I am? he'd thought. It didn't seem possible. He was just a guy who cared fervently about the environment, and who was willing to do things others considered beyond their reach in order to protect it. *Terrorist?*

But with the notoriety came funding, some from surprising sources, including anonymous corporate donors who'd been snubbed by the same lobbyists Stein's organization battled on a routine basis. The infamy also brought more volunteers than ever, and OLF's ranks had soon swollen to proportions that demanded attention.

As Stein learned how to manipulate the media through ever more reckless stunts, he became inured to the immorality of his actions. He knew only that the more outrageous his deeds and callous his attitude, the greater visibility and power his group attained. Underlying it all was a seething hatred, a genuine seed of mistrust sown that day in the Southern Ocean, thereafter to be watered, nourished, and pruned by every environmentally abrasive piece of legislation, every statistic depicting the irreversible loss of biodiversity at the hands of man, every Hummer-driving idiot who'd never rolled his leased wheels off the parking lot America had become.

What was destructive by all outward appearances was, for Stein, his life's work, nothing less than an art form that would lead to his own amputated future. He pictured it sometimes, his life, cut short by some glorious demise in the line of duty, and the fact was that it energized him. His life might be short, but it would be the perfect picture of his vision. No one, not even Anastasia—especially not Anastasia—would get in the way. Since the GreenAction trip, he had had no personal interaction with her. They would occasionally find themselves in close proximity for professional reasons—at a conference, a protest or rally, a political function—but there was no longer a relationship. She had affected him, once, but she would not be allowed to interfere now.

Through the walls of his ship he could distinguish Anastasia's voice on the megaphone shouting instructions, attempting to carry out her own vision, her idea of convincing the masses through academic work, interlaced with extravagant infotainment, that natural ecosystems were worth saving. But she was making it worse, Stein thought as he stood again and started to pace. Her actions reinforced the notion that nature was nothing more than a "resource" to be exploited on every possible level, from sustenance to entertainment. Her vision was incompatible with his own, and he determined, opening the cabin door, not to allow her TV show to become any more successful.

His moment of weakness passed, his resolve steeled, Eric sprung down the companionway toward the ladder that would lead him topside.

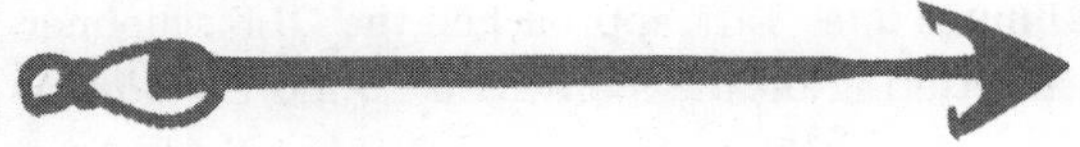

CHAPTER 17

ABOARD THE WIRED KINGDOM SCARAB

Anastasia threw the megaphone down. “Damn it! They're not moving.” She looked over at Tara, who stood on the side of the dock. The detective waved her cell phone. Anastasia called.

“Special Agent Shores, how may I help you?” It was Tara’s turn to be annoying.

“Can’t you do something about these punks? It’s illegal to willfully block a public waterway.”

Tara shrugged. “I’m not a traffic cop. Besides, it sounds like you know the guy. What’s the problem?”

“Old college fling gone bad. I’ll tell you about it later. Can you just get them to move, please?”

“Two minutes ago you wouldn’t stop the boat even long enough for me to get on. Now you want my help so you can leave without me?”

“Okay. Get those troublemakers to let us pass and you’ve earned your ticket.”

Tara saw Anastasia nod her head at a crewman, and a small tender launched toward the dock. A black guy in a *Wired Kingdom* T-shirt pulled up to Tara and steadied the launch while she stepped in.

Minutes later Tara approached the OLF schooner. Gilded lettering on the stern read *Pandora's Box*. As she drew nearer, Tara recognized the dreadlocked guy as the man in charge of the extremist environmental group. Although never convicted himself, he was widely believed to be responsible for influencing his members to commit a litany of serious offenses, always in the name of the marine environment. He was said to have a charismatic hold on his followers, not unlike a cult leader. Tara knew the FBI had an extensive file on him and his organization, and she found herself tensing as she drew near the schooner, trying to recall his name.

"Morning." She smiled. He stared back. "My name is Special Agent Tara Shores," she said, flashing her credentials. The sailor's eyes followed her movements, but he seemed disinterested at the same time. This guy is cold, Tara thought. Reptilian. She found herself almost subconsciously easing a hand near the pistol she wore in a hip holster.

"These guys gimme the creeps," the dinghy operator said, loud enough for the dreadlocked enviro-zealot to hear. "Maybe we should just call the harbor patrol."

"I'm hoping that won't be necessary," Tara said, also loud enough to be overheard. Then, turning back, she said, "Listen, Mr. . . . ?"

"Stein. Eric Stein."

It was the first time Tara had heard him speak. She was surprised to hear a rather thin, whiny voice.

"Mr. Stein, that vessel you're blocking is assisting the FBI in a murder investigation. Is there some reason you refuse to move?"

"Our organization believes that they've screwed around enough with the so-called wired whale, and that the animal is better off without them anywhere near it."

The Scarab drifted toward the schooner. Anastasia stood on the expansive bow deck, craning her neck to hear. "What's that lowlife idiot saying?" she called out. "Never mind. Just arrest him and get him out of the way."

"I'm not going to arrest him for—"

"Last summer you slaughtered a canoe full of Eskimos who were only hunting for food, retaining their cultural heritage," she said, pointing at him dramatically, "Remember that, Eric Slime? You didn't see our plane up there, did you? I know what you did last summer!"

This elicited a few chuckles from Stein's motley crew, but they did nothing more than maintain their casual state of readiness.

"Only one of them was an Eskimo," Stein replied slowly, "and that only on paper, as I understand it, due to some courthouse finagling to take advantage of Native American government benefits. He was as much an Eskimo hunting for food as you are a scientist studying whales with your ridiculous spectacle of a show. He collected cash from wealthy businessmen who flew into Alaska for the weekend to hunt walrus and whales the old-fashioned way for kicks: in a paddled boat, using hand-thrown spears. This 'Eskimo' didn't have any problem using protected, endangered animals as feel-good trophies for old men who wanted to believe they were young again."

"So you murdered them," Anastasia called across the water.

"They had a boating accident," Stein said, making no effort to conceal his visual appraisal of the sleek Scarab.

"That sounds like a threat!" Anastasia yelled.

It was the closest Tara had seen her come to being upset. And with OLF's rap sheet, Tara quickly reflected, she couldn't blame her. The group had grown progressively violent in recent years, and was on the verge of being formally classified as a terrorist organization by the U.S. government.

"Mr. Stein, as I was saying," Tara intervened, "I'm not here to investigate you or your organization. But if you refuse to let that boat pass, you'll be obstructing justice, and then I'll have no choice but to arrest you. I'm pretty sure you'd rather be out on the water saving the whales for the TV cameras than calling your attorneys for bail money and wasting precious time getting your vessel out of impound."

"So you don't care if we go out there?" Stein asked.

"Why should we?" Anastasia cut in with a taunt. "We'll be there and back by the time you get halfway to my whale in that old tub."

Tara frowned in her direction, then turned back to the schooner. "No, Mr. Stein. I can't stop you from sailing the ocean . . . as long as you stay peaceful. But you need to move. Now." It was a direct order, a challenge. She hoped he would move. If he disobeyed her, she'd have to call for backup. Then there would be some kind of action, which would mean reports to write up, not to mention jeopardizing attempts to rescue the whale, and she had no time for either.

Stein sat motionless for a long moment, but it was as if he was studying her, not considering what to do. Finally, he said, "You know, you've done something I've always wanted to do."

Here we go, Tara thought. *He's going to resist.* "What's that?"

"You swam in the ocean with wild Orca. I've been around the planet by water . . . what, seven times now?" He turned to consult with one of his crew, who ticked a count off on his fingers before shaking his head. "Okay, six and a half times. And I've never been able to do that, ever. None of us have. What was it like?"

"You can pay to see it on my damn web site, loser," Anastasia shouted. Tara cast her a sideways glance, surprised at the harsh language used so casually from such a well-educated professional.

"I'm not asking you, *Doctor*. You weren't even in the water, as I recall," Stein said.

Anastasia's face burned while Tara's mind lighted

on the powerful black-and-white mammals . . . the terror she felt . . . and yes, she thought, maybe even a fleeting moment of sheer child-like wonder that had found its way into her horrified mind when her bare hand brushed over one of their sleek hides. *So smooth, like velvet, yet so brutal at the same time.*

"The Shamu experience is definitely not for everyone. Seriously, it wasn't something I chose to do, or would want to do again," she said honestly. A few of the OLF crew were stepping forward to hear her, listening with interest. "I felt like I was in their way, like I didn't belong there."

Stein's eyes locked on hers for a second. No one said anything. Then he simply raised a hand, and two deckhands retrieved the anchors. Nothing more was said as the quiet hum of an electric trolling motor started and the sailing boat edged its way to one side of the channel.

The dinghy turned a one-eighty and motored back to the Scarab. Tara felt Stein's eyes on the back of her neck as a *Wired Kingdom* crewman helped her aboard the million-dollar racing craft.

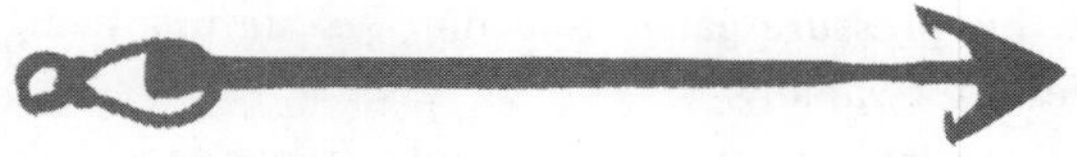

CHAPTER 18

33° 36' 25.8" N AND 119° 69' 78.4" W

When problems happen underwater they tend to start small. As experienced divers know, little problems left unattended have a way of becoming big ones, in a kind of snowball effect. For diver Carlos Mendonca, the snowball was already rolling downhill.

His first problem was simply seeing where he was going. The water was murky, visibility less than five feet. Hardly passable conditions in which to dive, let alone approach a hundred-ton monster. But thoughts of wealth propelled Carlos away from his better judgment and through the pea soup over the seamount. Just as the whale had been attracted to the baited net, he too was lured by what it now promised.

His second problem was technical. In the rush to get out of the plane he had slipped while jumping from the door and hit the aircraft's pontoon on his way into the water. He was unhurt, but his regulator mouthpiece had taken a hit. In the excitement of entering the water so close to their prize, he had been able to ignore it, but it now produced a steady burble of escaping air. And now, fifty yards and a few minutes of kicking later, his pressure gauge told him his air was being depleted too rapidly.

He pushed on. In his considerable experience, he'd faced far more dire circumstances—bull sharks, out-of-air situations in deep-lying shipwrecks, night diving in caves. This was practically a surface dive. He was not worried about air. Even so, he knew the risks he was taking. *Finish this dive and the risk-taking is over for good.* He would retire a gentleman farmer and raise a few head of cattle on his own ranch, with hired hands to do the real work associated with such an endeavor.

Problem number three was the whale itself. Where the hell was it? What was it doing? At first he had heard some low, mournful echolocations that seemed to come from everywhere at once, but now the sea was silent save for the rasp of his regulator.

He spoke into his communications unit: "*¿Dónde está la ballena?*" Replies of "*No sé*" were followed by a stream of technical chatter from the earpiece in his full facemask: his distance to where they last saw the whale from the plane, his compass heading, current and wind velocities, elapsed time since he left the plane—even his escalating breathing rate. He blocked it out and pushed on, mentally spending the extra reward Héctor had promised to the diver who handed him the tag.

It was then that the currents conspired for just a

moment to wash a stream of cold, clear water over the seamount. It was as if someone had wiped away the condensation from a warm breath on a cold window to catch a glimpse of the scene outside before it fogged over again.

Barely fifteen feet away, the animal stretched in both directions like a semi truck. Several awestruck seconds passed before he even recognized the shape in front of him as that of a living thing rather than some uncharted rock formation. It was an endless, dark wall until the whale rolled, exposing her belly to the sky, brightening the sea above. The Blue was so vast, so massive, that he couldn't be sure in which direction the creature's head lay.

He saw at once why he was able to get so close to the animal. The enormous fluke—the powerhouse of propulsion for this sea-going giant—was entwined in thick webbing. Invisible in single strands, the mesh now appeared an iridescent blue as it wrapped layer upon layer around the massive appendage. Making matters worse, great sheets of loose netting danced around the Blue in the currents like macabre shawls worn by invisible dancers.

He backed away in fright upon seeing the expressionless eye of a five-foot yellowfin tuna. The once magnificent fish was plastered to the indiscriminate wall of death as it was dragged past the diver's head. Carlos had time to notice that most of its fins, including the tail, had been amputated during the struggle to free itself. He tore his mind away from the grisly image. He had to find some open water. Should the whale roll into him, he would be crushed with the same force as if he had been hit by a car while walking down the street. The swaying mesh was also perilous. He would back off and get his bearings.

Then he saw it. As the whale shifted again, she all but disappeared as her dorsal side blended in too well with the shadowy chasm below. But the blinking red LED was unmistakable. He stopped moving and the currents instantly counteracted his progress, drawing him back to the cetacean.

He remembered the helmet light. Flipped it on. Almost worthless with the backscatter, the beam penetrated just enough to make out something altogether foreign on the Blue's dorsal fin. Picturing the textbook illustrations he'd seen, Carlos felt more in control for being able to orient himself to the colossal beast in his mind's eye.

The heated water circulating through his dry suit couldn't suppress a chill when something brushed against his neoprene-clad leg. He swatted at it with a hand but felt nothing. He craned forward to see, but the density of krill and detritus wouldn't allow it. He felt another downward tug on his ankle. Reaching, his gloved fingers felt a web of monofilament nylon snagged around the dive knife he wore inside his left calf. He tried to jerk his leg out of the netting, but it held fast. He was drifting in the current.

Where was the whale now?

Worried but not yet panicked, he undid the strap

on his knife sheath. He removed the blade, careful not to drop it, and sliced through the monofilament strands until his leg was freed. Then he looked up in time to brace himself with a forearm as he slammed into the Blue.

Dazed from the impact but unhurt, Carlos saw that he was only feet from the tag. Breathing very quickly now, he took precious seconds to reach into his vest pocket for the magnet that would trigger the release of the tracking device from the whale's body. His thick gloves afforded him warmth and protection, but not dexterity. Retrieving the oblong piece of metal was cumbersome. When at last he did, he was forced to grip the tag itself in order to stay with it.

Carlos started to swipe the magnet across the base of the tag in the manner he was shown by Héctor on a whiteboard diagram back in Cabo San Lucas—during the hasty pre-mission briefing, the procedure had seemed much simpler—when the whale lunged forward. The magnet slid out of its groove and was lost in the swirling murk. "¡*Mierda*!"

"What's the problem, Carlos?"

"I—" He was about to say he'd lost the magnet, but caught himself. He knew that any mention of problems would bring his colleagues to his aid, reducing his chances of being the one to bring the tag in. "*Nada*. I'm fine. No problem. I've found the whale and am about to remove the tag." He eyed the knife he still held in his hand. He considered the fragile-looking piece of electronic gear hanging from the Blue's dorsal, and thought about moving his family into a real house in a neighborhood with paved roads. He made his decision.

Carlos plunged the four-inch blade into the Blue's body just below the tag.

In the seaplane the standby divers alternated their gaze between the orange buoy that was tethered to the net trap and their boss, who occupied the pilot's seat. Héctor was doing his best to pretend he had more important things to do than listen to their exchanges. But they demanded to know why their colleague who had not been killed by Orca earlier was not still with them.

"If you knew he was bent, why did you not take him to a chamber?" one of them asked him.

Héctor rubbed his brow in exasperation before answering. When he spoke it was in a slow and deliberate manner. "I told you I did not know for certain that he was bent. He said to me before going to sleep that he was in only minor discomfort. I gave him oxygen as a precaution, and we both agreed that if he got any worse by morning, I would take him to the nearest chamber. As I recall we even debated which was closest—the one in Santa Barbara or on Catalina Island. But when I woke up, he had . . . passed on." He shook his head. *More lies. What am I becoming?*

"Perhaps. Or maybe you decided you wouldn't risk taking *my brother* to an American medical facility because they would ask too many questions."

Héctor sat bolt upright, shouting: "How dare you! I informed you and your brother of the risks this operation would pose. Get—"

At that moment the hefty orange buoy marker bobbing nearby was sucked abruptly beneath the surface, where it remained out of sight. The diver who had been watching the dive site whirled around.

"¡*Cállense*!" he shouted, pointing.

"What happened to the buoy?" the leader said, squinting at the sea outside.

"It was pulled under."

"Are you sure it didn't just break loose and drift away? It would take hundreds of pounds of thrust to—"

"I watched it disappear. The whale can do it."

The leader grabbed the microphone for the underwater communications system. "Carlos, what is happening?"

No answer came.

"Laptop . . . Get the satellite visual up on the laptop," Héctor commanded. He continued trying to raise Carlos over the radio while one diver scrambled for the computer and the other eyeballed the water. Before the laptop was open, they heard Carlos on the radio. There was no attempt to disguise the panic in his voice.

"Help! Help me!"

"Carlos, what is happening?"

The response was rapid-fire. "Get down here! Get down here! Help me!"

The diver whose brother had died on the island

shook his head and turned the laptop around so that the pilot could see it. Nothing distinctive was visible in the opaque stew on screen.

"Carlos?" The pilot tried to raise him without success. "Carlos!" He signaled his two standby divers. "Go."

Seconds later the pair was swimming toward the spot where the buoy had been. Héctor, now alone in the aircraft, continued to monitor the laptop and radio. Neither gave him any clues as to what was unfolding below.

He asked for a status check from the two divers who had just left to make certain his radio was functioning properly. It was. He had resigned himself to sit and wait when he heard the rumble of a boat engine in the distance.

CHAPTER 19

ABOARD THE WIRED KINGDOM SCARAB

"Are you going to throw up?" Anastasia asked.

Hunched over a seat in the Scarab's cabin, Tara nodded as she turned her ashen face upward. The seasickness had claimed her about ten minutes outside the marina. The swells weren't big, but the boat's incredible speed created a bone-jarring impact every time they slammed into another crest.

In her rush to meet Anastasia, Tara had forgotten her scopolamine patches.

"Can you make it outside?"

Tara shook her head no. Even if she could make it on deck, she didn't need the embarrassment of vomiting in front of a bunch of TV camera guys. They'd probably use it for the show. At least down here she was alone, except for Anastasia.

The bile in her throat made another upward surge and Tara retched. She stared at the floor, her hair hanging around her face. Her stomach clenched into a knot, her saliva grew thinner and more copious, a metallic tinge to it. The world started to swim around her. If Branson could see me now, Tara thought, one hand clasping hard against the floor. She heard Anastasia's voice, as if from far away.

"On the bright side, nobody's ever died from seasickness. They might wish they had, but they don't. Let me help." Anastasia pulled Tara's hair back, holding it away from her face.

A twinge of unease penetrated her nausea. Then Tara vomited again and was in no position to protest. And she *was* glad not to throw up in her hair.

While she knelt on the floor, hanging her head, she engaged Anastasia in conversation, to take her mind off of her embarrassment while she recovered. "I didn't know you knew OLF's leader personally." She wiped a string of spittle onto her shirt sleeve.

"Unfortunately, yes, I know him. It's something I try to forget," Anastasia said, continuing to hold back Tara's hair.

"We met while we were both junior marine biology majors at the University of California. He was a different person back then. We used to hang out. Study all night in the library. Drink a lot of coffee to get through midterms and finals. He's a bright guy, I'll give him that, but he never really applied himself. Always disillusioned with society and the government. He would get so angry during discussions about marine pollution and declining fish stocks, melting polar ice caps, stuff like that. He would berate the environmental studies majors for telling him to leave the lights off when he wasn't home. 'That's your big solution?' he would yell at them. 'Use less? Just accept the crappy infrastructure that's been put in place for us by shortsighted politicians? How about finding different energy solutions in the first place? Did you idiots ever think of that? You think if everybody leaves the lights off more or lowers the AC a notch that it's going to reverse global warming, stop the oceans from devolving into a primal slime where jellyfish are the only food source left? Go back to school.'" Anastasia shook her head in response to the memory.

"I see you recall it pretty well," Tara remarked.

"It's hard to forget when you hear him talk. He does have a gift for public speaking."

"Shame he's not putting it to use helping people."

"Yeah, I know it's twisted, but the way he sees it, he *is* helping people. He truly believes he's saving them from ruining their environment. So I stuck with him until . . ." Anastasia paused, choking back a painful memory, "until our Antarctica trip with GreenAction. He started Ocean Liberation Front shortly after that, and it changed him completely. And he always had so many girls around him, these wannabe environmentalists who volunteered for his organization, canvassing, putting up flyers, updating his website. I went to his apartment one night to tell him how upset I was that he'd made the local news for allegedly sinking a fishing boat that was known to be used to kill seals, and I . . . I caught him in bed with another woman."

"I'm sorry to hear that. Is that . . ." Tara hesitated.

"Is that what?" Anastasia asked.

"Is that when you broke it off with him?"

"Definitely."

Tara felt better to the point that she was no longer in danger of vomiting. She didn't pull away from Anastasia, though, because she was learning more about Eric Stein, someone she considered a mild person of interest in the case. But when Anastasia started massaging her neck, Tara clamped a hand around her wrist and stood up. She was about to say something when the roar of the Scarab's engines diminished, the boat fell lower in the water and they were pitched forward with the sudden decrease in velocity.

"Almost there," a crewmember called down. Anastasia calmly removed her wrist from Tara's grasp.

"Are we the first ones here?" Anastasia called up. There was a pause. Anastasia lifted an eyebrow before peeling her gaze from Tara. She looked up the stairs toward the deck. "Well?"

"We're the first boat, yeah, but we're not the first people here. You should get up here."

33° 36' 25.8" N AND 119° 69' 78.4" W

The Blue had gone as deep as the nets would allow. At one hundred feet, her fluke swaddled in mesh, she could descend no further. Eighty feet above, divers Juan Garcia and Fernando Jiménez hovered in the water column, slowly spinning in a circle, looking for the whale.

Their communications system did not permit them to talk directly with Carlos. They relied instead on Héctor for information.

"Topside, this is Juan. Anything from Carlos?"

"Negative. Nothing on the computer, either," Héctor replied.

"The marker buoy?"

"No time to look—there's a boat approaching."

Then they saw the line for the buoy slanting off into the darkness. But no buoy, just a big loop of braided yellow line. Juan grabbed it. He began to follow it down, signaling Fernando to follow. They heard the sound of the aircraft's engine fire up as the world darkened around them. At forty feet the water clarity improved. Juan felt Fernando clutch his arm. He aimed his light in the direction Fernando pointed. A wall of mesh, made easier to see by the many dead and trapped fish it carried, drifted lazily toward them in the slow-moving current. Its size meant that there was no time to get around it. Juan removed his dive knife. Fernando did the same, and they started cutting as they collided with the amorphous wall.

They drifted while they cut, but kept their focus on getting through to the other side of the net. Were it to wrap around them from more than one direction, they could be immobilized. Minutes later, they had each hacked their way through. Fernando took pity on a large bonito fish struggling spasmodically in the mesh, and sacrificed precious seconds cutting it loose. Juan held his hands up in irritation. The fish squirmed free, gave a few tentative shakes of its tail, and was gone.

They pressed on, looking for the buoy line again.

They found it by accident. A fishing rod arced past them, disappeared, and then reappeared a few seconds later. Juan grabbed and held it. They guided themselves along its monofilament. Twenty feet later they joined the buoy line, where a fluorescent pink lure was snagged. Juan cut the rod free and they resumed their descent down the thick rope.

At seventy feet they crossed a thermocline and the water became both colder and clearer. There was a lot of loose netting flying about here, and the two divers were nervous, their heads on swivels while they tried to monitor their three-dimensional surroundings.

Suddenly they could no longer hear the whine of the seaplane motor. Juan called the pilot. "Topside, what is your status?"

"Juan, I am in the air to monitor approaching boats. Maintaining a holding pattern. Over." Héctor made a low, tight circle over the dive site. From his vantage point he could see several boats en route to his divers' location. The Scarab led the way.

Cursing the fishermen who had broadcast the site's GPS coordinates, Héctor wasn't surprised to hear a voice asking him to identify himself emit from his radio. He weighed his options. Plausible misinformation, rather than stubborn silence, would give them more time to operate. He picked up the transmitter.

"Copy that, Scarab. We are from the South Coast Marine Mammal Rescue Network. Some of our members heard the fishermen's radio call. We thought we'd do a fly-by and see if there was anything we could do to help."

"Roger that, seaplane. Always nice to have an eye in the sky. We're from the television show *Wired Kingdom*. We've come to retrieve our equipment and will be filming our rescue of the whale."

"Okay. Let us know if there's anything we can do to assist."

"Just advise your people to stay out of the way and let our experts handle it."

"Copy that, *Wired Kingdom*. Be advised, I've got a bird's eye view of a whole lot of boats coming this way, including a Coast Guard cutter."

"Thanks for the heads-up. We'll get right to work."

"South Coast Marine Mammal Rescue Network? Never heard of it," a diver suiting up on the Scarab's deck said, looking at Anastasia.

The marine scientist looked up from her own dive gear. "No, but it's impossible to keep track of all those 'we love cute marine mammals' organizations. Some of them do legitimate work, but a lot are just amateurs who get in the way."

"I've never heard of them either," a cameraman said, snapping an waterproof case shut on a video camera.

"So what's your plan?" Tara asked Anastasia.

"The plan is to dive in and get an assessment of the whale's condition, see what we can do about it and, if possible, to try and get the tag back."

"Two ships on the way," a crewmember called out.

"NOAA and the Coast Guard," Anastasia said, squinting into the distance. "They'll want us out of the water. If we're going to dive, now's the time."

What transpired after he stabbed the Blue was a blur to Carlos. Things had happened too fast to recall them in order. He didn't remember blacking out, but here he was, strapped to the base of the Blue's tail by the mesh, one hundred feet down.

The alarming hiss of his regulator reminded him of the urgency of his situation. That, and the pain. His right arm was broken in two places, entwined in netting. Fire flared up in the limb with the whale's every move. How much air had he consumed while unconscious with a free-flowing regulator? he wondered. He checked his gauge: enough gas to last about ten more minutes at this depth. He would need to decompress after ascending to avoid the bends, but right now that was the least of his worries. Carlos instinctively reached for his knife and then remembered plunging it into the whale.

Recalling his communications link, he spoke into his mask. "*Jefe*, can you hear me?"

From the seaplane, Héctor saw more boats bearing down on them with every pass he made. Soon the area would be a zoo. And now his comm unit made a weird hissing and crackling noise. The Coast Guard cutter would be on site within minutes. He had three divers down. When or if they could meet their objective was unclear.

He pounded his fist on the instrument console as he made another circle. He picked up the transmitter for the underwater communications unit. "Juan, Fernando—do you copy? Over."

"*Sí, señor*. We have descended the buoy line. The whale—Carlos!"

"What is happening?"

"We see him. He is—"

Another voice punched through a standard marine channel. "Cessna seaplane, this is the United States Coast Guard cutter *Los Angeles*. You are flying too low and too close to a marine mammal in distress. I repeat, you are flying too close to a marine mammal in distress. You will be cited if you do not leave the area immediately."

The pilot allowed the plane to drift even lower while concentrating on how to reply. First he picked up the underwater comm unit's microphone. "He is what, Juan? He is *what*? The Coast Guard is ordering me out—can you get the tag and surface now?"

"No!" This from Fernando. "We need more time. Carlos is in trouble—tangled with the whale in netting, low on air.

"Does he have the tag?"

"I—"

The standard radio channel boomed, "Seaplane—

U.S. Coast Guard—Acknowledge at once. Over!"

The pilot switched over to the radio transmitter. "Copy that, Coast Guard. Will comply. I was passing by and thought I would mark the location for the rescue boats. Over."

"Roger that, seaplane, but we better see you leaving, now. We need to minimize all non-authorized rescue traffic—both air and sea. Over."

Looking off to his left, toward the coast, the pilot spotted the cutter plowing towards the site. A bright flash of light gleamed from it—perhaps a signal mirror—but no matter; they had made their point clear.

Knuckles white from gripping the steering column, Héctor grappled with the agonizing decision he faced. To comply with the Coast Guard meant leaving his divers behind in the water. Would they betray him if caught? Of course. Maybe he should disobey the direct order long enough to pick up the divers with or without the tag.

His arbitration was interrupted by the underwater comm unit. "I don't know yet if he has the tag, *señor*. We are almost to him, but it will take some time."

Time? There is no time.

The pilot broke his circular pattern and headed north away from the site. He was sure he would be forever haunted by the sound of Juan's anxious breathing suddenly cut short as the plane exceeded the comm gear's range.

CHAPTER 20

33° 36' 25.8" N AND 119° 69' 78.4" W

"Topside. . . . Topside!" Juan shouted into his mask.

"Why does he not respond?" Fernando asked.

"Don't know. Let's finish the dive."

They had seen Carlos' form strapped to the base of the Blue's fluke, but now the water grew murky. The pair followed the buoy line, which, due to the currents, took them along a horizontal path toward the end of the dark torpedo. The Blue constantly pitched and rolled as she struggled to free herself. They had to keep a safe distance from the monstrous body, yet at the same time not allow themselves to separate from their target.

The ghastly form of Carlos adorning the Blue's tail took shape as the pair neared the gargantuan fluke. A fast-moving current threatened to railroad them into the mass of netting surrounding the tail. They kicked against it, consuming more precious air, and inched their way closer to Carlos until they could see his dive mask.

His back was to the whale's body. To Juan and Fernando, Carlos appeared to be in a veritable fortress of nets. Not only was his arm lashed to the base of the whale's fluke, but at this close range they could see that the current had pushed a hornet's nest of loose mesh over his entire body. The whites of Carlos' eyes peered through black holes of fishing net like some bizarre aquatic mummy. Worse, they could see his lips moving, his pained facial expression, but could hear nothing.

Juan spoke first. "Topside, can you hear Carlos? He is talking now."

Only the mechanical rasp of their breathing broke the silence that followed.

"Topside, do you copy me? Over."

More breathing.

Juan and Fernando looked at one another in disbelief. Their communications link had malfunctioned, they thought. It wasn't unknown to happen.

Carlos continued to talk to himself behind the layers of nets.

Then the Blue attempted to harness the full power of her fluke. She felt a hunger for oxygen after being tethered by nets so long beneath the surface. The movement had the effect of thrusting the baleen whale only ten feet upward in the water column, when under normal circumstances the same exertion would have sent her gliding gracefully to her next sip of air.

For Carlos, the whale's unsuccessful attempt at forward motion had the same effect of a heavy bookcase toppling onto him. Fernando was astonished to hear Carlos' guttural outburst travel unamplified through ten feet of water to his ears. It sounded pitifully small against the vastness of the ocean.

Juan held up a white slate with a message he had written in grease pencil. He waved it in Carlos' direction, then held it steady for him to read: USE YOUR KNIFE.

Behind his shroud, Carlos shook his head.

"If he could use his knife, he wouldn't still be there," Fernando said. "We have to cut him out."

Juan nodded his head in agreement.

They waited for a gap in the netting to open up between them and Carlos. Then, sensing they had a window of opportunity, they power-kicked across the remaining distance until they clung to the monofilament sheet that threatened to become Carlos' tomb.

They could feel the Blue writhing beneath them, minor tremors portending a great eruption.

Juan scrawled another message on his slate and held it out for Carlos to read: TAG?

Again, Carlos shook his head. Fernando swayed in the currents, using the net to hold him in place. He saw Carlos' air hose threaded between sheets of mesh, hopelessly snared. Fernando managed to glimpse the gauge's face. Enough for maybe five minutes at their current depth. Fernando relayed the information to Juan, who was already sawing his way through the outer sheets of webbing.

The Blue remained placid.

Three minutes later the pair had managed to slice their way through the loose nets to where Carlos was lashed to the whale. The sight of him was far from encouraging. Thick ropes of snarled monofilament snaked through his gear. Carlos' eyes had begun to glaze over as he descended into a state of shock they feared would claim his life.

Suddenly Juan swam away, off to Fernando's right. Toward the Blue's dorsal.

"Juan, what are you doing?"

"Keep cutting, I will get the tag and be right back."

"No!" But he was already lost from sight along the leviathan's side. Fernando turned back to Carlos, who was too busy attempting to extricate himself to notice that Juan was no longer there.

Fernando remembered with a jolt that he had a second dive knife attached to his vest. He handed the small blade to Carlos. The tool gave the trapped man a sense of purpose, and together the two of them worked on cutting him free. The grinding of serrated metal on thick monofilament could be heard over their breathing, and they were rewarded with the occasional *snap* as thick bundles of line parted.

Juan was having difficulty locating the dorsal. He maintained a five- to ten-foot distance from the mammoth body, but it all looked the same to him. When the wall he swam along became white, he knew he had meandered to the belly. Then he would correct his course, swimming vertically until he was over dark hide once again.

Easy to miss in poor visibility, the Blue's dorsal fin was nothing more than a brief hillock punctuating a vast plane. Such a small fin for so humongous a creature, Juan thought.

The red LED gave the tag away. He swam to it. His eyes took in the knife embedded in the blubber just below the dorsal fin, but his mind saw only the piece of electronic gear.

His for the taking.

He would finish what Carlos had started.

Juan darted in. Gripping the implanted knife handle to steady himself, he added his own blade to the whale's flesh.

And the Blue's body heaved against the nets.

Fernando allowed himself to hope for the first time since finding Carlos. He had just hacked through two of the worst snarls, giving Carlos more freedom to operate. The biggest problem now was Carlos' lack of air. Their full facemasks were not designed for buddy-breathing, meaning that it was not possible for Fernando to share his mouthpiece with Carlos in the event that he ran completely out of air.

Another sawing motion and more monofilament fell from Carlos' body. As more of the netting came free, Fernando could see what was responsible for a great, spherical bulge adjacent to Carlos, also tethered to the whale. Fernando's dive light revealed a bit of orange peaking through the webbing: the marker buoy. Somehow it had become entangled with the whale when she dove.

Then the behemoth rolled away from Fernando, dragging Carlos with her. The netting holding the buoy strained with the movement before giving way. Fernando watched as the five-foot-diameter sphere broke free and rocketed toward the surface. Reeling in the net's slack with hundreds of pounds of force, the buoy peeled Carlos off the Blue's body upside down by one fin-clad foot. His broken arm was still viciously snagged on the whale. Fernando was scared that he would rocket all the way to the surface and suffer an air embolism—a rupture of the lungs caused by ascending too rapidly—but Carlos jerked to a stop about ten feet above him, dangling there in one horrifying moment as the sound of his joints dislocating popped in succession. His scream was only translated into a burst of bubbles from Carlos' regulator.

"Carlos!" Fernando cried, and lunged for him, knife in hand.

Juan returned from his expedition to the dorsal in time to see Fernando shoot forward. "Fernando, where—" He cut himself short as he saw Carlos, suspended upside down, and kicked up to him, ever mindful of the Blue.

They worked furiously to cut their colleague free of the whale, but Fernando could see Carlos' eyes locked in a glassy stare. His free arm dangled without purpose. His air was on zero.

ABOARD THE WIRED KINGDOM SCARAB

"One of the most widespread and persistent dangers facing marine mammals today is that of debris such as abandoned commercial fishing gear," Anastasia led off. She stood on the Scarab's deck in a black wetsuit, long hair in a ponytail, dive mask around her neck. The ocean sparkled and moved behind her as the cameraman zoomed in for a close-up of the TV show's host on location.

"So-called ghost nets can drift for years, killing everything in their path. Today this problem has become personal to us and to you—our faithful viewers who first alerted us to the wired whale's entanglement only a few hours ago. So now we're here in the Pacific Ocean about fifty miles west of Los Angeles to do what we can to save this venerable blue whale who has taught us so much about our own planet."

A confused look took over the cameraman's face, focused on a distant point somewhere behind her. He made a slashing motion with a finger across his throat and lowered his camera. Shouts of "Over there!" and "What's that?" called Anastasia's attention. She put on her best this-better-be-good expression and turned around in time to see three scuba divers surface about seventy-five yards from the Scarab.

Bobbing on the surface, Fernando ripped off Carlos' mask and then his own. He placed his ear to Carlos' mouth, feeling for breath. Nothing.

"Where's the plane?" Juan asked, spinning in a circle while looking upward, forcing his mind to accept the fact that the sky was empty.

"Help me lay him flat. Inflate his BC," said Fernando.

"OK, but where is Héctor?" Juan scanned the water for the aircraft but saw only a boat.

"I don't know, Juan! I wish I knew. Carlos needs CPR, right now."

"They see us—on the race boat."

"Different plane, but it's the same people who were on the whale yesterday," Tara said. It was the first time she'd spoken since being seasick. Crewmembers within earshot nodded in agreement. "Same gear, same modus operandi," she continued. "Seaplane, no boats, two or three divers with rebreathers. Somehow they manage to get to the whale before anyone else does."

"Whatever they're doing, I doubt it's helping my whale. It's been thirty minutes since her last breath," Anastasia said, consulting her dive watch.

"Bring us to the divers," Tara said. Anastasia nodded to a bearded man behind the wheel.

"Not too fast, we don't want to hit anybody," she said. Even at a slow crawl, the Scarab made short work of the remaining distance to the men in the water.

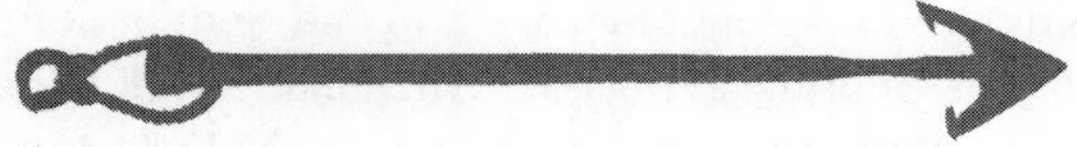

CHAPTER 21

33° 36' 25.8" N AND 119° 69' 78.4" W

Fernando pinched Carlos' nose closed and started breathing for him. "Hold him still, damn it."

"The boat is almost here," Juan said, distracted from his task of supporting Carlos' inert form in the water so that Fernando could administer mouth-to-mouth and CPR; difficult to perform in water, but not impossible. But the wake from the approaching Scarab was enough to push Carlos out of position.

"Forget the boat, Juan. This is it for Carlos—his last chance. Help me!"

Juan took one more look at the Scarab—sunlight glinted off a camera lens over its deck full of people—and turned back to Carlos. The unconscious diver's lips were pale blue. Juan steadied the body while Fernando, his dive vest full to the bursting point for maximum buoyancy, alternated between improvised chest compressions and mouth-to-mouth.

After another minute of CPR with no results, Juan lost his patience. He pulled Fernando from the body.

"It's over, Fernando. It's over."

Fernando swung a left hook at Juan's head, missing. He broke out of Juan's grip and went back to Carlos, attempting a final breath. Juan shook him violently. "Listen to me! Listen." Fernando looked up from the dead man's face. "We need to weight his body down so that they cannot find him." Juan jerked his head toward the Scarab, which had just cut its engine and was gliding up to them.

"But he is not dead—"

"Yes he is! He is *dead*, Fernando. And if you do not want to go to jail, we need to get rid of his body."

"He would want to be buried at home—"

"A burial at sea is respectable. And he would want us to succeed."

The crew on the Scarab was calling them directly now, asking them if they were okay. They could see one man hoisting up a first aid kit, another an oxygen bottle. The TV people would offer medical help, but there was no doubt that they would also turn them over to authorities. The divers had entered United States waters illegally, and they had harassed a protected marine mammal, a mammal that harbored a video of a murdered woman. Two—and now three—of their divers had been killed.

"Okay," Fernando agreed, mentally numb from watching a man die in his arms. They ignored the outstretched hands of crewmembers on the Scarab.

They hurriedly shoved some weights from their belts into his vest pockets, disregarding cries of "Hey, what're you doing?" from the boat and pulled the dump valve to release the air from Carlos' buoyancy control vest. Then they pushed Carlos' body below the surface and kicked for the bottom, head first, as the Scarab pulled up alongside them. Crewmembers' hands swiped at the water where their fins had been.

To the *Wired Kingdom* crew it looked as though the two divers were deliberately drowning their partner, dragging him below without a mask or regulator in place. Cameras rolled as the mystery divers retreated into the cloudy water.

"Find out if the tag is still on the whale—is it still working?" Tara asked Anastasia. The detective leaned over the boat's rail, peering into the water.

The scientist nodded. "Good question. Bob, check my laptop. Is the whale-cam still transmitting?" A skinny man in his late twenties with shoulder-length hair gave an informal salute on his way to the radio.

Tara looked to the sky, searching for signs of a seaplane returning to pick up the divers. There were none. It almost made her sick a second time to think that these men—whoever they were—seem to have evaded her yet again. But as she replayed her mental image of the three men struggling on the surface as the Scarab neared them, she paused the picture in her mind and zoomed in.

Something significant had happened this time. The diver's mask had been removed. She hadn't been close enough to distinguish his facial features, but she had seen his skin color. He was Latino, she thought, probably Mexican.

Juan and Fernando halted their descent at the dangerous depth of one hundred sixty feet, where the air they breathed was five times denser than surface air. They were deep enough to ensure that their co-worker's body wouldn't be returned to the surface by upwelling or currents. They scanned the area with their dive lights to be sure they were clear of the seamount's many pinnacles. Then they gave Carlos' weighted body to the sea with a final shove. When the corpse was out of sight somewhere below them, Juan broke the air-conserving silence they had held until now.

"Fourteen hundred pounds," he said, indicating he had just under half a tank of air remaining.

"Thirteen hundred," Fernando said, consulting his pressure gauge.

"Now what?"

The pair drifted slowly through the eerie twilight born of deep, cloudy water.

"We stay away from the whale. Just try to get away as far as we can underwater, then ascend and hope the plane is nearby."

"How?"

"Let's go up to forty feet, where we will use less air and get a chance to decompress. Then we'll follow the compass west out to sea, away from the boats." As if to emphasize his point, the faint whine of an outboard one hundred sixty feet above came to a muted crescendo as it passed over them.

"And when we run out of air?"

"We will worry about that then," Juan said, already kicking toward the light.

"They don't have the tag," Anastasia's long-haired crewman said. "The Blue's feed is still live. The guys on the bridge said you could see a diver with a knife come up to the tag, but he didn't get it, because you can still see the whale's body in the picture."

"Who's this?" Tara asked, nodding in the direction of a white ship drawing near the Scarab.

"NOAA?" a crewmember guessed.

They wouldn't have long to wonder. The ship deployed a Zodiac inflatable raft, which headed straight for them. Once there, a short man sporting a neatly trimmed black beard and prescription glasses held up a coil of line. He tossed it up to a crewman on the Scarab's deck.

"Hi, I'm Pete Pehl of the L.A. County Marine Mammal Disentanglement Network. I assume one of you two ladies is Dr. Reed."

Tara continued to scan the water and sky for any signs of divers or planes when Anastasia stepped forward. "That would be me," she said.

Pehl nodded. "From what we understand there's an adult female blue whale near these coordinates with a serious entanglement problem."

Anastasia was used to the Blue being referred to as *her* whale, or the wired whale, or some sort of deference to her connection with it, but the bespectacled man standing in the Zodiac offered no such recognition. Instead he only stared up at her, his expression betraying nothing but earnest professionalism while waiting for an answer.

"She's here, yes, but she hasn't surfaced in over thirty minutes. The video feed from our satellite tag on the whale shows her to be entangled in what looks like a monofilament trawling net. Her movements have been severely hampered since this morning, when the nets were first observed via biotelemetry."

"I see," Pehl said, his eyes roving for maybe a second too long over the curves of Anastasia's wetsuit before moving on to the gear assembled on deck. "Say, you're not thinking of using *that*, are you?" He pointed to the dart tag, this one both longer and newer than the one Tara had used in the helicopter.

Anastasia shrugged and pointed to Tara. "I'm assisting the FBI in their attempt to retrieve the whale's video-imaging tag for a murder investigation. The Blue's GPS is malfunctioning, so I brought along this simple tracking dart to try—"

Pehl shook his head emphatically. "No, no, no. Stow that, please. That whale is fighting for its life, and we need full control of the space surrounding it. It will not be shot with anything today."

Anastasia looked to Tara, who reluctantly nodded. Pehl waved an arm at the array of dive gear being prepared on deck. "No diving either, right? I mean, that would be extremely dangerous. This is all just for show, for the TV cameras. . . ."

Anastasia's cheeks flushed. "Look, Dr. Pehl, I can understand the tagging thing, but as far as diving goes, I'm well aware of the dangers involved. I appreciate your concern, but I'm an experienced diver. I'm a PADI instructor trainer, certified DAN O2 provider, Enriched Air Nitrox trainer, and I've got over two thousand dives logged, many of them with cetaceans in open water."

Pehl exchanged awkward glances with the operator of his Zodiac. "That's impressive, Dr. Reed, to be sure. But using our methods it's not necessary for anyone to be in the water to free the whale."

"Nobody?"

"That's right. Ninety-five percent of the time, anyway. The other five percent the whale is trapped at depth, and usually those are already dead by the time we get to them."

"We just want to get some establishing shots in the water over the seamount."

"Maybe you don't understand. No one is to be in the water during our operation."

"We don't need to approach the whale."

"Dr. Reed, I'm sorry, but it's simply not possible. Any presence in the water has the potential to negatively impact the whale, and bodies in the water will be in the way of our rescue equipment. We need to enforce a perimeter around the whale at this time."

"You can't stop me from going in." A camera operator maneuvered to get Pehl's reaction.

Pehl raised his eyebrows slightly but other than that seemed nonplussed.

"I'm afraid I can, Dr. Reed, not that I want to. I do respect your work. However, we are a contracted agent of the National Oceanic and Atmospheric Administration. As such, we have the authority to secure all marine mammal rescue sites as we see fit, according to established protocols."

"We'll pay whatever fines you throw at us," Anastasia said. She took a step toward the dive platform. The camera operators took it all in. Pehl was about to say something when they heard splashing.

The Blue surfaced fifty yards from the boats. Her great melon trailed masses of netting. She went under again and then feebly broke through to air a second time before falling back, her encumbered fluke unable to provide sufficient propulsion to keep her afloat.

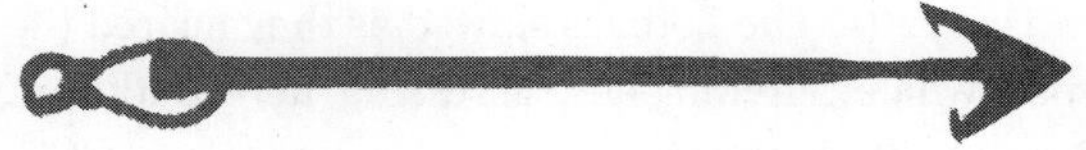

CHAPTER 22

Pete Pehl barked into his radio, “Fix that position. Get the buoys ready.”

“I’ll make you a deal,” Anastasia said. “Let us have a camera team on your boat to cover your rescue, and our team will stay out of the water.”

Pehl eyed her dubiously.

“Scout’s honor,” Anastasia said, flashing her best television hostess smile.

“Deal,” he said, scanning the water for the whale. His mind was already on the rescue. Anastasia nodded to two cameramen, who jumped into the Zodiac.

“You’re getting this, right?” Anastasia said to a third cameraman still on the Scarab. He gave her a thumbs-up in response, never taking his eye off the viewfinder.

Minutes later, not one but three Zodiacs deployed from the rescue ship. They headed for the Blue, which could still be seen struggling and thrashing to stay on the surface.

Each of the Zodiacs carried two rescuers—a boat

operator and an equipment handler. A mound of red buoys occupied the majority of deck space on the motorized rafts. The Zodiacs slowed as they neared the trapped whale, circling her, assessing her condition. Pehl spoke into his radio.

"Confirmed, adult female blue whale—*very* large individual—approximately ninety feet in length. Severe entanglement with monofilament." He paused while observing the Blue's condition through binoculars, then continued his report. "Netting obstructing the mouth is preventing her from feeding. Caudal peduncle and fluke areas are heavily wrapped. This is a dead whale swimming, people, unless we can cut her loose. Let's get to work. Keep all bystanders well clear; we don't want to spook her."

Pehl's boat cut its engines and drifted up to the Blue. Using an extension pole, a snap-hook on one end of a line was attached to a mass of netting trailing from the distressed beast's mouth. The other end was connected to a large buoy. The trio of Zodiacs proceeded to attach several more buoys to the Blue's mouth and fluke areas. The aim was to slow the creature so that it wouldn't panic.

With the buoys attached, Pehl called for the use of a specialized tool called a flying knife. A blade was rigged to be run along a line on the end of an extendable pole. This enabled the handler to cut material attached to the whale while the rescue boat remained as far as twenty feet away.

Netting was sliced as Pehl pulled the knife back in

along its line. All three boats worked in this way on the mouth area. The Blue occasionally lunged, but the running-line tools remained fastened to the netting.

As the rescuers worked, spectator boats began to congregate. They were escorted by the Coast Guard cutter *Los Angeles*, which launched a tender vessel to patrol the scene. The high-powered rigid inflatable boat, black with the unmistakable orange stripe denoting the military branch, flitted from vessel to vessel, checking registrations, safety equipment, and advising people not to interfere with the official rescue operation.

Passengers on boats coming within shouting distance of Anastasia's Scarab yelled stupid things and waved, making a scene for the cameras, hoping to get on television. Someone made a bad joke about the World Wide Whale "really surfing the net now." A few private marine mammal groups came in rented boats capable of making the offshore trip, their good intentions outweighing their equipment and experience. They were told in no uncertain terms by the Coast Guard, the NOAA support ship, and the *Wired Kingdom* Scarab to stay out of the way.

Once the Blue's head was free, the animal regained some measure of its natural movement and began to make small breaches. This brought cheers from the growing crowd of onlookers.

Pehl commanded his fleet to position themselves for the tricky job of liberating the fluke.

To a casual observer, the scene of three small boats

carrying men with metal spears and knives circling a beleaguered whale evoked images from another century. But for these modern men of the sea, their operation was a high-tech marvel which had been painstakingly developed after watching thousands of videotaped rescues, successful and otherwise. Some of the rescuers even wore helmet-cams so that afterward they could pore over every detail of the rescue like professional football players watching a post-game tape. Every advantage and disadvantage was noted, recorded, and organized into protocol. The result was the most effective whale disentanglement system ever developed.

The effort began to pay off as a modified grapple, designed to pull netting away from the whale's body so that it could be cut without injuring the animal, found its mark on the fluke. More mesh fell from the wired whale.

The Blue stirred. Her dorsal fin broke the surface and twin gleams of sunlight reflected off stainless steel.

"Look. You see that? She's got two knives sticking out from under the dorsal," a rescuer noted. In the Scarab, Tara and Anastasia heard the observation over the marine radio.

"Those bastards tried to *cut* the tag off her body with a dive knife!" Anastasia yelled. Crewmembers expressed their disbelief. Tara could see anger transforming Anastasia's face. "Turn that thing on," the show hostess demanded of a cameraman resting a camera on a bench while he stared at the enmeshed whale.

He scrambled to aim the lens at Anastasia. With a backdrop of the Blue and its three boats revolving around it like electrons around a nucleus, Anastasia launched into a tirade against animal cruelty, ending in a plea for the audience's help. "So if you know anything—anything at all—that might help law enforcement track down who's responsible for hunting our whale for its tag, call us at the studio right now. Or call the FBI."

Anastasia motioned for Tara to step forward. Wearing a dark blue windbreaker with the yellow letters FBI emblazoned on the back, a baseball cap and black sunglasses, she stepped forward. *Wonderful. National television after puking up my guts.* She wiped her mouth once on the back her sleeve, then spoke as rapidly as possible while still enunciating clearly.

"Anyone with information on either the apparent murder broadcast by the whale's equipment, or on persons using a seaplane and dive gear to approach the tagged whale, should contact the FBI immediately." She recited the hotline number and stepped from view, making it clear she would say nothing further on camera. Once clear of the lens, she couldn't help feeling that her words had been uninspired, even boring. This was reality TV, after all, she thought. *I should have said, 'call the hotline and press 1 if you think a murder was committed by someone in the seaplane . . . press 2 if you think no one really died . . .'* She was snickering to herself as she pictured Branson's reaction when she heard a noise.

Then the Blue exhaled—not the powerful geyser of spray Tara had witnessed the day before from the helicopter—but a ragged, wispy plume which was instantly lost to a light wind.

Tara considered the creature while Anastasia concluded her rant. The whale both terrified and amazed her. Some of its blood vessels were large enough for a child to crawl through. The car-sized heart pumped a miniature sea of blood, a sea within a sea . . .

"Look out! That's it. She's free. She's free." The voice of Pete Pehl boomed over the Scarab's radio. The Zodiacs propelled themselves away from the Blue at high rates of speed.

The whale breached, well out of the water this time, as if testing her newfound freedom. Applause erupted from the spectator boats. The Blue exhaled again, more forcefully this time. She rolled and righted herself, rolled and righted herself.

Then she went deep.

People quieted while they waited for the whale to show itself again. It did not.

Anastasia's satellite-connected laptop was produced on the Scarab deck. Tara and Anastasia could see dimly lit rock formations on its screen as the whale skirted the complex undersea topography of the seamount. Minutes passed while she remained at depth.

The Coast Guard began ordering the onlooking boats to return to shore, to give the whale space, and they slowly complied.

For several minutes everyone in the Scarab scanned the water in all directions, but the Blue was not to be seen. Boats continued to straggle away from the site. When only the Scarab and the rescue ship remained, the Coast Guard cutter also motored away, the seas safe once more for humans and cetaceans alike.

But as Anastasia debated with her crew about the most likely direction the Blue had gone, a sailing ship appeared on the horizon.

CHAPTER 23

WIRED KINGDOM TECH SUPPORT FACILITY

Trevor Lane's hands shook so badly he dropped his keys twice before stumbling into his office. He was beyond tired, physically and emotionally, but there was nothing for him in his crappy apartment. He didn't feel safe there. He almost wished they'd left him in jail. His blackmailers would know that he'd be willing to tell what he knew about them in return for leniency from the courts.

Trevor fell into his chair and fished around on his desk for an open can of Red Bull. His left eye throbbed, as it always did when he was under stress. He guzzled the half-empty can of warm, flat pop. He looked around at the computers, the damn Martin-Northstar manual that had gotten him into so much trouble, and at another PC on the floor by the wall.

He took from his pocket the paperwork he'd been given when his attorney bailed him out of jail. Summons to appear. Only two weeks away. The form looked innocuous enough, but under a section denoted

"Charge," a checkbox next to the word "Felony" was marked with an X. Description: "Attempted murder of a federal officer with a firearm." Funny how a little piece of paper could spell so much disaster, he thought.

But through the daze of his fatigue and distress, he remembered being fingerprinted. He'd even offered assistance to the fingerprinting operator when she couldn't get the computer to bring up the appropriate screen—having studied extensively the design of biometric capture devices, after all, before becoming interested in telemetry algorithms. Then his mug shot was taken, and his attorney, who had come courtesy of his employer, informed him in no uncertain terms of his likely fate: prison. The only question was how much time. The legal team might be able to uncover some loophole, perhaps relating to his treatment in the interrogation room, but unlike in the movies, his attorney had said it probably wouldn't happen to him. Then he'd told Trevor to get some sleep, stay out of trouble, and come in for a meeting on Monday morning.

Trevor bent down to the PC on the floor. Blinking LEDs on the front suggested activity within, but he snapped off a side panel from the case and reached inside. He extracted a roll of bills. He undid the rubber band and counted the money: two thousand dollars, mostly in twenties and tens. His emergency stash, tucked away a few bills at a time over the past several years. It wasn't much, but it would get him out of L.A.

First he would get out of the country, leaving no electronic trails of any kind, existing on cash. Then he would worry about everything else. He started to bring up Google to search for countries with no extradition to the United States, but then realized how incredibly guilty that would make him look. They would subpoena his Internet Service Provider for his online usage records, and his possible destinations would be given away. He didn't have time to take all the precautions that he knew would cover his digital tracks while searching the web.

Where to go? He drained the last drops of his beverage and threw the can on the floor, arguing with himself. Canada? No, everyone went there to run and it's too damn cold. Mexico? He didn't speak a lick of Spanish. He would need to blend in and could not afford misunderstandings due to a language barrier. The Caribbean? The Caribbean . . . lots of tropical islands, hundreds, no—thousands of them—close together. Hop over here and you're in one country; hop over there and you're in another. It had to make legal matters that much more complicated, which was just what he needed. Plenty of American tourists and ex-pats to fit in with. Women on vacation . . . He could skip from one palm-studded isle to the next, moving on when things became either too boring or too sketchy.

He thought about his situation. The TV show would probably only retain his attorney just long enough for them to find a replacement for him. As soon as they knew their web site was safe, they'd stop paying his legal fees and he'd be on his own with a public defender.

Could he make a deal with the prosecutor that would spare him a conviction in return for testimony against the Martin-Northstar insiders who had supplied him with engineering designs? "Reduced sentence" was the phrase his attorney had used. In a post-9/11 world, crimes related to national defense technology were not taken lightly.

No matter how much prison time he did or didn't serve, he was still going to be a convicted felon. He would never again be able to work in his chosen field. Who would—no, who *could*—trust him?

Trevor woke up the PC on his desk, looking for any distraction from his grim thoughts, and went to the *Wired Kingdom* site. The chat rooms were full, and a high percentage of subscribers were currently logged on. *Something must be happening*.

The whale's satellite feed took over his screen. He could see and hear a Zodiac boat zipping around the Blue. Other boats could be seen farther back in the field of view. He looked for landmarks but saw only open water.

White bubbles. The whale rolled and dove. Then she surfaced and he heard the sound of . . . applause? *What the hell is this?* Trevor reached for his desk phone, then stopped. Its blinking light told him he had messages, but they were no longer his concern. Now that he had no stake in it, Trevor grew bored with the whale. He exited the site.

Might as well check my e-mail one last time. He wasn't expecting anything good. Maybe something from Anastasia? He had mostly routine work-related messages that he left unopened. Nothing about his arrest. One had a .gov address he hadn't seen before, but it was the subject line that made him open the mail: GPS Interference Test.

He read with amazement:

To: Technical Director, *Wired Kingdom*

From: U.S. Coast Guard Navigation Center, Los Angeles

ATTN *Wired Kingdom*:

On occasion, the U.S. Federal Government is required to conduct Global Positioning System (GPS) interference tests, exercises and training activities that involve jamming GPS receivers. This is a courtesy notice to inform you that we are currently conducting such tests off the Los Angeles coast. It has come to our attention that you are operating a GPS unit which may be affected by our testing. The testing will begin on Friday, July 23 at 0500 and will conclude on Saturday, July 24 at 1700.

Additional information was given regarding the specific area of ocean covered by the testing. Trevor confirmed that the Blue had indeed been within the testing area since its GPS ceased to function. The wired whale had swum into a Coast Guard GPS jam-test zone—and only Trevor knew.

He checked his watch: 7:59 A.M. *So in about . . . nine hours . . . they'll be able to track the whale's position again in real time.* "Solved that problem," Trevor said aloud. Then he laughed like a maniac. He had racked his brain over that puzzle for hours on end, and the solution had turned out to be so simple. Not to mention completely beyond his control, like so much of the rest of his life at this point. *Too bad it doesn't matter anymore. Somebody's going to have the tag soon, but it won't be me. I'll be going off to jail.*

Tears welled in his eyes as he comprehended the gravity of his predicament. He shoved the computer monitor off the back of the desk, taking great satisfaction in hearing it crash on the hard floor. An act of pure frustration.

He got up and walked to the front door and picked up a coat rack, tested its weight in his hands. Then he walked back to the server room, opened the glass door and stepped into the chilly space. He looked at the stacks of machines, their blinking lights telling him that everything was okay. He begged to differ.

Trevor wound up and swung the coat rack into a rack of routers and switches. The loud impact startled him at first, but he became accustomed to it after a few more swings. He shattered one monitor after the next. He smashed through glass cabinet doors to get at the computers behind them. Over and over he swung the coat rack, obliterating the machines that had once supported his livelihood.

When it was done, Trevor let the rack fall to the floor. He slumped down next to it, his appetite for destruction momentarily sated, and picked a piece of transistor board out of his hair and flicked it away. He surveyed the server room, daring any lights to show themselves. He saw a green one on the floor that had somehow escaped his onslaught. He promptly extinguished it with a final blow.

Trevor dropped his tool and hurried back into the main office. He had taken the *Wired Kingdom* web site down. Millions of paying web users were now staring at a PAGE NOT FOUND message. The show's producers would be calling him soon. They'd paid a lot of money to bail him out to ensure the success of their online enterprise. When he didn't answer, they would send someone to the technical office to check it out.

It had been a stupid move, physically destroying the web site, Trevor knew, but he'd made a lot of those lately. He stood there in the office, head down, rubbing his temples hard, trying to concentrate.

Trevor rummaged through a desk drawer looking for his passport. He had been told not to leave the state, pending his court appearance, but he doubted that airport officials would be aware of his charges yet. He found the passport and put it in his pocket.

The desk phone rang.

He waited for the phone to stop ringing and then recorded a new greeting message: "Hi, this is Trevor Lane, *Wired Kingdom* technical director. If you're calling about the web site being down, it's just a minor problem that I should have under control shortly. If it's anything else, please leave a message. Thanks."

Let them think it's just a routine outage for as long as possible. He knew that they'd be able to restore the site, but hell if he was going to make it easy for them. Let the greedy bastards figure it out on their own.

Trevor grabbed the Martin-Northstar manual. *No reason to leave them a key piece of evidence while they work to nail me in absentia.* The phone rang again. He headed for the front door. He stepped outside as he heard his new message begin to play. He looked up and down the street. Seeing nothing suspicious, he walked to his car, a ten-year-old black Celica. As he opened the door his cell phone rang. *Wired Kingdom.*

After his first cell had been destroyed on the boat, he was pleased when he remembered his spare handset in the office. But as his thumb descended on the TALK button, he stopped himself. The handset would only be used against him at this point, to trace his calls, maybe even his whereabouts. He flipped it open and ripped it in half. He walked to a trash dumpster around the corner in an alley. He checked to see that no one was watching and threw the phone and manual inside.

As he started back to his car, an SUV Trevor had never seen before crept to a stop in front of his office.

ABOARD THE WIRED KINGDOM SCARAB

"We lost the damn connection," Anastasia said. She shoved aside the laptop, its screen black. The bad news was overshadowed by Ocean Liberation Front's schooner pulling up to the site. Once again, the schooner positioned itself broadside in front of the Scarab's bow. Eric Stein stood in the ship's pulpit.

"You're a little late, Eric Slime," Anastasia sneered. "Maybe next time."

Stein raised a can of Tecate beer in a gesture of cheers. He took a swig and said, "No hurry. We'll catch up. Radar sees a long ways off."

"Hit it," Anastasia said to a crewmember at the Scarab's wheel, who promptly put the engine into gear.

"What you're doing is wrong," Stein shouted in their wake. "Stay away from the whale."

Anastasia flipped him the bird, laughing as the Scarab sped off. They took the direction the Blue was last seen heading.

Five minutes later, when they were sufficiently far from the schooner, Anastasia ordered the Scarab to stop. All around them was nothing but unbroken, blue water. On the clearest of days, land might be visible from here, but now there was just enough marine layer to prevent it.

She fussed with the laptop some more. Perhaps a visual cue from the whale's current whereabouts would help. It would at least tell them if the Blue was on the surface. A few more minutes without a sighting and the whale would be lost again, she thought, and who knew when its GPS would be back online?

Anastasia tried again to log on to the Blue's feed. She cursed the error message displayed there. She handed the machine off to an assistant. "Call Anthony and tell him we're showing a 404 on the sat-feed. Ask him what he sees on the site now." The guy with the ponytail hurried off toward the marine radio.

The boat was oddly quiet while everyone on deck searched for the whale—some with binoculars, some with camera zoom lenses, others with the naked eye. Everyone, that is, but Tara, whose eyes searched from behind polarized sunglasses for a seaplane. She considered her own options while the call was patched through to Anthony. As long as they were in close contact with the whale, it made sense for her to stay out with *Wired Kingdom*. The Blue seemed to attract key elements of her case, after all.

But there were now other leads to follow. She could check to see the latest video from the tag—did it offer any additional clues about the divers or the plane? *The plane.* She could check with airport officials to try and trace it—she had a good enough description. The diver whose mask had been removed was Latino. That was something. She could request assistance from a marine unit. Relying on *Wired Kingdom's* modes of transportation was getting old. She was more of a bystander than anything else, able to observe but not act. Next time she saw the Blue, she wanted to be with an FBI dive team.

The ponytail guy left the radio and walked back on deck, shaking his head. “Anthony says the site’s down. They’re swamped with calls about it. Says he’ll get back to us when he knows something. He’s checking with Trevor now.”

There was an uncomfortable silence at the mention of Trevor’s name. The assault was only last night, but that kind of news travels fast. Eyes focused on Tara.

“Is the guy really going to be working the day after getting busted for attempted murder?” a cameraman asked no one in particular.

“For the amount we paid to bail him out, he sure as hell better be,” Anastasia replied.

There was laughter while Tara avoided any eye contact. She could not and would not discuss Trevor’s charges. She was here only to locate a central piece of evidence in what she now thought of as a murder case.

They motored south at low speed, towing a hydrophone array so that they might hear the Blue’s vocalizations, but the sea was silent. A sprawling, acrobatic pod of Pacific white-sided dolphins brought with them a moment of excitement, triggering a few seconds worth of B-roll footage, but the Blue was not making itself known.

After an hour of fruitless searching, there were no arguments about returning to shore.

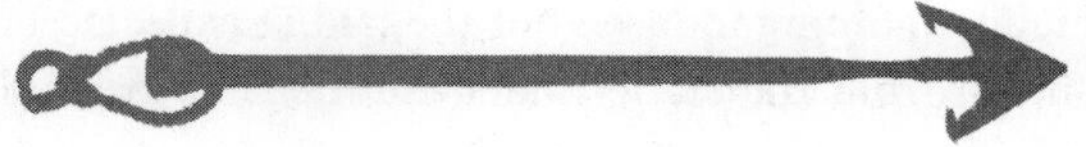

CHAPTER 24

FBI FIELD OFFICE, LOS ANGELES

While Anastasia and her crew headed for the studio to edit the day's filming for a network special on the wired whale's rescue, Tara checked in at her office. Although it was Saturday morning, multiple messages awaited her. Many were from reporters. One took the form of a note from the same assistant who had alerted her to the Blue being trapped: *Wired Kingdom* site entirely offline.

Tara logged onto the TV show's web site herself. SITE NOT FOUND. It had only been a few hours since Trevor was bailed out of jail. He probably hadn't been in the office yet, and there would have been heavy traffic for the Blue's rescue, which could have overwhelmed the site.

Another message was a memo from Imaging. Results of a frame-by-frame analysis of the murder video were waiting in the lab two floors below hers. Tara had been there several times before, usually to pick up enlarged prints made from convenience store or bank branch surveillance cameras. Submitting the whale video to Imaging had been something of a formality—nothing to lose—but she hadn't expected to get much from the static-ridden murder clip beyond the picture of the victim's body they'd already provided.

She hurried to the elevator, ignoring stares from passing co-workers. Her case was grabbing headlines. She reached a mostly empty break lounge where the television was tuned to Fox News.

She ducked inside, poured herself a small coffee and watched as the whale-cam's footage of a knife plunging into the whale's smooth flesh was replayed while the caption "Murder video sliced from tagged whale?" crawled across the screen. Tara ducked back out of the room before a pair of newly minted agents staring at her in awe could say anything. She found the elevator, mercifully unoccupied, and rode it down to Imaging. She presented her badge to a receptionist and handed her the memo. The receptionist waved her through the entrance area to the lab beyond.

Imaging Lab director Herb Shock's bald head popped over a divider. He smiled at Tara and waved her over. "Good news," he said as she walked around to his work area. Racks of video monitors and digital tape machines occupied most of his desk space. Computers took up the rest.

"What have you got?"

"Well at first, I didn't think we'd be able to get much of anything. The resolution is pretty good—

better than your average in-store security camera—but because it's underwater, there's a fair amount of backscatter. Add to that the intermittent static, the whale's constant motion, and it's a miracle we were able to get anything besides the victim photo I gave you for the case file."

Tara nodded patiently. Herb always had to preface what he gave her with a story.

He pecked at his keyboard and called attention to a color video monitor. The murder sequence played, and once again Tara watched as the unknown victim fought a losing battle for her existence. Tara wondered what the last day of life had been like for the dead woman. Had she had any idea she was in danger when she'd woken up that morning? That the white bikini she put on would be the last outfit she would ever wear? At least she looked good in it, Tara thought. She took a quick look down at her own boring outfit. *This is definitely not what I'd want to die wearing.*

"And here it is," Herb said, stopping the video.

A pale, shapely leg dominated the frame. Tara watched as Herb clacked away at more keys, zooming in on the lower part of the leg. After a few more seconds of manipulation he had the woman's ankle enlarged many times on the video screen. A splotch of color was visible on the ankle. It was heavily pixelated due to the image magnification, but was clearly a skin discoloration of some sort.

"This is as good as it gets here," Herb said, seeing Tara squint at the blurry image. "But if we move over *here*," he continued, switching his attention to a different workstation, "I'll show you the results of some software manipulation that you may find of interest."

Tara wondered why he hadn't just started with the software-enhanced version, but she understood that Herb wanted her to see for herself just how important his work was. There's nothing but a blurry ankle in that video frame, right? his expression suggested. Wrong! Look at this . . . .

"This is a ninety-nine-percent accurate rendering of that blob of color we saw on the ankle in the original video," he declared, striking the ENTER key with a flourish.

Tara stared at a purple dolphin.

"Tattoo!" she exclaimed, with great appreciation. Tattoos were a tremendous aid to law enforcement professionals, particularly when working with unidentified persons, both suspects and victims. She concentrated on the screen. The tattoo was small, not encircling the ankle but residing entirely on the right side. Granted, there must be thousands of women with dolphin tattoos on their ankles, but it sure was a good place to start. And this one was purple.

"We're not sure how true the color is," Shock said, reading her mind. "It looks purple, but it's underwater, so it could be due to the filtering out of short wavelength colors—your reds and yellows are the first to go."

"Print it out," Tara said. She didn't care what color

the damn dolphin was. Somewhere out there were people who would remember this woman. The tattoo artist . . . whoever might have been with her when she had it done. Finally, something concrete to go on for IDing the victim, she thought.

Shock handed her an enlargement of the tattoo.

Tara studied it while wondering what other secrets the video might divulge. "What about the audio track?"

"Still working on the sound. We're checking for voiceprint IDs now. I'll let you know if anything comes of that."

ABOARD PANDORA'S BOX

Eric Stein squinted at his radar screen. "The *Wired Kingdom* boat is heading back to the coast," he declared.

"Should we follow them?" asked a twenty-something man with a blonde crew cut. Unlike most of the Ocean Liberation Front crew, he sported no tattoos or piercings. The only name Stein or any of them had ever known him by was Pineapple, but they did know that he had a long rap sheet to counter-balance his squeaky-clean image.

OLF had once bailed Pineapple out of jail to the tune of $78,000 for "unauthorized swimming near a sea-based rocket system." Exactly what Pineapple's intentions had been that night was never made clear, even to Stein, but he'd been caught diving near the rocket's floating platform in Long Beach Harbor with underwater pipe-cutting equipment. He pled no contest in exchange for a suspended sentence of ten years in prison with five years probation. The judge was sure he'd see Pineapple again, and when he did, he warned, his sentence would be waiting.

In the days prior to Pineapple's arrest, OLF had staged public protests against the privately held rocket company. Founded by dot-com multi-millionaires, the outfit towed hydrazine-powered rockets on a barge from Long Beach, California, to a remote South Pacific atoll. There, it launched commercial satellite payloads into space. OLF, backed by a handful of reputable environmental lawyers, argued that the practice posed an "unacceptable risk" to the environment due to potential contamination by rocket fuel as well as the possibility of coral reef damage resulting from explosions or crashes.

Only later did it come out that this same rocket-launching operation was contracted to put two satellites into orbit in support of *Wired Kingdom's* whale-cam. Within OLF, this only raised the status of Pineapple, who merely said that he'd suspected something wasn't right about the rocket company.

Stein scratched the stubble on his chin and looked around at the open ocean before answering. "Why follow them? They're probably just going back to edit the so-called rescue footage they shot out here. Let's hang out for a while. Who knows, maybe we'll get lucky and run into the whale."

Stein hit the PLAY button on an iPod, and Bob

Marley's "Concrete Jungle" wafted across the schooner's deck. He watched the green blip of the Scarab slide off his radar screen, pleased with the empty circle it left behind. Sails hung loose as they drifted in a calm, uncluttered sea.

A barefoot woman in shorts and a bikini top, hair in corn rows, emerged from the cabin with a lit joint. Beers were produced from an ice chest, and the party was underway.

"Hey, who's on watch?" Stein called out, passing the joint. "Keep an eye out for the whale."

"And if we see it?" the corn-rows girl asked.

"We go for the tag," Pineapple interjected matter-of-factly. He refused the marijuana, as usual, but sipped an ever-present can of Tecate beer.

"What would we do with the tag if we did get it?" asked a skinny crewman who was climbing the mast for a better vantage point from which to observe the sea. Stein couldn't remember the guy's name; he was new to OLF and had landed his position by sheer persistence. Stein's office manager—one of the few people in the organization with an actual degree in environmental science—told him the man had literally slept in front of their headquarters until they'd given him a position going door-to-door in affluent neighborhoods, seeking donations. When he returned four days later with three thousand dollars worth of personal checks made out to OLF, he was hired. Stein didn't know he would even be here today; he'd just shown up at the docks.

"Let's just say we couldn't buy that kind of media coverage," Stein said, smiling.

"I'll drink to that," somebody said, and the members of Ocean Liberation Front toasted the possibilities.

After a couple of beers Stein began a patrol of the boat. Like a captain of an eighteenth-century warship, he knew that if he looked hard enough he'd find a few stowaways—women, in this case. That the crew had managed to keep them hidden while they approached the whale-trap pleased him, and so he didn't look as hard as he could have. Most of his crew worked for little or no pay above room and board, and so he needed to keep them happy. He made it quite clear, though, that despite the casual atmosphere his operation was a serious affair, and not the place for slackers or boat bums.

Stein had a temper. He kept it in check most of the time, but OLF veterans had all seen him blow up on one occasion or another, usually after he'd been drinking, and always out of the public eye.

As he left the partiers behind and went below decks, something gnawed at him. So far, his organization had failed to have any real impact on the juggernaut that was *Wired Kingdom*. In fact, Stein reflected as he ducked a bulkhead and entered the schooner's galley, that damned TV show was getting more attention than ever while the Blue remained tethered to its electronic leash. It irked him to no end. *That bitch . . .*

For a fleeting moment he wondered what his life would be like now if not for their college breakup. Would he have been able to sway Anastasia's opinions, get her to join OLF, harness her brainpower in support of his cause? He doubted it, which was why he hadn't committed himself to her. She was always so strong-willed. Whatever might have been was no more. Things were so vastly different now, he thought. He was no longer sure that he had the upper hand, as he had felt during their college years. His boat had been late to the trapped whale and she had laughed in his face. Her media exposure now dwarfed his own.

By the time he reached the bathroom, he had worked himself into a pre-rage state that was only a couple of drinks away from loss of control. The head was occupied. He was about to kick the door when it flew open. A long-haired, tattooed guy who looked like he belonged in a heavy metal band came out with a bottle of tequila in his hand and a smirk on his face. Stein had no idea who the guy was, which irritated him, but when he gave him the bottle Stein let it pass . . . until he went inside the tiny bathroom and found his girlfriend putting her shirt back on, hair a mess, cheeks flushed. Stein had been with her about a year, but they hadn't yet gotten serious about long-term plans. Still, the idea had never entered his mind that she could be seeing someone else.

But the thought made it past the booze now, and it occurred to Stein that Anastasia had been the woman most on his mind lately, even if in a negative way. Had his girlfriend picked up on this? There had been the time a few weeks ago when she'd had to repeat what she was saying, because he didn't respond. He had been staring at the muted television while Anastasia introduced another episode of *Wired Kingdom*.

"What the hell is up?" Stein demanded. "You okay?" If the guy had been forcing himself on her, he was dead. He took another slug from the bottle. If they both wanted it, he was still dead. The girl started to cry and pulled the door shut. Stein took a longer pull from the tequila, then he slammed the bottle on the doorknob, breaking it, spraying himself with glass and Cuervo 1800. "Open the door!"

"Leave me alone!"

He gave the door a violent kick with his bare foot and went back up on deck, where the party was in full-swing. He saw the guy who'd been in the bathroom with his girlfriend passing a joint back to a skinhead who'd done two years in prison for setting fire to a Monsanto plant. Stein trusted the skinhead, but this new guy? He'd never even seen him before. How did he know his girlfriend . . . or did they just meet today?

"Who the hell is Mr. Heavy Metal?" Stein asked no one in particular, but everyone stopped what they were doing. One of Stein's hands dripped blood from the broken bottle as he singled the guy out.

"Dude, take it easy," the guy said and then stopped as he put things together. "Hey . . . was that your girl? Look man, I had no idea—she didn't say—oh shit."

Stein snaked his hand into a recessed compartment and removed a flare gun. He aimed it at the long-haired guy, but someone grabbed his arm from behind and yanked it upward. The intended victim retreated to the safety of the stern deck, his face betraying bewildered shock, while Stein struggled to break free from his friends holding him back.

"Get him. . . . Get the flare. . . . Eric, chill. . . ." Ten people yelled at once as a struggle ensued. Stein had just elbowed one of his crewmen in the gut and dropped the flare gun to the deck, when they heard a voice calling from above.

"People!"

They looked up to see the lookout on the mast frantically waving his arms. The wind carried away most of what he said from that height, but when the melee died amid a chorus of *shush*es his words rained on their ears. He pointed to the two o'clock position off the bow.

"Two people in the water!"

CHAPTER 25

OFF THE SOUTHERN CALIFORNIA COAST

"I see a boat," Juan told Fernando. After drifting for almost two hours and being in the water for three, any kind of man-made object was a welcome sight. They had surfaced with empty tanks following a strenuous underwater swim. They were pleased to see no Coast Guard vessels or crowds of onlookers, but were alarmed at being adrift fifty miles offshore with nothing but their buoyancy vests. "Who are they?"

"Who cares?" Fernando looked around at the empty sea and sky. "If we do not get on that boat, we will die out here."

"What will we tell them?"

"Say we were part of a dive group in the islands and were left behind by our boat. It happens often enough."

"I think we should say as little as possible—like we are unable to speak much after our ordeal at sea."

The black schooner slid down a rolling swell before another hid it from view again. For a moment they heard music, and then it stopped. When the schooner reappeared a shirtless man on deck was tossing a life ring.

It landed within arm's reach of Fernando. He grabbed it. Juan could think of no arguments. He too grabbed the life ring, and the two divers feigned complete exhaustion, allowing themselves to be towed to the old yacht's side.

"They do not look like authorities," Fernando observed as they were hauled toward the small crowd gathering on the schooner's port rail.

"We could say we do not speak English."

"They might call Immigration."

"Maybe. What if the boss comes back to look for us in the plane?"

"What if he does not?" Fernando said through clenched teeth.

"Why wouldn't he?"

Fernando pondered this as a man with dreadlocks pulled them in. The man said nothing, but he nodded toward the stern as he began to walk the line toward the swim platform there.

Fernando lowered his voice to a near-whisper as they were dragged along the hull. "Why wouldn't he? Maybe he crashed. Maybe he was escorted to the mainland. The last thing he said was something about the Coast Guard coming."

"Or maybe he is halfway to Cabo San Lucas right now because he decided things have become too risky."

SAN FERNANDO VALLEY

Anthony Silveras rode shotgun in his Mercedes SLK, talking on the phone while an assistant drove. He knew better than to field so many phone calls while trying to drive at the same time, especially from George Reed, Anthony's boss and owner of *Wired Kingdom*.

Anthony explained that Trevor had left an outgoing message indicating he was working on restoring the web site. But, like his daughter when she was upset, Mr. Reed was not easily placated.

"I'm on top of it, George," Anthony said as they turned off Ventura Boulevard. "I'm on my way over there right now."

The assistant cringed as Anthony held the phone away from his ear. Even from the driver's side, the derision in Mr. Reed's voice could be heard as loud and clear as his words: "Remember that it was your idea to bail him out! The whole purpose of getting him out was to make sure the damn web site stays up."

"Right, and I'm sure he's dealing with it, George, but just in case he needs help, we're—"

"Listen to me, Anthony, and take this to heart. I don't want to hear your voice again until that site is up and making money. Just get it working. Is that clear?"

"Yes, sir."

Anthony flipped his phone shut and let his head fall into the headrest as the car accelerated. The driver, a production assistant who was hoping to work his way into a cameraman position, shook his head. "Anthony, let me tell ya something, man. I sure as hell hope you're getting paid a lot, because there ain't no way I'd take that kinda crap from nobody for less than fifty grand a year. No way."

Anthony smiled. "So you're saying for fifty grand you could deal with it? You put a price on how much crap you can take, is that it?"

"Well, yeah, I guess that's what everybody does, isn't? Even you—"

"Make a left here. . . . George is under a lot of stress. It's not personal."

The driver slowed as he turned onto a side street. A few cars were parked along both sides. Warehouses and storage lots dominated the area.

"Is this it?"

"This is the street—keep going."

"I thought a big show like *Wired Kingdom* would have fancier digs."

"George is smart. He doesn't spend money where he doesn't have to. Nobody sees the technical headquarters. It doesn't have to look pretty or be located on the west side, it just has to run well."

"Yeah, well so much for that. Maybe ol' Georgie cut a few too many corners this time and now he's blaming you. Ever think about that?"

Anthony gave the driver a sidelong glance. "Sometimes I think you're smarter than you look, buddy. Okay, pull up here. It's the brick entrance, there."

The assistant parked alongside the curb.

Anthony dialed his cellular as they stepped out of the car.

"Still no answer?"

"No. Just the message."

They walked toward the office entrance.

"What if nobody's in there?"

"You know anything about configuring high output schedulers with fiber optic uplinks and sever-side scripting?"

The assistant chuckled. "Nope."

"Me neither. I can get some IT guys out here from the main office, but this is definitely not your routine network admin—" Anthony cut himself off as he saw the black Celica parked at the curb. "Hey, all right, that's Trevor's car. He's probably got this almost licked by now."

They passed a dumpster and then made their final approach to the office entrance. The door was set back in a small alcove with two steps leading up to it. They came to the alcove, turned left, and Anthony tripped over something.

"What the—" the assistant started, staring at the body, which lay face down in a heap across the steps. "Is that . . . is that—"

"Trevor," Anthony said, kneeling down next to the inert form. "Call 911."

The assistant hesitated, unable to tear his eyes from the body, blood puddled beneath the head.

"Now, damn it!"

Anthony called out Trevor's name and shook

Trevor's body while the assistant produced a cell phone. No reaction. He flipped the body over and then flinched as dread mingled with revulsion.

"There's a man here, he's—"

"Trevor Lane. His name's Trevor Lane," Anthony said.

"He's unconscious and bleeding," the assistant told the emergency operator. "His name is Trevor Lane. . . . Um, the address is . . ."

"2119 Wilmot."

"2119 Wilmot. . . . No. He's— "

"He's been shot," Anthony said. The only apparent trauma was a single bullet wound high on his temple. A rivulet of dried blood ran down one side of his face and trickled down the steps where it pooled on the sidewalk. He put two fingers on Trevor's carotid artery, feeling for a pulse. Shook his head.

The assistant's voice cracked as he relayed the information to the operator. "He's been shot and he has no pulse."

Anthony took a look around. He saw no one. He could hear nothing out of the ordinary. The smell of congealing blood offended his nostrils. It appeared as though whoever had killed Trevor had come and gone. He looked at the door to the office and reached out to try the knob.

"Are you crazy? Don't go in there! What if someone is in there now?"

"Yeah, you're right. No good reason to leave my prints at a murder scene, now that I think about it."

BAJA CALIFORNIA COAST

Halfway down the Pacific coast of Baja Mexico, a blue seaplane emerged from a thick fog bank. It passed over an enormous, jutting finger of land, a remote and rugged area known as the "junkyard of the Pacific" because of the way currents washed ashore all manner of ocean debris.

The stinging criticism of Héctor's client assaulted him through the radio, preventing him from appreciating the majestic view. "So let me get this straight: after failing to meet your objective once again, you proceeded to leave the two remaining divers behind to be picked up? Or to die of exposure and have their bodies wash ashore so they could be identified?"

The seaplane pilot took a deep breath before he replied. "*Jefe*, what choice did I have? One man perished in the trap meant for the whale."

"Do not use that word!"

Héctor cursed himself, not wanting to do anything that would jeopardize the income that would mean so much for his little girl. But "whale" was not a word one was used to censoring in conversation. "Yes, I am sorry, *jefe*. The purpose of the dive could not be met. Why should I wait around to be detained by the Coast Guard, or be filmed by the television crew?"

"You are not upholding your end of our agreement. Should I put a stop on the wire transfer?"

"No! I am not—"

"Listen to me. I only need to know one thing. Will

you be able to complete the job, or do I seek someone else's services?"

The job had grown much more difficult than Héctor had anticipated. The thought of quitting had some appeal, but then he flashed to his daughter, bedridden in a hospital which could no longer help her. The potential rewards were too great to walk, or fly, away from.

"Of course I will complete it."

"I thought so. What are you doing now?"

"The package you sent arrived this morning. I arranged for my associate to drive it up and meet me in person at Ensenada."

"Excellent. It is time to put that package to use. And then?"

"After taking on more fuel and supplies I will fly back up to the last dive site and see if I can locate my divers."

"Don't go out of your way for them. Get what I'm paying you to get. Think of your daughter."

Héctor ducked a cloud layer, chasing a desolate stretch of brown sand south for miles.

CHAPTER 26

AVALON HARBOR, CATALINA ISLAND

Ernie Hollister was pretty sure he was making a mistake as he watched the pillar of black smoke escape from the engine compartment of his twenty-eight-foot Bayliner. The *Six-Pack* was so named not only for obvious reasons, but because it was designed to carry six fishermen on charter trips. That scenario had not come to pass for years, however, although Ernie yearned to put his charter business on a paying basis again.

After a breakfast of Spam and Budweiser spent poring over old issues of *Marine Mechanic*, Ernie had come to the realization that he knew how to rectify his engine problem without spending much money. Out here on the water, though, just outside the harbor, he was finding out firsthand that his fix was less than adequate.

Wiping the grease from his eye, Ernie tried the last trick he could think of, but still the engine sputtered, coughed and belched. Like a prairie dog chased from its burrow, he popped his head out of the engine compartment for fresh air. Around him the water was crowded with vessels of all types. It wouldn't be long before someone called the fire department. With a quiet curse, he inhaled all the air his lungs could handle before ducking back into the inferno.

He emerged again, this time with the last of the smoke, and reveled in the silence created by shutting down "the beast," as he had christened his boat's motor. Less comforting was the direction his craft took–toward a concrete docking pier used by the ferries known as "the mole." This wasn't good. With a sigh, Ernie pulled his cell phone from his pocket and placed a call to Avalon Marine Towing.

The tow service picked up on the first ring and Ernie explained his situation. After a little razzing about being a frequent customer over the years, the dispatcher asked Ernie for a credit card. Ernie read him the numbers while his boat drifted closer to the mole.

"Ernie, I'm real sorry, but your card was declined. You got another?" Ernie did not. "Geez, Ernie, you still owe us from before. There's no way the boss'll let me send someone out. If it's an emergency, you should call–"

"Yeah, yeah, the harbormaster or the Coast Guard, right. I'll see you around."

Ernie pressed the END button on his phone. The harbormaster would have a boat tow him in, especially if he got any closer to the mole, but then he would be billed an exorbitant fee for emergency services, as well as possibly being fined for posing a marine hazard. He looked around at the litter of beer cans on deck. He'd have to clean those up, too, before they got here.

He was dialing the harbormaster when his marine radio sounded. “Ernie this is *Deep View*, you read? Over.”

Ernie refrained from sending his cell phone call while he scanned the water around him. The *Deep View* was unmistakable because it wasn't an ordinary boat. The *Deep View* was a submarine. Ernie found it without any problem, about fifty yards up ahead along the mole. The lines of its sleek, white cigar-shaped hull and conning tower were unmistakable. And then Ernie saw the hatch pop open and a white-hatted head pop out. The figure wore pressed white pants and shirt—a captain’s uniform.

Ernie knew the man who threw him an informal salute.

Walter Johnson was the licensed captain of the island’s only tourist submarine, as well as manager of the sub operation. Walter had worked tenaciously to be the first person to bring passenger submarines to Catalina. He himself had collaborated with the Coast Guard to devise a commercial submarine captain’s licensing program. He was fond of telling people how a well-known U.S. astronaut from the Apollo days was one of the references listed on his resume. When California’s governor had requested an undersea tour of one of the state’s oil rigs, it was Walter Johnson who took him down in a submersible.

In his day, Johnson had traveled around the world on various oceanic projects. While he was somewhat of a maverick who liked to date women much younger than himself, liked to tell people how much he enjoyed living on a small island without a daily commute, and how he had once stayed up all night by himself on a remote Catalina beach cooking an influx of red shrimp with nothing but a butane lighter and some washed up scrap metal, he was not the reckless type.

Ernie scrambled to his marine radio and keyed the transmitter. He knew that if he didn't answer soon Walt would assume his radio didn't work. The radio was one of the only things that did work on his ramshackle vessel.

“I hear you, Walt. You read me?”

“I copy, Ernie. Looks like you're going just about wherever this big ocean wants to take you right about now. You want some help? Over.”

Ernie felt a wave of relief wash over him as he eyed the fast-approaching concrete mole and then turned an eye toward Walt's professional submarine operation, with its floating dock and twin support vessels. “Copy that, Walt. I could use a tow before I end up on the mole. Over.”

The reply was immediate and filled Ernie with confidence. “Copy that, *Six-Pack*. I'm sending Ted over in one of the inflatables now. He'll give you a tow back into the harbor. Over.”

Ernie could already hear the whine of an outboard

starting up somewhere behind the sub's floating dock. “Thanks, Walt,” Ernie called across the water. Then, into the radio, he said, “I'll get this taken care of and be back on the water soon. I owe you one.” Walt merely waved him off. Ernie having his boat in seaworthy condition anytime soon was not a bet he would have taken.

A runabout zipped by the sub, it's operator calling out, “Nice party the other day, Walt,” referring to one of the sub captain's summer seafood barbecues which had become the stuff of legend on the island. Walt gave him a thumbs up in return.

By the time Ernie had swept his beer cans into the bait well, Walt's tender vessel had arrived. His employee tossed Ernie a line and, amidst a barrage of good-natured ribbing about Ernie's calling as a mechanic, he slowly but surely towed the *Six-Pack* back into the harbor.

When Ernie's boat had been deposited at the dock and the tender's lines cast away, Ernie shook hands with Walter's employee. “Thanks again, Ted. Stop by The Nest tonight, I'll buy you a few rounds.”

“Thanks Ernie, but I'll have to take a rain check. Walt's sending all of us—the whole crew—down to the Bahamas for a week to start up a new sub operation there. Leaving tonight,” he finished, glancing at his watch.

Ernie thanked him again and was left standing once more in his docked boat. Not quite ready for the walk back into town, he lifted the lid on his engine compartment and reached into his bait well to retrieve another beer.

CHAPTER 27

ABOARD PANDORA'S BOX

The OLF crew gathered at the boat's swim platform to assist the two divers. First Fernando and then Juan were helped aboard.

"That's some serious dive gear," the lookout, now down from his perch in the crow's nest, noted.

"Rebreathers," Pineapple said, moving closer for a better look. "No bubbles—great for stealth missions. Let you stay down longer, too. Expensive stuff."

Stein put his hands out to remove Fernando's full-face mask. Fernando backed away, stumbled in his fins, regained his balance, and began to remove the mask without assistance.

"Hey, I'm just trying to help," Stein said, holding his hands up in a gesture of surrender.

"Maybe he doesn't want your blood on his gear," Pineapple said. Several crewmembers pointed out that Stein's hand was still dripping blood from the deep gash on his thumb. Stein looked around and found the long-haired guy he'd almost killed.

"Who brought him on the boat?"

The crew reacted with silence. No one wanted to say anything. The two rescuees were slipping their fins off, cautiously eyeing their new surroundings.

"I said, who brought him on the damn boat?"

Finally a crewmember pointed toward the cabin's entrance. "She did."

The girl from the bathroom emerged on deck. She glared at Stein.

"Oh great, my girlfriend, the party favor."

"Screw you, Eric. Maybe if you were home with me for more than two days at a time instead of out trying to tell people how to save the world like Mr. I'm So Freaking Important, I wouldn't feel the need to be with anyone else."

"You brought this guy on my boat without clearing it with anyone?" Stein said, cocking his head toward the long-hair.

"Hey! You two lovebirds can hash this out in therapy later," Pineapple interrupted. "Let's see what's up with these guys." He nodded at the divers, who had just removed their facemasks. No one spoke for a moment while the rescued men warily appraised the OLF boat and crew.

"You guys okay?" Pineapple asked tentatively. The divers returned blank stares. Someone produced a first aid kit and held its bright red cross logo out for the divers to see.

"First aid?"

To this the divers shook their heads no.

Someone offered a jug of water, which Fernando eagerly accepted.

"You speak English?" Stein asked them.

No again. Then Fernando said something in Spanish.

Stein, curiosity piqued, approached them slowly. He asked, "*¿Dónde está su barco*?" Where is your boat?

Juan was unable to contain his surprise. He had not expected any of their gringo rescuers to know Spanish.

"*¿Habla usted español*?" he queried Stein, just to be sure. Stein frowned as if insulted. He rattled off an account, in Spanish, of how he had grown up in Los Angeles, taken Spanish in high school and again in college before dropping out, and had used it many times during his extensive travels throughout Mexico and Central and South America. His command of the language was conversational, not perfectly fluent, but it more than got the point across.

Juan and Fernando, realizing they would have no choice but to communicate, began speaking rapid-fire Spanish at the same time.

"What are they saying?" Pineapple asked Stein.

Stein shook his head. "He's saying something about their boat hitting some rocks and sinking early this morning," he said, pointing at Fernando. "And he's saying they want to use the radio to make a call," he finished, indicating Juan. All three men stopped talking.

"They're full of crap about there being a boat," Pineapple said.

"How do you know?"

"You should turn on a TV now and then, Eric. Current events affect OLF whether you want to believe they do or not."

"Pineapple, just tell me what you know, okay?" Stein and his inner circle were concerned that Pineapple's criticism of Stein's leadership had become sharper in recent months.

"Sometimes I can't believe you guys," Pineapple said, turning to look at the crew gathered around the divers. "Yesterday when the FBI agent in the helicopter was in the water with the Orca . . . the guys that were already there trying to get the tag—"

"He's right!" a blonde hippie girl wearing a puka-shell necklace said. "I saw an article about it online. They had the same black re-what's it called?"

"Rebreathers." Stein prompted.

"Yeah. They had those, and it said they came in the plane that was shown on the whale's camera."

At the mention of the word "plane," Juan and Carlos looked at one another, knowing they'd been found out. A tense moment ensued for both sides. One of the divers had a knife strapped to his calf, but he was far outnumbered and knew that to even look at it would be a mistake. He wondered why the Spanish-speaking gringo was bleeding.

Stein stepped closer to the men they'd rescued, confident his crew would defend him should they attack. "Did you come by plane?" he asked.

They hesitated.

"Don't lie to me," Stein continued. "We are not from the television show that tagged the whale. We are against what they have done. But as the captain of this vessel, I cannot have anybody on my boat I don't trust." Stein couldn't resist turning back to look at his girlfriend and, hiding near the back of the group, her companion from the bathroom.

The two divers used the time to argue with each other, speaking in hushed tones. They became quiet after apparently coming to no decisive conclusion.

Stein pressed them. "Look, we don't know anything about the murder or whatever it was that the whale broadcast on the show's web site, okay? All we want—all we have ever wanted—is for marine animals to be able to live their lives in peace, without people like *Wired Kingdom* exploiting them and robbing them of their dignity." A few cheers went up from Stein's crew.

The divers appeared to relax, but the confused looks remained.

"I've got an idea." Pineapple jumped down from the rail he was sitting on to stand next to Stein. "Just hear me out," he said, reading Stein's impatience.

Stein nodded.

"Listen,"—the divers became noticeably on edge at the switch to English, but said nothing, waiting for a development—"I don't know what these guys' deal is, but if they're the ones who were after the tag yesterday—and it looks like today too—then they're not in any position to bargain." Stein's expression made it clear that he didn't understand. Pineapple frowned before continuing. "Their plane left without them. They were out here with without a ride until we came along."

This sparked several urgent conversations at once, and soon the divers were worried. But Stein wanted to keep them calm, so he stepped in. "Hold on. I want to hear Pineapple's idea."

Not expecting to be given the floor, Pineapple shot Stein a grudging look of respect before speaking. "Translate for me, okay?"

Stein nodded, as did the divers, recognizing the word.

"We can help each other," Pineapple began, and waited for Stein to communicate the phrase to the divers. "We can drop you off somewhere along the coast . . . instead of turning you in to the nearest port authorities . . . as required by law. . . ." When he saw the divers' eyes widen, he continued. "And in return . . . you give us all of your dive gear . . . rebreathers, communication gear, knives, drysuits . . . everything."

The divers turned to face each other and spoke to indicate their agreement while Stein interpreted. Then they hesitated.

"What's the problem?" Pineapple asked.

Juan spoke, and Stein interpreted for him. "How do we know you will not take our gear and throw us overboard?" Cries of "Oh, come on!" and "Give us a break" rang out across the deck. The members of OLF acted genuinely offended.

Stein waited for the outbursts to stop before responding. "Look, we've done some extreme things to stand up for the environment, but we don't kill people for dive gear. We'll take your equipment, sure. But as long as you agree to our conditions we'll make sure you get somewhere that works for you in one piece." The divers exchanged glances once more and then Stein drove the deal home. "We both want the tag off of the whale, just for different reasons. But we don't care what your reason is—you can have the tag for all we care. As long as it stays off the whale."

"And any other animals," the puka-shell girl said.

"*¡Excelente!*" Juan said and began removing his gear, handing it off to the crew. Fernando followed suit.

The same crewmember who had been lookout when he spotted the divers tossed them some shorts and T-shirts. "Have some dry clothes," he said. Fernando put on one of the shirts, which read *Señor Frog's, Cozumel, Mexico*.

"Eh, *Mexico,*" Fernando said, pointing proudly at the shirt. "*Bueno.*" Everyone had a good laugh.

Then Juan, his face becoming serious, waved at Stein to get his attention. The captain was watching his girlfriend out of the corner of his eye. "May we use your radio to contact our plane?"

"Why not?" Stein said. Then he addressed Pineapple, lowering his voice. "I'll monitor the transmission to make sure they're not calling out our position to a band of pirates waiting somewhere."

"Make sure they're on an air frequency, too. They said they needed to call their plane—not a boat." Stein nodded in agreement.

Stein informed the rescued pair that they could use the radio and led them to the electronics console. Juan placed a call, looking into Fernando's eyes as he broadcast the bogus call sign that identified them to their pilot. The rustling of manila lines against a wooden mast was the only sound while they waited for a reply.

After a minute, Stein couldn't help but notice that the Mexicans seemed distraught. He asked them what they thought had happened to their pilot. They replied that maybe he had been forced to make an emergency landing at sea and had already been rescued by the Coast Guard, who would have turned him over to Immigration or police. Stein told them that they were free to try the radio every thirty minutes. Juan and Fernando thanked him.

Tecates were offered and accepted, and for the second time that day a party started on *Pandora's Box* that would end badly.

CHAPTER 28

BEL AIR

Mr. George Reed gave up trying to ignore his wife.

"At least give me the courtesy of telling me who she is," Mrs. Reed said. "You expect me to go with you to another one of your tedious charity fundraisers while I pretend to know nothing about your latest affair?"

Mr. Reed walked away from the oversized plasma monitor mounted on the wall of their bedroom. The screen displayed a computer error message from the *Wired Kingdom* web site.

"You care more about that damn web site than you do about me *and* your new whore."

George had heard all the insults many times before. "We've been over this. Seven years ago I had an affair. I admitted that in the marriage counseling. Since then I've moved on, but I guess you haven't been able to."

She made a spitting noise. "As if that were the only one, George. You can't think I'm so stupid."

"Get ready to go, will you? The luncheon starts at

noon, and I'm speaking."

"Oh, you're *speaking*, isn't that wonderful? How lucky I am to get to hear you speak! Why don't you speak to me about who this woman is you've been screwing? Is she from one of your shows?"

Mr. Reed crossed the plush carpeting to their walk-in closet. He slid aside hanger after hanger, pretending to concentrate on selecting an outfit.

"Is she?"

"There's no one else, dear," George said in his best I-couldn't-be-more-bored tone. He removed one of his many designer sport coats from the rack with a flourish.

His wife shifted tack. "Will Anastasia be there?"

George knew that their daughter was the only hope of getting his wife to attend. And he did want his wife to go. Were he to show up alone, tongues would wag. "She said she has an important meeting at the university with the contracting agency for her whale project. That's at two o'clock, but she said she would try to be there."

"So she's not going."

"She didn't say that. She said she would try to make it. Can't you listen? She said millions of dollars in grant money are at stake, but she would try to squeeze in the event before her meeting."

"Did you talk to her yourself?"

George sighed and plucked a silk tie from a motorized rack. "Why do you ask me questions you already know the answers to? Anthony talked to her."

"Anthony? The guy who had to drive us home from the premiere that night because you were too drunk?"

"He wouldn't have had to if you would have driven."

"You know damn well I don't know how to drive a stick. I told you not to buy that car for that very reason. And we're not changing the subject."

George decided the tie clashed with his outfit and selected another. "You changed the subject, dear, not me. And yes, that's him."

"I'll go if Anastasia goes. But if it's just you, you can go to hell."

George exhaled heavily. He had always had the feeling that this statement summed up their entire marital union. For a few years, while Anastasia was excelling in college and graduate school, he and his wife had been distracted by the fruits of his Hollywood success. If not for Anastasia, his marriage never would have lasted this long. Even so, George had seen OLF protesting his show and had decided that it was not a coincidence his daughter's estranged college boyfriend was now targeting her successful enterprise.

"Did you hear me, George?" his wife demanded.

"Yeah, you're only going if Anastasia goes."

"Guess what, George. Remember that money I said I was using to dabble in the stock market?"

"Yes, you thought it would do you some good to have a hobby, and I agreed."

"As it turns out I made quite an investment, only it had nothing to do with Wall Street. I used the money to hire a private investigator to follow you around for a while."

Mr. Reed finished adjusting his tie and turned to face her. He shrugged. "Good. You should feel much better now that you know I'm not cheating on you."

"Don't think you're calling my bluff with that innocent act. This time I really did hire a P.I."

"Great! And what, pray tell, did your Sherlock Holmes uncover?"

Mrs. Reed walked to a night table and opened a drawer. She took out a manila envelope. George watched as she took her time removing its contents. She stared at a piece of paper, her face changing shape with her rising anger. Then she threw the martini she was holding—her third since breakfast—against the wall.

George asked to see what she was looking at. She looked at him as though she had forgotten he was there, and then she sidearmed the paper at him like a Frisbee. He held up a hand to shield his face and the paper sliced his palm. He ignored the paper cut and picked up what he could now see was a photograph. He stared at a close-up of himself lying on a beach, arms and legs entwined with those of a younger woman. It wasn't possible to tell by looking at the picture, but George knew that the beach was Pirate's Cove, an out-of-the-way stretch of Malibu sand forty-five minutes north of L.A. Forty-five glorious minutes of driving with the top down along the Pacific Coast Highway in his reconditioned Ford Mustang, a beautiful young woman in the passenger seat . . .

"Do you have anything to say for yourself?" his wife was screaming.

George didn't know which was worse—that his wife had caught him cheating and had hard evidence of it or that seeing the image triggered such pleasant memories that he was able to ignore his wife's tirade for just a few moments of remembered bliss. His temporary reprieve from reality would not last long.

"I want a divorce, George. I don't care who she is, what your story is. I want out."

George was back from the beach now, mind racing to think of something to say to his wife while trying to figure out who had taken the pictures, how he had been tracked. The multitasking proved too much for his shocked state. He said nothing.

"I'm afraid you won't be able to ignore this, George."

Mr. Reed only stared at the photo.

"All I'm asking for is an even split of our net worth. I'm not going to flush our money away on lawyers trying to get ninety percent, unless you piss me off. We shared twenty-two years of our lives, and a child, together. We can go halves on what we have now and walk away without hurting each other anymore. That's all I want."

He snapped out of it. "That's all, is it? Half of roughly a hundred million dollars? That's *all*?"

"That's what the law says I'm entitled to. And don't think I don't realize that your quoted figure of one hundred million doesn't include your points from *Wired Kingdom*—money you earned while married to me but have not yet received. That's mine, too."

Mr. Reed began to feel queasy. There was no way his wife had come up with that little financial insight on her own, debatable as it might be in the hands of a skilled litigator. She'd already consulted a lawyer. He half-listened while she blathered on.

"Since I'll be granted divorce on the grounds of your infidelity, slut that you are, it's quite possible I could get a good deal more. Maybe even everything. You never know how a spin of the legal wheel will turn out." She plucked a martini-soaked olive off the floor and examined it carefully before popping it into her mouth.

"I think you're getting a little ahead of yourself, dear. Maybe you should take a little nap to let the booze wear off, and afterwards we'll talk about this."

"Forget it, George."

"You really want to dissolve our fortune over this?"

"No fortune is worth being degraded the way you've done to me."

The phone rang. George started for the receiver but hesitated. Unable to think of any persuasive comebacks, he took the call. "This is George Reed. . . . Yes. . . . What! . . . How? . . . Uh huh. . . . So, where does that leave us?"

George's wife followed her husband's gaze to the error message decorating their bedroom wall.

"He *what*? . . . How long will that take?"

Mrs. Reed was becoming more interested.

"No, no. There must be some technical people who can restore it. Find them and get it back up. Don't worry about the fees." George slammed the receiver down. He glared at the non-functional web site on their wall, then at his wife. "Our technical director is dead, apparently shot outside of the Van Nuys office."

His wife fished a cigarette from a carton on the bed.

He continued. "Before he died, he, or somebody, smashed all of the servers and equipment that runs the web site. That's why it's down."

She blew a cloud of smoke at him in reply.

"I guess you don't care."

"Oh, but I do. I don't even know why you're standing around talking to me about it. The money you're losing by the web site being down is about to be at least half mine. So fix it George, and fix it fast. Or I'll sue you for deliberately dragging your feet to avoid having to pay me my fair share in the divorce."

"I think we should talk about that."

"There's nothing to talk about, George. I'll be staying in the beach house until the divorce is settled. All further communication with me will be through my attorney." Mrs. Reed picked up her purse to leave. "I hope she was worth it."

"Hold it. You can stay here if you want. You don't have any clothes in the beach house. There's no food there. I'll sleep on the yacht." The Reeds owned a luxury sailing yacht, which George had dubbed *Prime*

Time, berthed in Marina del Rey.

"Oh, the yacht, huh? Was that where you liked to do your hussy? Maybe you can meet her there tonight." She walked across the floor, stopping when she reached the picture of George and the girl. "Look at this tramp," she said, grinding the woman's head in the photo with her shoe. "Tattoos and everything. Does that turn you on, George? Dumb bimbos? Wannabe starlets with piercings and 'body art'?" She shook her head and stalked out of the room, pausing to extinguish her cigarette on the door on the way out.

"Stay on the yacht, you bastard," she called back as she walked down the hall. "Don't let me see your lying face, or I don't know what I might do."

George was too stunned to respond. He watched her leave. Then bent down to pick up the photo. It was a close-up, obviously shot with a high-powered zoom lens from far away. A tattoo of a butterfly adorned one shoulder. George's body blocked the view of her torso, but the woman's toned thighs and calves dominated the picture. They contrasted painfully with George's hairy, spindly limbs. One of the woman's legs was bent at the knee, her foot in the air.

A dolphin tattoo graced the ankle.

CHAPTER 29

WIRED KINGDOM TECH SUPPORT FACILITY

His eyes looked the same in death as they did in life, Tara thought, looking down on Trevor Lane's corpse. Big and brown, maybe a little sad, although she might have been projecting that melancholy on the deceased man.

By now she'd heard the initial reports: victim found dead, single gunshot wound to the head, no known witnesses, body discovered by a *Wired Kingdom* producer and assistant. Anthony Silveras and his apprentice were still on the scene answering questions from eager police officers, some of whom were on their first murder scene.

Tara recognized Silveras from the television studio the night before. She had no reason to disbelieve what he told police. He was on his way to check on Trevor after the web site had been down for more than an hour. When he arrived at the technical office, this is what he found.

Presently a uniformed beat cop came trotting up

from around the corner, out of breath. "No side or back entrances, or even windows," he declared, looking in Silveras' direction. "He's right."

Anthony puffed up his chest, indignant. "Of course I'm right. Didn't I just tell you the front door is the only entrance?"

"Cool it pal, he's just doing his job." This from a fifty-something, white-haired police detective who never took his eyes off Tara while she examined the body. He would have loved to tell her not to touch anything, but he didn't have to. Professional, even by FBI standards, he noted. He watched as she slipped a credit card-sized digital camera from a pocket and took her own photos of the corpse from several angles, not wanting to wait for the professional shots.

She put the camera away and stood up. The police detective nodded at Silveras, who removed his keys and approached the office door.

"You check the roof?" Tara asked the policeman as Anthony reached the door.

"The roof?" Several faces tipped skyward.

"No," the police detective answered, irked at being tested, not by a woman so much as by someone considerably younger than himself. "But I have men posted on the building corners and more casing the neighborhood. If anybody was up there when we got here," he said, turning his head toward the roof, "they're still up there."

"One time I was on a case where the perp was hanging out on the roof while we were collecting evidence inside. Saw him when he stepped over a skylight thirty minutes after we'd been in. We're photographing the dead body of a guy he shot, and he's up there watching the whole time."

The police detective quietly indicated for two of his officers to keep sharp eyes on the roof. The others readied their weapons as Anthony approached the door with his key.

There was an uncomfortable silence before Tara continued.

"The entrance wound indicates to me that the shot was fired relatively straight on. The shooter probably came in a vehicle and left in the same. But you never know," she finished, comfortable enough that there was not a shooter lurking silently above them to ignore the roof and focus on Silveras unlocking the door.

Nothing happened. The key was inserted but wouldn't turn. Some nervous laughter made its way around the group while the producer double-checked his keys. He shook his head. "Lock's been changed," he declared.

"You sure?" the police detective asked.

"Positive."

"When's the last time you used that key?" a different policeman asked.

"Maybe three months ago," Anthony admitted.

"Makes sense," Tara interjected. "Lane wanted to keep everyone—even his employers—out of what he probably came to think of as *his* office."

"So now what?" Anthony asked. He flipped open

his cell phone. "I can have a locksmith here . . ."

"Forget it," the police detective said. "Sully, Harris—"

Two cops hurried over to the trunk of a squad car and returned with a battering ram.

"Wait a minute is that really neces—"

"Yes it is," Tara said. The policeman gave her an appreciative look. "Whoever killed Lane could still be in there. It's worth the price of a door."

"Especially a piece of shit door like that," one cop said. The wooden entrance, although stout, was warped and peeling. Crude graffiti covered it from top to bottom.

The door to *Wired Kingdom*'s technical headquarters blew off its hinges on the second thrust from the steel-encased concrete ram. Tara stood to one side with the officers, her weapon drawn but not aimed. She did not expect anyone to be inside. The position Trevor's body lay in told her that he was hit from streetside. Plus, she was beginning to believe Trevor's story, or at least parts of it. He was afraid of somebody. In Tara's experience, violent crime involving business outside of drugs, sex or street weapons tended to be highly targeted. They wanted one guy dead. Now he was dead. They wouldn't mess with anyone else.

The cops all had their weapons pointed inside. Tara let the cops enter first, covering each other as they went. When she heard a round of "Clear!" she walked slowly up the steps, dodging Trevor's corpse, and over the battered door into the dead man's office.

Destruction was evident. Pieces of glass and electronic debris trailed outside of the server room as if coughed up by a gigantic robot. In the main room, bookshelves had been toppled and computers knocked to the floor.

Taking in the chaos, one cop said, "Looks like somebody tossed the joint and left. The deceased worked here, right? Maybe he tried to stop 'em."

Another officer emerged from the server room, following a path of blood drops on the floor. "Somebody really did a number in there," he said, shaking his head. "Everything smashed. Don't slip," he said to Tara, who made her way past him to look inside.

She found it hard to believe it was the same space where Trevor had first given her the copy of the whale's video. The entire floor was a jumble of shattered circuit boards and shards of glass. Loose wiring jutted forth from mangled plastic like uprooted plants.

Mentally picturing the tenacious ferocity it would have taken one man to do all this in a short amount of time gave Tara the chills. For she knew it was one man. . . . Her thoughts were interrupted by Anthony, who stared with incomprehension over her shoulder.

"Now we know why our web site's down," he said.

"Yeah," his assistant said, surveying the debris field of electronic waste. "I'm no webmaster, but I do know that the computers are supposed to be in one piece to work."

While the officers huddled about various piles of

ruin, Tara slowly made her way to Trevor's desk, where she saw one PC still standing—not on the desk, but on the floor. Kneeling down, she was surprised to see a screensaver still working on the violently displaced screen. Somehow she found the dancing geometric shapes disconcerting as they floated across the upended display. Tara found the keyboard still attached to the PC. Donning a pair of white latex gloves, she gingerly hit the SHIFT key. Thankfully, the parade of fractals making its way across the screen vanished, replaced by innocuous-looking text.

Tara's eyes caught on the .gov e-mail address displayed in the "From" field of what she realized was an open e-mail account. Aware that this could very well be the last e-mail Trevor Lane had read before he was murdered, Tara read the message. She tilted her head sideways because she didn't want to move the monitor from its oddly angled position on the floor. *Coast Guard GPS Interference Test.*

She recognized the testing zone coordinates as being similar to those she gave the helicopter pilot yesterday on their first trip to look for the Blue.

She checked her watch. If what she read was correct—and she would have it verified by staff at the field office—the testing was set to conclude in . . . *under six hours!* But what difference will it make if the whale-cam's GPS works when the entire web site is down? she wondered. *How will I see the what the damn coordinates are?*

"Find something, Special Agent Shores?" The

police detective stood next to her, taking in her peculiar posture with equal parts amusement and concern as to what she might be observing.

Tara straightened and tapped keys to close the e-mail program. She knew when the whale's GPS would be broadcasting again; she didn't need a room full of cops to know it too. "Checked out recently opened documents. Just routine fax and memo templates. Sorry, I'll get out of your hair."

She was glad to see Anthony exit the server room, heading in her direction. She excused herself from the police detective and pulled the producer aside. Lowering her voice, she asked him, "How long do you think it will be before people can see the whale-cam online again?"

"Wish I knew. Few hours, at least."

"As I recall, Trevor said the data on the servers wasn't backed up anywhere else. Is that true?"

"Yes. The entire site will have to be built from scratch."

"Can you get a bare-bones version of the site back up sometime today?"

"In theory, but it depends how long it takes to assemble a technical team and acquire the equipment." He looked at his watch. "I'd better get going."

"Good luck."

"Thanks." He turned to leave but then paused, adding, "Hey do me a favor, will you?"

"Depends on the favor," she said, smiling.

"If you talk to Anastasia—I know you're consulting

her to look for the whale—don't mention I said it might take a while for the site to be back up. I'm already catching enough crap from her Dad. I don't want to hear it from her too. She's got some meeting at the university today, after she gets through editing, so hopefully I can have it running again by the time she's free."

"No problem. If she hears about it, it won't be from me." Anthony left and Tara wondered if he'd meant any innuendo when he said she was "consulting" Anastasia.

Tara walked past the server room, samples of blood on the floor now being collected by crime scene technicians. She flashed upon her conversation with Trevor.

Anastasia . . . Anastasia's lab . . . A.N.A.S.T.A.S.I.A . . . Data on the university computer . . . but no video. . . . Forget the video, GPS is data! . . . We can find the whale!

As technicians photographed a blood-spatter pattern, Tara recalled something else Trevor had said about Anastasia. "*She doesn't want anyone to get the tag . . . Interrupt her precious data stream? No way.*" She found it hard to believe anything Trevor Lane had said. This was, after all, a man who had gone to great lengths in order to deceive her. But there was such conviction in his voice. . . .

Tara could see no advantage in going to Anastasia for the GPS coordinates yet. Too early. And it would tip everyone else off about the Coast Guard testing.

Better to use the time to organize an FBI dive team. When the whale-cam's GPS started broadcasting again, she would be ready with her own marine force. *No more riding shotgun.*

She would end this today.

Tara stepped outside and threaded her way through a gathering crowd of onlookers to her Crown Vic. The coroner unit was on scene now loading Trevor Lane's sheeted body onto a stretcher.

CHAPTER 30

FBI FIELD OFFICE, LOS ANGELES

"I told you to keep me informed," Tara's boss exclaimed as she entered his office. He was holding the phone, receiver cupped in one hand.

"Trevor Lane's been murdered," Tara said, taking a seat in one of the chairs in front of Will Branson's desk.

Branson nodded and continued speaking into the phone. "Have him call me back. I'm in a meeting." He started to hang up when Tara could hear his secretary trying to tell him something. "Then cancel it!" He slammed the receiver in its cradle.

Branson leaned back in his chair. "I heard, Shores. News agencies around the world are picking up on this whale murder. We're flooded with calls. I hope you've got some leads on this."

"That's what I'm here for, sir," she said.

"Tell me."

"It's not apparent who killed Lane, or even if his death is related to the whale-cam murder. But in the course of investigating Lane's office, I learned that the GPS malfunction of the whale's telemetry unit was caused by scheduled U.S. Coast Guard GPS interference testing."

"If it was scheduled, how come the TV show didn't know why their GPS was out, or were they bluffing?"

"They didn't know it was out because Trevor Lane didn't tell them. He received an e-mail from the Coast Guard but never passed the information on."

"Why wouldn't he pass it on?"

"Maybe by the time he saw it he was under too much pressure to get the tag himself. Something related to the blackmail he was involved in over the whale-cam's core technology."

Branson tented his hands, looked around his desk at the growing stacks of inquiries regarding the whale case, his blinking phone lights, and sighed. "So now what? What's our next move? I need something solid for the press."

"Sir, I'd like to put in a request for the FBI's underwater unit to take me to the whale's location as soon as its GPS coordinates are known again."

Branson started to protest, then caught himself and changed tack. "Wait a minute. I've been getting reports that the whale's web site has been taken down."

"Right. Lane destroyed the servers in his office before he was killed. At least I'm pretty sure it was Lane. Blood work will confirm that." For some reason the image of blood drops spattered across broken electronic equipment caused her to shudder involuntarily.

"So even if the GPS is working, how would you see the coordinates without the site up?"

Tara smiled. She was glad she worked for a smart man. "Excellent point, sir. But I've thought of that. Dr. Reed, the nature show's host, has a lab at USC. I have yet to confirm this, but I was told she has a computer there that receives a telemetry data stream—data that would include GPS—from the whale."

"And who was your source on that?"

Tara hesitated before coughing up the answer. "Trevor Lane." *Now there's a pillar of reliability.*

Branson said nothing. He simply stared at her as if he might be evaluating her in some way. He broke the silence as Tara was about to speak in self-defense.

"I expect a UCLA gal might be able to find her way over to SC, am I right?"

Tara smiled at his reference to the storied football rivalry. "I know the way, sir."

"Good."

Tara got up to leave.

"Just one more thing," Branson said.

"Sir?"

"Once you get the GPS coordinates of the whale's position, assuming that pans out, I want you to turn them over to the underwater unit and let them handle it from there."

Tara sank back into the chair as she let the words register. *Let them handle it from there.* After all she'd been through, she wouldn't even be on scene when the crown jewel of evidence in the case was recovered.

"I don't understand, sir," was all she could manage. But of course she did understand. Perfectly well. He lacked confidence in her, or was trying to protect her.

"I don't want you going back out on the water, Agent Shores. You've been through enough. Let the professional underwater people recover the video camera, then they'll give it to you so you can continue your investigation."

So I do all the work and some sea-going glory hounds get to come in at the last minute and take all the credit. "Very well, sir." She made no attempt to disguise her disappointment.

"You get us those coordinates, Shores, and I won't forget that."

"I'll have them in"—she checked her watch—"four hours."

"Good, Shores. Anything else?"

She wanted to tell him to let her go with the team, that it was the only way to . . . A part of her was glad she wouldn't have to go, however, and so she told Branson about her visit to Imaging and the victim's dolphin tattoo.

"Excellent. That lead to anything yet?"

"I ran the dolphin tattoo against missing persons reports. I'm awaiting results now."

He nodded his approval. "Get some rest if you can. You look like hell, if that's possible. I'll coordinate the underwater team."

SOUTH ROBERTSON, LOS ANGELES

Even before Mrs. George Reed stumbled out of her car into the alley behind the office of Roger Carr, P.I., her black Mercedes convertible attracted attention. The South Robertson area of L.A. was not one she normally frequented. Broken glass and trash littered the street below a canopy of graffiti-strewn billboards. Mrs. Reed was certain that any number of drug deals were taking place right now within a one-block radius.

Beverly Hills was home to plenty of private investigators, and with much cushier offices than Roger Carr's, Mrs. Reed might add, but with the unsavory surroundings came privacy, and privacy meant not having to suffer the humiliation of her fellow socialites and tennis club pals knowing that her husband had cheated on her. *Again.*

She made her way to the back door of Mr. Carr's establishment. She had told Carr that on occasion, when she must stop by, she would only use the back door. Explaining her presence here would be difficult. Not that it mattered much anymore. The look on George's face when he saw the photo had made it all worth it.

One more visit. She would have George tailed for one more week, just to make sure he wasn't up to anything else, keep the pressure on. Then she would sweep this whole business under the rug. She wanted to have the upper hand for what he'd done to her, but secretly, she didn't want to ruin their marriage. For years they had drifted apart, but when *Wired Kingdom* had started she'd begun to see a difference, especially in their relationship with Anastasia.

Inside, Mr. Carr looked at the black-and-white closed-circuit TV monitor on his desk and cringed. He took the phone off speaker and grabbed the receiver. "I don't know how I'm gonna spend all the money yet, Marty, but I do know there's a couple of island girls waiting for us in Aruba, okay? Oh, listen," he said, putting an end to the hearty laughter on the other end of the line, "I gotta go—a client just walked in."

Mr. Carr hung up the phone and stood behind his desk as Mrs. Reed entered. "Elsie, I wasn't expecting you today. How are you?" Carr knew that Elsie wasn't Mrs. Reed's real name, but she insisted on using an alias.

"You just took pictures of my husband cheating on me, Roger. How the hell do you think I am?" She looked at Carr, an aging hippie-type in a loud Hawaiian shirt with longish blond hair and a face rough with stubble.

Mr. Carr cowered back into his ratty desk chair. As soon as he was seated he wished he had remained standing, for there, just beyond arm's reach on the edge of his desk, was a magazine he wanted Mrs. Reed to see least of anyone.

"Well, I mean how are you, all things considered?" Carr managed.

"I want you to follow my husband for one more week."

She tossed a roll of bills on the desk. Almost as if hypnotized, Carr couldn't stop his eyes from watching the money's progress as it rolled to a stop on the edge of the magazine that had just changed his life. The detective-for-hire knew it would seem out of character for him not to count the cash right away, so he reached across the desk, as if for the money. He couldn't help but glance up at Mrs. Reed as he started to pull the magazine toward him along with the bills. Their eyes locked.

Then Mrs. Reed snatched the glossy magazine out of Carr's hand and read it: CAUGHT CHEATING! trumpeted the cover in ridiculously large type. There was still room on the page, however, for a small inset photo of Mr. Reed in a tuxedo, raising a glass with Mrs. Reed at some after-party. And there was also space for a much larger picture of a semi-nude George Reed with his arms wrapped around a shockingly younger, bikini-clad woman.

It was the same picture Mrs. Reed had shown her husband earlier today, taken by Roger Carr, P.I.

She read the headline a second time, tears falling. Carr kept starting to say something and then stopped himself, as if thinking better of it. "I . . . It's just . . . I didn't think—"

"Tell me, Mr. Carr, *private* investigator," Mrs. Reed said, the last two words dripping with sarcasm, "how much did this sleazy rag pay you for this picture, this picture that *I* paid for you to take, and therefore own?"

"Look, Mrs. Ree—I mean Elsie . . . " He shifted his eyes from those of Mrs. Reed while stalling for something to say, and they landed on his two small suitcases in a corner. A Caribbean travel guide lay on top of one of them. Mrs. Reeds' eyes followed his until she too was looking at the packed bags.

"Interrupting your travel plans, am I?"

Carr gave up all pretenses. He looked around at the crappy little office where he'd labored to get by for so many years—the rust stains on the ceiling, the shabby furniture scavenged from alleyways and thrift stores, the hard-to-reach corners that served as thoroughfares for unseen vermin. He pictured his once-anemic bank account now bubbling with funds thanks to a few beach shots he never would have taken had it not been for his angry client. Then he conjured up a mental image of his new bank balance and he imagined himself floating away on that delightful train of zeroes, all the way to some tropical island where he could drink and screw himself to death at his leisure and never pick up another camera as long as he lived.

"Sorry, Mrs. Reed," he said, walking out from around his desk. "I'm no longer in business."

"You can't just leave! That picture is mine! You had no permission to sell it to anyone!"

"So sue me," Carr said, picking up his bags. He walked out with his suitcases and just left her standing alone in his office. She could have it and everything in it, for all he cared.

CHAPTER 31

MEDICAL CLINIC—LOS CABOS, MEXICO

A doctor hovered over a young girl lying on an operating table. Unconscious and barely breathing, her condition had taken a turn for the worse over the last few hours. An EKG machine fluttered, alarms rising in pitch, then flatlined. A nurse stepped to the table with defibrillator paddles. “Clear . . .”

Minutes later the doctor shook his head, removed his mask, and exited the operating room.

In the waiting room outside, a grieving mother jumped to her feet upon seeing the doctor. Even before he spoke, his body language told her the news. “We did everything we could, *señora*.”

MEXICAN-AMERICAN BORDER

The mood in the Cessna was jovial as Héctor crossed back into American airspace. Two new recruits rode with him, one up front and one in the back. The man in the rear shared floor space—the seats had been ripped out to create sufficient cargo room—with a host of new equipment. A heavy, oblong crate occupied the tail section.

Héctor held up a hand to silence his divers, who were high-fiving each other on crossing from Baja California into California, U.S.A. The radio was making noise.

The pilot listened closely to the marine band for any signs of news about Juan and Fernando, whom he regretted leaving behind. There was plenty of the usual fishing and boating chatter, but the frequency he had set aside for Juan and Fernando remained stubbornly silent. He did not let this worry him too much. They were, after all, still very far away.

Héctor's satellite phone began to ring and he checked the caller ID: his wife. He had not even had time to see her while he was back in Mexico. She would not be pleased. He was about to answer the sat-phone when he heard new voices on the marine radio. *She will have to wait.* He silenced the sat-phone. He had to monitor the radio for every possible shred of information that might help them locate Juan and Fernando. The trio became quiet as they settled into the flight and contemplated the unusual mission that lay ahead.

As they flew north, Héctor was blissfully unaware that his personal motivation to obtain the whale's tag no longer existed.

ABOARD PANDORA'S BOX

The decks of the schooner *Pandora's Box* were awash in midday sun. Drifting lazily under the crew's watch, the boat followed the offshore current south. Not knowing where the whale was, Ocean Liberation Front and the two castaways they had picked up had no immediate destination, but liked the idea of a pleasure cruise while they decided on one. At some point Eric Stein had thought it a good idea to ply Juan and Fernando with tequila.

In between radio checks, the Mexican divers traded shots with the OLF crew who were not on immediate duty. Everyone knew there was drinking on OLF cruises, but Pineapple urged Stein not to have anymore tequila after he had nearly shot his girlfriend's companion. Stein initially took offense to this, but they reached a compromise when Stein agreed to have margaritas instead of shots.

Those on board had clustered themselves into three main groups. The largest group, occupying the stern deck, was centered around the Mexican divers. Stein and Pineapple continued to converse with them in Spanish, interpreting for the rest of their inner circle and a few hangers-on.

Stein's girlfriend was being consoled by several of her friends who sat cross-legged in a loose circle on the smaller bow deck. The guy she'd been with in the bathroom also sat in their group, although not next to her, to avoid inciting Stein any further. The third group was the on-duty crew, who kept track of the ship's position and monitored the radar screen and radio channels.

Stein had just finished telling the Mexicans yet another story highlighting the heroic deeds of his organization while patently ignoring the criminal derring-do they were infamous for, when Juan looked at his dive watch. He signaled Fernando. Time to check the radio again. Fernando said he would go after finishing his beer—he was grateful for the cold Tecates and got a healthy laugh from the crew when he told them he would have traded his dive gear for a six-pack.

At the radio Fernando monitored several channels he knew their pilot would know to use. He could hear the others holding their voices down while they strained to listen.

"*Nada*," he said, giving up on the instrument. He turned to face them. Juan returned his gaze, contemplating the unspoken question. Hours had passed since last contact with their pilot. This floating fiesta could only last so long.

Where would they be—and what options would they have—when it ended?

FBI FIELD OFFICE, LOS ANGELES

Tara ate lunch at her desk, reviewing missing persons alerts and hoping for a call from the techies who ran the tattoo database, when her assistant stopped by.

"You won't believe this," the young woman said, tossing a magazine next to Tara's mahi mahi sandwich. Tara always found it odd that she loved seafood even though she hated the ocean.

"Caught cheating," Tara read aloud, not sure at first what she was supposed to be reading. Then she realized who it was on the cover and put down her food. Her eyes went straight to the mystery woman's ankle.

She shoved her lunch aside and placed Imaging's tattoo enhancement and the gossip rag side-by-side on her desk. Then she produced a magnifying glass and studied the ankle tattoo in each photograph.

"Mr. Reed . . ." Tara said to her assistant while still peering through the lens. "Find out where he is, please."

CHAPTER 32

BEVERLY HILLS HOTEL

Mr. Reed took the podium to a hearty round of applause. Flashbulbs sparkled as the celebrity-studded audience settled into their seats. The crowd of five hundred had paid a thousand dollars per plate (with the exception of the celebrities who were comped in return for their appearance) for the privilege of donating to charity while dining in the company of Hollywood mogul George Reed.

George had been told about the tabloid cover by a hotel events coordinator. He wasn't pleased, but he refused to let it rattle him. He'd been in the public eye during periods of personal stress many times over the course of his career, and he was not about to let it deter him now, at this new height of success.

Eager reporters were kept at bay by a small army of hotel security staff working with private bodyguards. Nothing that might distract Mr. Reed was to be allowed in the room—with the exception of Mrs. Reed—only she wasn't there. She was supposed to be sitting at a front-row table with a close circle of George's most trusted associates and their wives, girlfriends, or escorts, as the case may be. But even though the lights and flashbulbs made it difficult for him to see, it was clear that they had found a seat-filler to take her place. A striking female seat-filler, George couldn't help but notice.

In light of the tabloid, George wasn't surprised that his wife hadn't shown. He figured she'd leaked the photo to the press in order to publicly humiliate him and had known all along she wouldn't be going to the event. No way she'd want to be seen here with that smut circulating.

"C'mon, George, you old dog, don't keep us waiting!" one of his colleagues cat-called from the table at which Mrs. Reed should have been seated. Mr. Reed realized he had been just standing there at the podium, staring off into space.

He recovered quickly, though, and launched into one of the politically incorrect, joke-laden speeches for which he was known. "For those of you who are not here from the network," he said at one point, "we've got a new little show by the name of *Wired Kingdom*." George paused a moment, letting the expected wave of applause peak and recede. "I'm thinking of putting one of those web-cams on my wife, it's impossible to track her down!" This was met with raucous applause.

But in the silence that followed, before George should have started speaking again, a small commotion ensued at a secured rear entrance intended only for staff.

Knowing exactly when to bring a suspect into custody was a tricky business, but one for which Tara Shores was well regarded. Bring them in too soon and you run the risk of being altogether wrong. Bring them in too late, on the other hand, and you give them time to cover their tracks, flee, commit more crimes, or all the above. Tara also knew that the timing of an arrest could weigh heavily on a suspect's willingness to cooperate. There were those who preferred to keep things nice and quiet, to maintain a façade that all is well. These suspects tended to put up a pretense of cooperation by continuing to respond amiably to requests to come down to the station, answer phone calls, all while lawyering up and continuing business-as-usual. As long as the case doesn't rear its ugly head high enough, they continue with their lives. But there were times when it was advantageous to knock the suspect off balance. And right now, Tara decided, was one of those times.

By taking George Reed down in his own backyard, in front of his colleagues, peers and Hollywood at large, Tara would be ensuring that he couldn't hide behind an anonymous wall of high-priced attorneys. Paparazzi would capture the whole encounter. It would make the evening news. He'd want to settle it immediately, do whatever he could do to get his life back to normal. At least that's what Tara was counting on as she burst through a second contingent of security guards, her badge parting the way like a swordfish through a school of mackerel.

Mr. Reed may be unconnected to the girl's death, Tara thought—the fact that he had a relationship with her did not mean he'd killed her—but with no other leads, he was at the very least a "person of interest."

Tara hadn't expected so much attention from the paparazzi directed her way, but the word spread once she showed her credentials. She strode past women in designer dresses. Nothing that impressed her. She was fairly blinded by flashbulbs by the time she emerged though a short hallway, out a door, through a gauntlet of security personnel, entertainment reporters and paparazzi, to the main floor.

The podium at which Mr. Reed spoke was elevated on a small dais. Tara watched the man in between the bright spots floating across her eyes from the flashes. She could see him looking in her direction, but he continued his delivery without breaking stride. Those in the front rows, however, could plainly see that something was going on. Soon many were indicating for him to look to his right.

Tara merely stood watching Mr. Reed speak—something about how he was really going to give the network's investors something to look forward to once the next Nielson ratings came out—like a cat stalking her prey. There was no need to pull him off the podium in mid-sentence. He was simply being brought to the field office for questioning.

Then the audience was clapping, some even standing up to do it, and Mr. Reed was thanking them for being there, reminding them how important they were to the cause of the moment—something about preventing animal cruelty. When George stepped down from the dais, Tara was there to greet him. He tried to breeze his way past the special agent, throwing her a wave as if she was just another fan. Tara had expected no less.

"Mr. Reed, I need to speak with you," she said, raising her badge high. When he ignored her, continuing to walk past, she grabbed his arm and squeezed. "Now, Mr. Reed." She waved the tabloid photo in his face. "Who is this woman?" He stopped dead in his tracks.

"Lemme see that," he growled as he took the photo. He appeared to study it for a moment, then said, "No comment." He started away. Tara grabbed him again, more forcefully this time.

"I'm not a member of the press, Mr. Reed. Your response is not optional."

"What? What's going on here? Am I under arrest?" The paparazzi were really going crazy now, circling tighter, straining to hear the exchange.

"If you don't come with me and answer some simple questions, you will definitely be under arrest. Comply with our investigation, and you'll be back in time for desert." *Unless I can prove you're guilty.*

He started to say something, then saw a reporter swing a boom microphone over, and thought better of it. He leaned in close to Tara and asked, "What about my attorney?"

"Do you think that's necessary?"

"I—look, I don't think this is an appropriate place to talk about his," he said, fishing his sunglasses out of his jacket and putting them on.

"Shall we go, then?" She motioned toward the exit.

"George, what's going on?" one of Mr. Reed's associates called out.

He waved him off. "Talk to you in a bit, Klaus." He turned back to Tara. "Look, Agent . . ."

"Shores. Same as it was when we spoke yesterday."

"Agent Shores, that's right, yesterday you were a guest in my house. I answered your questions then. I think that demonstrates my willingness to cooperate. I'd like to oversee my event here. How about you give me your card and I'll stop by your office tomorrow? Say about twelve—hey, we could even do lunch. I know this excellent Caribbean cuisine place that just opened over on—"

"Keep moving your feet, Mr. Reed, if you do not want to be arrested under suspicion of murder right now." An exclamation of surprise rippled through the crowd. Tara had raised her voice intentionally, knowing Mr. Reed would be more uncomfortable the louder she became.

"Okay, okay, just keep it down. There's no need to make a scene."

"Making scenes is what you're all about, isn't it, Mr. Reed? Lead the way out, please."

The man *Time Magazine* once labeled "the most successful executive producer in Hollywood" ran a gauntlet of paparazzi and reporters to the street outside. Along the way Mr. Reed spat out statements that did nothing to quell the crowd's curiosity. "Excuse me, I'll be right back" seemed to be his favorite, followed quickly by "Some routine business to take care of."

Tara had heard it all before and recognized the signs of a nervous man. Surrounded by their peers and on public record, a lot of people feigned cooperation. But after some time to think about it on the drive to the field office, they would stonewall every effort to elicit valuable information, making her jump through every legal hoop they could conceive. George Reed would be no exception.

They reached the door to the street, where a small gathering was already beginning to congregate. Tara's Crown Vic was there, the FBI placard in the windshield allowing her to park in the red zone.

"I'll have my driver bring my car around," George said, preparing to dial his cell phone. "That way when we're done I can just—"

"Please get in the car, Mr. Reed. I promise that as soon as our business is concluded you will be dropped off right back here."

"You're arresting me, aren't you? I mean, no handcuffs, but I don't have a choice about this, do I?"

"You're not under arrest at this time, Mr. Reed, but we need you to answer some questions."

"At this time? At this time!" George trilled.

"Get in the car." She opened the front passenger-side door. He hesitated a moment, peering into the vehicle, as if unsure of what it contained. Then he turned around and waved to the crowd. "Go back inside, have fun. I'll be back shortly to join you." And with that he got inside the car.

Tara made a quick radio call to inform her field office that she was coming in with a suspect. The coded language kept Mr. Reed from knowing exactly what was said, but he could tell it was about him. She drove fast. She wanted to get her suspect into the controlled setting of an interrogation room without delay.

"Okay, I've been good enough to play along with you. I demand that you tell me what this is about!" Mr. Reed said sharply. "Should I have my attorney meet me at your office?"

He removed a cell phone from his jacket. Tara kept a close eye on him, and had to swerve back into her lane.

"Who was the woman you are having an affair with, Mr. Reed? What is her name?"

He hesitated, glancing out the window.

"The woman in the tabloid photo, Mr. Reed. You are having an affair with her, correct?"

"Yes, but that's not illegal is it? I mean, well yes—I know it is, since I'm married—but since when does the FBI treat people with marriage difficulties as criminals?"

Tara pulled up to a red light separating them from a short freeway ride to the field office. "Tell me about your marriage difficulties. It seems like you and your wife had been fighting when I interviewed you yesterday."

Mr. Reed appeared aggravated. "Look, my wife told me this morning she hired a private investigator to follow me around. I guess he shot the picture that ended up on the tabloid today. Probably split the money he got for it with my wife, for all I know."

"So your wife knew about your affair with—what's the woman's name?" Tara did her best to appear to be concentrating on the road. This was a big moment, and one for which she would prefer to be in the field office, but she had him talking now, and would keep him talking.

"Crystal. Her name is Crystal." Tara immediately picked up on the use of the present tense. "Crystal what? What's her last name?"

George Reed blushed in the front seat of the special agent's car. "I don't know," he said, anticipating, and getting a doubting stare from Tara. "I know it sounds bad, but I don't know her last name. I don't think I ever knew it. We only went out a few times."

"Was she a stripper?"

"A stripper? Why would you ask such a thing?"

"Sounds like a stripper name. They only use their first names. And older married men only want one thing from younger women. . . . While younger women want only one thing from older men. . . . A stripper fits that profile."

"She wasn't a stripper, as far as I know. I don't know her life story; I only dated her for a little while."

"What's a little while?"

"I don't know, maybe two, three months."

"Was it closer to two, or closer to three months?"

Tara exited the freeway and turned right.

"Three, I guess. Look, I really don't see the point of all this. Maybe this was a bad idea."

"We're almost at the field office. When we get there I'd like to show you a photograph."

"Fine. Let's just get this over with."

CHAPTER 33

SANTA CRUZ ISLAND

Channel Islands National Marine Sanctuary ranger Ben Stacy pulled his Land Cruiser to a stop on a gravelly switchback. After patrolling this natural laboratory all morning—checking for poachers of wild boar, foxes or pheasants; looking for illegal campers or boaters in trouble—Ben needed to stretch his legs.

He particularly liked the scenic vista at which he now found himself. Not many people visited this part of the island. There were boaters who camped on the side facing the mainland, but most of the land mass was off-limits to all but park personnel and visiting scientists brandishing research permits. The impact of humans was restricted.

To get a sense of what California looked like hundreds of years ago, before it was heavily settled—when it was populated primarily by Native Americans—one would do well to visit Santa Cruz Island. At ninety-six square miles (four times the size of Manhattan), Santa Cruz is California's largest island. Lying about twenty-two miles off the Santa Barbara coast, its rugged coastline protects a dynamic interior. Beyond the jagged cliffs, sea caves and empty beaches, the island supports diverse habitat types including two mountain ranges with several peaks over 2,000 feet, low-lying grasslands and a forested central valley.

At the base of a narrow canyon lay one of the most striking beaches the ranger had ever laid eyes on. Though he had witnessed it countless times in his decade of employment with the park service, he swore that the hypnotic crescent of light brown sand grew more impressive each time he saw it. In the foreground of Ben's view were yellow flowers tumbling down a green hillside. The far end of the beach seemed to melt into a cascade of rolling emerald hills, well over a mile away. Heavy, demanding surf drummed in from a dark blue ocean that stretched all the way to Japan.

In such a harmonious environment it was easy to notice when something was amiss. Far below on a beach devoid of footprints, he saw a pile of something unusual. That was how he described it in his own mind, just a pile of . . . *something*. But he'd been here yesterday and it hadn't been there then. He knew what everything was around here. He knew what it was not: it wasn't a pile of kelp (too light), and it wasn't part of a shipwreck (not angular enough).

And so it was that park ranger Ben Stacy was prompted to put down the fresh halibut sandwich he'd been eating, jump down from the Land Cruiser's hood where he'd been sitting, and go for the binoculars he kept in the glove box.

FBI FIELD OFFICE, LOS ANGELES

"Have you seen this before?" Tara directed the question at George Reed, who somehow managed to look dignified sitting in one of the interrogation room chairs. He and Tara were the only two people inside the room, but George was correct in his assumption that they were being monitored closely by agents in adjoining rooms.

An eight-by-ten of Imaging lab's frame capture from the whale's murder video sat on the table. Mr. Reed hunched forward to study the picture. He cocked his head to one side. "It's a tattoo. A dolphin," he said and looked up from the print. "So?"

"Have you seen it before?"

"Why would I?"

Tara's heavy gaze tempered Mr. Reed's defiant attitude.

"I—if this has something to do with Crystal . . . she had a tattoo on her shoulder. A butterfly. And . . . and a dolphin on her ankle." Tara glanced toward the one-way glass pane. "How did you get this picture? She's not in some kind of trouble. . . ."

"Mr. Reed, this is a frame capture of the video taken by the whale-cam. Of the murder," Tara added quickly.

He remained impassive for a moment, the expression on his face revealing the process of deduction working in his mind. “What are you saying?”

“We believe—”

“You’re not telling me that Crystal’s dead. That she was murdered. . . .”

“Mr. Reed, please—”

“Wait a minute.” He began to stand, raising his voice. “You’re not suggesting that *I* had anything to—”

“Mr. Reed!” He froze, his mouth open, twisted in fear and pain. “Sit down!” He sat. Hung his head. Tara walked around the table to stand opposite him and began again. “The tattoo in this picture was taken from the whale’s web-cam. It appears to match the one in the tabloid shot. If that proves true, then Crystal was the victim in the whale’s video.”

“This shot came from the whale video?” Mr. Reed asked without looking up.

“Yes, Mr. Reed. It did.”

George shook his head as if confused. “I’d say they’re the same tattoo—I’m not denying that. In real life—on Crystal—the color was more purple than it looks here.” George flashed back to his tongue tracing the outline of that tattoo, looking up to see Crystal giggle at him . . . telling him to have his fun while she watched herself on TV. *Just until the next commercial* . . .

He forced himself back to the present. “It could be her. I don’t—but I have no idea how she would have ended up in that video."

"Let's talk about that for a moment, shall we, Mr. Reed?" George shifted uncomfortably in the stiff chair. Those watching from the other side of the one-way glass noticed he was looking a bit less dignified now. More like a subject settling in for what he knew would be a long day of questioning.

"So if Crystal wasn't a stripper, what was she? What did she do and how did you meet her?"

Mr. Reed took a sip of water before answering. "She was a part-time actress who had a couple of minor parts on one of my reality shows a while back, before *Wired Kingdom* started."

"Which show was that?"

"*Sex Coach.* It was a show where sex therapists made house calls to married couples looking to spice up their love lives. On some segments there were models who would . . . simulate various lovemaking positions for the couples. Crystal was one of those models."

If Mr. Reed was embarrassed by the type of programs he did before *Wired Kingdom*, he didn't show it. Tara could almost hear the snickering from the other side of the observation glass.

"I see," she said. "And the personal relationship you had with her—was it sexual?"

He was back on the couch with Crystal again, watching TV . . . "It was."

"And she knew you were married?"

"She did."

"What about her? Was she married? Any boyfriends, anyone close to her besides yourself?"

"She said she'd never been married and I believe her on that. Said she didn't have a boyfriend. But it's not like I was with her all the time, so who knows." He ran his hand through his hair. "Can I smoke in here?"

"As long as you answer my questions, sure."

Mr. Reed produced a cigarette and lit up. Tara disliked being around smoke, but hoped that if her suspect was more comfortable he'd continue talking.

"Mr. Reed, did Crystal know, or was she ever introduced to Trevor Lane?"

George gave Tara a condescending smirk. "Not that I know of. No. They didn't work together. And to my knowledge they never met in a non-working capacity, either. Why—"

Tara cut him off. "Had she come into any large sums of money recently?"

George paused while he appeared to think about this. "Well, I bought her some nice things, if that's what you mean, but large sums of cash? Not that I'm aware of, no."

"When was the last time you saw her?" The question hung in the air with George's cigarette smoke while he pondered the answer.

"Actually, the day this photo was taken was the last time I saw her," he said, nodding at the print on the table.

"And this was taken two weeks ago?"

"Correct."

"And during the course of your relationship how often did you typically see each other?"

"Not very often. Maybe once a week."

"Did you want it to be more than once a week?"

He looked surprised. "No," he said rearing back in his chair, "of course not. She was a temporary diversion. It never should have happened. I was under stress from putting together the *Wired Kingdom* deal, and *Sex Coach* was coming to an end. I suppose she was a little tense, too, and we just . . ." He tapped his cigarette into an ashtray.

"But didn't you call her after a week went by? That would have been per usual, right? Why haven't you seen her since this?" Tara said, pointing to the tabloid photo on the table.

"I don't . . ." Mr. Reed held his head in his hands, as if trying to remember. "Okay, I did call her—twice, I think—but she never returned my calls. I figured maybe she was busy with another acting job, plus my wife was beginning to suspect an affair—as you can see," he said, indicating the tabloid. "So I didn't pursue it. Next thing I know, you're telling me it's her in that ghastly whale video."

"So you're saying you've got no idea where she is now?"

"None whatsoever."

"What's her phone number, please?"

George stared at the cell phone that had suddenly materialized in Tara's hand. He opened his mouth before shutting it again without having said anything. Then he gave her a number. Tara dialed. She enabled the speaker mode so Mr. Reed and the agents listening in could hear. A bubbly, high-pitched voice said, "This is Crystal. Do your thing at the beep."

At that moment there came a knock on the door. She ended the call and opened the door. A case worker waited, holding a fax. The young woman appeared out of breath as if she had been running, which in fact she had.

"Special Agent Shores," she began, "a park ranger on Santa Cruz Island found the partial remains of a body on a beach about an hour ago." She looked down at the paper in her hands, making sure she got it right. "Says it looks like a female Caucasian shark-attack victim."

Tara took the fax and read it over, turning toward the glass and giving a thumbs-up to her concealed colleagues when she was done. Then she turned back to her assistant. "Get me a warrant for the address that corresponds to the billing for this phone line." She handed her a piece of paper with Crystal's phone number. "We're looking for latent prints—maybe she has a record. And get her toothbrush, hairbrush, things like that we can use for DNA. We'll be looking for a match with the body on the beach."

Then Tara's boss, Will Branson, appeared in the doorway behind the case worker. "You know what this means, right Shores?"

"Sir?"

"In terms of jurisdiction. All of Santa Cruz Island is a—"

"National Park," Tara finished for him. "That's why the park service notified us so quickly—which makes the Jane Doe who washed up a federal case!"

"Exactly, Shores."

Tara felt an adrenaline surge. She'd been worried that after she had done the leg work in the case, when she had uncovered all the evidence, she would find it was out of her jurisdiction. They'd had no way of knowing when they were first alerted to the video. Now she was one ID away from unchallenged authority over the most publicized murder case in the country.

She looked at the reality television mogul, who appeared to be digesting this new development. "Mr. Reed," Tara said, "anything you'd like to add at this point?"

He rested his head in one hand and muttered, "I can't believe it."

Tara and her boss exchanged glances. Was he about to confess?

"Mr. Reed?" Tara prompted. George shook his head as if to clear his mind.

"I didn't have anything to do with Crystal's murder," he declared. "I had an affair with her. It was consensual. The last time I was with her was on the beach in Malibu. I know nothing about what happened in the whale video."

"You'll want to call your attorney, Mr. Reed," Tara said, "because right now you're under arrest for the murder of Crystal—last name as yet to be determined."

George Reed bolted up from his chair. "You're out of your mind! I'm leaving this instant." He started for the door but was smothered by no less than six agents who poured past her into the room, wrestled him to the ground and restrained him in handcuffs.

Tara raised her voice to be heard over the scuffle. "If the ID determines the body that washed up is not that of the woman you had an affair with, then you'll be free to go at that time."

"I didn't do it. I wouldn't hurt her."

"Then you better pray we get our hands on that whale's web-cam unit, Mr. Reed, and that it shows someone besides you committing the murder."

That reminded Tara. She glanced at her watch. In less than four hours the whale's GPS would be functioning again. Branson, reading her mind, signaled for her to step outside. "Good work in there, Shores."

"Thank you, sir."

"I've already got our underwater unit on ready alert status. We need those coordinates as soon as they come in."

"I know it, sir. I'll send an evidence unit to Santa Cruz Island to collect possible fingerprints and DNA from the body to submit to the lab for testing. While they're doing that, I'll go myself to get the GPS data from Dr. Reed's lab."

CHAPTER 34

USC CAMPUS

Tara could hardly contain her excitement as she drove onto the University of Southern California campus. An oasis of collegiate tranquility amidst one of L.A.'s rougher neighborhoods, the private school was home to the laboratory of esteemed scientist, Dr. Anastasia Reed.

Tara had told herself on the drive over that Branson's handling of the actual extraction of the whale-cam was a good thing. She had been delivered from that part of the case, and now needed only to present the underwater team with the GPS coordinates of the whale's position. When that was done, she'd have satisfied her obligations to this case—another notch on her belt.

An armed security guard in a kiosk checked her credentials and handed her a campus map. A gate arm lifted. Tara had called Anastasia's cell phone and her *Wired Kingdom* office but had received no answer.

Tara parked her Crown Vic in the visitor lot for the

Department of Biological Sciences and walked into the building. She checked her watch. Three hours now until the Coast Guard GPS jam-testing ended. She found the main office and was surprised to find it buzzing with activity on a Saturday.

A secretary, casting a surprised glance at the badge Tara wore on her belt, asked how she might be of service.

"Afternoon, ma'am. Special Agent Tara Shores, Federal Bureau of Investigation. I need to see Dr. Anastasia Reed, please. Her father told me she was working here today."

Several secretaries looked up from copiers, workstations, and phones to stare at the real-life special agent in their midst. The eldest of them, apparently the office manager, addressed Tara. "She's in a meeting now, until about three o'clock." The secretary cocked her head, indicating that the meeting was taking place in a room just down the hall.

"I'm sorry, but this matter cannot wait. I need to see her now. Can you get her for me, please?"

There was no way Tara could wait for two hours. She needed to confirm with Anastasia that her equipment would, in fact, be receiving the GPS data stream once it was available.

A silver-haired man who'd been standing in a corner conversing quietly with one of the secretaries stepped forward. "Pardon me," he said to Tara, "my name is Peter Young. I'm the chair of this department. Is there something I can help you with?"

Used to being deferred to higher-ups, Tara patiently repeated the purpose of her visit.

"She's in an important funding meeting right now. It's the reason we're all here this morning. Any chance you could come back after three? Or I could have her get in touch with you?"

"I'm terribly sorry, Mr. Young, but it's critical to our investigation that I speak with her now."

The department chair looked uncomfortable for a moment, but then seemed to snap out of it. "Do you mind stepping outside with me for just a moment, Agent Shores?" He turned back to the secretary he'd been talking to. "Take in a fresh pot of coffee and the chips and things at the top of the hour, please."

He and Tara stepped outside the office into an empty hallway. Peter Young spoke in hushed tones as if he wanted to keep this matter as private as possible. "Allow me to ask, if you please, detective, whether this is about the complaints filed against Dr. Reed."

"Complaints? What complaints are those, Mr. Young . . . or is it Dr. Young?"

"Doctor, yes, but that's quite all right. How can I put this . . . ?" Tara waited for Dr. Young to formulate his thoughts. Whatever it was he was trying to say, it was clearly uncomfortable for him. "Anastasia's brilliant, the finest researcher our department's ever had. Her publishing track record is unprecedented, but we have had . . . social issues with her, although they've been more than offset by her remarkable scholarly output."

"What was the nature of these 'issues,' Dr. Young?"

"In the last couple of years we have had two separate complaints filed by two different students, complaining of . . ." He paused awkwardly yet again, as if unsure how to phrase what he was about to say.

"Complaining of what, Dr. Young?" Tara prodded.

Young craned his head around to make sure no one was within earshot before continuing. "Complaining of unwanted sexual advances to students during office-hour visits," he finished, looking her straight in the eyes.

Tara did her best not to look surprised. "And these complaints were found to be legitimate?"

"Yes, unfortunately they were. One of the students even retained an attorney at one point, threatening the university with a lawsuit, but the matter was settled out of court."

"The student who settled, did he have a past history of these kinds of problems?" Again, Dr. Young appeared extremely uncomfortable, almost blushing, Tara thought.

The secretary emerged from the office with a tray of coffee and snacks. Dr. Young waited for her to pass down the hall before continuing.

"The students who lodged the complaints were both female, detective."

Tara's mind lighted on her interactions with Anastasia the past two days. "I see." Tara forced herself to stay focused on getting the GPS coordinates. She was less than three hours away from wrapping the case, after which she'd be free to go back to the more familiar robberies, identity-theft rings and counter-terrorism operations she was used to. "But I'm not here to investigate that, Dr. Young. My reason for being here has to do with the whale tagged with Dr. Reed's device."

"Oh," Young said, letting the news sink in. "OH!" he repeated, his tone brightening as he realized the investigation was not centered around his department's brightest star. He cleared his throat.

"I do need to see her right now," Tara reminded him.

Dr. Young frowned for just a second and then motioned for Tara to follow him down the hall.

ABOARD PANDORA'S BOX

***Pandora's Box* floated** on a calm sea. Drifting for hours now with no sign of the Blue, the crew were showing signs of impatience. The beer and tequila had run out. Bodies lay in various states of repose around the deck, some sleeping, some just plain drunk. Only Eric Stein, Pineapple, and the hired divers were still alert.

Pineapple wanted to turn the ship around and head for the marina. He spoke in a low murmur, so as not to wake the crew—or panic the Mexicans—but his voice retained a sense of urgency. "If we can't find this damn whale, Eric, no one else will be able to either.

"I know that."

"So why don't we pack it in for now?"

"What about these guys?" Stein gave a subtle tilt of the head toward the divers. "What if they freak out when we get close to port?"

"We can't stay out here forever just because we picked these guys up. We saved their frickin' lives, we don't owe them anything. Let's drop their asses off!"

At this the divers, who had been semi-dozing on a pile of wetsuits, sat up and openly paid attention.

"Chill. They know we're talking about them."

"I don't care, Eric. Look at you, man, you're still bleeding all over the place."

Stein looked down at his thumb. A jagged, crusty ridge of caked blood snaked its way through the web between his thumb and forefinger. There were new blood splatters around the deck where his hand continued to drip. "No worries. I'll go patch it up."

"The first aid kit's out of gauze because some girl, who's not supposed to be here anyway, cut her foot on the bottle you broke."

"Okay," Stein said, picking off a protruding flap of skin and flinging it overboard. "Maybe we should just go in."

"I agree. However, we've got illegal aliens on board, and everybody, including you, the captain, is completely drunk. We don't need another Coast Guard citation, Eric. They'll take our boat. What I'm saying is that we need to plan out *how* to go in."

"You're just full of good cheer, aren't you, Pineapple?"

"Hey, at least I'm taking some responsibility here. You're not doing jack."

Stein drained the last of his beer and let the bottle drop to the deck. "What the hell is your problem, Pineapple? You don't like OLF anymore? Then leave. I don't care. Go start your own deal."

"Maybe I'll do that. Your organization's losing steam anyway."

"What's that supposed to mean?"

"We just haven't done anything. This whale thing seemed like a good idea at first, but it's making us look bad. The media's making us out to be a bunch of punk losers more than environmentalists. Our approach isn't working."

"Maybe you're not working."

Pineapple took a step back, glancing around to see if anyone was watching. The divers were. Everyone else was more or less comatose. "Great, Eric."

"You know what, maybe I'm sick of your BS. You should just take the tender back to shore." The tender for *Pandora's Box* was an eight-foot Boston Whaler with a five-horsepower outboard. It was fine for ferrying passengers around a marina or in to a beach from anchor, but nearly fifty miles out to sea it would be like playing Russian roulette with the weather.

"Yeah okay, Eric, I'll leave that for you to try."

"You're getting in that Whaler, Pineapple. We'll tow you in behind us, just like they used to do in the olden days when crewmembers had to be punished."

"Punished? Will you listen to yourself? Are you

all right?"

The Mexicans were chortling now, but concerned.

"I'm dead serious." Stein yelled a crewmember's name. A sleepy first mate poked his head out the cabin. "Tommy, prepare the launch."

"Listen, Eric, I don't know what the hell's the matter with you," Pineapple said, "but I'm not getting in that boat."

"Then I'll throw you in it," Stein said. "Yo, Tommy, Wes, help me out." Eric took a step toward Pineapple, who backed away toward the Mexican divers.

Suddenly they heard the sound of an engine, its clear and unmistakable buzzing at complete odds with the quiet world of a drifting ship. Juan and Fernando sprang to their feet. Juan turned his head skyward while Fernando hopped around the heap of dive gear on deck.

"Radio, *señor*," he said urgently to Eric and Pineapple, pointing to the sky as he did so.

Pineapple was glad for the distraction. "C'mon, let's go," he said, leading the way. Stein's curiosity over the plane had him willing to forget about his plan for the tender.

Just then Juan called out, "*Lo veo*." I see it.

At the radio, Fernando flipped to the channel he'd used before with his pilot.

Silence.

Pineapple turned an eye toward Stein as the inebriated skipper approached the radio console.

A string of rapid-fire Spanish burst from the

speaker. Fernando's eyes went wide as saucers. "Juan," he called back to the stern, "Juan! It's him."

Juan was jumping up and down on the stern deck, waving his hands. "He's circling. What's he saying?"

Fernando white-knuckled the transmitter while he shouted and frothed into the microphone. Pineapple frowned at him. Was this guy going to lose control? Right here and now, in the middle of their cramped cabin with a bunch of drunks passed out all over the boat, fifty miles out to sea?

He looked uncomfortably at Stein. "Tell him to ask if they're alone," Pineapple said. Stein interpreted the question. Fernando uttered some words and shifted his eyes nervously as he waited for an answer.

When the reply came he relayed it to Pineapple. "They only have one plane, but they have more divers with them," he said.

Around *Pandora's Box*, people were coming to life, lulled from their collective stupor by the sound of a low-flying aircraft and all the shouting.

"He's landing," Fernando said before running back out to the stern deck.

Pineapple addressed Stein. "They could pirate us, you know. You wanna play around with pretending you're an old-time sea captain, well this is for real. Modern-day piracy."

"Come on. They came back for their divers."

"After six hours? Such concern. They really pulled out all the stops."

"Why'd they land by us at all, then? Why even acknowledge the radio calls if they don't want their divers back?"

"Maybe they just came back with more divers so they could get the whale's video. You ever think about why they want the damn video so much in the first place, Eric?"

"You're overreacting."

"Maybe they killed that girl," Pineapple speculated.

"So? What's that got to do with us?"

Pineapple looked incredulous. "What it's got to do with us is that they're about to land next to our ship, which, I might add, is dead in the water until some kind of breeze comes up."

"We're helping them. They won't want to hurt us."

"Yeah, right. Once those guys get on the plane, how do you know they won't shoot us all and set *Pandora's Box* on fire? Get rid of all the witnesses?"

"Because, my friend," Stein said, "we're going to help them in a way they won't be able to deny. A small plane by itself is one thing. A ship by itself is one thing. But a ship and plane working together . . . think about it."

"I don't know. . . ."

"Come on, they could fly search patterns while their divers rest on the ship. We can provide all the diver support. Greater efficiency. Less risk."

Stein extended a hand to Pineapple. Pineapple shook it. "Okay. OLF, man."

"OLF!"

The two men stepped out on the stern deck in time to see a blue seaplane cut a white swath across the cobalt sea.

CHAPTER 35

DOWNTOWN LOS ANGELES

Even as he poured four Tylenols from the ever-present bottle in his pocket, Anthony Silveras cracked a smile for the first time in two days, then quickly erased any show of emotion from his face. He did not want those around him to perceive anything less than a total sense of urgency for the task at hand.

But it was working! "Forget about all the bells and whistles," Silveras had told his lead Information Technology man, "just get the live feed and subscription-taking software back up without delay."

He stood in the middle of a glassed-in room whose walls were lined with racks of computers and tape drives behind glass cabinets, ten times the size of the one Trevor had destroyed. Outside the room, the entire thirty-ninth floor of the Arco Tower, downtown Los Angles—cubicles, computers, network and all—lay at his disposal.

A loan processing center had been forced to shut down as a result of a class-action suit stemming from illegal practices. The IT consultant he'd contracted to get the *Wired Kingdom* web site back online as fast as humanly possible had informed him that they might be able to take over the space at a bargain price.

Since the expenditure would show up on Accounting's radar as a large blip, Silveras had tried to call George Reed, thinking he should be out of his fundraiser. He'd gotten no answer. He saw no other way to get the site back online so soon, so he'd gone ahead with it without waiting to hear back. His IT guru had just informed him that he should have the live feed back up within minutes, with the subscription services to follow shortly.

Silveras watched as a small army of technology workers buzzed about the machines like bees about a hive. Trevor Lane had been wrong when he'd said no one else would be able to figure out the complex architecture behind the whale's live feed, Silveras realized.

Dead wrong.

DEPARTMENT OF BIOLOGICAL SCIENCES, USC

Dr. Anastasia Reed was having a bad meeting. As principle investigator for the highly funded Pacific Pelagics Telemetry Tracking Study, she was responsible for delivering the asked-for reports with supporting research. Now in a conference with National Science Foundation funding partners to report progress on the project, she was finding out that her people had made anything but sufficient progress in the last reporting period—a time when she herself had been busy with *Wired Kingdom*.

Minutes earlier she had openly tried to place the blame for the lagging project on a graduate student she'd left in charge, berating the young man in front of the group. The contractors reminded Anastasia, however, that she alone was accountable for submitting project deliverables on time, not her students or employees.

Anastasia's request for a project extension had just been denied when there came a knock at the conference room door. It was opened by a student.

Tara Shores flashed her badge and asked to see Dr. Reed. The surprised student beckoned the detective inside.

A pudgy bald man was standing at the head of the table, addressing the group in irritated tones, gesturing incessantly. "We asked for 'A' and you're giving us 'A'-prime."

Anastasia sat at the middle of the rectangular table, flanked by assistants, her back to the door. "The no-cost extension will allow us to—" she began.

"Why should we give you more time? Your extracurricular activities are clearly affecting your job," the NSF guy said over her, unaware that Tara had made her way into the room. "We notice that in the coming months, the schedule for your television show is more, not less, demanding. What's going to change?"

Heads around the room swiveled, fixing on Agent Shores as she stood just inside the door. Anastasia stood up, her chair clattering to the floor. "I'll tell you what's going to change: you can get someone else to head up your study. I have plenty of other projects to choose from."

"Yes, we know, like TV game shows. That's very—"

Tara made eye contact with another of the NSF reps, who indicated for his associate to turn around. He cut himself off in mid-sentence when he saw the special agent.

Anastasia, wondering what put a stop to his angry reply, turned to see Tara's badge held out in front of her. Seeing Tara, a smile slowly spread across her face. "Special Agent Shores, to what do we owe this unexpected pleasure?" She turned so as to address the group at the table. "Agent Shores accompanied our film crew this morning during the rescue operation I told you about."

The NSF guy rolled his eyes. "Maybe if you weren't out playing detective and interacting with pseudo-environmental thugs, you'd be able to complete your contracted work on time."

Anastasia's face reddened. She thrust a finger at him. "Perhaps if you—"

Tara cut in. "Excuse me, ladies and gentlemen. I'm sorry to disrupt your meeting. Dr. Reed, I need your assistance immediately. This cannot wait."

Anastasia stood up, collecting the papers in front of her. "Gentlemen, this meeting is over. Please inform me of your decision in writing. Good day."

Anastasia's assistants shot each other bewildered looks that said, *I hope she knows what she's doing, or else we'll be looking for new jobs!*

Tara led Anastasia out into the hall. "I understand you have an office here. Can we speak there? I'd like to keep this matter private."

"Thanks for getting me out of the meeting, but what's this about?" Anastasia said, forcing a fake smile at Peter Young as he cautiously approached the conference room.

"I have reason to believe the whale's GPS coordinates will start broadcasting in the next few hours."

"How do you—"

Tara held up a hand. "Please. Your office?"

Anastasia nodded to several people who gave her curious looks coming out of the meeting. She looked back at Tara. "Lab. I have a lab. Let's go."

Tara couldn't see why Anastasia's lab was called a lab and not an office. There were no racks of glassware, microscopes, centrifuges, or any of the high-tech equipment Tara associated with research laboratories. Only computers. Lots of them. In rows along the lab benches. Several graduate students looked up from LCD displays as the lab's namesake entered with the federal agent.

A wooden door with a frosted glass window and a nameplate reading "Dr. A. Reed" led to a small office within the computer lab. Anastasia unlocked it and Tara followed her inside. One wall of the large inner-office contained the now-familiar racks of computer servers and related equipment. The other walls were lined with books. Two desks occupied the room—one with a PC and one dedicated to paperwork, cluttered with journal articles and various printouts. A few chairs were scattered about the room. Tara took one as Anastasia sat behind her desk.

"So what makes you think the GPS unit will broadcast again so soon?" Anastasia asked.

Tara told her about the Coast Guard e-mail she'd read in Trevor's office.

Anastasia shook her head. "Doesn't surprise me he would keep that a secret. He always wanted the tag for himself. Wanted to sell it to some third-world government where it would represent an overnight quantum leap in communications technology. Looks like he got what he deserved."

Tara tried not to appear taken aback by such a callous remark. "As you know, the web site for *Wired Kingdom* is still down," she said. "But if I'm not mistaken, your lab receives a direct GPS feed from the whale that does not depend on the web site, correct?"

Anastasia nodded. "Yes, it's like Trevor said. Here I get the data-logger feed, including GPS coordinates, but no video. So if what you say is true, we should have the whale's position as soon as the testing stops."

"Right. In about"—Tara consulted her watch—"two and a half hours."

"And what would you like to do until then?" Anastasia looked deep into Tara's eyes. Tara wondered if she was reading more into the question than she ought to be.

"I'd like to wait right here."

"That's an awfully long time. Hey, my dad's holding a charity lunch at the Beverly Hills Hotel. We could check that out for a little while and come back here."

"Thanks for the invitation but, first of all, believe me when I tell you I'm not dressed for it, and second, getting those coordinates is critical to my investigation. If it's okay with you, I'd like to just wait right here until I get them." *Make sure the data feed is physically secure.*

"Well, there might be something we can—"

The desk phone rang. The scientist clutched the phone as a panic-stricken voice trilled on the other end. Anastasia appeared concerned at once. She threw the phone onto the desk.

"You arrested my father?"

"Anastasia—"

"You arrested my father for murder! After I assisted you for the last two days with your invest-tigation. And then you have the nerve to come here asking for my help?" Her voice was steadily rising in tumultuous waves. Tara recognized that on the heels of the finance committee meeting stress was mounting for the scientist.

"Anastasia, listen."

"No, Special Agent Shores, you listen. I want you to get the hell out of my lab this instant."

"Dr. Reed, do not address me in that fashion. I—"

"I said get out! You have no—"

A soft knock came at the door, followed by footsteps padding quickly away. Tara guessed it was a student who had decided now would not be a good time to review the latest test material.

"Tell me what you know about your father's affair."

"You can forget about any help from me. Get out or I'm calling security."

"Do you think he's innocent?"

"I know he's innocent."

"Then the best thing you can do for him is to help me get that video from the whale. If there is any possibility of identifying a killer other than him, then you should be every bit as eager as I am to get at it."

Anastasia gently put the phone back in its cradle.

"Thank you. And no fooling around this time. I've got a Bureau underwater unit on standby to handle the extraction. All I need to do is feed them the coordinates."

"This kind of stress could kill him, you know."

"He'll be okay. I'm sure he's made bail by now."

"He has. . . ." She drifted off, pondering something.

"You okay?" Tara asked.

"Yeah. I'm sorry I blew up at you. I was just thinking how sad this is. I mean, not the murder—I know he didn't kill anyone—but the fact that he was cheating on my mother."

"You had no idea?"

"No. I mean . . . not this time. Years ago he

cheated. There was a time, right after I got my PhD, when I didn't speak with either of my parents, things were so bad."

"Why not talk with your mother?"

"I blamed her for driving him to it. For never being at home—always out shopping or on some cruise with her friends while he was at the studios making deals."

"So you weren't close?"

"We were always different people. Neither of my parents ever understood why I wanted to 'toil away in a lab,' as they put it," she said, waving an arm toward the book-and-computer-lined office. "Especially since they have a trust fund for me and reminded me that I didn't need to work such a demanding job. But I wanted to. It was the only thing that got me away from them—mentally, by forcing my mind to deal with academics, and physically, by spending a lot of time in the field on oceanographic cruises."

Tara nodded, sympathetic. She couldn't help but wonder if the success she'd had in her own career was the result of filling the void left when her parents' car had plunged into the canal in Florida so many years ago.

"So you stayed in school to avoid dealing with the reality that your parents had a less-than-perfect relationship."

Anastasia laughed. "To avoid dealing with the reality that they had a completely dysfunctional relationship. When I defended my dissertation, my mother was on a cruise in the Greek islands. Dad was in Palm Springs with some tart who was a backup dancer on one of his stupid shows. Neither of them even knew I'd completed my PhD until about a year later when I had started teaching here at USC."

"It seems like you're on better terms with them today. You work with them, in a way."

"Right. That's what brought us back together."

"*Wired Kingdom*?"

"Yeah. It allowed our two worlds to meet: my science and their Hollywood glitz."

Tara nodded. Anastasia gestured to a pot of coffee. She offered Tara a cup and the detective surprised herself by accepting. Usually she avoided anything offered to her while in the field. But the coffee smelled great, she was tired, and there wasn't much to do until the GPS came back online.

Then came another knock at the door. Anastasia glanced at the clock on the wall. "Office hours. I won't be able to hold them off any longer," she said smiling. Inwardly, Tara cringed as she recalled the conversation with the head of Anastasia's department. "There's a couple of hours left until the GPS is back," the professor continued. "You're welcome to wait here, if you don't mind hearing me explain the basics of marine population dynamics to aspiring biologists."

"Thanks, I think I will. I need to be the first one to see the coordinates when they become available."

Tara took a seat at one of Anastasia's desks and settled in to wait.

CHAPTER 36

33° 32′ 34.8″ N AND 119° 60′ 56.4″ W

"I know Fernando's voice when I hear it."

"I hope you are right," Héctor said to one of his new divers, without taking his eyes off the schooner. "We will know soon enough." Héctor was grateful his men had been rescued. But by whom? Had the authorities already been called? It bothered Héctor that he could not pigeonhole this nautical curiosity. Old yachts weren't typically used by any kind of law enforcement. And they were much too far from shore for day sailors; long-distance cruisers, maybe, but the black ship didn't look like something the yachtie set would be caught dead on. Well used, not pretty to look at . . . *almost looks like a pirate ship.* Héctor told himself to look on the bright side. *Two more able-bodied men to work with now.*

The seaplane settled lower in the water as it cut power a few yards from *Pandora's Box*. Héctor looked back at his men, fresh recruits from Mexico who were eager to earn the bonuses offered them. They were itching to get out of the hot plane and get to work.

The two divers were both about twenty-five years of age. They wore military-style buzz cuts. One complained of seasickness. After so long in the air, slogging along on the water like a small boat was anything but smooth.

"*Silencio,*" Héctor said as they taxied toward the schooner.

"But *señor,*" one of the men said as he strained to look through the plane's small windows at the schooner, "there is no room for two more people in here. What do we do if it is them?"

"*Sí,*" his associate said, wincing as his head struck the crate in the converted cargo space behind him.

The pilot cut the plane's engines. They bobbed and rolled and seesawed through the swells until they drew alongside the wooden ship. "Say nothing. Let me talk. Be ready to defend us if we are attacked," Héctor commanded.

ABOARD PANDORA'S BOX

Eric Stein watched as the pilot opened the seaplane door and waved to them. Stein could see that Juan and Fernando recognized their leader immediately. The two rescued divers shouted strings of hyper-fast Spanish toward the plane.

Stein couldn't make it out clearly. He could see, however, that the two passengers inside the plane made no move to show themselves. He warned

Pineapple to be alert. Piracy was rare in American waters, but not unheard of; they were fifty miles from land with only sail power to rely on.

If the divers they had rescued were planning on some kind of coordinated attack with those who had just arrived in the seaplane, they were good actors, Stein thought. Juan and Fernando had tears streaming down their cheeks as they bear-hugged one another. Stein thought he could make out, *He came back for us*!

Héctor's eyes swept across the people lining the schooner's deck. He looked at Juan and Fernando and made a questioning gesture. *Which one's in charge?* Fernando pointed at Eric Stein. "*El capitán,*" he replied.

Stein was inwardly pleased that the pilot—the leader of this potentially adversarial group—could not contain his surprise once he laid eyes on him. This shirtless, dread-locked gringo with blood-smeared skin and tattered shorts was the leader of the unusual vessel.

"Captain, we request your permission to board," Héctor said in English. Pineapple smiled at once. He knew it would please Stein to be formally asked in the traditional seafaring manner. It also put his mind a little more at ease, since most pirates did not ask permission to board, even as a ruse.

Stein nodded to a pair of young men standing by the tender vessel. "Splash it," he commanded.

Minutes later Héctor González stood on the rear

deck, embracing Juan and Fernando.

"*Amigos*," he began, "I am so sorry I had to leave you." He spoke in Spanish but his words were roughly conveyed by Stein to the group who had gathered to witness this curious reunion. "I had no choice. The authorities . . . I was counting on the good deeds of fine sailors such as these men." He swept an arm at the gathered crew of Ocean Liberation Front.

Juan said, "I knew you would come back for us, *jefe*. I knew it all along."

Applause broke out on deck as the men reconciled with one another. Then the three Mexicans huddled and conversed in muted tones.

Héctor, still wearing a John Deere ball cap with mirrored aviator sunglasses and a dirty T-shirt that proclaimed, "Does not play well with others," pointed to his plane. "Captain Stein, I believe you and I have something in common."

"What's that?" Stein replied, eyeballing the two shadowy figures still inside the floatplane.

Before Héctor could answer, a deckhand emerged from the cabin with two more twelve-packs of Tecate beer and said, "Secret stash!" Cheers as the cans were passed around.

After Héctor cracked his beverage, he addressed Stein, who had already sequestered a second beer. "*La ballena, amigo*. The whale."

"You're looking for the wired whale?"

"*Sí, señor*. For two days now." Stein couldn't believe what he was hearing. It was all out in the open now.

"So it was you who set the net trap that almost killed the whale today?"

"We did not mean to harm the animal, only to get the tag it carries. But we will do what we must."

Pineapple, who'd been listening in over Stein's shoulder, stepped forward. "Why do you want the tag so bad?"

Héctor looked at his divers, then back at Stein. "This, my friends, I cannot say. But our goals are compatible. You want the tag removed from the whale, yes?"

A roar from OLF's crew confirmed a response in the affirmative.

"So do we. The only difference is that—correct me if I am wrong—you would prefer for the whale to remain alive after the tag is retrieved."

"Of course!" one woman shouted.

But Stein shrugged. "It would be better if it lives, but if one whale's death is the price we have to pay to keep all other whales free, then that's the way it has to be."

Murmurs of agreement trickled through the gathering.

"So besides rescuing your divers, how is it that we can help you?" Pineapple asked.

"If you allow us to load our equipment onto your vessel, our plane will be much lighter and able to fly farther. I can perform aerial searches for the whale and hopefully direct you—with my men and special equipment on board—right to it."

Pineapple looked at Stein as if to say, *I told you so.* Stein frowned. “You could have murdered the girl in the video, for all we know,” he said.

“True, señor, although I assure you that we did not. But if you prefer, we can part ways at this time. We are forever in your debt as it is.” The two divers nodded solemnly toward the crew circled around them. Beyond the ship’s rails, a mild, almost imperceptible breeze started up, dimpling the water’s surface. “We would not blame you if that is your choice,” Héctor continued, “but if your goal is to locate the blue whale and remove its tag, then my men and I will be of invaluable assistance.” He looked at his watch. “But we must hurry.”

Pineapple addressed the crew gathered around them. “What do you think?” There were a few shouts of “Yeah!” and “Why not?” But there was also a chorus of boos.

“Dissension in the ranks,” Pineapple said to Stein. “So what’s it gonna be, Captain?”

All eyes were on Stein. The creaking of rigging and slapping of wavelets against the ship’s hull were the only sounds until Stein spoke. “I remember I had this girlfriend once, and her Dad was like fifty-five years old,” he began.

Héctor, unsure where Stein was going, wore a confused expression on his face, but he interpreted for Juan and Fernando. In the plane, the pair of newly arrived divers waited with diminishing patience. One stuck his head out a window, straining to hear what was happening on deck.

"He worked as a cop for thirty years or something. Anyway, one time I was at his house, and he was asking me what I was going to do with my life, what my plans were. This was after I had dropped out of college but before I started the Front. I told him I wasn't sure yet what I wanted to do.

"He didn't much like that, and he started calling me a bum and a loser not fit to take care of his daughter. I kept my cool though—didn't lose my temper with him or anything—and then he started talking about his morning routine to get ready for work and what a great sense of order it gave him.

"He told us that there were exactly thirty-seven things he had to do each morning in order to get himself off to work. Ordinary little things, like turn on the shower, shampoo, rinse, turn off the shower, dry off, get dressed, put his watch on, feed the cat, lock the door on the way out, start his car . . . stuff like that. But he knew the precise order of all thirty-seven of them. Ticked 'em all off like they were imprinted on his freakin' eyeballs or something."

"Some life," one of Stein's crew said.

Stein nodded. "I always thought it was sad. The guy died a couple years later of a heart attack. I couldn't help but think that somehow, those thirty-seven things were the most significant part of his life, and yet in the end they added up to nothing. I don't want that to be me."

A few rumblings of "No way" and "Hell no" made

their way around deck.

Stein pressed on. “I want to do something that matters. If I die young, then so be it, but I want to leave this world knowing that I died trying. That was why I started OLF. To make a difference in how people perceive the importance of the environment—at any cost.”

Héctor nodded at Stein, as if to confirm the veracity of his story, but he needed no lectures on what was most precious in life. For him, such significance took the form of his Rosa and her tenuous hold on existence that pervaded every moment of his being. The gringo was concerned only about himself, Héctor thought, and how important he was considered to be by others. It was a kind of selfishness that, for the pilot, had died along with the birth of his daughter.

Héctor nodded at the short-haired diver who had eased up to the schooner in the launch boat. The new diver waved amicably. A large wooden crate towered above him in the launch. The other man still waited in the plane. Juan and Fernando helped their new associate to load the crate onto the schooner's stern deck. Héctor caught a crowbar thrown by his man in the skiff and approached the crate.

“You might just get your chance to make history, *amigo*,” he said to Stein, wrenching the lid off the unmarked crate. All eyes were on him now as crew and divers alike gathered to have a look.

Next, Héctor pulled away some plastic sheeting from some kind of metal tower. Stein and Pineapple continued to stare at the strange-looking apparatus, walking around it in a slow circle, taking it in from every angle as the remaining sides of the crate were pulled away. They could see it was some kind of weapon. Almost six feet high and mounted on a swiveling turret, the cannon was painted a drab shade of olive.

"What the hell is that?" someone inquired.

"Anti-aircraft?"

"A LAW—Light Anti-tank Weapon?"

The seaplane pilot chuckled as his new recruits continued to fuss over their package.

"Have you not been to other parts of the world where commercialized whaling is still legal?"

Stein felt incapacitated just looking at the weapon as the Antarctic memories it triggered came flooding back. "It's a harpoon gun," he said, softly at first. He repeated it, louder. "Grenade-tipped, probably ninety-nine-pound grenades, right?"

"I see you know this weapon, *Capitán*," Héctor said, surprised. "You have used one before?"

Stein shook his head. "No. Had them used against me. It's a modern-day commercial whaling harpoon gun. Not easy to come by in the West. Japan uses them . . . Norway, Iceland, Russia. How did you get it?"

"eBay," the pilot said, cracking a smile.

Stein raised his eyebrows.

Héctor remained impassive, then pointed to the bow of Stein's ship. "With your permission, Captain, I would like to mount it."

Stein nodded. "Let's do it."

"Hey!" It was Stein's girlfriend, the one he'd just caught in the bathroom with the long-haired guy. "Eric," she began sternly, "we've always been about protecting whales. Now you want us to shoot them? What the hell?"

"We're only going to shoot one whale, and that only if we have to. But if we want to show the world that this invasive tracking technology is unacceptable, then this is the way to do it."

"It's going too far," someone else said. "People won't understand why we had to kill an endangered species."

"Think about it," Stein said. "Every part of our lives are on computers now. There is nothing governments or corporations don't know about each and every one of you. Your online banking, credit history, taxes, shopping, web surfing, searches, e-mails—they know frickin' *everything* there is to know about you. Even the companies who babble on about their privacy policies and how they never sell any data—sooner or later the government will subpoena them and make them turn the data over."

"So?" Stein's girl asked.

"*So*? So, the citizens of this country are being *tracked*, just like this whale is being tracked. A digital leash. Only difference is the whale doesn't deserve it, and it's still early enough in the game to do something about it. So we're either going to set it free, or sacrifice it to prevent the enslavement of more innocent animals."

No one said anything.

Héctor nodded and his men gathered around the harpoon gun.

CHAPTER 37

33° 20' 40.0" N AND 118° 26' 41.0" W

The Blue stopped swimming for the first time in hours, coming to rest on a green sea surface. She was in different water now. Shallower and more devoid of life than the nutrient-rich deepwater channels she favored when not being chased about, it even tasted unusual. She heard the sound of boat engines more frequently now.

After taking in several deep breaths, she swam again.

DEPARTMENT OF BIOLOGICAL SCIENCES, USC

The second the clock struck five, Tara followed Anastasia out of her office and into the main lab. There were two students working there, but Anastasia asked them to leave. Then she went to a computer terminal displaying an old DOS-style interface. A cursor blinked next to the green letters, MS ANASTASIA

REED. The program's namesake entered her login credentials.

"This is my telemetry program. I had a big breakthrough with it when the journal article came out last year. It stands for Marine Science Animal Network—"

"And Satellite Telemetry-ASsisted Information Archives of Real-time Environmental and Ecological Data," Tara finished for her.

"Wow. How did you know that?"

"What else could it stand for?" Tara joked. "Trevor told me about it when I went to get a copy of the murder tape."

"Okay. Well, this is where I get the telemetry stream," Anastasia explained. "If the GPS transponder is working, we'll see the coordinates right . . ."—she tapped some keys—"here." Anastasia stepped away from the display to give Tara a clear view and waited.

"It's working!" Anastasia said. "These coordinates are different. That should be where the Blue is right now."

Tara reached for her cell phone as her gaze fell upon the critical numbers on the screen: 33° 21' 83.0" N and 118° 12' 42.1" W.

"Where is that?" Tara wondered aloud.

"I'm looking," Anastasia replied, already digging for a marine chart under the piles of notebooks and technical handbooks that swarmed the lab bench.

"Got it."

She cleared a space on the bench and unfolded a chart, laying it out flat. A concerned look occupied her features. "Oh, geez. I thought those numbers looked familiar," she exclaimed.

"Why?"

"This is not good," she said, shaking her head.

"*What* is not good?" Tara was itching to call Branson with the coordinates. Her thumb rested on her phone's keypad.

"Let me double-check this," Anastasia said, going back to the chart. She turned back to the screen once more, refreshed the coordinates, then went back to the chart on the bench. "It's right," she muttered, almost to herself.

"Dr. Reed, please tell me where the hell the whale is!"

The scientist got up from the chart and turned to face Tara. "Sorry, I'm being a tease. It's uncharacteristic for such a large rorqual during this time of year, but she's not far from Avalon Harbor, Catalina Island."

Like everyone who lived in Southern California, Tara had heard of Catalina: the popular summer spot with a cute little town, though Tara had never been there herself.

"That's pretty far away from where we last saw her, isn't it?"

Anastasia refreshed the coordinates again. "That kind of daily travel distance is at the upper limit of what *Balaenoptera musculus* can do, but it's not unheard of."

"Let's hope she'll be tired from all that swimming and the underwater team can get to her."

"Underwater team?"

"Special FBI unit on standby waiting for the coordinates. Excuse me while I make a call."

Tara speed-dialed her cell. Branson answered immediately. "Talk to me, Agent Shores." His booming voice was clearly audible in the room even though he wasn't on speakerphone.

"Sir, the whale's GPS data is transmitting again."

"Excellent. What's its location?"

"The Avalon end of Catalina Island."

"Are you serious? Catalina?"

"Yes, sir. How soon can the underwater unit be there? Are they ready?"

Branson nearly snorted into the phone. "Trust me when I say they're ready. They should be there within the hour. And Shores, you should see some of the equipment they've got—they've got one of those—" Tara heard a male voice interrupting. "Okay, it's show time, Shores."

"Let me read you the coordinates."

"Go ahead."

Tara looked at Anastasia and nodded at the computer monitor. "Refresh. . . . Please." She wanted Branson to be able to give the underwater team the latest available data. Tara knew the researcher might be miffed at having a simple command barked to her, but Tara was here to work, Anastasia to cooperate in hopes of freeing her father. Thankfully, Anastasia complied. Tara relayed the numbers to Branson.

"Got it. Good work, Shores."

"Thank you, sir."

"Now listen to me. I need you to continue to feed us the coordinates, say, every fifteen minutes, or if this big-ass fish starts to move. Understood?"

Tara tried to avoid looking disappointed in front of Anastasia. "Understood."

"Let's get this thing done."

"Yes, sir."

Branson clicked off.

A phone rang from the adjoining office. The renowned researcher trotted out of the lab to pick it up.

"Yeah," Tara heard. "You're kidding. Already? . . . No, I certainly wasn't expecting it. . . . Let me check. . . ." Tara heard her clack away on the keyboard. And then, "Yes! How did you do that? . . . Well I hope you only use those powers for good, Anthony! . . . No, thank *you.*"

Tara walked into the office as Anastasia put the phone down, in time to see the *Wired Kingdom* site with the whale's video feed playing. "Is that real-time?" she asked.

Anastasia whirled around in her chair. "Sorry, detective, I didn't know you were off the phone."

"Is that the Blue, off Catalina right now?" Tara squinted at the GPS numbers in the lower left corner of the screen. But it was the video that commanded Tara's attention. Shifting rays of light pierced the opaline water, playing over what they could see of the Blue's sun-dappled body. A beautiful, tranquil scene, though they could see that the water was not as clear as it had been farther north, with the exception of the seamount. On screen, the whale's expansive melon faded into cloudy obscurity, whereas in the previous days' video the outline of her entire body was crisply defined against the openness of the crystal-clear sea.

"Yes, that's her. I can't believe it, but one of our producers got the commercial site back up already. I have to tell my Dad."

Tara could see Anastasia starting to become uncomfortable. The scientist stared off into space.

"Hold on," Tara said, wanting to bring her back. "So it's not just back up for you, everybody can see this?" Tara knew that the divers she'd seen would likely be monitoring the web site as well, waiting like pirates with a treasure map for it to come back online.

"Exactly!" Anastasia replied, perking up at the thought of it.

Tara contemplated this. With the telemetry unit broadcasting its position to the world, it wouldn't be long before the Blue was surrounded by curious boaters.

Anastasia threw open a metal storage locker and pulled out a waterproof dry bag.

"What are you doing?"

"Going sailing."

"To the Blue?"

"No, to Hawaii. Yes, to the Blue! I've got to see

what happens to my girl."

You mean you've got to see what happens to your million-dollar tracking instrument and to the ratings of your show after you appear live on the scene.

"You wanna go?" Anastasia asked without looking up from zipping her bag. Tara, transfixed by the Blue's greenish surroundings, said nothing.

"It'll just be you and I. No cameras. No crew."

"Without the crew?"

"My personal sailboat. C'mon, it'll be fun. And you'll be on site to monitor things."

Tara shook her head. "I can't."

"Why not?"

"I told the field office I'd stay here to feed them the coordinates."

"The web site is live now. I've got a laptop with a wireless connection that'll work the whole way over there. You'll always know the coordinates, and you'll be able to see what the whale sees."

Tara thought about what happened the last time she trusted someone to lead her to sea with a laptop. "I agreed to stay here."

"No, what he actually said was, 'I need you to continue to feed us the coordinates,' to which you replied, 'I understand.' You never said you'd stay here."

Tara watched the Blue on screen. She was moving, diving deeper into an emerald cathedral, the greenest water Tara had ever seen.

"Well, are you coming, or what?"

CHAPTER 38

AVALON, CATALINA ISLAND

Fifteen minutes after the Blue's webcast began, a line of boats formed at both of the picturesque harbor's fuel docks. She was close and getting closer, came the word from Avalon's many watering holes where the televisions ran the news channels after the owner of the town's only Internet café had put out the word.

For many it seemed like just another island day. At the end of the town's pier, passengers boarded a glass-bottom boat for a tour of the nearby kelp forests, where towering columns of giant brown algae, the fastest-growing plant in the world, stretched from the seafloor to the surface. At the other end of Avalon Bay, scuba divers entered the water in front of the Casino Point ballroom, many as part of classes to obtain their certification.

Inside The Pelican's Nest, Ernie Hollister lit up a Camel as he flapped an arm in an attempt to quiet the clientele. Somebody cut the volume on the jukebox, and Jimmy Buffet faded to the background.

"Hey, hey, hey," Ernie began. "I just was over at the Internet café and they're all taking about how the wired whale–you know the big Blue they have that TV show about–well that whale is here, right now, right off Avalon."

The television over the bar was tuned to a baseball game.

"So, you wanna drink to the whale, Ernie?" somebody wisecracked.

"I wanna take my boat out for whale watch tours," Ernie said, "but I need a first mate. And maybe someone to help with the customers. Collect money, show 'em on board, that kind of thing."

There was nothing but stunned silence.

"Your boat working, Ernie?" Bill the bartender asked.

"Been working on her all day. Needs a little tweaking, but she'll do. All we gotta do is take some looky-loo's just outside the harbor to take a gander at this whale."

"Ya gotta bring 'em back, too, Ernie," somebody pointed out to rowdy guffaws.

"Hey, I'm serious," Ernie continued. "There's thousands of people walkin' around out there right now. All the big boats are in for the day. I say we offer whale watch trips for forty bucks a head. We can probably fit ten on my boat, that's . . ." He struggled with the calculation.

"Four hundred bucks, Ernie," Bill finished for him.

"Four hundred, for a piddly-ass little boat ride! Maybe we can squeeze in three or four trips. Set a time limit. Since we can track this whale on the computer, we can keep making runs as long as it sticks around."

"Four hundred ought to just about cover your bar tab and the damage your cart did to my door," Bill said, cocking his head toward the entrance. At this there was much cackling but also a few boat captains who nodded, beginning to see Ernie's logic—except for one small problem.

"Ernie, your boat's not ready." This from submarine pilot Walt Johnson, making a semi-rare appearance at The Nest. While he was known to stop in for a brew or two now and then, he was not a permanent fixture like the majority of its patrons.

They all knew that Ernie, back in the day when The Pelican's Nest logo on his cap was still legible, had run a small charter fishing operation. In his pleasantly inebriated state, Ernie saw the wired whale as his way to get back into the fishing business.

Ernie spun clumsily on one heel and faced the bar. "That's it, Walt! The sub! Let's take tourists out to see this whale from the damn sub!"

Walter set his beer mug down on the bar and turned around. "Sub's in for the day, Ernie."

"You know how much we can charge to take people to that whale in the *sub*? Probably five times more than a boat."

"She's done for today, Ernie. Her batteries aren't

even fully charged yet, plus my regular crew is leaving right now for the Bahamas to train their local guys on how to run a new submersible operation there," he added, looking at his dive watch.

"I know, Ted told me when he towed me in. I'll be your crew. Weather's good. This is a special occasion. The whole point of a submarine is to explore the underwater world, right?"

Walter nodded, discarding some peanut shells on the floor.

Ernie went on. "So here's a blue whale sitting within easy cruising range. Imagine the publicity your operation will get after a bunch of super-happy people get off your sub and talk about how they saw that whale underwater."

A few of the other patrons nodded in agreement.

The bartender said, "That would be something if you got close enough to the whale in that sub, and the folks out on the Internet could see the people inside the sub wavin' at 'em."

Walter stared into the depths of his beer for a moment, reflecting. He *was* more than an underwater bus driver, wasn't he? He knew he wasn't getting any younger, and the scenario—or anything *close* to it, like the one Bill had just outlined—would mean a lot of bragging rights, even to Walter Johnson. He looked up from his glass.

"Well, after today I know your boat needs some work, Ernie, and the last thing I want to see is you trying to take it out before it's ready. And I would like to help you get back on your feet again. So, okay, I'll do it. But I get half of the take," he declared. "*And* you stop drinking—right now."

Returning from his first sortie away from *Pandora's Box,* during which he had seen no indications of the Blue, Héctor González splashed the floatplane down beside the old black schooner. She was a warship now, the explosive-tipped harpoon gun riding menacingly atop her prow, but it was a change of a different kind that commanded his attention. As he taxied up to the ship and cut his engines, he could see that something had happened while he was in the air.

A crowd was gathered around a young woman cradling a notebook computer. Eric Stein was gesturing wildly. Héctor tossed a line to a deckhand on OLF's boat. When the plane drew near enough, he jumped aboard.

"We've got the coordinates!" Stein shouted at the pilot as soon as he boarded.

"And so does everyone else," Pineapple said. "We need to hurry."

Stein explained to Héctor that the Blue's GPS and web feed had come back online at the same time, and that the whale was now just off Catalina.

"Not good," the pilot said. "For the plane, it is not very far from here, but there will be many people."

The girl with the computer nodded. "I already saw two boats," she confirmed.

"Get your divers over there. We'll be right behind

you with the big gun," Pineapple said.

"Whale ho!" Stein shouted, pointing the way to the island.

Pineapple rolled his eyes. He knew Stein was acting out his fantasy of being a sea captain in days gone by, when killing whales rather than studying them was a way of life. Stein's enthusiasm was contagious, however, and the ship became energized as everyone scrambled to do their part. Héctor ordered his two newest divers back into the plane to make the trip with him. Juan and Fernando would remain on the schooner.

Its spotter plane airborne, the first operational whaling vessel to ply American waters in decades set its sails for Catalina Island.

CHAPTER 39

MARINA DEL REY

Driving into Marina del Rey again did little to calm Tara's nerves. To take her mind off it as she followed Anastasia's Range Rover in her Crown Vic, she placed a cell call to the Imaging lab.

Herb Shock's enthusiastic voice answered. Without being asked, he started to tell her about some state-of-the-art equipment he'd be getting next month.

"Listen, Herb, I can't talk long now, I'm about to board a boat. I want to know if you turned anything up on the audio track analysis of the murder video."

"Short answer: no. But we did isolate an unusual signal—non-vocal—that's being processed now for ID."

"How long?"

"Too early to tell, but aside from myself and the technicians doing the work, you'll be the first to know."

Tara thanked him and killed the call, watching as Anastasia parked a few stalls ahead. The marine biologist stepped out of her truck, waving for Tara to take the adjacent spot.

"My boat's right over here," Anastasia said, pointing at a nearby dock whose slips were occupied by small- to medium-sized sailboats.

Tara parked and exited her car.

She gazed at the row of boats but found it impossible not to stare through their bobbing masts out to the water beyond; water which had claimed her parents, and which now seemed all too eager to claim her, too. She reminded herself that she didn't have to go. She had fulfilled her obligation to the case by providing the whale's coordinates to Branson's team. But there was a part of her that knew she had to go, that if she didn't, she would always be a prisoner.

"Come on, Detective." Anastasia hopped aboard a white sailboat. The vessel was neat, but obviously well-used, unlike some boats in the marina, which were in pristine condition because they were never taken out. "Watch your step coming aboard. Welcome to my ketch."

Tara stepped gingerly aboard. The instant both of her feet were set on deck, she realized that she'd forgotten her scopolamine patches. Again. "I know a ketch is a kind of sailboat," Tara said, deliberately diverting her thoughts from the fact that another bout of seasickness was likely in her near future, "but what is it, exactly?"

Anastasia pulled a canvas cover off of a winch and made some adjustments to a line as she answered. "A ketch is a sailboat that has two masts, with the one in the rear, called the mizzen, shorter than the forward mainmast."

"So most sailboats only have one mast?"

"Most smaller ones do. Like the one right there." Anastasia nodded toward a boat a few slips away where four middle-aged men were preparing to sail while they passed each other beers from a cooler and fiddled with the radio.

Tara gave the boat a quick appraisal. She recognized that the men aboard were weekend warrior types. Their boat was considerably smaller than Anastasia's but even with four of them aboard, they still looked like they wouldn't be ready to sail anytime soon.

"How long is this boat?" Tara asked, watching Anastasia undo a line from a cleat without even looking at it while her eyes focused on a radar ball atop the mainmast.

"Forty-two feet. I think we're ready." The marine biologist pulled a small remote from her pocket and clicked it. An electric trolling motor fell into position up on the bow.

"Well isn't that fancy," one of the men on the neighbor boat said.

"Look at that, she's outta here before we even got a sail ready," another replied. "We need to make a run to the chandlery to pick up another line."

Anastasia waved to the men. "Have fun shopping, boys. We're going sailing." As Anastasia led her boat out into the main channel, the would-be sailors had a good laugh at the name printed on the transom as she motored away.

Ketch Me If You Can.

33° 22' 73.2" N AND 118° 13' 45.0" W

The Blue was 175 feet down, rubbing her back against a rock outcropping to scrape the barnacles from her thick hide. Even at this depth, the animal had no trouble hearing boat motors buzzing overhead. She had been here for thirty minutes, and in that time a throng of boats had gathered at the site of her last GPS reading. She would not transmit another GPS data point until she surfaced again. Until then, the boaters circled aimlessly, wondering where the celebrated beast had gone.

After a final scouring of her miniscule hitchhikers, the Blue made her way to the surface in a lazy spiral. Entering the world of air, she exhaled a geyser of mist which announced her position to the boaters. "Blow, eleven o'clock!" Boats maneuvered around one another in order to best see the famed creature.

Those on the water were so intent watching the Blue that they failed to notice a C-130 Hercules cargo plane approaching from the east. Passing low over the water, the huge aircraft lumbered directly toward the Blue. As it flew over the boats that now formed an almost complete circle around the wired whale, the letters "FBI" stenciled on the plane's fuselage were clearly visible.

While people craned their necks to look at the aerial intruder, the giant plane dropped even lower. Flying only feet above the water, the C-130's cargo bay doors opened and a stunned crowd of boaters watched in disbelief as the aircraft disgorged a speedboat.

The sixteen-foot craft fell from the plane's rear doors and hit the water with a splash about two hundred feet from the circle of marine onlookers. Remarkably, the boat landed on an even keel. Bristling with antennae, radomes, and other apparatus not readily identifiable to the average recreational boater, there was something odd about the dropped vessel.

This feeling was confirmed when a male voice issued from loudspeakers atop the boat's antenna mast. "Attention boaters: This craft is an unmanned surface vehicle operated by the Federal Bureau of Investigation. The whale and its tracking equipment are part of a federal investigation. All persons found to be interfering with this investigation will be charged with obstruction of justice and prosecuted to the fullest extent of the law. All boats and persons are ordered to stay at least one hundred yards away from the whale at all times. . . ." The message repeated in a loop.

The boaters realized that with such sophisticated equipment in use, the FBI meant business. In fact, the drone, or Autonomous Surface Vehicle (ASV), represented counter-terrorism technology developed in the wake of 9/11. A few of the spectators began to depart.

Overhead, the cargo plane circled back toward the Blue.

MARINA DEL REY

With sails tight as drum heads, Anastasia's ketch flew across the channel, passing several larger sailboats on the way to the popular island. To Tara, watching the Blue's feed on a wireless netbook connection, it wasn't fast enough.

She placed a call to Branson. "You have a boat on the Blue?"

"We have an unmanned drone boat on site, and guys in the air."

"What good's the drone?"

"It lets us stay with the whale even though we're not there, give warnings to anyone approaching it, and it's taking video."

"How are—"

"We've got a high-speed inflatable boat en route now. Should be there in about fifteen minutes. Dive team's on that." Tara couldn't suppress a twinge of disappointment. After all she'd been through for the case, she probably wasn't even going to be there when the whale's video was recovered.

"Where are you, Shores?" Branson asked, breaking the silence. "What do I hear in the background?"

"Those are sails, sir. I'm about halfway there in a sailboat piloted by Dr. Reed."

"Shores, you were supposed to be maintaining watch at Dr. Reed's data feed."

"What you told me, sir, was to keep you informed

of the whale's coordinates. I've done that—am doing that. When the web site came back online with working GPS, there was no longer any reason for me to remain in Dr. Reed's lab, since I knew you'd be made aware of that."

"Listen, Shores, I appreciate your effort—we all do—but now I need you to let the team do its work out there."

"Of course, sir. But I thought it wouldn't hurt for me to be on site with an expert marine mammalogist on standby."

"Okay, Shores. Just stay clear of the whale. You've had enough action in the last two days."

"Yes, sir."

Tara ended the call and stood up in the small but nicely appointed cabin. Standing, she found she had a couple inches of headroom. The walls and furniture of the compartment were blonde tropical hardwood. Framed posters like "Whales of the Pacific," a map of Baja California, and "Creatures of the Kelp Forest" adorned the walls. A smaller framed print above the miniature stove showed Anastasia as a child with her parents. She was at the wheel of a sailboat, her father, George, with his arm around her, pointing at something unseen out on the water.

Tara exited the cabin and stepped out on deck, where Anastasia minded the helm. "So you've been sailing for some time?"

"Yeah, my father started teaching me when I was

eight. I bought this ketch as a present to myself when I got my first professorship. It's great for quick get-aways. You should come with me up to Santa Barbara one weekend."

"Look, Dr. Reed, there's something I need to get straight with you." She didn't know how to put it delicately. "I am not lesbian, or bisexual. My interest in you is strictly professional as it relates to this case."

Anastasia smiled. "Relax. I won't bite. You're not married. I don't see a ring on your finger. You have a boyfriend? Are you seeing anyone at all?"

"Not at the moment, no. I've been caught up with my work lately. I'm sure you understand."

"Yes, but I've found that people make time for what's really important. At our age, most women are involved with someone."

"Well I'm not, okay?"

"Detective, correct me if I'm wrong, but it seems as though you're harboring some kind of stereotypical resentment against lesbians."

Tara shrugged. "What happens between consenting adults is their business. It's what happens among non-consenting adults that usually becomes mine."

Anastasia nodded while she scanned the seas ahead of them.

"How much longer?" Tara asked, wanting to reiterate her all-business persona. A faint, mountainous outline was visible to the west.

"About an hour. How's the Blue?"

“Being circled by a robot boat sent to keep an eye on her until the dive team arrives.”

“Robot boat?”

“Yeah. Dropped from a cargo plane. Autonomous, but can also be controlled from a plane or boat, like a life-size radio-controlled toy.”

“Sounds like you’ve got a lot of resources on this murder case. With all the hype surrounding the show, how did you manage to convince them it was real?”

Tara’s respect for Anastasia crept up a notch. At least she recognized a key investigative difficulty surrounding the case. “It wasn’t easy, but after those divers were seen on camera, it was obvious that the video was extremely important to somebody.”

“And now you think that somebody is my father.”

Confident the gesture wouldn’t be misinterpreted, Tara put a hand on the boat captain’s shoulder. “Anastasia, he admitted to being involved with the victim. So he had a motive. Any law enforcement officer would have brought him in for questioning.”

“How’s being involved with someone in and of itself a motive?”

“He was having an affair. Sometimes in affairs both partners are not in agreement about a breakup. People act on emotions without thinking. I see it all the time.”

“And so that’s it? Because he had an affair he gets prosecuted for murder?”

“He’s not being prosecuted for murder, at this point. There were other factors.”

"Such as?"

"He owns a large boat, the *Prime Time*, capable of making the trip to where the murder occurred, so he had the means. Motive and means. We're looking into his opportunity now. Apparently your mother says he was home at the time of the murder, so he does appear to have an alibi. But we're going to get the video, and if it shows conclusively that it wasn't him, he'll be vindicated."

Anastasia fell silent, her glum expression fixed on the outline of Catalina looming ever closer ahead of them.

CHAPTER 40

OFF THE CATALINA ISLAND COAST

Héctor approached the Blue's coordinates, which were fed to him by his man in the back seat with a satellite-linked notebook computer. The precision that the GPS afforded was unneeded, however, since the ring of boats now visible around the whale gave away its position.

"Ready," he announced. The two divers prepared their gear. In addition to their full-face masks and underwater communications equipment, each man carried a snub-nosed speargun and multiple knives strapped to various places on their gear.

Héctor raised *Pandora's Box* over a secure marine channel.

"PB here," Eric Stein's voice came back.

"PB this is Seahawk. We have reached the target. Now preparing two divers for entry. What is your position and velocity? Over."

Stein relayed his position, speed, and heading.

"You're making better than expected time."

"We found a way to mount the outboard from our tender vessel. We should be there in thirty minutes. Get your divers in the water. We'll see how things look when we get there. *Buena suerte.*"

"Good luck to you, too, my American friend," the pilot said. And he meant it more than he knew Stein would ever believe. He signed off, and his satellite-phone rang just as he spotted the Blue's surface activity on the water. He noticed one boat in particular circling tight around their quarry. He turned around and faced his divers.

"It is time to go." The divers gave him the OK sign.

Héctor answered his sat-phone.

"Hello—hold on, please," he said into the mouth-piece without listening.

He wanted to take the call—it might be his client—but right now he needed to focus on bringing his plane in for a smooth landing. He needed to be far enough away from the crowd of boats so as to have sufficient open space to land, but not so far that his divers would have a time-, air- and energy-consuming swim to reach the Blue.

Héctor didn't know what to do about the closely circling boat; that would be his divers' problem. But the cargo plane he now saw plodding into view ahead was definitely his concern.

Into the phone, he spat, "One moment, please," before guiding his plane down for a landing.

The plane up ahead had distracted him, and he landed at a higher than usual speed. The seaplane bounced once, then dug a wingtip in the water, which wrenched it onto a new course, sending it skipping directly toward the Blue—and the assemblage of boats.

His men shrieked at him to turn. Héctor leaned on the steering column and gave it full rudder. And for a moment Héctor thought the plane would surely flip. A vision of his daughter lying in the hospital bed passed before him. But soon the aircraft settled into a familiar rhythm and he knew the landing would be only a near-disaster, not an actual one.

When the engines fell to an idle, however, the sound of angry voices told him he'd come much too close to the boats.

"Idiot!"

"What're you doing!"

"Trying to kill somebody?"

Héctor looked to the two-o'clock position from his windshield and saw the Blue roll over and raise an immense pectoral fin as if in greeting. Sheets of water cascaded down the outstretched appendage.

One of his divers opened the rear door facing the whale.

"Go, go, go!" Héctor commanded.

The scuba men hit the water just as the drone boat completed another oval circuit around the whale and headed for the plane.

The pilot threaded his way between two cabin cruisers, seeking open water. After a wobbly taxi and a false start, where he almost clipped the tuna tower of a large sportfisher, he was airborne once more. Merely being in the air wasn't enough to escape his problems, however.

Héctor remembered the satellite-phone and snatched it up. "*Bueno*," he said, doing his best to sound to his boss as though everything was under perfect control. He was greeted instead by the sound of his wife's sobbing. Before she uttered a coherent syllable, he knew. It was a moment he had hoped would never come, but had been half-expecting for a long time.

He asked her to slow down and tell him. His daughter. In the hospital. Pronounced dead an hour ago.

"Rosa," Héctor whispered, crossing himself. The sky seemed to dissolve around his plane. Nothing made any sense. For several seconds, the plane was functionally pilotless. A frenzy of hysterical radio chatter brought him back enough to address his wife. He told her he loved her and that he was on his way home. There was nothing here for him anymore. The money had lost its significance. He needed nothing—he had nothing—except his wife and the simple life they had once lived.

Héctor felt little loyalty toward his men. They were nameless, unknown to him before their current mission. He and his wife would quickly and quietly relocate to mainland Mexico, where they could live out their lives in peace. Besides, the pilot rationalized as he set a course due south, the *loco* environmental gringos would be arriving soon in their sailboat with the rest of his men. They would pick up the divers.

These new thoughts coursing through Héctor's mind now guided him just as the instruments on the dash guided the plane. The only thing standing in the way of these best-laid plans was a C-130 Hercules cargo plane bearing down on his single-engine Cessna. Héctor ended the satellite call with his wife and concentrated on the stream of irate chatter that continued to burst forth from his radio.

The FBI co-pilot in the cockpit of the Hercules identified himself yet again to the seaplane.

The fleeing pilot said nothing. Héctor was now running, running from everything—from the men he'd hired to do a job for him, from his boss, from the American FBI and, he supposed, from the death of his only child. Then his mind wandered back to that moonlit rocky beach on Santa Rosa Island to the north. He heard his feet crunching on the gravelly sand as he made his way to the foliage-shrouded plane. Inside, Guillermo lay dying as his hands snuffed the life from his body. *Your share of the money will go to your family. They will be taken care of for the rest of their lives. I promise you, I promise you that*, he had said.

This was the only thing which gave him pause. Would he be able to live with himself after not delivering on a promise made to a man he had killed?

He wasn't sure.

Momentarily Héctor considered suicide, kamikaze style. He cackled as he imagined pointing the nose of his plane straight down and barreling full speed into the Blue's back. Obliterating the tracking device would be satisfactory to his boss, allowing him to accomplish a last mission, a last piece of work in his life that was useful to someone. But then he thought of his wife, so utterly alone right now, waiting for him to return home.

He had just steeled his resolve to fly back to Baja when the FBI plane buzzed him, close. His only consolation was the fact that they probably wouldn't want to shoot him down over such a crowded coastal area.

"Cessna seaplane, there is an airport on Catalina. Approach 127.4 at altitude 1,500 feet. We are ordering you to land there, now. Repeat . . ."

Catalina's Airport in the Sky was an asphalt landing strip with a restaurant, souvenir shop, and taxi service. Occupying a grassy plateau atop Catalina's highest point, it was the only place for planes to land on the island.

Héctor struggled with the decision to land and be detained, or continue flying south and hope they didn't shoot him down. He was nearing a panic state. He felt the way he thought drivers attempting to run from police cars felt as they drove and drove, unsure of what to do next, but also not ready to stop and confront the consequences of their actions.

AVALON PLEASURE PIER,
CATALINA ISLAND

The submarine *Deep* *View* was taking on a full load

of paying passengers at the end of the Avalon Pleasure Pier. Ernie collected hefty cash-only payments for what the sub's captain, Walter Johnson, described as an "off-the-books specialty dive," meaning that his business partners who had invested in the sub would not have to know about it unless it was a success. To the passengers, the ride had been billed as an underwater whale watch.

Ernie had no trouble raising sufficient interest. Shortly after his talk with Walter in The Pelican's Nest, he'd run home to shave, gargle mouthwash, and put on a mostly clean T-shirt. Then he had raced his battered and hastily repaired golf cart down to the waterfront where he began soliciting vacationers for submarine rides to see the wired whale. *Yes, that's right, my island friends, the adventure of a lifetime leaving right now!*

Enjoying an eight-beer buzz, his gregarious demeanor aided his rapport with potential customers. In fact, the sub was presently at its licensed maximum passenger capacity of sixty-four, with a long line of eager tourists still clamoring to be let aboard.

Walter, who had been readying the sub in its control cabin below, stuck his head up through the crew's entrance at the bow of the craft. Normally the sub carried a crew of four—pilot, co-pilot, and two cabin crew. For this trip, however, it was only Walter and Ernie, the latter of whom had never even been in the sub, much less worked on it. With Walter's regular crew abroad, they were short on time to get a full crew ready, yet wanted to maximize profits.

Walter scrambled up on deck and trotted over to Ernie. “We’re full down there, buddy. We’ve got to turn the rest away for this trip.”

Ernie looked at the long line of families and couples stretching down the pier, seeing lost opportunity. “Aye aye, Captain. Go ahead and start her, I’ll get the lines and the hatch.”

Walter leaned in closer to make sure no one else would hear. “You sure you know how to close the hatch, Ernie? You remember how I showed you on the diagram? Make sure it’s—”

“I remember. Don’t worry.”

Walter gave Ernie a hard stare, then smiled as he looked up at the waiting passengers. He could hear excited talk emanating from the main cabin. Those already on board were catching their first glimpses of marine life as bright orange Garibaldi—California’s state marine fish—darted past the portholes and around the pier pilings.

“Okay, Ernie, let’s rock and roll.”

Ernie gave Walter a thumbs-up and watched him until he had retreated back down into the control cabin. Then he turned back to the waiting line. “Folks, we’re about full at this point, but we do have standing-room-only space available, at a reduced ticket price, of course. If you’re interested, the first twenty with the money get the spots.”

There was a minor stampede as those who didn’t

understand what it would actually be like to stand for an hour in an understaffed, overcrowded metal tube stepped forward. Ernie let twenty more people on before informing those remaining that they may be able to make the second trip, provided the wired whale was kind enough to stick around.

Then he clamped down the hatch as he had been instructed, hopped up onto the pier to undo first the stern and then the bow lines, and finally descended the bow ladder into the control cabin. Though Ernie had just closed the main cabin hatch, Walter insisted on securing the control cabin's hatch himself.

After asking Ernie four times if he'd closed the other hatch correctly, Walter activated the sub's thrusters.

CHAPTER 41

OFF THE CATALINA ISLAND COAST

With the excitement of a seaplane plowing through their midst, most people on the boats failed to notice the two divers now surface-swimming toward the Blue. As the divers prepared to descend, the drone boat completed another lap around the whale and headed toward them.

Instead of veering off on its course around the Blue, the ASV careened straight toward the divers, who attempted a rapid descent. One of the divers managed to submerge just deep enough to avoid the oncoming boat. But the other was struck, his skull smashed by the prow of the robotic sentry. The sound of the impact was so loud in the surviving divers' headset that he was rendered temporarily deaf. He couldn't force himself to look away from the body of his friend slowly turning in a spreading cloud of blood just beneath the surface. Then he broke his gaze and spastically propelled himself into the depths to avoid the same fate.

High above him in the Hercules, a technician seated inside the ASV's control van smiled to himself as he used a joystick to take the drone on another pass around the Blue.

The remaining diver leveled out at a depth of forty feet, taking stock of his situation. Where was the whale? The water clarity was not terrible, but not good, either. He was suspended in an empty blue void, the bottom being too far below him to discern while the surface—not actually visible—was just a haze of white light.

He tried without success to raise his boss, the pilot, on his communications link. Not sure what to do, he checked his compass and kicked off to where he thought he last saw the Blue. He could hear the creature's haunting moans, but they offered him little in the way of directional clues.

A rigid-hull inflatable boat carrying six FBI divers parted the spectator craft, its loud-hailer booming for everyone to make way. As it approached the Blue, the drone boat moved aside, controlled by the FBI divers' colleague in the Hercules.

"Be advised, you have divers in the water," came the word via radio from their eye in the sky. "One possibly injured in a collision with the drone."

The inflatable slowed as it neared the Blue. The enormous creature was entirely submerged now, but still visible a few feet below the surface. A body appeared on the waves, its boxy rebreather making it easy to see. The FBI boat pulled up to it, pistols drawn.

The diver's skull had been broken apart by the drone's hull. Gobs of his brain drifted away in the currents, drawing schools of anchovies to congregate in a frenzied boil to pick at the gray matter. One of the FBI divers, experienced at recovering corpses from many different bodies of water, retched at the site of it.

But their primary mission today was not body recovery.

"We'll keep an eye on the floater. Go for the asset," came the word from above. The man piloting the rigid-hull boat was all too happy to turn away from the drifting corpse and head closer to the Blue.

Out of habit, they scanned the surface for tell-tale bubbles, but they knew that the diver down, like his deceased partner, also wore a rebreather, which meant that there would be no visual trace of his presence below.

Shouting came from the spectator boats. A few had satellite laptop connections and had been viewing the whale's live feed. Earlier there had been some clowning around as people tried to show off their boats—and the swimsuit-clad people on them—for the whale's camera, but the drone had put a stop to that.

This was something different.

The men in the Hercules also had a monitor on the whale's web-cam, and they advised their divers in the boat. "The remaining diver is approaching the asset. Repeat, remaining diver is approaching the asset. Make your entry now. Over."

The divers entered one pair at a time. The first was dropped off on one side of the Blue, then the boat circled around the whale's head. Once on the other side, the next two divers flipped backwards over the edge of the inflatable. Two men remained in the boat—one to drive it and the other to act as lookout and remain on standby.

Underwater, the two pairs of FBI divers began to converge beneath the Blue. None of them had ever dived with an animal the size of a commuter jet before, and for a couple of minutes they all hung there, staring at the spectacular beast while assessing their safety related to its presence. Its entire length was not visible at any one time because they could see only about forty feet in the greenish murk.

They were too close to the fluke. This became immediately apparent when the whale stirred and moved forward. Only a casual motion of its mighty tail, the Blue's movement was enough to send the FBI men tumbling in the after-wash of the massive appendage.

They regained their bearings, giving a wide berth to the tail. As the whale's dorsal slid into view, the team spotted the figure of the Mexican diver, his silent but bulky rebreather visible while he faced the whale.

Like his associate before him, this diver had given up on the notion of using the tag's intended release mechanism. He possessed neither the time nor the patience for screwing around with precision electronics.

The diver unsheathed a large knife. Guiding him to his mark was not only the tag itself, but two knives already protruding from the whale's blubber—a memento of Juan's and Carlos' earlier attempts to cut the tracker free.

The diver was about to make his incision when the whale surfaced for breath, abruptly leaving him in open water . . . face-to-face with two divers wearing stock yellow rebreathers. One of them had been facing the other direction when the whale ascended, and now his buddy urgently tapped his shoulder. He turned around, but not before the Mexican saw the dark blue lettering stenciled onto his rebreather: FBI.

He looked up to make sure he was clear of the Blue. The beast rested on the surface a safe distance away. A wall of boats bobbed beyond that. He couldn't see the drone that had killed his partner, but he knew it was up here somewhere. Time to move.

He spun around. Two more FBI divers were only feet away. He hollered into his facemask mic, "*Jefe*, I am being chased by four FBI divers. Meet me on the surface by the whale, now!" The fleeing would-be thief bolted for the surface as he saw one of the FBI men aim a speargun at him.

To get to the surface he had to work his way out from under the Blue. Once clear, he broke the surface and spun about wildly, looking for the seaplane. He didn't see it, but between the water draining from his mask and the lack of time to look, he wasn't alarmed.

He put his face back in the water, one arm

stretched out in the direction of the whale, as if he could stiff-arm the mega-ton beast away should it roll into him. But right now it was the humans who worried him most. Looking down he saw that the two pairs of divers had become a quartet. They came for him now in a tight-knit group, ascending purposefully.

The Mexican repeated his desperate message into his mic. No reply was forthcoming. He didn't wait for one. Glancing back down at the approaching feds, he removed his weight belt. Designed to counterbalance the positive buoyancy of his wetsuit and air tank, the belt was strewn with 5-pound squares of lead. He dangled the belt from a hand, held away from his body so it wouldn't snag on his person on the way down. Then he let go of it.

The lead missile sank so fast that the FBI divers had no time to avoid it. One of them looked up just in time to have his full facemask shatter on impact. Since his regulator was built into the mask and not a separate unit, he was now without an air source, his bloody face instantly encased in cold seawater.

The injured diver shot to the surface, trailing a gushing burst of bubbles as his breathing gas emptied into the surrounding water. Essentially blind, he was followed closely by the FBI diver who had been paired with him. They reached the surface some distance away from the suspect, who now had only two professional divers to immediately contend with.

Those two divers were armed, vengeful, and coming fast.

He checked the sky. *Where is the plane?* The drone boat whined as it leaned into a turn at the farthest point of its elliptical trajectory.

Suddenly the Blue slapped her gargantuan fluke against the water. The percussive explosion reminded everyone in the vicinity—especially the hunted diver—that they were dealing not merely with a set of GPS coordinates at sea, but with a wild animal that possessed a will of its own.

The diver who had been hit with the weights was being rescue-towed by his buddy on the surface away from the whale. The Mexican knew they wouldn't come for him.

But the other two had also come up, and their spearguns were pointed his way. One of the aquatic feds pulled his mask off and demanded, "Diver, FBI—stay where you are!"

CHAPTER 42

ABOARD DEEP VIEW

The paying passengers aboard *Deep View* clamored for their money back. It wasn't that they didn't get to see the wired whale. The vantage point from which they observed the animal was first rate, affording them a prime glimpse of one of nature's supreme wonders that they would likely never experience again. But after forty-five minutes in a packed vessel that bordered on claustrophobic to begin with, even witnessing an incredible sight was not enough to stifle their mounting unease.

The sub's seating was designed such that there was a porthole viewing window for every one to two passengers. Normally this ensured that everyone had ample opportunity to see without craning their necks or not being able to see over someone's head. Ernie had so packed the vessel, however, that people were standing in the narrow space between the benches on either side of the sub. Once in range of the "ginormous whale," as one boy put it, window space was quickly occupied. A fight broke out after a man forcibly removed a twelve-year-old boy who had broken free from his parents to get a better look at the whale.

Ernie tried to maintain order but it quickly became apparent that he lacked on-the-job experience. Passengers complained of the heat, and that it was becoming more difficult to breathe. Some demanded to speak with the captain himself.

Walter, who was worried enough about 100 tons of whale accidentally slamming into his packed sub, became even more concerned after hearing a knock on the control room door. He had told Ernie not to disturb him while submerged unless it was an emergency.

Walter consulted the sub's instrument panel. Depth was okay. No alarm lights. He peered out of his bow-mounted viewing port. The Blue was on the surface. He could see her on sonar too, but preferred to keep the animal in visual contact. Satisfied things were under control for at least the next few seconds, Walter opened the door.

"Hurry, close the door," Ernie said, stumbling inside. An angry mob stormed behind him. Walter heard shouts of "Take us back" and "I want my money back."

"Ernie, what the hell is going on? There's way too many people on board!" Walter exclaimed after seeing the overcrowded cabin for the first time.

"Sorry, Cap'n.

"You should be, Ernie. I'm going to bring us back. You know what a Coast Guard citation would mean for me?"

"That's fine. We can bring 'em back now. They saw the whale."

"Ernie, if they ask for their money back, we'll have to give it to them. There's twice as many people back there as there should be."

"Okay, well, hopefully they won't all want their money back."

"Get out there and tell them we're preparing to surface. And stay out there with them. You brought 'em aboard. Make them feel safe. The last thing I need is a mutiny on my hands, not to mention some kind of reckless endangerment lawsuit."

It was the Blue who gave the hired diver a chance to escape. As the two speargun-wielding FBI divers split up to approach him from either side, the whale executed a shallow dive, arching yards and yards of her broad back out of the water before slipping beneath the waves.

She submerged beneath the humans and then glided gently back to the surface. The Mexican found that he now had the Blue's vast bulk between him and the divers from the elite underwater unit. What's more, he was damn near face-to-lens with the whale's web-cam. Perhaps his people—wherever they were—would see that he was literally reaching for their reward and come to get him.

He moved closer to the cam, dive knife in one hand. He took a last look around for his pursuers but couldn't see them. He carried a diminutive snub-nosed speargun strapped to the inside of one calf, but it was no match for two well-trained divers carrying full-size shafts.

The Blue exhaled a cloud of spray, lolling peaceably on the surface. The diver surveyed his three-dimensional surroundings—underwater, sea-surface and air. His biggest threat was either the Blue itself or the swiftly approaching drone boat. The sea-going robot had broken from its elliptical path. It now made a beeline straight for him at a high rate of speed.

The diver decided he had just enough time. He scissor-kicked toward the living wall, reaching out a gloved hand, and grasped the million-dollar piece of technology on the whale's dorsal fin. Steadying himself, he prepared to commit the knife in his other hand when his eyes picked out the fresh scar leading away from the tag to one of the embedded knives. He could hear the drone bearing down on him. He could discern bits and pieces of English in a broadcasted message issuing from the ASV's loudspeakers: "FBI . . . stop . . . whale!"

He plunged his knife, more of an attempt to wedge the foreign device from the whale's body than it was to slice it cleanly off. The whale executed a shallow dive as the knife entered the blubber at the base of its dorsal. The diver hung on, riding the beast as it submerged.

Underwater, the Blue accelerated. The diver tightened his grip. Should he be torn from the whale, he could easily find himself in a position to be smashed by its fluke. If the whale dove too deep, however, he would have no choice but to let go.

He was relieved when the ocean-dweller leveled out at a depth of only twenty feet. He tried to take away the tag as he was dragged along but the animal moved too fast. Were he to loosen his grip for but a moment he would be cast off the mammoth body.

As he looked up from his botched cetacean surgical procedure, he spotted the FBI buddy team, ten feet above him and to his right. Their eyes were as wide as saucers as they reached for their spearguns, far too late. He flew past them attached to the massive creature like a remora on a shark.

Then the Blue set herself in a near-vertical posture and rushed the water's surface until she breached. Her entire body except for the fluke cleared the sea.

Breaching was common behavior for medium-sized whales, such as the grays, which migrated up and down the Pacific Coast. But blues rarely breached, possibly due to their enormous bulk.

The congregation of mariners was delighted by the spectacular performance, although not all of them could see the Blue's hitchhiker. The diver hung on, still clinging to the tag and his embedded knife, sheets of water draining over him as the whale reached the apex of her jump. But as the Blue started to fall back into the water, she canted over backwards such that the diver was falling back first, his eyes to the sky.

Then the laws of physics kicked in. The knife came

loose under the diver's increasing inertia, and as the diver separated from the whale, his knife dragged across the Blue's hide in front of the dorsal, slicing it but finding no real purchase. Although he had no way of knowing it at the time, the wound his knife made ran perpendicularly through the existing incision left by Juan during his earlier attempt to net the leviathan. The resulting disfigurement was a perfect cross; a crucifix symbol hacked into the whale's back.

The diver fell from the whale. Viewers of the Blue's live web-cam feed around the world saw the unreal view of blue sky with a cross carved into the image's foreground. The Latino community immediately started talking. It was as if an image of the Virgin Mary had appeared on a tortilla in East Los Angeles or in the pattern of a jaguar's coat in Costa Rica.

For the diver, perhaps the cross represented his own miracle, for he was uninjured as he fell into the water and the hundred-ton body landed beside him rather than on top of him, missing him by mere feet.

The Blue sounded, diving deep. She left the diver alone on the surface, cartwheeling in her backwash. The Mexican knew that it wouldn't be long before the FBI divers realized he'd been shaken loose from the whale and came after him.

To make matters worse, the drone was back, angling toward him, now flashing an array of strobe lights atop its unmanned bridge. If that weren't enough, the Hercules cargo plane lumbered by overhead, a helmeted crewmen peering out of the open bay doors through a pair of high-powered field binoculars.

The diver tried his comm unit. His string of urgent Spanish went unanswered.

Then something unexpected happened.

As he treaded water, calculating how long it would take him to swim into the mass of spectator boats where he might be able to lose himself among them, perhaps even board one and hide without being detected, a white flash appeared just beneath the surface. For a split second he thought it might be a large shark. He felt a stab of adrenaline jolt his system, and then his brain saw that whatever it was, it was much too big for a shark, even a great white.

The alabaster form grew larger, rising. The diver kicked back to avoid being directly over it. Then it materialized from the deep, and he could see that it was a man-made object: a submarine.

Water cascaded from the sub's rounded edges as it pushed its way to the surface. At first the diver assumed the underwater boat was coming for him, another weapon at the Americans' disposal with which to hunt him down. But as he appraised the curious ship, he wasn't so sure.

The whole sub was white—not a very stealthy color. Sections of the outer decks were plastered with no-slip grip tape, and a stainless-steel railing ran around the entire perimeter of the vessel. It was the sub's name, however, that really gave it away.

A blue logo was airbrushed on the sail, or conning tower, and although the Mexican couldn't understand the words *Deep View*, the swirling bubbles around the letters told him it was a tourist craft. In fact, he'd seen them before in Cabo San Lucas—not exactly the same as this one, but close enough.

He put his face back in the water. The two FBI divers were looking up at him, maybe thirty feet away, swimming fast.

He swam for the sub and kicked hard up over the slippery deck until he could grab the rail. He used precious seconds to rip off his fins and shed his rebreather. Then he stood up, holding the railing for balance.

People on the boats had noticed the sub, and now they pointed at him. He could hear both the whiny, high-pitched buzz of the drone and the low rumble of the Hercules. He didn't bother to look for them. He scanned the sub's smooth, glistening surface. There was no opening of any kind except for the sail. He had almost gotten to it when a hatch flipped open at the top of the sail, and a cap-covered head appeared. The diver saw the metal rungs leading up to the man.

He began climbing.

"Wait a minute, pal, we're not taking on passengers," Ernie said. The Mexican continued up the ladder. When he was eye to eye with Ernie at the top of the sail he jabbed a finger downward. "We've got people who want to get out," Ernie protested. Exasperated cries came from the passengers below.

"Down," the Mexican insisted. He looked over his shoulder. The FBI inflatable approached after having picked up the diver who had been injured by the dropped weight belt. The diver unsheathed his speargun and leveled it at Ernie's face.

"Down now," he intoned.

"Whoa, take it easy! Okay. Come down." Ernie backed down the ladder. As he neared the bottom, some of the passengers became even more incensed.

"You're blocking the air!" one said.

"Let us out!" shouted another.

"Sorry folks," Ernie said, stepping off the bottom of the ladder into the main passenger cabin with his hands up. He wanted a drink. Just then the door to the control cabin swung open.

The captain appeared. "What's going on, Ernie? Why aren't they going topside?"

"Ask him," Ernie said with a shrug. "He's got the gun."

The mercenary dropped from the ladder, spear at the ready. He swept the weapon around the main cabin, as if expecting someone to physically challenge him. No one did. Then he settled on Walter, who, in his starched white captain's uniform, made for an easy target.

"Back!" the diver commanded. He stepped forward while Walter walked backwards into the control cabin, pushed back by the spear point a few feet away.

"What do you want? Who are you?" Walter demanded.

The diver gestured to the open hatch in the main cabin. "Close," he said simply, followed by the more ominous, "Dive."

Walter commanded Ernie to close the hatch.

The underwater pilot couldn't believe it. He was being hijacked. *Who in their right mind would hijack a tourist submarine?*

The passengers were screaming now, hysterical.

"Dive now!" the diver said, his English perfectly comprehensible. He spun his speargun around to the passenger cabin, his other hand clenching a small dive knife guarding Walter's direction.

Two passengers who had been creeping for the exit ladder stopped cold in their tracks. The sub had gone quiet at the sight of the weapon aimed at the passengers. The sound of Ernie clanging the hatch into place reverberated throughout the metal tube. It had a certain finality about it that pushed some of the passengers over a mental precipice.

Choked sobs emanated from somewhere near the stern.

"No, please—I can't breathe," a woman cried.

"Let's rush him!" one man suggested. No one agreed with him.

"Close now. Dive!" the hijacker repeated.

Walter could hear Ernie banging the hatch door shut, but couldn't see him. He hoped he wasn't trying some kind of trick that would get somebody killed. "That's it, Ernie, close the hatch. Just do it." Walter watched as his woefully inadequate crew reappeared at the bottom of the ladder, having prepared them for what was shaping up to be a dive into Hell.

"It's okay, people," Walter said, "we've taken on some fresh air. You'll be fine."

The passengers' collective response indicated they felt otherwise.

Walter stood nearly toe-to-toe with the armed stranger. "Where do you want to go?"

"Dive."

"Dive *where*?"

"Mexico."

In spite of the situation, Walter laughed. "The motors on this submarine are electric. Run on batteries. Not enough juice to get that far. Six hours running time, tops."

If the hijacker understood the English being spoken, he was unmoved. He thrust the speargun at Walter's neck in a menacing gesture. "Dive now. Then south."

Eyes wide, Walter shuffled at spear-point back into the control cabin.

CHAPTER 43

OFF THE CATALINA ISLAND COAST

News of the commandeered sub burned across Catalina like a brushfire and replicated itself around the Internet like a virus. Media correspondents who were initially dispatched to Avalon to report live on the wired whale were now covering what they speculated—and later confirmed—to be the first-ever hijacking of a tourist submarine. To the rapidly converging journalists, it was an irresistible development, made even more so by the blue whale herself.

After sinking into a shallow dive, the Blue found herself next to the sixty-five-foot cigar-shaped machine. The whir of the sub's electric motors was much quieter than that of the combustion engines on a typical boat. As the titanic rorqual glided past the underwater vehicle, a child, perhaps unaware of the danger he was in, plastered his face and hands against one of the sub's many viewing ports, gazing at the whale outside. He became an instant Internet sensation, the undersea traveler's expression being the perfect embodiment of humanity's sheer wonder at the natural world.

The media were not the only ones interested in the hijacking. The FBI team quickly learned what had happened and were able to shadow the sub's progress from the surface. Walter managed to get out a brief radio message that was punctuated with heavy impacts and forced grunts. The FBI could make out the words "Overpower . . . gun . . . southeast 159—" before the channel fell silent.

The FBI underwater unit shifted plans. Shepherding the wired whale was out; saving human lives in full view of the national media was in. The Hercules flew a search pattern, its spotters probing the depths for the sub's tell-tale white glow while those in the cockpit monitored communications channels for more updates from the sub's pilot. The cargo plane was trailed by the inflatable, once again carrying a full complement of FBI divers. Only the drone was left to circle the mighty Blue and her asset.

ABOARD KETCH ME IF YOU CAN

"Avalon, dead ahead." Anastasia checked her compass heading and made a slight course correction. Catalina's sprawling coastline loomed before them.

Tara pried herself from her FBI radio for the first time in ten minutes. She had learned from her assistant that the phone records search had turned up the victim's last name: Wilkinson. She emerged from the protective shelter of the ketch's cabin, doing her best to ignore the water rushing along the craft's sides as she made her way topside and found Anastasia at the helm.

"Can this thing go any faster?"

Anastasia looked up from the wheel. "Not without a change in the wind, no, but we're making good time. What's the rush?"

"A tourist submarine has been hijacked outside of Avalon. The FBI team sent to deal with the whale has now been diverted to assist with the hijacking."

"Is the Blue still there?"

"Yeah, but with only the drone boat to guard her now."

"Why did somebody hijack a tourist sub?"

"Guess they wanted to play Captain Nemo for a day. Got me. But this means that once we get there, I'll need to be more involved."

"Shouldn't be long now," Anastasia declared, peering over her vessel's bow.

Tara watched the scientist's brow furrow with concern.

"What is it?"

Anastasia said nothing while she pulled a pair of binoculars from the console. She held them to her eyes and focused. "Damn it!"

"What?"

"OLF."

"You sure?"

"Positive. Black schooner. And they're flying the skull-and-crossbones now."

Tara took a turn with the binoculars. As she focused in on the black ship, she could indeed make out the Jolly Roger fluttering atop the schooner's highest mast.

The ketch continued to fly with the wind, and soon one of the island's famous landmarks came into view. The Casino, an immense, white circular building with a red tile roof, built in the 1920s as a dance hall, continued to beckon visitors to Catalina to this day. Soon after sighting the Casino, the raft of whale-watching boats could be seen, like a floating city outside the harbor. Upon seeing the rag-tag flotilla, Tara was motivated to action.

"I need that laptop so we can see the Blue's feed," she told Anastasia. She recalled with a shudder Trevor Lane's satellite-connected notebook—now on the bottom of the sea—from which she'd e-mailed the location of their sinking boat.

"In the cabin. Should be on the galley table."

Tara ducked back inside and found the machine. She lit the thing up and navigated to the wired whale's webcast. Her breath sucked in sharply as she saw the cross carved into the whale's hide. *They're getting close.*

The Blue inhabited shallow water. Cascades of bubbles roiled across the creature's camera; the light was intense. A cacophony of boat engines made her reach for the volume control. Still, the device transmitted, she thought. Her evidence was still intact.

Tara ran back outside and read off the Blue's GPS coordinates to Anastasia, who adjusted the ship's course accordingly.

ABOARD PANDORA'S BOX

"We have to get them off!" Pineapple said, lowering the tender into the water.

"We're wasting time! We've got a fix on her, let's go," Eric countered.

Another crewmember, consulting a laptop, nodded in agreement. "Whale's right over there," he said, pointing off the bow. Other crewmembers, including the two Mexicans, gathered around the screen to watch.

Pineapple stood up from his job of lowering the tender and turned to Stein, exasperated. "Eric," he began, "listen to me. What we're about to do is highly dangerous. We didn't know ourselves we'd be getting into this when we left the marina this morning. A lot of these people snuck aboard for a half-day party-cruise. We have to give them a chance to leave if they want to."

"I suppose most of them would only be in the way," Stein conceded. Pineapple nodded wholeheartedly.

"Okay people, listen up," Pineapple said to the crew assembled on deck. "Things are about to get violent. We want to give everyone a chance to leave now who might get upset at what we're about to do."

"What are you about to do?" someone called out from the rear of the ship.

"We're going to shoot the wired whale's dorsal with the harpoon gun," Stein declared. Immediately about a dozen people poured onto the tender, filling it to capacity. Stein was surprised to count the two Mexicans among them.

"*¿Cuál es su problema*?" Stein asked them. The divers told him to look at the whale's video. The cross. A sign, they said. They wanted nothing to do with it. "So that's it, you're just going to leave? What about the reward money from your boss?"

"No reward is worth that," one of them said. They both nodded and crossed themselves.

Stein snorted derisively. "It was your own divers who cut that cross into the whale!"

"There are some things we cannot fight," Fernando said. "We leave you our equipment, as promised."

Pineapple looked at Stein and shrugged. There was nothing they could do. Pineapple pointed the way to Avalon Harbor, and off the tender went, some of the other environmentalists in the small boat calling out, "You guys suck!" in their wake.

"We still have a rowboat if anyone else wants to get off," Pineapple said. Six more people stepped forward. Stein felt a pang of jealousy at seeing his girlfriend make her escape with her new beau. She glared at Stein as she boarded. Pineapple shoved them off toward the harbor with instructions to give the whale a wide berth.

Stein looked around *Pandora's Box*. Including himself and Pineapple, there were now six men to operate the ship and launch the attack. Should be nice and efficient, he thought, finding it hard to keep his mind from lighting on his girlfriend, now being rowed to Catalina where she would doubtless spend the night with that creep in some hotel. . . .

"The good news is that Juan and Fernando already got the harpoon ready," one of the crew said. Stein looked away from the retreating runabouts. *Let them go*. The culmination of his life's work was here and now.

Stein said, "Okay, good. Go up there and study it. Make sure you'll be able to rig it again after the first shot is fired. Holler if you have any questions." The young man skipped off toward the bow, and Pineapple stepped up to Stein.

"You ready for this?"

"Ready to let the world know that it's not okay to enslave God's creatures with technology for the benefit of a few already-spoiled rich jerk-offs?" Stein replied. "How many grenades do we have for the gun?"

"Six, but it'll be hard to get that many off. It takes an experienced whaling crew sixty seconds to swap harpoons, but you can bet it'll take us at least twice that."

It was unfortunate for them that they'd lost the Mexicans, who had received special training on the use of the harpoon before leaving Baja. Although Stein and Pineapple had seen harpoon guns in action, they had always been on the receiving end of them, and had never actually fired one themselves.

"Not a huge problem. If we can score a hit anywhere near that tag, it ought to do the trick."

"Right, but once the first one is fired, you can bet that the Coast Guard will be on us. Maybe even the pleasure boaters. We need to be effective with the first one or two. I don't think we'll get to fire more than that."

"We'll want to stay low and out of sight too, in case someone shoots at us," Stein said grimly. Pineapple's eyes widened somewhat but he said nothing, only nodded.

The ship was already moving, turning. Toward the Blue.

At the bow, the crewman Stein had assigned to the gun studied Juan and Fernando's work. A neat coil of rope lay at the base of the weapon, and a grenade-tipped harpoon was loaded into the launcher. The explosives that would propel the deadly projectile were primed and ready.

A strangely empty-appearing *Pandora's Box* approached the throng of boats. The Blue cavorted playfully on the surface, maybe a hundred yards from the prow. The whiny pitch of the drone made itself heard as the robotic sentry's circular pattern brought it toward the approaching gunship.

"Any idea who that is?" Pineapple asked, peering

out from the slit opening above the salon door.

Stein fixed binoculars on the approaching craft. “Looks pretty high-tech whatever it is.”

“I don’t see any people on it. They must all be below.” The drone continued to approach *Pandora’s Box*, breaking from its previous pattern.

“It’s coming right for us,” Pineapple observed.

“We could harpoon it,” Stein offered.

“Do you want to shoot the whale, or a boat?”

“Take it easy. I’m just kidding. Let’s see what they want.” That task was made unnecessary by the drone itself, which blasted a high-decibel message through its loudspeakers. “Attention watercraft: You are too close to the whale, which is now under the protection of the Federal Bureau of Investigation. Move away from the whale. . . . Attention watercraft . . .”

A crewman appeared and knelt in front of the salon door, asking Stein what he wanted to do.

“Is the harpoon ready?” Stein asked.

“Looks ready to me,” the crewman responded.

“Is there a laptop visual on the Blue?” Stein asked Pineapple.

“Yeah. Continued surface activity, about a hundred yards dead ahead. Thick circle of boats around her.”

“Go ahead and turn us away as if we’re going to comply,” Stein commanded. “Then, after this FBI boat leaves, swing us back around and we’ll go in for the kill.”

The crewman was nodding and about to leave when Pineapple called out. “I found something,” he said, squinting his eyes at a message board on the *Wired Kingdom* web site. "People are saying here that the boat circling the Blue is an unmanned FBI drone," Pineapple said, eyes widening. They could hear the drone bleating its message just outside. Apparently the robotic craft had idled up to the schooner and was not leaving.

A smile crossed Stein's face. "See if you can get somebody to jump aboard that thing and disable it—rip off the antennae, the speakers, whatever damage can be done," Stein finished. "Hurry up, it might not sit here for long. Hell, they might even have a microphone on that thing to hear what we say."

"Aye aye, sir," the crewmen said, grinning in return before running off.

"And kill that music," Stein called out. The party tunes were silenced.

The schooner picked up speed toward the Blue.

CHAPTER 44

ABOARD PANDORA'S BOX

"Hey, you're too close to the whale!"

"Get back!"

These cries were ignored by Stein and his crew, hidden as they were below decks, while *Pandora's Box* plowed toward the wired whale.

Stein gave the command, "Fire!"

The first shot went high and right. The Blue didn't even move as she basked in the surface sunlight. Neither did the twenty-six-foot cabin cruiser with the misfortune of drifting behind the Blue's dorsal fin, in a direct path with that of the grenade-tipped harpoon. The projectile struck the cruiser astern, igniting a fireball which engulfed the rear half of the boat.

Screams of terror rent the air as two boaters jumped overboard trailing smoke and flames. A third made an attempt to quell the inferno with an extinguisher, but it was like trying to put out a forest fire with a squirt gun. Soon that man, too, abandoned ship, leaving the burning craft unattended.

Other boaters hurled angry invectives and collided as they maneuvered to put distance between themselves and the ticking time bomb the burning boat had become.

Leaving Pineapple with the laptop at the helm, Stein half-crawled to his gunners on the bow. He was pleased to see them already at work loading another harpoon.

"Ready the gun," he told them.

"Aye aye, Captain."

Stein watched as one worked to load the harpoon into the launcher while the other primed the explosive. He was filled with pride at the sight of these two young men risking prison time to achieve his objective. He made a mental note that were they to survive, these harpoon gunners would be promoted through the ranks of OLF in a very tangible and visible way.

"What the—" Pineapple muttered to himself as he peered from a salon window, watching the melee unfold around them. It was pure chaos. The cabin cruiser had become a wayward fireball, still drifting in the easy breeze after being abandoned by all hands. Vessels lying in its path cleared the way, fishing the fated crew from the sea. Others showered it with their own fire extinguishers to little effect.

And then there was the drone boat, which had taken on a passenger as it went back to circling the Blue. Pineapple watched in amazement as his crewmember—a shirtless guy with long hair in his twenties, whose name he couldn't recall—stood on the drone's deck, attempting to rip off one of its myriad antennae. Pineapple winced as he saw a wire aerial, bent all the way down to the deck, suddenly whip loose, striking the man across his back and head. The young activist went down and rolled off the deck, but caught himself on a support strut and struggled back up.

Pineapple feared it wouldn't be long before the FBI came to protect their autonomous investment. He switched on the marine radio, hoping to intercept some useful chatter. He was encouraged to hear that the FBI's underwater unit was still fully engaged in the submarine rescue. As best Pineapple could tell there had been some sort of struggle in the sub's control room, and the underwater craft now lay motionless on the bottom in ninety feet of water.

Stein and his gunners on the bow no longer needed Pineapple to confirm the whale's position. They were the same distance away that a recreational whale-watching vessel might maintain. What surprised Stein the most was that after all the commotion the Blue still remained in the same place on the surface, seemingly without a care in the world. Maybe whales weren't as intelligent as people made them out to be, he mused.

The man loading the harpoon stepped aside, making certain his feet were well clear of the coil of rope which would soon be unraveling at breakneck pace.

The explosive charge was prepped.

"Aiming . . ." his colleague said.

"Whale is holding position," Stein said for

confirmation. "Anytime you're ready."

Stein was afraid to take his eyes off the whale to look and see if anyone might be approaching them. He would have to leave their defense to Pineapple and the two other crewmen.

". . . and firing. Stay clear!"

The discharge of the explosive grenade was but a mere champagne cork pop compared to the concussive blast that rocked the water at the same moment.

The blaze on the stricken boat had reached its main fuel tank, causing a fiery detonation whose explosive force launched would-be rescuers from their decks. A nearby sailboat that had sustained a hit to its hull from a piece of debris began to sink. Flaming shrapnel rained from the sky.

For the Blue, the shockwave meant one thing: dive. And that she did, moving in time to evade the harpoon's grenade-tipped lance as it passed scant inches over her back. In seconds she had reached a depth of fifty feet.

ABOARD KETCH ME IF YOU CAN

"It looks like a . . . harpoon gun!" Tara said from behind her binoculars.

"Impossible," Anastasia said, scanning the fiery seascape from the ketch's helm. "Where would somebody get one of those in the Western world today, unless it's an antique?"

"Doesn't look old. Whatever it is," Tara added,

"they're working fast to reload it."

"Where's the Blue?" Anastasia asked.

Tara turned her head with the binoculars, covering a swath of water between their boat and *Pandora's Box*. Where their quarry had been seconds before there was now only a smooth patch of water with an oil-slick appearance known as a whale's "footprint."

"I think it got tired of the surprise party and left."

"I'm afraid what those psychos might do if we try to get any closer to our whale," Anastasia said.

"Anastasia, Stein was once your boyfriend. Can't you talk to him?"

"You heard him the other day. He's become too radicalized over the years. Probably piss him off even more to hear from me right now."

Tara took a deep breath. "If you can get me close to the schooner, I can try and neutralize the shooters," she said, barely believing the words coming out of her mouth. Even if OLF had no other weapons besides the harpoon, she was on the wrong end of that firepower contest. Her best weapon would be the element of surprise. OLF would be on the lookout for law enforcement vessels and aircraft, not slow-moving pleasure boats. Tara wondered if the Hercules could do a high-precision strafing run, but she knew it was busy searching for the hijacked sub.

"I can try," Anastasia said, gauging the distance to the OLF gunship before turning the wheel.

Tara trained her binoculars on the schooner. She could see the gunners on the bow, although she couldn't make out their faces. They were searching the water, no doubt looking for the Blue. How close would the ketch be able to get to them before they took action?

Tara flipped on her FBI-issue radio. Its stream of chatter told her that the underwater team was still very much involved with the sub rescue. They were preparing to put a dive team in the water to swim down and visually evaluate the situation on board the sub. Coast Guard vessels had also been dispatched to deal with the explosions and boat fires reported by dozens of terrified boaters. Tara's eyes swept the area but saw no sign of the Coasties or any other assistance.

It's just me and this whale again.

Suddenly the Blue reared her head above the surface halfway between the ketch and the schooner. Instinctively, Tara turned to look at the whaling ship, but her view of the eco-terrorists was obscured by the whale's blow as it exhaled.

"We're in their line of fire! Get out from behind the Blue!" Tara shouted. Anastasia throttled the ketch's motor into high and brought her boat toward the Blue's tail so that they were no longer behind the dorsal area. By that time the mist from the Blue's breath had cleared. Tara aimed her binoculars at the gunship's bow.

"Harpoon's loaded," she said to Anastasia, keeping her eyes behind the binoculars. She struggled to keep her voice steady. "They're—they're going to fire!"

Tara took a quick look around. No support of any

kind in sight. The Blue lay exposed on the surface. The schooner had drifted even closer to the pleasure boaters, ruling out any thought of firing on the gunners.

Anastasia picked up her marine transmitter. Probably to call OLF, Tara thought somewhere in the back of her mind. A last-ditch effort at reasoning with Stein.

There's a chance.

It took several moments, perhaps not until Anastasia said the words *Pandora's Box,* for Tara to realize that the marine scientist was speaking in Spanish. Tara could not understand what was being said—the words were spoken too rapidly—but she could pick out a word or two that she recognized. Many numbers were spoken. They sounded to Tara like they might be an ID number of some kind, judging by the careful and deliberate way Anastasia spoke them.

Tara's mind reeled, trying to figure out why Anastasia would speak in Spanish to OLF, or why she would speak Spanish at all, for that matter, when Eric Stein's voice broke through the speaker in English.

"Wait a minute. I can *see* you. In the ketch."

Tara could see Stein peering back at them through binoculars of his own. His bewildered voice continued to pour out of the radio. "Anastasia? Juan and Fernando told me the code words, but I was expecting them to come from the seaplane pilot. They said he might call back."

"What happened to my men?" Anastasia asked. Then the scientist cast a quick glance at Tara, as if to see if she'd noticed her slip back into English.

Tara's blood ran colder than the ocean swirling beneath their boat. *My men*? At the same time, she was very aware that the harpoon had not yet been fired.

OLF was waiting on the conversation, their Jolly Roger fluttering in a light breeze. It gave Tara the creeps, this modern-day pirate-whaling ship indiscriminately killing people in the waters of L.A.'s favorite marine recreational area. And meanwhile, *her* sanctuary was the private sailboat of a woman she plainly did not understand half as well as she thought she had.

"Like I said," Stein continued, "the pilot left in the seaplane, and nobody knows where he went. One of his divers hijacked the tourist sub, which I'm sure you heard about by now. We had nothing to do with that."

"Juan *y* Fernando?"

"They got spooked by the cross cut into the whale's back and went ashore. Left about thirty minutes ago."

Anastasia continued speaking in Spanish to Stein. Tara noted the urgency in her voice. *What doesn't she want me to hear?*

Tara was forcing her mind to accept the fact that she had vastly mischaracterized the scientist when the conversation with Stein demanded her attention.

"It's my harpoon now," Stein responded. "And you can speak in English now, Dr. Reed, I'm sure Special Agent Shores would like to hear this little chat. That is her on deck, isn't it?"

Tara gave Stein a wave. If the moron had a single viable brain cell left in his head, she thought, he would never fire on a ship.

The scowl on Anastasia's face didn't escape Tara's notice. "Fine, Eric, you can have it," Anastasia said. "Just don't use it anymore, okay?"

She's given up all pretense, Tara thought. *Something is sure as hell going on here.* For the first time since the exchange began, Tara's mind went to the details of using her sidearm: the angle her body should assume to best shield the weapon from view . . . the simple but practiced motion of drawing it . . .

"It's already mine," Stein said. "Your divers gave me all of their gear, including the harpoon, in exchange for saving their lives. Your pilot left them for dead, you know."

"Eric, I'll remove the tag from the whale. Just don't destroy it. Please. I need it to prove my father's innocence."

"Yeah, you'll remove it all right," Stein said, voice dripping with sarcasm. "And then you'll use it to enslave some other innocent sea creature for your own personal gain, so you can buy more luxury yachts."

"I don't need any more yachts, Eric."

"You might if you don't move that one out of the way. Prep the harpoon, soldiers!"

"Eric, no!"

"I'm telling you now to get out of the way. Agent Shores, you are a witness to that instruction. Move your boat or risk being hit. That is all. Over and out."

"Eric! You already hurt me once before. Wasn't that enough? *Eric*!"

Radio silence.

The Blue was moving slowly on the surface now. Tara could see the gunners swiveling the harpoon on its base, tracking the beast.

Anastasia had taken the ketch around the whale. They now motored straight for the black schooner. Tara could hear Stein shouting commands to his gunners. She watched through binoculars as one of the harpoonists gave the other a nod.

Here it comes, Tara thought. She thought about taking a shot, just out of effective range, but were she to miss, there were scores of innocent bystanders just beyond her intended target. Not to mention that once they realized where the shots were coming from, it wouldn't be long before that harpoon gun was trained on their little ketch. They were defenseless against such an attack. The risk was too high.

"Can you shoot them?" Anastasia shouted, as if reading her mind.

Tara was about to reply when she was interrupted by the shriek of an outboard motor being accelerated far beyond its ability to respond. Here come the vigilantes, she thought. They watched a small speedboat carrying four sunburned recreational boaters—all of them yelling with fists raised in the air—ram into the schooner's bow.

The collision didn't do any serious damage to the much larger ship, nor did it stop the harpoon from firing, but the impact did distract the gunners enough to throw off their aim. The grenade-tipped harpoon splashed into the water just short of the Blue, slicing into the deep without detonating.

Anastasia stopped the ketch dead in the water, unsure of what to do next. Tara didn't need binoculars to see that all hell was breaking loose on OLF's flagship. The rec boaters had stirred a nest of angry hornets. With the help of one of his men, Eric Stein dropped *Pandora's* anchor onto the deck of the tiny runabout ten feet below. Tara winced as she heard a man scream.

The vigilantes had had enough. Two of them tossed the anchor over the side while the man on the outboard put them in high-speed reverse, away from the schooner. Tara heard them shouting, heard the word "hospital," as they retreated into the throng of spectator boats.

And that was when the Blue surfaced alongside the ketch, not more than one foot away.

CHAPTER 45

ABOARD KETCH ME IF YOU CAN

Tara forced herself to take a deep breath and exhale slowly. OLF's gunners were reloading the harpoon again. The enormous whale had just surfaced at the side of the ketch facing away from *Pandora's Box*, perhaps seeking shelter from the hunters. But even with so much happening, Tara's brain continued to process details of the case. The sound, for example. She didn't mean to listen for it, but as the ketch lay still in the water, its sails luffing in the light breeze, she recalled the unknown sound from the murder video, her mind matching the two.

Sails. It was sails flapping in the wind, when Crystal died.

That didn't mean it had to be Anastasia's boat, but because of her interaction in Spanish with Stein and the fact that she'd thought the Mexicans were on his boat, she was certain that if she looked into Dr. Reed's past research trips to Baja California, she would find that she had hired Mexican pilots in the past. And that, in conjunction with the fact that she owned a sailboat, and that a sailboat could be heard on the murder video, was enough to put the detective on extreme edge.

Tara watched Anastasia walk away from her, slowly and deliberately, to the ketch's port side, where the Blue was. Tara's hand was on her Glock, but the scientist made no threatening moves.

Tara stole a glance at *Pandora's Box*. The whaling crew was at the ready, but straining to find their target. Stein was gazing intently through binoculars. The animal was a good fifty feet longer than the sailboat, but its head and dorsal were blocked by the craft while the rear portion of its body hung down into the water. OLF had no shot.

Anastasia leaned over the ketch's rail and extended her right hand, which now held a small, rectangular piece of metal. She swiped it across the base of the Blue's dorsal fin, extended her left hand over, and then stood upright again in the ketch . . .

Holding the tag.

Tara struggled to accept what had just happened. After all they'd been through—the helicopters, the boats, all of the professional divers who had been killed—Anastasia had simply walked over to the whale and plucked the web-cam from the giant without even getting wet. The small metal cylinder held in Anastasia's hand dripped seawater onto the deck. For a moment there was no sound save for the splatter of the drops. For millions watching the scene unfold live on the web, the view the whale's camera now afforded was bizarre, for they were looking not at water, but at the deck of a boat.

Then at an attractive woman wearing a cap with the letters FBI, pointing the barrel of a Glock directly at the camera's lens.

"Hold it right there, Dr. Reed," Tara said, her words picked up clearly by the tag's microphone. Those watching online could both see and hear the action unfold. Tara was also aware that the device may well be capturing the details of her arrest procedure, and so she was hyper-conscious of the fact that she would need to do everything by the book.

Anastasia froze. "It was me. It wasn't my father. I'll give you the tag."

"What was you?"

"I wanted to get the tag because it proves that my father had nothing to do with it. Yes, he had an affair with Crystal, but he didn't kill her." Tara nearly winced at Anastasia's use of the victim's name.

"Who did?" She had to coax it out of her. All the while, she braced herself for the possible impact of a grenade she prayed would never come. Out of her peripheral vision, Tara saw the Blue still floating near the ketch. "If it wasn't your father, then who was it?" Tara prompted.

"We should get out of the harpoon's range," Anastasia suggested.

She's getting evasive.

Tara knew she had to act. "Dr. Reed, you are under

arrest for the murder of Crystal Wilkinson. You have the right to remain silent. Anything you say can and will be used against you in a court of law. You have the right to an attorney. . . ." When Tara read the part about an attorney being provided if one cannot be afforded she thought, *Yeah, right, this lady will have the finest legal team money can buy.* "Do you understand these rights?"

"Yes."

Tara reached back and produced a pair of handcuffs. She dangled them from the hand not holding the gun. "I need you to turn around and place your hands behind your head."

Anastasia just stood there, looking like she wanted to say something.

"Do it now, Dr. Reed. Nice and easy."

"I didn't want to do it, you know."

"Do what, Dr. Reed?" Tara continued to address her formally, to remind her of the seriousness of the situation.

"For years, I had no contact with my father."

"I know that."

"We had no respect for each other. I was a scientist and he was a producer of trashy Hollywood TV shows. And my mother *and* my father wanted to disown me ever since . . . ever since college."

"Your parents told me all that," Tara lied.

The Blue made short, breathy gasping sounds as it rested behind the shelter of the ketch.

"But *Wired Kingdom* changed all that," Anastasia

continued, remaining still. "It brought us together again as a family."

"And then what happened?"

"Crystal was an actress on one of my Dad's shows. I saw her on TV. I thought she was gorgeous and vibrant and captivating. I went down to the studio on a day I knew my father wouldn't be there so I could meet her. I introduced myself as George Reed's daughter and took her out for drinks. We hit it off and I dated her for a few months . . . until I found out she was also having an affair with my father, which she had kept a secret from everyone, including me. My mother began to suspect, but she never said anything to me about it. I think she was also happy we were finally a family again."

"Go on," Tara said. *Give me the details.*

"And then, on this very boat, Crystal told me that she intended to marry my father. I tried to convince her to break it off with him, explain that she was ruining a twenty-five-year marriage. You know what she told me?"

"No Dr. Reed, what did she tell you?" As long as she was providing more details about the case, Tara saw no reason to apprehend Anastasia immediately. People—especially wealthy people—had a way of clamming up under their lawyer's advice once they saw the inside of a jail cell. *Let her run her mouth for a bit.*

"She told me that girls were just a phase for her, and that I'd grow out of it when I found the right man, like she did."

"And for her that 'right man' was your father?"

"So she said. Our family was finally back together again, and now it was being torn apart by someone I thought had cared for me. And so . . ." Anastasia trailed off, her face a mask of anguish and confusion.

"And so you shot her and pushed her overboard."

A tear fell down Anastasia's cheek. The whale-cam began to tremble in her hand. "I'm sorry," Anastasia said. More tears chased after the first. Eventually they mingled with the seawater dripping from the whale-cam.

Tara was dumbfounded. How was it possible that so keen a mind—such an extraordinary intellect—could also be so primitive in its capacity for human relationships? *She's lonely. Coming off a painful rejection. . . . Stein cheated on her. . . . I rejected her. . . .* But that would be for the psychologists to theorize over later.

"What about Trevor Lane? Were you involved with him in any way?"

"No," she said, sniffling now. "He came to my father saying he invented a telemetry device small enough, rugged enough, and powerful enough for long-term deployment on wild marine animals. I guess it turns out that he stole the design from some black-market defense-tech ring, but we didn't know anything about that. That was his world."

Tara had heard enough. "Okay, Dr. Reed, I need you to turn around, put your hands behind your head, and get on your knees." Anastasia slowly turned around, facing away from Tara.

"On your knees!"

As Anastasia started to kneel, Tara heard the distinctive *CRACK* from the harpoon gun. Tara hit the deck, covered her head with her arms.

A second later the grenade-tipped projectile struck the ketch amidships. The blast knocked a hole in the upper portion of the ship's hull.

Tara sprung from the deck and turned back to Anastasia, who was gone. "Dr. Reed!" she called out. "Don't make things worse than they already are." It made Tara nervous to think about just how far away from her field office she was right now, so she pushed the thought from her mind.

In the distance Tara could hear the *whump-whump-whump* of helicopter rotors. Worried they may be sinking, she took a precious second to glance at the side of the boat where the harpoon had struck. They did not appear to be listing or taking on water. The sound of the helicopter grew louder, but she did not want to take her eyes off the deck a second time to look for it.

Tara's gaze swept the vessel from bow to stern. No sign of Anastasia. She had not heard any splashes. She had to be somewhere in the cabin.

Tara walked around the ship's side. She jumped on top of the cabin where there was a small sundeck. As she climbed over the railing there, she lost hold of her pistol and dropped it, then heard the clatter of metal on metal followed by a splash as it went overboard.

Her mind screamed one question: *Did Anastasia hear it?* She didn't think so. She hoped her suspect didn't have a gun somewhere in the cabin. She must have had one at some point to shoot Crystal, Tara thought, but it was likely she would have disposed of it afterwards. *Probably threw it overboard in the same water Crystal died in . . . 1,600 feet deep.*

Tara imagined Crystal running around the ketch for her life, perhaps over the same sundeck on which she now crouched, Anastasia close behind. Tara made a mental note to have the boat searched for forensic evidence—bullet holes, blood that might be revealed by the chemical luminol, any signs of a struggle . . .

The helicopter was loud now. Tara looked up. There it was, a big, beautiful Coast Guard bird, bearing down fast on the black schooner. She lamented the fact that she'd left her radio in the salon.

"I can't go to prison, you know," Anastasia called out from inside the cabin. "You know I couldn't live like that."

Tara didn't respond. Why give away her position? The fact that Anastasia remained in the cabin was encouraging. But that didn't mean the scientist was unarmed.

And then it was too late. Anastasia popped her head and shoulders out of a covered hatch at the bow end of the same sundeck Tara crouched on, aiming a crossbow directly at her. "Your turn to freeze, detective," Anastasia said.

"What do you think you're doing? You think if you

kill me, that you'll just be able to sail off into the sunset?"

"I don't know. But I'd rather die out here on the ocean, where I belong, than spend the rest of my life in a cage."

At that moment the Coast Guard helicopter buzzed in low over the OLF gunship. Two flash grenades detonated, one after the other. Then a team of heavily armed men rappelled onto the deck of the schooner, covered by automatic weapons fire.

Anastasia said, "Looks like we won't have to worry about them anymore."

"What do you want me to do?" Tara asked, hands in the air.

"There's not much you can do. I know it's your job to bring me in. But I cannot allow that to happen, Tara. It's ironic, you know." Anastasia carefully climbed up through the open hatch cover. To do this she had to hold the crossbow with only one hand, but she never lowered it, and Tara didn't think for a second that there was a decent opportunity to charge her. Anastasia stood on the sundeck next to the hatch, both hands now back on her weapon, still pointed at Tara's heart.

"What's ironic?" Tara was buying time—anything to avoid being shot with that god-awful looking thing. She noticed a rope that trailed past her along the deck and between Anastasia's feet.

"'I intend to get that hard drive, Dr. Reed.'" She mimicked the tone and inflection of Tara's voice almost perfectly. The effect was chilling. "Do you remember saying that to me, in the studio?" Anastasia pressed.

Tara only returned her stare.

"Well, you were right. You are going to get it. This is the tag delivery system I used to implant the device into the whale. But a whale has about a foot of blubber to absorb the impact. You don't look like you're packing that much fat," she said, looking Tara's body up and down.

"Please don't. That won't solve anything." Tara said. The crossbow's dart, to which Anastasia had attached the tag, certainly looked lethal enough at such a close range. Anastasia had the bow drawn all the way back. Tara had taken enough ballistics courses to know that the speed of its projectile would be measured in hundreds of feet per second, the force of its draw in hundreds of pounds.

FBI FIELD OFFICE, LOS ANGELES

Tara's boss, Special Agent in Charge Will Branson, stood in front of a computer monitor set up by staffers to keep an eye on the wired whale's feed. "How the hell did this happen?" he bellowed. An assistant replied something about the underwater team being preoccupied with the hijacked submersible. "Never mind. Get some of that underwater team on that sailboat. Now, damn it! We've got an agent one-on-one with an armed murder suspect in a close-quarters environment. Get them the hell over there! And where's the Coast Guard?"

"They're in a gun battle with the environmental terrorist group, sir," another staffer reported.

"Tell them to send more men!"

"Sir, I'm getting word that the team is working on raising the sub, using air bags," a different staffer, monitoring a secure communications channel, said.

"Give me that." Branson took the handset.

"Listen to me, agent . . . No, you listen to *me*! I am Special Agent in Charge Branson, L.A. Field Office. I don't care if you're saving eight *hundred* citizens. Don't tell me you can't spare two men to save one of our own. Now get somebody's ass on that ketch, right now!"

He slammed the phone down and turned his eyes back to the monitor, where part of a crossbow could be seen in the foreground, with Special Agent Shores kneeling with her hands up in the background. He had no doubt that the underwater team would comply with his orders.

He just hoped it wouldn't be too late.

CHAPTER 46

ABOARD KETCH ME IF YOU CAN

Tara and Anastasia could hear gunfire as the Coast Guard tactical team shot OLF into submission. Screams of agony punctuated the barrage of bullets. It was not easy for Tara to stand with her back to the carnage unfolding only a hundred yards away, but she dared not take her eyes off Anastasia. She couldn't help but notice the Blue, however, swimming away from the ketch toward the open sea at a leisurely pace.

"I'd say Eric Slime and his crew are getting what they deserve right about now," Anastasia said. "And now I'm afraid it's your turn, Detective."

"Great, will you make up a cute little name for me, too?"

"Believe me, I've thought of a lot of cute little names for you, dear."

"I never hurt anyone," Tara whined. "Why do I deserve to be killed? I didn't even have to come out here today, you know that? I *volunteered* so that I could help you prove your father's innocence." Tara did her best to trace the path of the rope running between Anastasia's feet without moving her eyes as she blathered on in a pathetic monologue.

Although she had no way of knowing it, the riveted web viewers had inundated television news networks with calls and e-mails about the life-and-death struggle of an FBI agent broadcasting live off Catalina Island's eastern shore.

CNN was first to put the telemetry feed live on the air, and soon other networks followed. In Times Square, New York, the jumbo screen carried the live drama from the whale's former tag. Thousands of people stood outside in the street, staring up at the tense situation unfolding on screen.

"You leave me no choice. Incarceration is not my destiny. As soon as OLF is taken care of, I'll be next on the FBI to-do list." On the whaling ship, the gunfire ceased. The silence that followed fell heavily upon them. The decks of *Pandora's Box* swarmed with Coast Guard men. She could see that at least one OLF member had been taken alive, pinned as he was to the deck by four Coasties. "I've got to get going."

Anastasia steadied the crossbow.

"Goodbye, Tara Shores. I'm sorry it had to be this way."

In the distance, the high-pitched whine of an outboard running at full throttle, grew louder. Anastasia shifted her focus from Tara and watched in horror as the crewman from *Pandora's Box* who had commandeered the FBI drone raced directly toward his mother ship with no apparent intent of changing course. The support helicopter hailed one warning before it opened up its arsenal, pumping hundreds of rounds per minute into the threatening craft and its pilot, who performed a brief macabre jig as he was shredded beyond recognition.

And then she watched as the lifeless, mutilated body of the OLF saboteur rolled off the riddled drone, leaving the wreckage to drift on the swells.

Before Anastasia could regain her composure Tara dropped to the deck, her right hand shooting out to grab the line, and pulled it taut with all her strength. The line snagged the inside of Anastasia's thigh and rocked her off balance. She didn't fall to the deck, but the unexpected movement caused her to bobble the crossbow.

That was all Tara needed.

The special agent shot across the sundeck with surprising speed.

Hands went to the crossbow, wrenched it down, spraining Anastasia's finger in the trigger guard but failing to dislodge it from her grip. She followed up with a strike to the nerve bundle beneath her ear but missed her mark.

Anastasia wrapped her hand in Tara's hair and jerked her toward the deck, but she maintained her balance and countered with a nasty kick to the knee, which brought Anastasia to the deck.

Tara fell on top of her, one hand going for the bow.

The two fighters rolled over one another. The crossbow was on top of them, then it was pinned to the sundeck beneath. Then it emerged once again, pulled in all directions by desperate hands.

They reached the edge of the small sundeck, Tara on top of Anastasia, throwing fists and elbows while trying to gain control of the weapon.

Both secured a hand on the grip, but it was Anastasia who gained control. Tara watched the bow's dart swing toward her face from below. She could feel Anastasia pulling the trigger back, her hand over Tara's. Tara knew she would not be able to stop it.

Then she swung one of her legs over the edge of the sundeck. In an act of desperation, Tara pulled both of them over the side of the sundeck.

They tumbled over one another onto the main deck six feet below, both landing on their feet but quickly falling to their knees, with Tara pinning Anastasia's back to the cabin wall.

Anastasia's hand was knocked away from the bow's trigger during the fall.

Tara belted her in the stomach. Anastasia doubled over. Tara swung the bow around to point it at Anastasia, who spit in her face and lunged forward. And the next thing she would be able to recall was the soft *thud* of the dart penetrating Anastasia's body high on her chest, just beneath her right shoulder. Tara backed away, half surprised. She felt the saliva slide down her lips.

Anastasia gasped. Her mouth dropped open as she looked down. The whale-cam dangled from underneath her right clavicle, firmly implanted there. Tara was surprised at how little blood there was.

Anastasia closed her eyes. Tara thought she was about to pass out. But suddenly the killer bolted left, toward the ketch's stern deck. Tara sprinted after her, not wanting her inventive mind to come up with some other makeshift weapon.

She slipped on blood that had begun to flow as she rounded a corner, landing hard on her elbow. She cringed in pain as the arm went numb.

Tara expected Anastasia to either jump on top of her or run back into the cabin, but she did neither. She ran to a set of scuba gear already assembled in a tank holder against the starboard rail. She threw on a weight belt while Tara struggled up from the deck. She was shaky.

By the time Tara was back on her feet, Anastasia had managed to back up to the tank and slip into its attached vest. She would have been unable to lift its weight on her own in her injured state, but with the gear held in place by the tank holder she was able to wriggle into it. Tara rushed at her, but Anastasia jumped over the side just as the detective reached the rail. Tara saw the pair of swim fins still on deck next to where the tank had been. Anastasia hadn't had time to put them on. She wouldn't be able to move very fast without them.

In the water, Anastasia was strapping on a full-face

mask—the same type that the Mexican divers had used.

"Care for a swim, Detective?"

Tara bit her lip.

"I'm not wearing flippers; you'd catch me for sure. . . ."

"How long have you known?"

"About being afraid of the water? Since our little adventure in the helicopter." The two women exchanged searching glances, each wondering what past events had brought the other to this moment.

"Communication unit's next to the radio," Anastasia called out before pulling the mask straps tight and sinking beneath the waves.

Tara took a quick look around. Coast Guard—and now police boats—still hovered around *Pandora's Box,* containing the situation. The spectator boats had been ordered to disperse, and a long line of vessels could be seen returning to Avalon Harbor. Near the site of the raised submarine, Tara could see an inflatable boat with blue flashing lights atop its control console heading her way, fast.

Here come the cavalry.

Tara stared down at the water she so hated and feared, watching the murderer make her escape. *Are you going to let this happen?* For a moment she struggled with the question, but by the time Anastasia's head went underwater, she had made up her mind.

No way.

Tara dove overboard after Anastasia, almost landing on top of her.

Without equipment of any kind, still dressed in pants and a shirt, Tara could do nothing but reach down and make a grab for the fleeing criminal. She could see her retreating form just beneath the surface. Anastasia was venting the air from her buoyancy control vest to sink more rapidly.

Tara thrust her face in the water, keeping her eyes open against the sting of salt, until she saw the blurry figure beneath her. She reached down and, feeling something besides water, latched onto the shoulder strap of Anastasia's vest. She clutched her fist tight, seeking purchase with her other hand. As she grabbed onto the tank valve, she felt Anastasia's arm on one of her wrists, trying to rip it away.

The diver continued to descend. With her weight belt intended for use with a thick, buoyant wetsuit that she was not wearing, and a purged buoyancy vest, gravity was on her side. Anastasia began to pull Tara under with her.

The special agent held on. She struck and clawed at Anastasia's equipment, unable to see exactly what she was doing but attempting to inflict damage nonetheless.

FBI FIELD OFFICE,
LOS ANGELES

Branson was livid. He stood in the middle of a now even larger contingent of employees gathered around a row of monitors set up to view the telemetry feed. The data logger's depth was displayed in the lower right-hand corner of the video.

"She's ten feet underwater!" Branson exclaimed. "Where the hell is my backup?"

On screen, only a commotion of flailing limbs could be seen as the two women battled each other in the liquid realm.

"Underwater team tells me three men are on the way to the ketch now in an inflatable, sir," a headphone-wearing assistant said. He held up a finger, as if receiving new information. "The rest of the underwater unit has entered the sub. The hijacker has barricaded himself and the pilot inside the control cabin, but they're evacuating the passengers and a crew now."

"Tell that inflatable unit that Special Agent Tara Shores is in the water near the ketch. Depth *twenty* feet," he said, eyes glued to the video feed.

The pressure in Tara's ears grew more painful by the foot. Somewhere around twenty feet, Tara began to want for air. She did not panic; she simply recognized a biological need and acted accordingly. She would not be able to drag Anastasia back to the surface. Her situation now was a matter of releasing herself from the killer's reversed grip, to avoid being hauled into the deep forever.

Tara let go of the tank valve with her left hand, her right hand still clutched in both of Anastasia's hands.

She yanked violently to free it, but without success. Then, at a depth of twenty-five feet, she used her free hand to find the rubbery texture of Anastasia's face mask. She pulled on it, trying to rip it away. She was unable to do so, but the attempt had scared Anastasia enough that she pushed Tara off.

Tara swam for the light while the lone diver continued on into the depths.

Tara gulped air the second her mouth broke the surface. She treaded water for a minute, grateful to be breathing again. She spotted the white ketch adrift a few yards away and swam for it, wondering if Anastasia would come up and grab her from below. She didn't look down. She just swam her clumsy crawl stroke to the boat.

Tara knew there was a step ladder on the stern. She went to it. She climbed the ladder, now seeing the boat's name on the transom—*Ketch Me If You Can*—in a whole new light. She stepped onto the sailboat's deck and looked out over the water where Anastasia had been and a smile materialized. She had not panicked. She had dived into the ocean, made a serious attempt at apprehending a murder suspect (on streaming video for the whole world to see), and come back to the boat again. She stood there dripping water onto the deck, amazed.

I'm not afraid of the water! I am not afraid!

She felt like jumping back in again just to prove the point, but she knew that this would be tough to explain. And besides, here was the underwater team.

Tara waved both hands at the approaching inflatable. Then she remembered the last thing Anastasia had said before submerging—something about a communications unit.

CHAPTER 47

ABOARD KETCH ME IF YOU CAN

In the cabin, next to the standard marine radio, Tara found a small electronic unit with a receiver attached. She flipped its switch to the ON position and turned its volume knob to the right.

"Hellooooooooo, can anybody heeeear me?"

Anastasia's voice startled the detective. She picked up the transmitter, pressed the button, and spoke. "I hear you Dr. Reed. Special Agent Shores here."

Laughter emanated from the unit's speaker. "Like I don't know who you are. How could I forget the woman who tagged me with a whale-cam?"

"Where are you, Dr. Reed?"

"Well, let's see, I'm about . . . 100 feet below you." The sound of Anastasia's raspy scuba breathing punctuated her sentences. Tara felt like she was talking to a ghost.

"There's nowhere for you to go, Dr. Reed. We've got divers ready to follow you. We've got boats to follow you. And the submarine is under FBI control, in case you're planning to team up with your hired help to make your escape."

This was met with a cascade of laughter. "Oh my, that's a good one, Detective. That really is priceless." She giggled some more. "I'm not sure if it's the nitrogen narcosis setting in, but that *really* cracks me up."

"Why don't you come back up now? You're only delaying the inevitable."

Another labored breath.

Tara saw Anastasia's laptop sitting on the galley table where she'd last used it to monitor the whale-cam and woke it up.

"Oh, but there is, Tara. There is."

Tara heard the rasp of the regulator again and went back to the comm unit. Suddenly she heard heavy footsteps on the ketch's deck.

"Special Agent Shores—FBI underwater team on board. Are you okay?" a man called out.

"Yes, I'm okay. In the cabin. I'm in communication with a fleeing murder suspect." While the FBI men made their way through the boat, clearing each compartment, Tara turned back to the underwater communications unit. "What are you talking about, Dr. Reed?"

The comm unit crackled to life. "There's one direction where I can go a long, long way, babe. That would be down."

Tara couldn't suppress a chill as she grasped the scientist's meaning. "Hold on, Dr. Reed." She picked up the laptop and brought it to the radio area. At a depth of 175 feet, the available light was scant enough that the camera's night-vision had been auto-enabled. Tara was startled to see Anastasia looking down at her on screen, her smiling face cast in an unearthly greenish glow. The numbers on the video's depth readout continued to increase.

"Dr. Reed . . . Anastasia, don't do this. Please come back up now."

Two FBI men eased into the cabin, pistols drawn. "Special Agent Shores?"

Tara didn't move but motioned to the badge at her hip. They asked if she was all right. She assured them that she was and explained the situation with Anastasia.

One of the FBI men announced that he would take over the job of sailing the ketch, and left the cabin. The remaining agent extended a hand. "Michael Rietti, FBI underwater specialist," he said. Tara shook his hand, taking comfort in the firm grip. He explained that a third team member was with their inflatable and would remain near the ketch, should they need it.

"We could go down after her," he suggested.

Tara showed him the depth readout: 200 feet and gaining. "She doesn't intend to come back," she said. "How deep is it here, anyway?"

Michael found a fish finder next to the radio and flipped it on. He frowned. "Deeper than 800 feet," he said. "That's the max depth on this thing. But I know that the Catalina Channel hits depths of 4,000 feet.

Besides, if she's breathing regular air, anything beyond 200 is suicidal. If she's got a gas mixture of some kind, like maybe Nitrox, she could go deeper, but not for very long."

Tara pressed the TALK button. "Dr. Reed, are you breathing air or something else?"

She heard a long *hissssss* in reply. "Pure air, baby, all the way."

The depth readout now displayed 225 feet.

The FBI man shook his head. "She trying to kill herself?"

"Unless she's grown gills."

"She might be trying to get us to believe that and then head for the surface somewhere else."

Tara nodded at the video feed. "Kinda hard to do that when you've got a web-cam and GPS unit pegged to your chest, isn't it?" He had no way of knowing she wasn't using a figure of speech.

"Hey, let me take a look at those cuts," he said, moving closer to Tara. She had sustained a bloody nose and a cut over one eye during her brawl with Anastasia, as well as a nasty gouge on the back of her right hand. Agent Rietti rummaged around the cabin's cupboards until he found a first aid kit. He tenderly cleaned and disinfected Tara's wounds before bandaging what he could while she monitored Anastasia's descent.

Suddenly a shadow of movement on the laptop caught their eyes. Because of the upward angle of the web-cam, there was still sufficient light at this depth to see things in the background beyond Anastasia's masked face. A tremendous form made its way across the field of view, becoming larger as it approached the lens. With a start, Tara realized they were watching the Blue.

The great whale soared above Anastasia's head, free of the camera that she was now burdened with. Tara couldn't help but think that although things had gone badly for Eric Stein he would be most pleased with this turn of events. The special agent was saddened, though, by these former classmates drawn together by a shared love of the sea, and now destroyed by it.

The two FBI personnel could only stare in awe at the remarkable spectacle playing out on screen, as did the millions of web and television viewers watching worldwide. Then, as suddenly as it had appeared, the Blue was gone, vanished into its own wireless kingdom. And it occurred to Tara that this time it really *was* gone. Free.

"So what do you want us to do?" Rietti asked, pulling her back into the reality of the moment. "I could have a couple of divers down at 100 feet, in case she decides to come back up again. If she does, she'll probably need help. I don't know how much air she has left, but at those depths you're talking mere minutes. We can bring her extra air tanks so that she can decompress."

They both glanced at the depth readout: 300 feet now. Her rate of descent was increasing.

"Leave me one agent to sail the ketch, please. Then you can tether the inflatable to us. That leaves two of you to dive."

"Roger that, Agent Shores. Mind if I talk to her before we go?"

Tara handed him the transmitter. She didn't see how it could hurt.

"Hello, Dr. Reed, my name is Michael Rietti, underwater specialist with the FBI. Do you copy? Over."

"I do," came the reply.

"You've gotten yourself into an extremely dangerous situation, Dr. Reed. You need to ascend immediately."

"No can do, Michael, Mikety-Mikey," she said in a sing-song voice.

Rietti turned to Tara. "She's narced. Nitrogen narcosis—it's like she's had four or five martinis by now." He went back to the transmitter. "Okay, Dr. Reed. Listen, please. Try and understand what I'm saying. I want you to know that myself and another diver will be going down to 100 feet and standing by to render assistance. All you need to do is ascend to 100 feet and know that we'll be there—we'll find you."

"Alrighty then, Mikey. Over and out."

Rietti looked at Tara, shaking his head. "Keep talking with her, but don't be surprised if she passes out. We'll do our best." With that the underwater specialist turned and strode from the cabin, already calling to his men outside.

Tara picked up the transmitter, wondering what to say. She glanced at the laptop. Anastasia's depth was an astounding 400 feet. The monitor showed dark water surrounding the wanted woman's moonlit face.

"Anastasia, it's Tara again." This time there was no sassy reply about knowing who she was.

"T-T-T-Tara. Hi, Tara." Anastasia's teeth were chattering, and Tara realized how cold she must be at that depth without a wetsuit.

"Please come back up. Our divers will help you."

"N-N-N-No." Her breathing was shallower and more rapid now, Tara noticed. She looked at the laptop. Anastasia's eyes remained alert. "Are you w-w-w-watching me?"

Tara found this disquieting, but it was her job to bring the suspect into custody alive, if possible, so she kept talking. "Yes, I can see you." She glanced at the depth: almost 500 feet. "How much air do you have left, Anastasia?" Maybe a jolt of reality would knock some sense into her.

Raaaaaaaaaaaaaasp. "N-n-n-not enough . . . for a round trip, babe."

Tara began to give up. It was true, after all, that Anastasia faced life in prison—perhaps even the death penalty, since her evil deed seemed to have been carefully pre-meditated—were she to return to the world above. She tried a different tack.

"Dr. Reed, is there anything you would like to say to anybody—any last words? This is being broadcast live on the web, you know." Maybe *that* would get to her, Tara thought.

"The d-d-d-deep sea," came Anastasia's voice over the speaker, "is the most common environment on our p-p-planet, yet is also the l-l-l-least understood."

She's gone now, Tara thought. Like a malfunctioning computer program, her brain was spewing random bits of stored information according to broken lines of code somewhere deep within.

"For years . . . s-s-s-scientists have had only tanta . . . *rassssssp* . . . lizingly short glimpses . . . into this m-m-m-mysterious realm. . . ."

Tara could stand it no longer. She screamed into the transmitter, "DOCTOR REED, STOP IT! STOP IT NOW!"

Another breath whispered its way through the communications system.

No more words came.

Tara looked at the computer screen. Depth was a staggering 700 feet. There were mini-subs that weren't rated to that depth. Even the water above her was dark now—not enough photons reached the camera's optics for it to see beyond the self-illumination of its night vision.

Anastasia's eyelids began to flutter. Tara ran her hands through her hair, rubbing her temples. There was *nothing* she could do. Anastasia may as well be on the surface of the moon. She repeated Anastasia's name into the transmitter.

No reply.

800 feet came and went.

On screen, Anastasia's eyes were open, but she said nothing. Her breathing came in shallow, rapid pants. The sound of her continually chattering teeth could be clearly heard over the sound system.

For the next two minutes Tara spoke Anastasia's name into the transmitter. She even said a few things, some of which she would never remember except in her darkest nightmares. When she had exhausted her repertoire of one-sided dialogue, Tara looked again at the telemetry feed.

Anastasia's eyes were closed. Her breaths were very few and far between now. Tara checked the depth: 1,100 feet. The water beyond the reach of the web-cam's night vision was utterly black in all directions; a complete absence of light. And then, under immense pressures it was never designed to withstand (only the sperm whale could dive to such depths), the telemetry device began to fail.

Tara cringed as a crack snaked its way across the video feed.

1,250 feet.

Tara's hand went to her mouth. Seawater still dripped from her hair and body onto the floor around her.

1,300.

The single crack spiderwebbed across the entire field of vision.

1,350.

Anastasia's eyes opened. One was obscured by a thick fracture in the lens, but the other orb could be seen staring out through a maze of fissures. Tara could swear the eye winked at her.

Then a piercing *pop* was heard, and the screen, like the sea that swallowed Anastasia, went black.

EPILOGUE

FBI FIELD OFFICE, LOS ANGELES

A Saturday morning not long after her eventful day at sea found Tara Shores in her office at the Bureau. There was one piece of business she wanted to take care of.

The days following her ordeal had been a whirlwind of briefings and media interviews. There were reams of reports to fill out. There were medical and counseling appointments to make sure that she was still the same Special Agent Tara Shores she had been prior to her involvement in the case.

She wasn't, of course, she had been forever changed. But she knew it was for the better. She had received many heartfelt congratulations from friends and colleagues, and had even received a commendation from the FBI director himself. Even better than that, Will Branson announced that he would be retiring soon, and there was serious talk of naming her as the new special agent in charge of the Los Angeles field office.

Tara shuffled various papers on her desk, looking for something. A post-incident briefing on the OLF whaling-ship fiasco reminded her of Stein's fate. The environmental extremist had been killed by automatic-weapons fire when the Coast Guard had attempted to take the combative captain into custody. Pineapple had been taken alive and now awaited a lengthy prison sentence.

Another briefing, this one on the tourist submarine hijacking, caught her eye. She had contributed to it, but had not been the sole author, since the underwater team had handled most of that nightmare. In the end though, she noted as she skimmed the report, it had worked out okay. All of the passengers had survived, as she was told by Michael Rietti on the ketch, and so had the pilot, Walter Johnson. Even the hijacker had survived, she had been surprised to find out. He now awaited trial in federal custody, and was cooperating with authorities to help bring his employer, the seaplane pilot, to justice, although he had been unable to produce the pilot's name or address.

Michael.

A smile crossed her face as she read his name in the report. She had spent some time with him after their work together; he had taken her out for dinner and drinks. Almost every night this week, in fact. You could even say we're dating, Tara thought happily.

Ah, there it is. She located a flash-drive taped to a note from Imaging Lab director Herb Shock, which read:

Tara, Huntress of Whales:

This video file contains the original images, recovered from the telemetry device's hard disc drive, corresponding to the timecodes you requested. Glad to be of assistance,

Herb

P.S. Audio analysis I promised from the broadcast video: the sound that can be heard from timecode 070709:14 - 070709:21 has been confirmed to be that of Dacron sailcloth commensurate with those usually found on boats approximately 32'-42' in length.

Tara inserted the drive into her computer. She had come into work early on a Saturday for this. She recalled how badly she had wanted to see through all that static. Here was her chance.

She never expected to have this opportunity. But although Anastasia's body had not been recovered, the tag had worked its way loose from her remains, perhaps by currents on the seafloor, where her weighted corpse would have ended up. The tag was designed to float, so that if it ever came loose from the whale, it could be recovered.

After Anastasia had disappeared and the tag's video and data transmission ceased, it was thought that the device had been completely ruined, but miraculously, when it reached the surface the GPS started signaling again. It was found floating halfway between Catalina and Long Beach by a day sailor, who turned it in to Anastasia's university, who in turn handed it over to the FBI.

The GPS and the hard disc drive components of the telemetry device, buried deep within the titanium housing as they were, had withstood the pressures of the deep—only the exposed camera and sensor elements of the device had been destroyed. So Herb Shock in the Imaging lab had been able to recover the original video recorded on the high-capacity disc drive.

Now Tara brought up the original murder video. She hunched forward over her desk, watching intently.

Then she let out an exasperated sigh.

Where there was static in the broadcast version, this original video showed only blue sky, a few clouds, expanses of empty ocean, and some glimpses of the sun—nothing incriminating. The clip revealed nothing significant that hadn't been seen on the web. The killer could not have been deduced from this video. George Reed might still be in jail had Anastasia not confessed to the crime.

Tara shook her head in amazement. How much deceit, destruction, and death had resulted from the race to obtain these images, which, in the end, revealed nothing new at all?

For the last time, Tara watched Crystal Wilkinson struggle in vain for her life. Then she killed the video and headed for the door. Outside it was a beautiful day, and she had recently purchased a new toy.

She drove her Crown Vic down to Marina del Rey,

where she used her key card to gain entry to Dolphin Basin, where her new ketch waited in its slip. No, not Anastasia's. Tara had learned that the Reeds would be putting it up for sale—it held too many bad memories—after it was released from the forensic lab, and the Reeds' divorce was finalized. But she had purchased one just like it, painted sky blue.

Tara decided to permanently conquer her fear of water, once and for all. She wanted to take Michael out on it soon, so today she would practice her first solo sail.

Stepping onto her new boat, she smiled at the name painted on the transom.

Dot Calm.

FURTHER READING / SUGGESTED RESOURCES

Books

Bortolotti, Dan. *Wild Blue: A Natural History of the World's Largest Animal*. New York: Thomas Dunne Books, 2008.

Calambokidis, John and Gretchen Steiger. *Blue Whales*. Stillwater, MN: Voyageur Press, 1997.

Scientific Literature

Calambokidis, J., J. Barlow, J.K.B. Ford, T.E. Chandler, and A.B. Douglas. 2009. Insights into the population structure of blue whales in the eastern North Pacific from recent sightings and photographic identifications. *Marine Mammal Science* 25:816-832.

Calambokidis, J., G.S. Schorr, G.H. Steiger, J. Francis, M. Bakhtiari, G. Marshall, E. Oleson, D. Gendron and K. Robertson. 2008. Insights into the underwater diving, feeding, and calling behavior of blue whales from a suction-cup attached video-imaging tag (CRITTERCAM). *Marine Technology Society Journal* 41(4):19-29.

Lord-Castillo, B.K., Wright, D.J., Mate, B.R., and Follett, T. (2009). A customization of the Arc Marine data model to support whale tracking via satellite telemetry. *Transactions in GIS* 13(s1): 63-83.

Mate, B., R. Mesecar and B. Lagerquist. 2007. The evolution of satellite-monitored radio tags for large whales: One laboratory's experience. *Deep-Sea Research II*. 54: 224-247.

Other

American Cetacean Society blue whale fact sheet: http://www.acsonline.org/factpack/bluewhl.htm

National Geographic, March 2009 issue.

National Geographic documentary, “Kingdom of the Blue Whale”: http://channel.nationalgeographic.com/episode/kingdom-of-the-blue-whale-3302#tab-blue-whale-facts

Oregon State University’s Marine Mammal Institute, Whale Telemetry Group: http://mmi.oregonstate.edu/wtg

Also from Variance Publishing

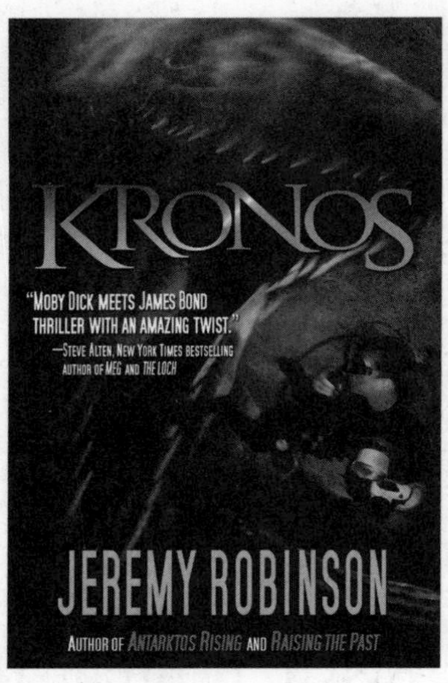

"Robinson's latest is a Moby Dick meets James Bond thriller with an amazing twist."
-- Steve Alten, NY Times bestselling author of MEG

"Jeremy Robinson is an ORIGINAL and EXCITING voice."
-- Steve Berry, NY Times bestselling author of THE PARIS VENDETTA

AVAILABLE NOW!

About the Author

Photo credit: Tabbatha Chesler

Rick Chesler holds a Bachelor of Science in marine biology and has had a life-long interest in the ocean and its creatures. When not at work as an environmental project manager, he can be found scuba diving or traveling to research his next thriller idea. He currently lives in Honolulu, Hawaii, with his wife, cat and some fish.